Anne Allen lives i
three children and l
nearby. Her restless
the longest stay bein... ... ..........,
falling in love with the island and the people. She contrived
to leave one son behind to ensure a valid reason for
frequent returns. By profession a psychotherapist, Anne has
now published three novels and the fourth, The Family
Divided, will be published in 2015.
Find her website at www.anneallen.co.uk

Praise for Dangerous Waters
'A wonderfully crafted story with a perfect balance of
intrigue and romance.' *The Wishing Shelf Awards, 22 July
2013 – Dangerous Waters*
'The island of Guernsey is so vividly evoked one feels as if
one is walking its byways. An atmospheric and tantalising
read.' *Elizabeth Bailey, author of The Gilded Shroud*

Praise for Finding Mother
'A sensitive, heart-felt novel about family relationships,
identity, adoption, second chances at love... With romance,
weddings, boat trips, lovely gardens and more, Finding
Mother is a dazzle of a book, a perfect holiday read.'
*Lindsay Townsend, author of The Snow Bride*

Praise for Guernsey Retreat
'I enjoyed the descriptive tour while following the lives of
strangers as their worlds collide, when the discovery of a
body and the death of a relative draw them into links with
the past. A most pleasurable, intriguing read.' *Glynis Smy,
author of Maggie's Child.*

# Also by Anne Allen

Finding Mother
Guernsey Retreat
The Family Divided

# Anne Allen

# Dangerous Waters

**The Guernsey Novels Book 1**

Sarnia Press
London

Sarnia Press
Unit 1, 1 Sans Walk
London EC1R 0LT


A catalogue record for this book is available from the
British Library
ISBN 978 0 9927112 2 1
Typeset in 11pt Aldine401 BT Roman by Sarnia Press

*For my mother, Janet Williams, with love*

And just as he who, with exhausted breath
Having escaped from the sea to shore, turns
back
To watch the dangerous waters he has quit
So did my spirit, still a fugitive
Turn back to look intently at the pass
That never has let any man survive.

*Dante Inferno Canto 01*

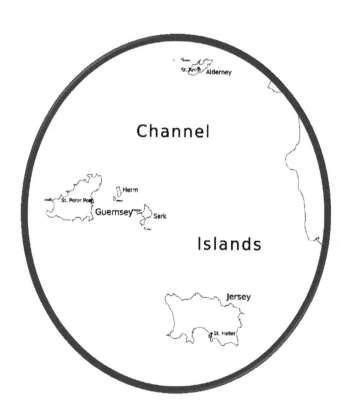

# chapter 1

Jeanne stepped out on deck as the spring sun broke through the clouds. A warm glow spread across green and gold jewel-like Herm and its big sister, Guernsey, patchworked with fields and granite buildings.

The salt-laden air enveloped her like an old, trusty coat. Taking a deep breath, she closed her eyes and was a child again, playing on the beach with her parents. The image was so powerful that tears formed and she blundered, unseeing, towards the railings.

As her vision cleared she found herself staring at Herm and, without warning, was overwhelmed by such a strong feeling of fear that she had to hold onto the rail. Jeanne's heart began to race, blood pounded in her head and her breathing came in short, painful gasps. *Oh my God, what's happening to me? After all this time, please, not again!* Struggling to breathe she was on the verge of passing out. Letting go of the rail she stumbled, crashing into a man walking past.

'Hey, steady on! Look where you're going!' he shouted, grabbing hold of her to stop them both falling. 'Overdid the dutyfrees, did you?'

Stung by his accusation, she took a deep breath before replying. 'No...no. I just lost my balance.' His hands gripped her arms so hard that she could already imagine the bruises. 'Hey, that hurts!'

His grip loosened and he guided her back to the rail. She clung on, filling her lungs with sea air.

'Sorry, didn't mean to hurt you. Okay now?'

Jeanne nodded. As the man stepped back she took in, through a still blurred gaze, dark brown hair, deep blue eyes and the muscled arms of a man unlikely to be a pen-pusher.

Responding to his warmer tone, she managed a tight smile before straightening up and walking, unsteadily, to the starboard side.

*What on earth was that? Is this what I can expect now? Perhaps I shouldn't have come back. Not that I had a choice...*The thoughts whirled around her pounding head and she shuddered as she leant against the railings as Guernsey came into full view. While the ferry headed towards St Peter Port harbour, it seemed as if she were approaching a strange, unknown country rather than the land of her birth. The whole of the northern sea front, from Les Banques into St Peter Port, had been transformed. Towering edifices of granite and glass replaced the remembered old, tired mishmash of warehouses, scruffy hotels and shops. With a gasp, she realised that even the elegant landmark of the Royal Hotel had been supplanted.

*Wow! What's happened?* It was as if a natural disaster had occurred, flattening the old front and replacing it by buildings more reminiscent of London than of the parochial island of old. She'd never have thought that Guernsey would move into the twenty-first century with such a bang.

The dramatic transformation which lay before her seemed to Jeanne to be an echo of the change in her own life and she felt a stranger here. She wished she had stayed in the familiar, dull Midlands town which had been her home these past fifteen years. For a moment the urge to remain on the ferry and return to England, without setting foot on the island, was overwhelming. Her face must have mirrored her inner turmoil as a middle-aged lady standing nearby asked, 'Are you all right, dear? Only you've gone very white.'

'I'm fine, thanks. Just not very good on boats.'

The older lady nodded her sympathy. 'My Tom gets seasick too, has to fill himself up with beer or the odd whisky or two before he'll set foot on a boat. Just as well I can drive or we'd be marooned on the ferry till he's sobered up!' She laughed.

Jeanne forced a smile.

'Aren't these waters supposed to be dangerous?'

'Yes, they can be, if you don't know where all the rocks are,' Jeanne replied. Yet again, her heart hammered against her chest and her breathing quickened. She fought down the feelings of panic to add, 'but these big boats are perfectly safe,' wondering who she was really trying to reassure. Jeanne joined the throng of eager passengers heading towards the car deck, found her car and sat there feeling sick and trapped in the echoing bowel of the ship. She would just do what had to be done here and then go back – but where? Her body arched over the steering wheel with the painful memory of her loss. Going back would be as bad as going on, she realised. The sound of car horns blaring behind her brought her back to the present. She started the engine and joined the queue towards the gangway and whatever lay ahead.

Emerging from White Rock, Jeanne followed the steady stream of cars up St Julian's Avenue and turned left into Ann's Place. She smiled on seeing that the Old Government House Hotel was still there and was lucky to find a nearby parking space. It was only a short walk to the advocate's office but she decided she needed a coffee first. Ideally she would have preferred a couple of vodka shots to calm herself, but didn't think it would be appropriate to meet her lawyer with glazed eyes and a stagger, especially as she'd already been accused of hitting the duty-frees! The thought made her frown as she walked down Smith Street, side-stepping the tourists intent on window shopping.

Jeanne began to feel more at home at the familiar sight of Boots at the bottom of the hill. It was where she and her friends used to meet up before going on the prowl in Town. On her right was a smart and inviting looking café with squashy leather chairs.

She sank, with a contented sigh, into a chair and ordered a cappuccino from the young waitress.

'Anything to eat with your coffee? We do have some scrummy chocolate cake guaranteed not to put on an ounce.' The girl grinned.

'Can't resist!' Jeanne smiled back, pleased that at least one of the natives seemed friendly.

Sipping her frothy drink and conscious of the resultant milky moustache flecked with chocolate, Jeanne thought about her impending meeting with the advocate. She had been receiving gentle but persistent reminders from Advocate Marquis that there were important legal issues to discuss, not least that of her grandmother's cottage. Her mind, unbidden, took her back to that awful day five months ago…

The phone was ringing as she and Andy arrived home, glowing after their holiday.

'Oh, Jeanne, thank goodness! I've been trying to get you for ages and left so many messages…I'm so sorry, but it's your gran…' Molly's voice caught on a sob and Jeanne's stomach clenched as she anticipated the dreaded news.

'She died in her sleep, Jeanne. It was peaceful, just as she'd have wanted,' Molly continued as Jeanne's eyes filled with tears.

'The…the funeral?'

'It was yesterday. I'm so, so sorry. The advocate and I kept trying to contact you but she died over two weeks ago and we didn't know where you were or when you'd be back. I did try your mobile but it was switched off.'

'We've been in Tenerife for three weeks. It was a bit last minute and I forgot my mobile charger. But Gran had seemed so well! If only I'd known…' The tears now flowed freely.

'Jeanne, you couldn't have foreseen it. None of us did. She slipped away quietly. No pain, no fuss. We weren't sure what to do for the best, but in the end the advocate, as her executor, thought he'd better organise the funeral. But you'll be over soon? To sort out the cottage and everything?' Molly's voice was calmer, more urgent.

'Yes…I guess so. I'll get back to you later. Thanks…Molly.'

She collapsed onto the sofa while Andy made some tea and muttered a few ineffectual words of condolence before he opened the post. As she sipped her drink she remembered the feisty old lady, the last link to her past life in Guernsey. Although her gran had been over a few times to see her, Jeanne had not been tempted to return. It would have been too painful…

But now she was back and without any known living relatives in Guernsey. Apart from the cottage, the only sign of the family's roots here were the headstones in the graveyards. Jeanne shuddered at the thought of her loved ones lying cold and unvisited in the earth and felt the tears threatening. *It wasn't fair!* She gripped the coffee cup tightly, self-pity heightened by her guilt at staying away so long. Catching sight of a young, laughing family walking past the café only made her feel even more sorry for herself. *For heaven's sake girl, get a grip! Stop being maudlin and get on with what you came to do. You owe it to the family.* With this thought she straightened up and finished her coffee.

Glancing at her watch, she saw that she'd better get a move on and, after paying the bill and freshening up in the Ladies, walked the few yards to the advocate's office.

As the receptionist led her down a corridor Jeanne glanced at the watercolours on the walls. With a pang she recognised the local bays with cabin cruisers – *oh, just like*

5

*Dad's!* –bobbing on the waters as families gathered on the beaches. She could almost smell the sea and the pungent tang of seaweed on the rocks. Her thoughts were interrupted by the girl opening a door and announcing, 'Miss Le Page, Advocate.'

'Good afternoon. How are you?' enquired the man who came forward to shake her hand.

'Well, thank you, Mr Marquis. I'm sorry for the delay in coming over. There's been a lot happening recently and certain...' she paused, 'events have meant that I couldn't travel. Now I'm ready to settle everything before I go back to...England.' She had nearly said 'home' before remembering she no longer had one.

'It's quite straightforward. Your grandmother's will leaves everything to you as her sole beneficiary. Once we've gone through the various papers I'll need you to sign some forms, then you'll be the legal owner of Le Petit Chêne as well as the money your grandmother left.'

After much reading and signing Jeanne was presented with the keys to the cottage and Mr Marquis arranged for the monies to be transferred to her bank account. Mm, didn't realise Gran had as much as that in the bank. But she'd never been a big spender, not bothered by material things. Just her beloved cottage and garden. Especially the garden. A lump formed in her throat as Jeanne realised that Gran's savings might come in very useful until she sold that beloved cottage.

'Where are you staying while you're here? In case I need to contact you.'

'I'm staying with Molly and Peter Ogier for a few days until the cottage is more habitable.'

'Good. I believe they were close friends of your family?'

'Yes, I've known them since I was a child.'

Jeanne hesitated and then said, 'I have to ask, Mr Marquis, have there been any...developments with the investigation? Have the police found anyone yet?'

He shook his head. 'No, there's been no progress at all. Technically the case is still open, but I don't think the police have found any more evidence. It's difficult without any witnesses and after all this time…Have you remembered any more of what happened?'

'No, I've had nightmares over the years but I've never been sure whether they've been caused by actual memories. Perhaps coming back will stir things up, memory-wise.'

She bit her lips as she recalled what had happened on the ferry.

'I don't really want to remember any more, but if I did, perhaps we would find out who killed my parents and nearly killed me.'

# chapter 2

Jeanne left the office and headed back to her car. Distracted by her meeting with the Advocate, she bumped into a woman burdened with shopping, causing her to drop it.

'Watch out!' the woman cried, scrabbling to retrieve her errant purchases.

'Oh, sorry! Here, let me help.' Jeanne smiled apologetically as she collected up the rest of the items on the pavement. Within seconds, order was restored and the woman nodded and went on her way.

I must get a grip, Jeanne thought as she reached her car. Bumping into people is becoming a habit. She decided as it was still light for a while yet, she would go and see her cottage (odd thought that – now it really was hers) before going on to the Ogiers.

She swung the car into The Grange to take the road out to the west coast and the old cottage which had once been so important to her. A place full of so much love and laughter, before her world had fallen apart.

Driving southwards along the west coast from Vazon, she glanced towards the beaches on her right. People were still out walking in the afternoon sunshine, some with children skipping alongside and others with dogs bounding ahead, making the most of the fine weather and bracing sea air. Surfers rode the waves, particularly strong on this stretch of coastline. It was idyllic. *Oh, to be a carefree tourist enjoying this beautiful island instead of a self-pitying, grieving saddo like me. She pulled a face. Where's that tough ol' Guernsey spirit you were once so proud of? It's about time it resurfaced and brought back the smile to your face, my girl!*

From the winding coast road she turned left into a

narrow lane rising uphill and dotted with cottages on each side. About 200 yards inland she pulled into a drive belonging to a detached granite cottage with a mossy tiled roof. Her heart raced as she switched off the engine and looked at what was now her house. She knew the cottage dated back at least two hundred years and had been built by a fisherman, as had most of the others in that area. He must have been particularly successful because it had the largest plot in the lane with a good-sized garden to the rear and a spacious orchard to the side.

The central front door peeped out from under a gabled porch thick with clematis and roses growing up the trellised sides. Pairs of small-paned sash windows upstairs and downstairs either side of the porch created an attractive symmetry. Looking at it, Jeanne felt the house was watching her – and waiting. But for what? She shivered. In her heart she knew that by rights this shouldn't be her cottage. It should have been her father's and perhaps ultimately hers, but many years from now. That would have been the natural order of things, but in her family that natural order had been destroyed fifteen years ago.

Squaring her shoulders Jeanne walked to the porch and, after inserting her key, pushed open the stiff, creaking door. It had never been used very much, as the usual entry for all and sundry had been the back door, never locked, this being Guernsey. The low, beamed ceilings made the cottage somewhat gloomy as dusk approached so Jeanne had to switch on the lights, relieved that the electricity had not been disconnected. As she entered the sitting room on the left she was assailed by a musty, damp smell and this, together with the blast of cold air which hit her full in the face, prompted her to force open the windows to let in warm, salty fresh air. She gazed around at the room she had not seen for what felt like a lifetime.

The familiar, now dusty pieces of furniture, were still in

the remembered places. Her grandmother had been a creature of habit, rarely moving things around for the sake of a change. Jeanne walked round, lightly touching the solid oak furniture which had been in the family for generations. The more modern sofas she remembered as being marginally more comfortable when piled up with cushions. But now they looked old and shabby. The picture of neglect was reinforced by the threadbare carpet on the oak floor and the thin curtains which looked as if they would not survive much more pulling to and fro. An ancient wood burning stove squatted on the granite hearth in the inglenook fireplace surmounted by an old blackened beam. There was no central heating as her gran had not approved of such "new fan-dangled" innovations and had not wanted her home cluttered up with radiators, pipes and a boiler. She had been happy to clean out fires in the main rooms all her life and made it clear to anyone who would listen that it was much healthier than central heating, even though the smoke did blacken the walls and ceilings.

Crossing the hall Jeanne entered the kitchen.

The chill from the slate floor struck up into the soles of her trainers as she walked round the large room. Jeanne ran her fingers along the wooden tops of the two freestanding cupboards, leaving a trail through the dust. Under a window sat the old stone butler sink with tarnished brass taps which she now turned on – yes, there was water, she discovered. Good.

Next to it was the blackened range which she recalled as consuming coal at a prodigious rate. As she touched it she realised, with a shock, that this was the first time that she had ever known it to be cold. The range had been the true heart of the house. The absence of its warmth spoke such volumes that Jeanne shivered, whether from the cold or her grief she wasn't sure.

The smell of the kitchen felt wrong to her. It was musty

and the air tasted brackish, like dirty water. It had been so different once, with the smells and tastes of baking, especially bread. Closing her eyes she could picture a familiar scene.

A wonderful aroma of freshly baked bread filled the kitchen as a young Jeanne, hands covered in flour with white streaks on her face, frowned with concentration as she kneaded the mixture in the bowl. Her mother stood next to her, hands in a similar bowl as Gran pottered about, calling out instructions.

'Now, not too firm or the mixture'll be too dry. But not so light as t' leave it uneven. Mm, you're getting the hang of it, Janet, but I'm not so sure about our Jeanne!' She chuckled and her plump, smiling face brought a small grin to the girl's face.

'I'm no good at this, Granny. I'll just watch Mummy.' She looked at her mother who smiled her lovely wide smile, tossing her long, dark hair out of harm's way. The hair that Jeanne had inherited.

'Never mind, darling. I'm sure you'll be a great cook when you're older. I'll teach you what Granny's teaching me, which I have to say, is rather a lot!' She smiled at her mother-in-law who then explained the next stage in preparing a perfect Guernsey Gâche.

Jeanne's eyes watered as she remembered the words spoken so lightly by her mother years ago. She had not had the chance to teach Jeanne very much, who never did master making Gâche.

After a quick rub at her eyes she opened the doors of the two wall cupboards which still contained the everyday china her gran had used. She turned to gaze at what had been Gran's pride and joy, a dust coated, but still beautiful, enormous solid oak dresser. Handed down through generations, it had been made locally by a master cabinetmaker, whose name, Martin Le Mesurier, had been carved on the back. The best blue and yellow porcelain was laid out on the shelves giving a welcome, cheerful air to the otherwise stark kitchen.

Jeanne reached out and carefully picked up a plate, gently stroking away the dust to reveal the oh-so-French pattern she remembered well – a legacy of her gran's Norman ancestry. With a sigh, she replaced the plate on the shelf and moved over to the old pine table in the centre of the room.

The top was scored by the knives used over the years by busy housewives as they chopped, sliced and pared. Six pine chairs of varying design were drawn up around it, used for most family meals with diners huddled next to the range for warmth in the winter and in summer basking in the sun pouring through the opened windows. Jeanne traced the marks on the table with her fingers and found, on one edge, the initials she had laboriously carved as a child – J.L.P. They were barely visible and she grinned at the memory of what she had once thought of as her 'secret'. But her gran had found them and her usually smiling face had looked so hurt that Jeanne had burst into tears, and promised not to be a bad girl, ever again. But of course there had been more scrapes, inevitable for the tomboy she had been.

Just off the kitchen, well away from the range, was a walk-in pantry in which had been stored milk, cheese, butter, meat, eggs and all other perishables. Gran had never had a fridge but the pantry had faithfully preserved the family supplies. Jeanne was thankful to see that any fresh food had been disposed of as the vision – and smell – of five months' old milk and bread didn't bear thinking about. All that now graced the shelves were empty storage jars and the old-fashioned tins so beloved by her gran for storing home-baked cakes and biscuits.

Suddenly feeling chilled and despondent, Jeanne decided to leave the rest of the ground floor and climbed the solid wooden staircase to the landing, off which lay four bedrooms, the bathroom and airing cupboard.

She opened the door to what had been her grandparents' bedroom; a reflection of the shabby discomfort of the sitting room, it had the same musty smell. Although the room was a good size it only possessed a double bed with a small side table, a wardrobe and a chest of drawers with a chair beside it. Possessed of few ornaments and with no signs of feminine vanity except for the small wooden mirror on the chest. Gran had been a warm, lively woman but she had not been concerned with her appearance and wore the same old clothes till they fell to pieces.

Jeanne picked up a framed black and white photo of her grandparents on their wedding day, their faces smiling self-consciously at the camera.

'Hello, Gran, I'm back,' she said softly, running her fingers over the picture.

Taking a deep breath she then lifted up the only other photo, a large colour one of her laughing parents. Her eyes were drawn to her mother, proudly cradling her baby self. Involuntarily, her left hand went to her own stomach and as she replaced the photo on the chest, her throat tightened.

'Oh, Mum, how I miss you! There's so much to tell you and it really hurts…'

Her stomach clenched as waves of grief swept over her and her breath was reduced to short, hard gasps. She couldn't bear it, she really couldn't! No-one could. Falling onto the bed, Jeanne gave in to all the pent-up emotions brought to the surface by her return. She had to be strong and face the demons before they destroyed her. Easier said than done when you felt like shit.

It was a while before she felt anything like calm again but time was pressing. After glancing into the two other double bedrooms she checked out the bathroom which was as austere as she remembered. Still painted a horrible green, it possessed a chipped enamel bath on claw feet, an old fashioned WC and a big pedestal washbasin.

She walked across the cold, cracked lino – an even more bilious shade of green – and tried the tap on the bath. Rusty brown water trickled out, nearly drowning a spider slumbering near the plughole. After a few minutes the water cleared and Jeanne switched off the heavy tap and repeated the process with the washbasin. As she let the water run she scrutinised herself in the foxed mirror, hardly large enough to hold an entire face.

Reflected back was a mass of long, dark hair framing a pale face dominated by what were normally large, bright blue eyes, but now reddened and puffy. Under the somewhat ordinary nose, her mouth was unsmiling and the overall effect was almost sullen. *God, I can't meet Molly and Peter looking like this,* and splashed cold water onto her face, wiping it off with a tissue. A quick repair job with the makeup in her bag, a tentative smile and the transformation was complete. It was if another person entirely had stepped into her skin. Feeling pleased with the improvement – as after all, she didn't want to depress her hosts – she went onto the landing.

Jeanne hesitated, her hand on the stair rail, but instead of going down as she had intended, she went along to the last and smallest bedroom and opened the door.

An icy blast nearly knocked her off her feet and she braced herself before stepping forward. The room was colder than the rest of the house by at least fifteen degrees. It was like walking into a cold store. The smell that caught at the back of her throat was a mix of mustiness and something she couldn't quite place which left a metallic taste in her mouth. She gave only a cursory look at the room she had hated since a small child. Her eyes travelled over the single bed, cupboard and small chest of drawers set out on the bare, dark oak floor.

She had always been puzzled by the increased chill factor which she had felt whenever she had been obliged to enter this room. Thank goodness she had never had to sleep there, her parents' modern house having been only a short distance away. Unfortunately, it had been the room used for storing surplus bits and pieces, occasioning the odd foray to find things her gran had needed.

With a feeling of relief Jeanne shut the door and ran down the stairs and out of the front door. As she locked up she again thought back to the happy, carefree days spent here so long ago. As a child she had not noticed the cold or shabbiness, it had been so full of the love and warmth of her family. It had seemed like a wonderful place to her then and looking back she realised it was her loving family which had transformed the ordinary house into a memorable home.

Jeanne had known for years that one day she would inherit the cottage and had, more recently, imagined returning with Andy to help lay the ghosts. She had envisaged them playing at happy families with their children running about in the orchard, laughing and shouting at each other. But now that dream had been cruelly shattered and the thought of living there alone was too awful. She had to sell the cottage and move on – but where?

# chapter 3

The narrow, arched entrance to the Ogier's cottage was a challenge to drive through and Jeanne was anxious to avoid scratching her car. However, most cars in Guernsey sported dents and scratches as the granite walls bordering the narrow lanes often seemed to jump out and hit the unwary motorist.

As she switched off the engine Peter and Molly appeared at their front door and with broad smiles reached out and hugged and kissed her in turn.

'At last! You're here! Peter and I've been so excited since you phoned.' Molly beamed at Jeanne.

'I'm so happy to see you both again, it's been too long–'

'But you're here now and looking so grown up!' Peter said

Although I'd have recognised you anywhere. Come in, come in,' Molly cried.

'Thanks. Mm, what a wonderful smell.'

'Yes, dinner's ready to serve and I'm sure you're starving.'

'Sure am, ready to do justice to your renowned cooking!'

Molly gave Jeanne a quick squeeze as they headed for the dining room. This opened through to the kitchen so that anyone cooking could still talk to those eating and as Molly ushered Jeanne into a chair at the polished oak table Peter went into the kitchen to open the wine.

'Red or white?'

'Red, please, Peter,' Jeanne called, breathing in the heady aroma of what she felt sure was beef cooked in wine.

Molly and Peter brought the food through and soon the table was covered in dishes heaped with steaming potatoes, mixed vegetables and the pièce de la resistance, Molly's famous *Daube de Boeuf Provencale*. Jeanne began to relax properly for the first time that day, soothed by the warmth of her welcome. The Ogiers had, from childhood, been like a surrogate family.

'Santè! And welcome back,' Peter said as they clinked glasses.

'Mm, delicious, Molly. Haven't tasted anything as good for ages.' Jeanne smiled her appreciation.

'Thanks. The recipe was Janet's, passed down by your grandmother. So it's rightfully yours now.'

'I'll be looking out for Gran's recipes when I go through the cottage. Might encourage me to improve my cooking skills.'

Mentioning her gran reminded her of why she was there.

'I…I'd like to thank you both for what you did for Gran. And after–'

Molly squeezed her hand.

'It was nothing, we were happy to help. You know how much we cared about her.'

Silence reigned for a few moments as they focused on their food and Peter topped up their glasses.

'So, how're Phil and Natalie these days? We seem to have lost touch with each other.'

Peter smiled wryly. 'Even we, the parents, don't hear much from them. Both pretty independent, aren't they, Molly?'

'You can say that again! But we do know they're both well and happy, that's the main thing. Phil's in London now and Natalie's just moved to Oxford. Last time we heard they were both seeing someone but I gathered that neither was serious. So, how's your Aunt Kate? Keeping well?

'She's fine, thanks. Been a rock these last few months. I don't expect she thought I'd end up on her doorstep again.'

Molly frowned. 'We were so sorry to hear about you and Andy. You must have been together for what, four years? Quite a while.'

Peter took himself off to the kitchen to find some more wine.

Jeanne realised she was twisting her hair round her fingers, something she did when upset or stressed, and stopped.

'Yes, we were. But these things happen, don't they?'

'You'll meet someone else one day, I'm sure. When you're ready.'

'Perhaps.'

'Could even be someone here.'

'Not sure about that! Just being here – it all seems to come flooding back.' Jeanne sighed. 'All of it.'

'That's not really surprising,' Molly said gently, 'and if you wished, I might be able to help you?'

Jeanne looked at Molly with affection and knew that if anyone could help, it would be her. Not only had she been like a fond aunt over the years but she was a psychotherapist, well versed in dealing with problems such as hers.

'Thanks, Molly. I'll bear that in mind.'

Peter arrived back after taking an inordinately long time opening more wine.

'More food, anyone?'

'No thanks. That was plenty. And absolutely delicious.'

Molly also refused any more and she and Peter started clearing away the debris before serving the dessert. Jeanne was not allowed to help and was left with her thoughts.

She watched Molly bustling about in the kitchen. She must be in her fifties now, just as her mum would have been. The thought provoked the familiar ache in her solar plexus. Molly was so different to her mother – cheerfully plump with a broad, smiling face and fair, now greying, curly hair – whereas her mother had been slim and dark and more serious, though still loving. *Wonder what she'd look like now? Ah, don't go there! Just don't.*

Jeanne pushed down the unsettling thoughts and forced a smile as she watched her hosts bustling in the kitchen. Peter had also aged, but still had a good head of hair and his boyish grin.

The pan containing the dessert, Crêpes Suzette smothered with flaming liqueur, was borne in by a red-faced Peter while Molly carried a jug of cream. Obviously no-one worries about diets here, thought Jeanne.

'Now, coffee everyone?' asked Peter after the crêpes had disappeared. Molly made a pot and they went through to the sitting room.

The cottage was similar in design to Le Petit Chêne and Jeanne remembered how hard the Ogiers had worked to transform it into the warm, bright and comfortable home it now was. They had done a lot of the work themselves and could be proud of the result, she thought, noticing even more improvements since she'd last been there. Compared with the cold, damp and shabby cottage she had inherited it was a veritable palace.

'This is lovely, Molly. You've done wonders with this room,' she exclaimed as she gazed around the sitting room. The walls, a warm peach colour, were covered in bookshelves and paintings and the main focus of the room was a large restored inglenook fireplace. Jeanne gave a little sigh – *oh, wouldn't it be wonderful to have a home like this!*

'Thanks, we love it. So cosy, particularly in the evenings,' replied Molly.

Peter fetched a bottle of Calvados and poured out three generous measures.

'Have you considered renovating your cottage, Jeanne? You could achieve what we've done here, no problem. And the garden was always stunning,' he said, handing Jeanne a glass.

'Thanks. It's a thought, I suppose. But it would be such a huge project and cost a fortune to get it like this,' she said, waving her arms around the room. 'And I don't have a fortune. To be honest, I wasn't planning to stay long. Just tidy up the cottage ready for sale and then go back to England.' She twisted her hair, noting Peter and Molly glance at each other.

'I know it must be difficult for you, my dear. Coming back after so long and after losing your gran, but wouldn't you like to try and settle here again? After all, you must still have friends from school and we're here to support you in any way we can.'

Jeanne sighed. 'I don't know, Molly. It would be a big step and I'm not sure…I have to admit there's not much for me in England at the moment. Feel I'm between the devil and the deep blue sea!'

'Perhaps you need to sleep on it.'

'Mm.'

'You could always get some builders' quotes. If the figures stack up and you do still sell, you might make a tidy profit.'

'Typical man! Thinking of money, as usual.' Molly laughed.

Peter took a sip of the fiery liquid before saying, 'I'm sure Jeanne's not averse to making some money, are you?'

'No, not at all. But it does depend on what's involved.' Suppose it might make sense if she could make a profit, she thought, swirling the amber liquid round her glass. And she really hadn't anything to go back for.

Peter nodded. 'Well. How about us going round the cottage with you tomorrow? We could jot down a few ideas.'

'You're obviously keen for me to stay! I guess it won't

hurt and you'll be more objective than me.' She thought for a moment and then added, 'By the way, I know you've both been round the cottage a number of times. Have you ever felt anything a bit odd about the small bedroom?'

They looked at each other, puzzled.

'No, not really. What sort of 'odd'?'

'It's probably just me then, but I've always felt a real chill in that room and hated going in there.' Jeanne shivered at the thought.

'Can't say I've noticed. Have you, Molly?'

'No, I haven't. Perhaps it's just your vivid writer's imagination!' Molly smiled at Jeanne. 'Which reminds me, I meant to tell you how much I enjoyed that story of yours in last month's *Woman and Home*. Are you writing anything at the moment?'

'No. Thought I'd give myself time off to come here, although I've brought my laptop with me just in case. But I do have various stories and articles being published over the next few months.'

'Good – I shall look forward to reading them. Even Peter likes to read your stories despite the fact that they're aimed more at us females.' Molly grinned at her husband.

He looked slightly embarrassed as he turned to Jeanne.

'Well, I don't see why men can't read them. We can cope with a bit of romance if there's also some suspense. Particularly if there's a sting in the tail, which you're so good at. Where on earth do you get your ideas from?'

Jeanne shrugged.

'I don't know. They just sort of pop into my head and I write them down as the story develops. I'm glad you enjoy the stories, Peter, as I'm not at all sexist.'

They finished the Calvados in companionable silence and as first Jeanne and then Molly started yawning it was decided to call it a day. After loading up the dishwasher they headed upstairs and Molly went with Jeanne to the pretty guest room complete with a tiny en suite shower.

Jeanne turned to Molly and gave her a hug. 'Thanks, Molly, for letting me stay. It's just what I need at the moment.'

'You're welcome, my dear. It's lovely to have you here after all this time. And I think you need mothering just now.'

Jeanne's face crumpled.

Molly looked mortified.

'Oh, Jeanne! How tactless of me!'

Jeanne shook her head and gave Molly a hug.

'No, don't be silly. It's just me feeling a bit maudlin, that's all. Coming back…'

'Of course. I understand. And so soon after Andy as well…'

Jeanne sniffed. 'Yes, it's not been a great few months. And I had what I'm sure was a panic attack on the ferry, just as we neared Herm.'

'Oh no! Did you remember anything?'

She shook her head. 'No. Just a terrible fear gripped me – as if I was going to die!' She shuddered.

'Oh, my dear, how awful for you. After all these years it's still affecting you.'

'It's bound to, isn't it?' Jeanne said sharply. 'It was bad enough to lose my parents but not to know what happened…'

'I know, I know,' Molly soothed her. 'Would you like me to help? Perhaps we could use hypnosis to recover your memory?'

Jeanne was twisting her hair round her fingers.

'Perhaps. If it stopped the awful nightmares…' She sighed and gazed at Molly.

'I'm not sure I'm quite ready to face it all just yet. Too scared about what I'll learn. Even the police aren't really sure what happened. After all, initially it was thought that

Dad had misjudged his bearings and landed on the rocks by mistake, even though he knew those waters like the back of his hand.' She took a deep breath and the hair twirling intensified.

'Then when they found that dent on the starboard side it pointed to us being hit by something. So the police decided that some drunk in another boat had caused the accident and we'd been forced onto the rocks.'

She stared at Molly, white faced. 'What really upsets me and has always puzzled me, is why didn't the other boat stop and help us? Why didn't they rescue Mum and Dad before it was too late? Before they died?'

# chapter 4

That night the dream returned. She was lying on the floor somewhere, her body leaden and still. She knew she had to move – it was vital, somehow, that she got up but she just couldn't. Someone was shouting but the sound came and went in waves. Waves! That was it! Waves were crashing against whatever it was she was lying in and she could feel water lapping around her inert body. Oh God! She was going to drown!

Jeanne woke up, her heart hammering and her body drenched in sweat. The nightmares were back. She'd hoped that maybe, just maybe, they had finally left her alone. But no. It must be coming back here, she mused, crawling out of bed to fetch a glass of water and a towel. After a quick rub down and some sips of water she felt better. Was it a real memory or was her mind playing tricks on her? There was no way of knowing, which made it so frightening. Pulled unconscious from the wrecked boat, her memory of what happened on that fateful evening had never returned.

Still feeling disorientated Jeanne gulped down the last of the water before standing under a hot shower to wash away the numbing cold she had felt in the nightmare.

As Jeanne walked into the kitchen Molly was just putting the kettle on. Seeing Jeanne's white face, she turned and gave her a hug.

'Bad dream?'

'Yep. One I haven't had for years. I guess it's because I've come back,' Jeanne replied, feeling safer now in Molly's warm embrace.

'Well, that's possible. Do you feel up to telling me about

it?'

Over a cup of strong coffee Jeanne described the dream as clearly as she could and Molly looked thoughtful for a few moments.

'I think it could be a buried memory rather than a bad dream. It fits with what we know about how you were found that night. It's too much of a coincidence to be otherwise.'

She reached over and squeezed Jeanne's hand.

'You know I'll help you when you feel ready to learn more.'

'Thanks, Molly. I've just got to feel a bit stronger first.'

'Of course. You've got a lot of things on your mind at present. Don't want you going into overload.' Molly smiled.

If you only knew! Jeanne thought, forcing a smile.

Just then Peter came downstairs and gave Jeanne a big bear hug. She sighed, envying Molly for having such a loving partner.

His size belied his gentle personality. A senior teacher at the grammar school, he was well liked by pupils and fellow teachers alike. He never had to raise his voice with an unruly pupil. He just looked at them with a rather sorrowful expression and the child, abashed, would mumble an apology and get on with their work. Jeanne had been at the Grammar but had not been taught by Peter, for which she was glad. He had known her too well!

Peter released her and scrutinised her face.

'We need to get some colour in those cheeks. How about a brisk walk on the beach after lunch, before we go to the cottage?'

'I'd love that thanks. I've so missed walking by the sea. Not many beaches in the Midlands!'

After a light lunch they grabbed their walking shoes and sweaters. It was another lovely, sunny day but there was a cool breeze coming off the sea. They walked down the lane to the coast road and along it until they could cross over onto the beach at Vazon. The tide was out, exposing a large stretch of golden sand.

'Oh, this is heavenly!' cried Jeanne, taking a deep lungful of ozone-laden air and spinning around, her arms spread out. 'I'd forgotten just how wonderful this sea air is. Boy, does it clear away the cobwebs!'

Peter and Molly smiled indulgently and together they all walked at a brisk pace up the beach in the direction of the kiosk. At times they had to scramble over rocks, but it all added to the enjoyment of the walk. Jeanne felt like a child again as she gazed into rock pools, looking out for tiny crabs and silver fish. She let the small crabs crawl over her hands, the tickling sensation making her laugh. Iridescent shells, pearl and silver, sparkled in the sand and she started to collect them, together with tiny round shells of varying shades of pink and brown. Her pockets were bulging as they arrived at the kiosk.

They opted for tea and as they sat on the sea wall drinking, a group of young men arrived. They wore wetsuits and carried surfboards as they joked together. One of them, a tall, fair-haired man in his early thirties, spotted them. He came over and said to Peter, 'Hello, sir. Good to see you. Enjoying your walk on the beach?'

'Yes, Marcus, thank you. Let me introduce my wife, Molly, and you remember Jeanne Le Page from school, I'm sure?'

'Pleased to meet you Mrs Ogier,' he nodded at Molly and, turning to face Jeanne, started slightly. 'Yes, of course I remember Jeanne. Weren't you in the year below me?'

'Yes I was and I remember you, too.' Jeanne felt herself redden. *Oh no, it was The Crush from school!* She used to dream of him asking her out, but he'd seemed to prefer a leggy blonde in her class. *And he's as gorgeous as ever.*

'How are you Marcus and...what are you up to these days?'

'I'm good, thanks. I've recently been promoted to Senior Manager in a trust company and the top of the ladder's getting nearer by the day,' he boasted.

She remembered that Marcus had always been full of himself at school but he was also very charming and his lop-sided grin took the sting out of his bragging.

'I'm impressed. Have you...settled down yet?'

'No fear!' He laughed. 'Too busy earning money and enjoying myself to get tied down. Guess I will one day. How about you? Have you hitched up with anyone?'

She shook her head, trying to curb the blush which threatened to creep up her face. *God, hope he thinks it's the walk that's made me flushed.*

'So what are you doing now? I knew you'd left the island after that awful accident. Have you...come back for good?' he asked, looking serious.

'No, I'm not planning to stay long. I'm back to sort out my grandmother's cottage which I've just inherited. Once I've sold it I can go back to England. As for my work, I'm a freelance writer.'

'I see. Sounds interesting, being a writer. Good for you. So, where are you staying?'

Jeanne nodded towards the Ogiers, who had walked away out of earshot.

'With Peter and Molly. My cottage is uninhabitable at the moment but I'll stay there once I've cleaned it up.'

'Well, perhaps I could give you a ring sometime? A group of us are planning a beach barbecue next weekend, if you'd like to join us?' He flashed his most charming smile.

'Yes, thanks. I'd...like that,' Jeanne replied, feeling the heat rising again. *Oh, stop behaving like a lovesick schoolgirl. Ridiculous at your age.*

'Great. I'll ring you later in the week, then. Be seeing

you.'

Jeanne nodded and he walked off to the kiosk where his friends were drinking as she re-joined Peter and Molly.

'Well, you two seemed to have a lot to talk about,' Peter grinned at her.

'Yes, suppose so. We were just catching up with each other. He might ring me about a beach barbecue next weekend.'

'That's great, Jeanne. Just what you need – a bit of fun with old friends,' Molly said. 'Now, we'd better start walking back if we're to go round the cottage in daylight.'

As they turned into the lane leading up to Le Petit Chêne, Jeanne looked intently at the cottages.

'Some of these seem empty.'

'Yes, most of them are now self-catering cottages and as it's early in the season they're not yet let. Your cottage is one of the few that's still a permanent home and it would be a shame if it were to become like the others. Housing's in such short supply on the island it makes it difficult for youngsters to get on the ladder,' Peter said, frowning.

'No, I wouldn't want it to become one either. When I sell, it'll only be to people who want their own home. It's ideal for a family and children would have a wonderful time in the garden, just as I did,' Jeanne said, wistfully. Part of her mind still insisted on picturing herself there with her own children around her, playing in the orchard.

'Right then, let's see what needs to be done. Got my pad and pen ready.' Peter tapped his pocket.

Jeanne had left some windows open – not too much of a risk in Guernsey, she'd hoped – and the air in the cottage was a little warmer, and a hint of the sea flowed through the rooms. The musty smell was slowly being dislodged. She sniffed in appreciation. Peter made notes as they explored. They concentrated on what seemed to need more urgent attention: the wiring – 'as old as the hills' according to Peter

– the plumbing, the kitchen and the bathroom. There were no obvious signs of damp or real decay and Peter volunteered to climb up into the attic to see if there were any holes in the roof. He hauled in a ladder from the shed and carried it up to the landing, setting it under the hatch to the attic. He had had the forethought to bring a torch for his inspection.

While he was crawling around above them, Jeanne and Molly went through the bedrooms. As Molly opened the door to the single bedroom Jeanne braced herself for the chill she had come to expect. Molly went in and, without hesitation, started opening cupboards and drawers.

'Are you sure you don't feel particularly cold in here? I certainly do!'

Molly turned round and shrugged. 'No, to me it's no worse than the other rooms. Why, you're shivering!' Molly exclaimed.

'I know. I can't help it. It's freezing! I'll wait for you in Gran's room.'

Why was she the only one to feel it? Jeanne asked herself as she hurried along the landing. Surely it wasn't just her imagination as Molly had suggested. She had such a sensation of great sadness about that room. Perhaps something awful had happened there in the past, to one of her ancestors. The cottage had been in her grandmother's family for generations and her gran was born there. Perhaps something had been passed down in the genes, she mused, like people who were regressed to apparent past lives, but might actually have been reliving the life of an ancestor. All fascinating stuff for a writer, but it wasn't very pleasant to live with, she thought, shivering.

Peter came back down the ladder, looking dusty, with cobwebs sticking to his sweater. He gave Jeanne a reassuring smile. 'The roof looks sound to me. Couldn't see any big gaps anywhere, though to be on the safe side it'd be best to get it checked by a builder. No damp patches and everything's quite dry. There's loads of boxes and things up there, but it's all floored so it'd be easy for you to have a look.'

'Oh, that's a relief! Thanks. I'll have a hunt around when I move in as I need to go through Gran's papers and things. Might as well leave the ladder up here.'

Returning downstairs they went out through the back door into the garden. Next to the cottage, sheltered by the walls, were the neglected herb beds of which Gran had been so proud. Herbs had always played a big part in her cooking and herbal remedies and she had planted dozens of varieties including borage, comfrey, chamomile, tarragon, mint, basil, rosemary, thyme and sage. Bay trees stood like sentinels either side of the back door. Edging the paths were lavender bushes of different varieties – white, blue and deep purple – looking healthy despite needing a prune.

As they walked, Jeanne and Molly absentmindedly picked stems of lavender, discharging the heady aroma around them.

'Oh, this takes me back!' exclaimed Jeanne. 'Do you think I could get these beds into shape again?'

'Well, don't see why not. But apart from all the weeding, digging and pruning you'd have to re-plant a lot of new herbs as some are definitely past their sell-by date. And there's so much else to do,' Peter replied, eyeing the rest of the garden.

It was very much a traditional cottage garden with areas set aside for fruit and vegetables, alongside herbaceous borders displaying the spring flowers of tulips, flag irises and hyacinths amongst others. They made a bright show of red, yellow and purple peeping through the weeds and overgrown deadwood of previous seasons. In the summer, Jeanne remembered, there would be agapanthus, poppies, roses, hollyhocks and foxgloves, offering a similar display of bright colours. The mild climate of the islands also encouraged the planting of sub-tropical plants and palms. Yuccas, with their deep green spiky leaves and woody trunks, sat alongside soft feathery pampas grass, lining paths and fronting crumbling granite walls. It was this mixture of the traditional and the more exotic which had made the garden such a joy in its heyday.

Gazing around now, it was obvious to Jeanne that it would need quite a blitz to get the garden back into peak condition, but it would be worth it. The peace and seclusion provided an ideal outside living space with scope for a patio and pergola. She began to visualise summer barbecues with people milling around, a glass of wine in one hand and a plate of chargrilled (or cremated if she cooked it) food in the other. Oh, God, there she went again –imagining herself living here. Stupid girl! She shook her head at the thought.

'Shall we explore the orchard?' Molly asked. They braved the long grass encircling the apple, plum and fig trees. At least it was dry as they pushed their way through.

'The trees look healthy enough, anyway,' Molly said. 'I think there'll be a good crop of fruit later this year.'

'I can't remember if Gran ever used chemicals on them.'

'She didn't use them at all. Didn't want the taste of anything edible spoiled. Quite right, too,' Peter replied. 'Everything grown here is organic. Your gran used to follow the Guernsey tradition and sell the excess fruit and vegetables by the roadside, charging a bit more as it was organic,' he added.

'Ah, useful to know. If I'm still around later on in the summer I could earn myself a few pennies!' grinned Jeanne.

Peter and Molly laughed as they continued their tour of inspection. After satisfying themselves that all the hedges and walls were in reasonable shape, they made their way back to the cottage.

'Have you seen everything you wanted to?' Peter asked.

'Yes, thanks. I'd forgotten quite how big the garden is, though. How on earth did Gran manage when Dad was no longer there to help her?'

'She had some help with the heavier work from a fisherman who'd worked for your grandfather. He would keep the hedges and walls in good order and cut the grass in the orchard. I think she used to slip him the odd bottle of whisky in return,' Peter smiled. 'If you want to restore the garden properly, you'll need to get professional help to give you a start. I can recommend a good chap who's worked for me, if you'd like.'

'Thanks, it's too much for me, but I'd love to see it as it should be. Gran spent most of her time out here and it meant so much to her.'

Jeanne locked up and closed the more vulnerable windows when Peter pointed out that Guernsey was not quite as safe as it used to be. Still much safer than the mainland though, he reassured her. They walked back to the Ogier's home and all voted for another cup of tea. Molly brought in a big teapot and plates of Guernsey Gâche, a favourite of Jeanne's. A fruit bread served with lashings of rich local butter, she decided it was best not to count calories as she took a bite.

'What do you think now that you've had a really good look at everything?' Molly asked.

'Confused! As a home it's got great potential but there's so much needs doing and it will cost thousands,' she sighed.

'I don't wish to pry, but do you have any capital you could use?' Peter asked.

'Well, some. There's a bit left from the sale of Mum and Dad's house. As my income's been erratic as a freelance, I've had to dip into my capital at times. But Gran left me some money so it's not all bad.' She was thoughtful, twisting her hair around her fingers.

'If you could raise the money, what would you do?' Molly asked.

'Not sure. It's really a question of whether I would want to stay here until any work's completed. And I could be risking my capital. Or I could sell it now and have enough money to buy something in England. That would definitely be easier and a lot more sensible.'

'It would be easier, for sure. But if you got some builders round to quote for the work you'd have a better idea of what's involved. The bonus might be that, fully renovated, the cottage could fetch more than you'd spent on it. If you did decide to stay here and work on the cottage, remember we're here to help, aren't we Molly?'

'Of course. Any help or advice freely given. Not so good on the practical side these days, I'm afraid. We discovered that we're absolutely useless at plastering but we can wield a paint brush if need be. And if you did stay here for a few months, Jeanne, you'd be able to make friends and have some fun, wouldn't you?' Molly raised her eyebrows at Jeanne and smiled.

Flushing, she replied, 'I guess it *might* be worth thinking about. But if it proves to be too big a job or costs more than it's worth, then I'll just sell up and leave. As I'd originally planned.'

# chapter 5

As they all tucked into a cooked breakfast on Sunday morning, Jeanne explained that she planned to start cleaning and airing the cottage so she could move in within a couple of days. From the way that Peter and Molly glanced at each other, Jeanne sensed that they were not particularly happy about her plan but were wise enough to keep quiet.

'I can lend you a vac and mop. And I've got plenty of cleaning materials and cloths. Are you going to light any fires?'

'Thought I'd light them in the sitting room and dining room and try and get the range going. There's a load of coal out the back under cover I can use. I'll make a list of essentials to buy tomorrow when the shops are open. Of course, back in England I'd be able to buy everything today.'

'Yes, we're a bit out of step here with Sunday trading. But at least we can now buy petrol and alcohol on Sundays, which we couldn't when you lived here,' Peter replied. 'I'll give you a hand with the range and the fires if you like. The range might be a bit temperamental after all this time.'

'That's kind of you Peter, but I don't want to deprive you of your day of rest. You already gave up most of yesterday for me.'

'Nonsense. As Molly will tell you, I just hunker down with the papers and she can't get a word out of me for hours. I can work off this fattening breakfast I've just enjoyed. And it shouldn't take too long.'

The car was loaded up with everything they needed and they quickly drove down the lanes to Le Petit Chêne. The weather was still holding and the sight of blue sea, golden sand and blue sky lifted Jeanne's spirits. She was secretly glad that she did not have to tackle the fires and the range herself as she had never done it before and had not wanted to appear completely useless. Housework had never been top of her favourite occupations, always preferring the result to the process.

After unloading all the cleaning paraphernalia into the hallway Jeanne went around opening doors and windows while Peter fetched the coal.

They decided that the range was the priority as it provided hot water for the ground floor, leaving Jeanne to nip up to the bathroom to switch on the old immersion heater. As it took ages for the miracle of hot water to occur she decided to vac and dust the other rooms first, beginning with the dining room.

It had been little used in her grandparents' time except for important meals like family celebrations and, more recently, funerals, Jeanne remembered sadly. Glancing at the large oak beamed fireplace she started on seeing the desiccated body of a starling among the scattered ashes of the hearth. Yet another reminder of death. When would she be able to forget?

*Come on now, get on with it or you'll have Peter wondering what's the matter,* she chided herself. Dominating the room was a large, and in Jeanne's eyes, ugly, oak gate-leg table with six hard oak chairs spaced around it. The chairs were well made but uncomfortable. The worn rug couldn't stop the cold striking up from the stone floor and into Jeanne's feet as she worked.

She went across the hall into the third reception room, a small study which had been used by her grandfather as his snug, where he could escape with his pipe, newspapers and books. Her memories of him were limited as she was only ten when he died, but she had always held a mental image of a jovial man with twinkling blue eyes, curly white hair and a strong body. As he was a fisherman she'd seen him as like Captain Birdseye, but without the beard. An only grandchild – her father not having siblings – her grandfather had made much of her, allowing her the honour of joining him in his snug. He could tell such stories…

'Go on, Granpa, tell me a story about those pirates you had to fight.'

She must have been about five or six, sitting on his knee, big eyes wide open as she listened enthralled.

'Well, m'dear, there was about eight of 'em, and they just came out o'nowhere. But I was ready for 'em and…'

His tales were ones he had heard as a child and others he made up as he went along, like the pirates story. They were so real to her that she had been constantly on the look-out for pirates, expecting them to jump out from behind trees and rocks as she walked the cliffs with her parents. Jeanne sighed as her eyes swept over the dusty desk, battered easy chair and bookshelves. She could have sworn that the smell of fish which had always clung to him was still in the room, along with a hint of his tobacco. Shaking herself, she quickly dusted and vacuumed before going into the sitting room.

She was making good progress when Peter shouted, 'I've got the range working!' Joining him in the kitchen she heard the familiar rumble of the old Rayburn. A dishevelled looking Peter was beaming with the pride common to men when they've got any gadget or machine working against the odds.

'Brilliant, Peter. Thanks. You'd better show me what to do in case it goes out.'

Peter made a start on the fires while Jeanne went upstairs to clean the bedrooms and get out of his way. When the fires were glowing downstairs he went home, leaving her to work on.

She decided to just, very quickly, dust and vacuum the

small bedroom and was in and out in five minutes, shivering the whole time. *Perhaps if I bought a small electric fire for the room it would make a difference?*

The water upstairs was now hot so Jeanne was able to give the bathroom a clean before going downstairs to the WC by the back door, a room best described as functional and uninviting. Drab green painted walls matched those of the bathroom, enclosing an old-fashioned pedestal wash basin and a large antiquated WC with the original chain and tank. Jeanne grinned at the thought of her grandparents buying what must have been several tins of that awful paint and not letting any of it go to waste. After giving the room a good scrub and mop she turned finally to the kitchen, which was now actually dirtier than when they had arrived that morning, thanks to Peter's work on the range.

By five o'clock Jeanne had had enough and was glad to shut up the cottage for the night. She checked the fires were safe and the range was stoked up before leaving. Starting the car she caught herself thinking about what Peter had said about renovating the cottage. *Perhaps maybe, just maybe, it might be worth doing. After all, it could be exciting to bring it to life, as Peter and Molly have done at their cottage. Images of smart kitchens and bathrooms flashed through her mind. Hey, steady on, girl! There's a little thing called money needed here, remember. And you'd have to live here for some months – not what you'd planned, was it? Mm, I need to think about it.*

Arriving at the Ogiers', Jeanne ran upstairs for a shower and a much needed change of clothes. Refreshed, she went into the kitchen to give Molly a hand and told her how much she had done that day.

'It looks and feels so much better already. Amazing what a difference it makes when a house is warm. I should be able to move in on Tuesday if I can keep the fires going and buy what I need tomorrow. It'll be a real adventure!'

'If you're sure, my dear. You know you're welcome to pop back whenever you want. Now, let's go and sit down with a cup of tea and check on Peter.'

In the sitting room Peter was surrounded by what looked like all the Sunday broadsheets and he appeared to have nodded off, quickly coming to with the rattle of cups. As they sipped their tea Peter mentioned that the gardener would be happy to meet Jeanne at the cottage at about four o'clock the next day.

'His name's Jim Le Prevost and has a young lad working for him. They're both hard workers and Jim won't rip you off.' Taking another sip, he added, 'Do you want to talk to any builders yet? The chap who helped here was pretty good and you can mention my name if you phone him.'

'I'll do that, thanks. Perhaps tomorrow.' Jeanne stared at them both. 'This doesn't mean I've made a decision to renovate yet, you know. I'm just getting the facts. I might still sell, take the money and run.'

Peter and Molly assured her that they understood and the newspapers were passed around for the women to peruse.

It was a quiet, but enjoyable, evening as they tucked into a traditional Sunday roast with all the trimmings, accompanied by Peter's excellent smooth red Rioja. I could get used to this, Jeanne thought, as the food and wine soothed her aching body. They made an early move to bed and this time, Jeanne slept a deep, dreamless sleep.

Monday morning dawned a little duller though it remained mild, clouds scudding across the sky propelled by a light easterly wind. Peter had already left for school but Molly was not working until later in the morning and she and Jeanne sat down to enjoy a healthy breakfast of cereals and juice.

'You'll probably find all you need at the Bridge, Jeanne.

Quayside is more or less a one-stop shop for anyone setting up home. The Co-op supermarket is just down Nocq Road which I think was being built when you left. There's some nice little cafés too if you want to treat yourself to a coffee break. Oh, and by the way, I've just remembered the phone's been disconnected. I'll give you the directions for the telephone office so you can get back online.'

'Thanks. I'll buy a local SIM card for my mobile while I'm at it. The Bridge is a good idea. I remember it as being a great place to shop. It'll give me an excuse to drive around the coast and see what's changed over the years.'

Jeanne gingerly reversed the car out under the arch before driving down the lane to the coast road and heading north. This was one of her favourite stretches of road, following the sea right up towards L'Ancresse in the north of the island. She hummed to herself as she watched the waves crashing against the rocks at Cobo. There don't appear to be too many changes around here, she thought. Keeping the car at a steady 35 mph, the maximum allowed on the island, she turned inland at L'Islet to join the road leading to the Bridge. This was the area around St Sampsons harbour composed of shops, banks and restaurants and it was usually easier to park there than in Town, as St Peter Port was known.

After buying everything on her list from Quayside she went on to the supermarket. Not having a fridge or freezer meant that she could only buy a small quantity of perishable foods but she stocked up on store cupboard staples to last for a few weeks, in case she stayed longer than planned.

Glancing at her watch she decided to take Molly's advice and have a coffee and walked down the road to a smart-looking café on the corner she had noticed earlier. It looked busy but she found an empty table in a corner and ordered her favourite cappuccino. Sitting there listening to the chatter around her she thought how nice it would be to belong somewhere again, being able to meet friends for a drink and a gossip. It was so long since she'd done that. It had been lonely working from home and she'd lost touch with friends, particularly after moving in with Andy. She had devoted all her time to him – a classic mistake made by so many women, she thought sadly.

*Whatever happens now, I must change my life so that I spend more time socialising, and it would be good for my writing as well.* She loved people-watching and often made mental notes of interesting characters. Overheard snatches of conversation triggered off ideas for her stories. *Perhaps I could make a start by going to the barbecue this weekend. She flushed at the memory of Marcus at the beach. Mm, he's very attractive but do I really want a new relationship? No, I don't, it's much, much too soon after…but a friend would be nice. Surely it's possible to be just friends with a man? Mm, not sure about that.* She sighed, picking up her cup.

As tables around her cleared Jeanne became aware of two men sitting nearby. Sipping her drink she glanced up at the man facing her. There was something familiar about him – what was it? Late thirties, she guessed, with dark, curly hair and thick eyebrows framing deep blue eyes and a firm mouth. His complexion was slightly olive with the extra colour of someone who spent a lot of time outdoors. She wracked her brains. *Oh no, it's Muscles, that man I bumped into on the ferry!* Without thinking she rubbed her arms where he'd gripped her. They had come up in bruises as expected. The conversation drifted towards her as Muscles spoke.

'I'm sorry for the delays, Mr Evans, but my hands are tied. I can't work without the materials I need and you did keep changing your mind about whether you wanted teak or mahogany.'

The man with his back to Jeanne looked rather large. He

started waving his arms about, nearly knocking over his coffee cup. Clearly angry, he said in a loud voice, 'I don't give a toss about your problems and how you sort them, but I still want my boat ready by the end of the month, as agreed. I'm paying you a small fortune and I'm entitled to change my mind about which wood I want. Now I've chosen teak you can get on with it! I don't care if you have to go to Timbuctoo for it, that's your problem, not mine. Understand?'

Although Jeanne could only see his back she could sense the glare on Mr Evans' face as he thumped his fist on the table. She peeped up at Muscles from behind her raised cup and he looked flushed, his jaw tightly clenched in an apparent effort to stay calm. Not surprising, she thought, considering what a horrid man this Mr Evans seemed to be.

'Okay, Mr Evans, you'll have your boat ready as agreed. But there can be no more changes to the design or finish now.' His deep voice was cold.

Mr Evans stood up and as he moved to the side Jeanne saw that he possessed the belly of the over-indulged and the cut of his blazer and sharp-creased slacks proclaimed him to be wealthy as well. A florid face hinted at too great a love of alcohol which she knew to be one of the hazards of being a social go-getter on the island. Assuming he does live here of course. Perhaps he was a tax exile with money to burn and not much else to do except boss around those with less, she thought. Her hackles were rising on behalf of Muscles. She found this amusing as he had been so brusque with her the other day. Calling her drunk, indeed! But he seemed able to take care of himself, rising to shake hands, briefly, with Mr Evans who, with a grunt, marched off. Muscles sat down, letting out a deep sigh as he drank his coffee.

Glancing up he saw Jeanne looking at him and he scowled, quickly finished his coffee and left. Jeanne continued drinking her cappuccino and thought about what she had just witnessed. The man she thought of as Muscles appeared to be a boat builder and it looked like Mr Evans was a rich man who needed bringing down a peg or two. Hope he gets seasick in his new boat, she smiled grimly. Muscles still seemed to be a bit grumpy but at least he had a reason to be, with clients like that.

Leaving the café she went back to the car and drove down towards Town and the telephone company's office. She was impressed when told that the phone would be connected by the following day.

After Jeanne had unloaded all her purchases into Le Petit Chêne she went round feeding the fires and the range, enjoying the warmth permeating the cottage. Plugging in her shiny new electric kettle – her gran had rarely used anything electrical – she made some tea to go with the sandwich she'd bought.

It was time to start properly on the kitchen and most of the contents of the cupboards and larder ended up in black sacks. The majority of her gran's pots and pans were definitely past their use by date, being very heavy and blackened from years of constant use. Once the cupboards had been cleaned, the new pots were safely installed and the food put away on the scrubbed marble shelves in the pantry.

Jeanne went upstairs to Gran's bedroom. It was certainly the best room to choose, in spite of the memories. The sea could be seen from the front window and it was brighter than the other bedrooms. The mattress was in reasonable condition. It didn't seem damp but it was a bit musty. Jeanne filled up two new hot water bottles and placed them on the bed, covering them with a clean blanket.

She then brought up the largest electric fire she had bought and plugged it in, setting the thermostat on high. She also carried up the new bedding and put it on top of the clean blanket. Going downstairs again – this was better than a step class, Jeanne thought, grinning – she fetched the two smaller heaters. The bathroom heater she plugged into a socket on the landing and placed just inside the room. It was a pity she couldn't have it on when having a bath but she didn't fancy electrocuting herself. Her gran might have seen that as her comeuppance for using an electric fire, of course. She put the other heater on, full blast, in the small bedroom and quickly shut the door. Well, if that doesn't warm it up, nothing will.

There was still some work to do in the kitchen and it was all beginning to look much fresher and brighter when the doorbell rang. Jeanne opened the door to find a well-built man of about forty, with a ruddy, outdoors complexion and wearing gumboots, a well-worn sweater and muddy jeans.

'Afternoon, Miss Le Page. I'm Jim Le Prevost. Peter Ogier asked me to call round,' he smiled, stretching out a dirt-encrusted hand.

Jeanne gingerly shook his hand as she said, 'Thanks for coming, Jim, and at such short notice too.' Ushering him into the hall, Jeanne led him down towards the back door where she slipped on her boots before they went into the garden.

'What exactly would you like me to do?'

Jeanne discussed her ideas for tidying the garden, including cutting the grass and hedges.

Jim nodded and rubbed his nose, deep in thought.

'Right then. I reckon it'll take me and the lad about three days to do what you want. We could start next Monday, if that'd suit.' He named his price, which Jeanne thought was reasonable in view of the hard labour involved.

'That's fine, Jim. I look forward to seeing you next week then.'

In the kitchen, Jeanne emptied the dresser of her grandmother's best china and washed it carefully. She left it to drain as she polished the dresser with some newly purchased lavender-scented beeswax. Once dried she re-arranged the china on the now gleaming shelves, pleased to see the whole dresser shining with renewed life and colour.

It was now late afternoon and she went upstairs to check on the bedrooms and bathroom. All were fine except the small bedroom which she was shocked to find was still freezing although the fire was blasting out heat. How odd, she thought, unplugging the fire. No point in wasting electricity in here, anyway.

Downstairs she topped up the fires. The rooms were warming up a treat, the thick walls helping them to retain the heat.

Once back at the Ogier's, Peter helped her to unload the car before they joined Molly in the kitchen and Jeanne described what she'd achieved and that she was now ready to move into the cottage the next day.

Peter chipped in. 'Would you like to ring the builder now? You could say I've recommended him.'

The builder, Martin Brehaut, agreed to come round at 4.30pm on Wednesday.

By the time Jeanne had made her call, Molly had finished cooking the supper and they all chatted companionably as they ate. Peter then disappeared to work in his study and Jeanne lent Molly a hand in the kitchen. While Molly made a pot of tea Jeanne wandered into the sitting room. On one of the shelves were small framed photos of Phil and Natalie as babies. She picked them up and the dreaded memory was awakened. Pain shot through her as that awful day was re-played in her mind.

'I'm going to keep my baby, whatever you say!' Jeanne cried as Andy stood over her, his face taut with anger.

'You've done this on purpose, haven't you? Trying to trap me into something I'm not ready for. Well, you've made a big mistake, my girl. I told you what to do and if you insist on having the baby we're finished. You'd better start packing your stuff and find somewhere else to live. I'm off to the pub and I'll be back late.'

Jeanne collapsed on the bed, shaken to the core. Andy ran down the stairs, slamming the front door.

*Oh my God! How's it come to this? How can I have so misjudged his reaction to my pregnancy?* She'd thought he had wanted children as much as she did. While they were in Tenerife she'd been sick with a tummy bug and this must have affected her Pill. She'd found out she was pregnant a month later and had been ecstatic. Andy had been anything but.

'What! I don't want to have kids yet. I'm not ready to be tied down with all that domestic stuff. In a few years' time, maybe, but not yet.' Andy, normally laidback, was red-faced, pacing up and down the kitchen as Jeanne sat heavy as stone on the stool.

'You did this deliberately, didn't you? Forgot to take the Pill?'

'No, of course I didn't! I was sick, remember? That must have stopped the Pill working properly.'

'Well, you'll just have to have an abortion then. If you want us to stay together that's what you have to do.'

*An abortion! I can't do that. It's my baby we're talking about here. Surely he'll come round in time? I'll just humour him for now.* She felt miserable.

'Okay, I'll...I'll look into it.'

Andy had calmed down and they had not talked about it for a while. She had known it was weak of her. She should have discussed it with him but had been scared. Scared that he would leave her if she had their baby. She hadn't wanted to push him into walking away, believing he would accept the idea eventually.

But on that fateful day, two months ago, they had had a row and she had blurted out the truth – that she was keeping the baby…

As she was lying on the bed, wracked by sobs and wondering what on earth she was going to do or where she was going to go, the doorbell rang.

Andy. He must have forgotten his key. She jumped off the bed and headed to the stairs. She was so sure it was him and he'd come back to say sorry that she didn't look where she was going…her eyes were  blurred…she was barefoot and slipped on the wooden stairs, crashing to the hall below. She landed heavily, twisting her ankle. Trying to stand was agony so she crawled to the front door, crying out, 'Just a minute, I'm coming, Andy!' before pulling herself up to open the door.

'Thank God, you've come back…' Only it wasn't Andy, but their neighbour, Mary.

The disappointment was so intense it hit her like a physical blow. Then waves of stomach cramps took hold and she gasped with the pain.

One look at her face and Mary called an ambulance.

It was too late.  By the time Jeanne had arrived at the hospital she knew she had lost her baby.

# chapter 6

The next morning, burdened with an armful of flowers, Jeanne picked her way through the graves at St Saviours Church. It was completely still and peaceful. The church was quite high up, providing far-reaching views over the fields to the sea. Jeanne sighed as she trod carefully past ancient stones, thinking what an idyllic place to be buried, the quintessence of 'Rest In Peace'.

Some of the more recent graves displayed splashes of colour from fresh flowers while others bore the dying sticks of blooms brought weeks or even months ago. Jeanne vowed that while she was on the island she would bring fresh flowers weekly. The sight of the dried-up, colourless skeletons was so depressing.

It took a while for her to find her parents' grave with its beautifully polished black granite headstone standing proudly and protectively at the head. The grave had been unmarked when she had left the island in such a hurry fifteen years before. Reading the gold-lettered inscription brought tears to her eyes.

In Loving Memory

Of

Owen Le Page

1946–1990

A much loved Son and Father

And His Beloved Wife

Janet Le Page

1947–1990

A Much loved Mother

Died tragically together at sea

Forever in Our Hearts

## God Bless

Blowing her nose and wiping her eyes, Jeanne found memories of her parents crowding into her mind, evoking their happy times as a family. Images floated in: of the three of them when she was a little girl, together on the beach, building sandcastles or splashing in the sea; fishing with her father from his boat as she got older, triumphantly reeling in a sea bass; her mother waving goodbye at the gate as she started her first day at the grammar school, proud of her new oversized uniform; her parents beaming with pride as she collected a prize that last school year. There was so much that her parents had missed since then and Jeanne felt an urgent need to share everything with them.

'I'm back, Mum – Dad. I don't know for how long. There's so much to tell you! I managed to get good grades in my GCSEs and I went on to study A levels at the Sixth Form College near Aunt Kate. I...I couldn't stay here after . . .and Kate offered to have me. Looking back now, Mum, I realise how brave it was for her to take me on. I was a pretty stroppy, unhappy teenager who'd just lost her beloved parents.'

Jeanne stopped to take a deep breath as she recalled that most unhappy of times. Her decision to leave had distressed her gran, for which she was sorry. But she couldn't see beyond her own pain, which she now realised had been selfish of her. The need to escape the scene of so much grief and horror had been too strong. Kate, her mother's older sister, had never married and was a recently retired English teacher, still living in the Midlands town of their birth. Initially they had been an unlikely pairing. But after the first few decidedly edgy months, they had settled down into a mutually supportive friendship.

'So,' Jeanne continued, 'we got on really well and Kate encouraged me to go to university. I read English, gaining an upper second. After graduation I went into journalism. Then a few years later I met Andy.' A lump formed in her throat and tears pricked at her eyes as she forced herself to go on.

'We…lived together for a while…but we broke up recently, so I've come back. I'm at Gran's cottage and have to decide what to do next.'

Jeanne sat on the grassy mound as she talked. The desire to feel close to her parents was so overwhelming that it was like a power surge – she had to make a connection of some kind.

'I…I'd like to ask you both to help me make the right decision. I think I'll cope better if I know you're there, watching over me.'

Her face softened and her shoulders dropped as she had the intense feeling that her parents were standing either side of her, holding her in a warm, loving embrace.

Quickly brushing away the remaining tears, Jeanne unwrapped the flowers and filled the inset vases with yellow freesias and pink roses. Then she moved off to find her grandparents' grave, which bore a weathered grey granite headstone with a black lettered inscription. The last few lines recording Gran's death looked so much brighter. Kneeling on the grass she offered a quick prayer for them both.

'Oh, Gran, I'm so sorry I wasn't here when you died. Please forgive me. And thank you for the cottage. I'll do my best to look after it, especially the garden. Honest.'

Jeanne couldn't suppress a sheepish grin at the possibility of central heating going in to the cottage and decided not to mention it to Gran. The phrase 'turning in her grave' came to mind – might disturb Granpa, she thought.

Feeling a bit brighter, she filled the holder with the cheerful flowers and stood up to leave. She felt so much closer to her parents and grandparents that she began to think that it was right for her to be back. Everyone wanted to feel they belonged somewhere, she thought, as she went back to the car. This small island held her history and that of her father's family. Her maternal grandparents had died before she was born so this family was all she had really known, apart from Kate. They seemed to be calling her back to her birthplace. If this was so, then surely she would be able to renovate the cottage and live there? However, the thought of living on her own in the cottage conjured up all her fears. As she pointed the car in the direction of home she knew that there were still many ghosts to be laid.

Jeanne had been distraught the previous evening when the horror of her miscarriage had engulfed her yet again. Molly had come in with the tea and had held her tightly while she had poured out her story. Her friend had been great. Jeanne knew she needed to let it all out. With Molly's arms like a soothing blanket around her, it had not been difficult. Painful, yes. Of course. She had so wanted that baby! And coming so soon after losing her gran and then Andy…

Her hands gripped the steering wheel even harder. *Come on, girl, get a grip! It's been awful, yes, but you must move on. What was it that Molly had said this morning?*

'You have to let go, of both Andy and the baby, Jeanne. Of course, you're still grieving and that's natural but it's important to focus on the present. So you can heal.'

'I'll try,' Jeanne sighed. 'At least I've got the cottage to focus on and if I do go ahead with the building work, I'll probably not have any time to think at all.' She paused. 'Could getting involved in major building work be considered therapeutic, do you think?'

Molly laughed. 'People usually need therapy after they've had the builders in, so I wouldn't think so! Still, you're right in seeing it as something to focus on, instead of the past.'

It was late morning when Jeanne arrived at Le Petit Chêne. The sun skittered about behind soft, white clouds. Promising to be another warm, spring day Jeanne itched to be out in the garden or on the beach but she had other priorities.

As she carried her case inside, it struck her – *this is it! This is the first house I've owned – this is mine!*

Buoyed by the thought, she banked up the fires and unpacked her case upstairs, laying claim to the bedroom with her few personal possessions. After putting the kettle on for her daily caffeine hit she hunted out some vases, filling them with the remaining flowers and placed them in the kitchen, sitting room and bedroom. She smiled. Much more homely. As she sipped her coffee she wrote her "To Do" list, a habit which had helped her to stay organised throughout her adult life.

Phone calls headed her list and she was relieved to hear the familiar dialling tone as she lifted up the handset. It was time to phone Kate.

'Cleo's been wondering where you are. She slinks into your room and lies on a sweater you left on the bed. It's looking more like mohair by the day,' Kate chuckled.

'I miss Cleo too. I might get my own cat eventually so that I'll have someone to talk to and cuddle. Should have smuggled her over with me.' She paused. 'Kate, I might be longer than I'd thought. Will it be a problem to leave my things with you for a few more months?'

'No, of course not. You must do what you have to do, my dear. I've always thought of Guernsey as your true home. What are your plans now?'

They chatted for a few more minutes while Jeanne brought her up to date.

She replaced the phone, picturing Kate in her book-lined sitting room doing the same. A kind, quiet woman, Kate had come out of her shell in the role of surrogate mother. She later admitted to Jeanne that she had been happiest when she had lived with her.

When Jeanne and Andy had broken up after the loss of the baby she had fled to Kate for succour and healing, staying until she had felt strong enough to go back to Guernsey. Kate had been adamant that she should not put it off any longer.

'You must go, Jeanne. You owe it to your family to finalise your gran's affairs. I think it would be good for you to pick up the old threads again. If you do decide to settle there you can always build me an auntie wing!'

They had both laughed as they knew that nothing would entice Kate away from her beloved home and friends. She was an active member of so many groups and clubs that there would be a riot if she tried to leave.

It was now lunchtime and sitting at the old table, cosy by the range, Jeanne savoured the first proper meal in her cottage. As she finished her salad, the kitchen was suddenly suffused with the smell of baking. Jeanne felt the hairs on the nape of her neck stand on end. Closing her eyes, she saw her grandmother, be-floured and aproned, beaming her big warm smile.

'Thanks, Gran,' Jeanne whispered. The aroma receded, to be replaced by the tang of the sea floating through the window. This fresh smell induced her to go for a brisk walk on the beach.

That evening Jeanne prepared a simple stir fry to the background of Robbie Williams. Without a TV the evenings could have been lonely, but the new micro stereo she had bought at the Bridge would keep her company.

She read little of the latest Maeve Binchy before she started yawning. She went upstairs, smiling as her eyes took in the cosier bedroom. The flowers and bright new bed linen gave it a warmth lacking just days earlier. Jeanne switched off the heater and climbed into bed. Would Guernsey be able to offer her the healing she so badly needed? She had loved it once. Perhaps the spark was still there. She hoped so. Turning over she was asleep within minutes.

But her sleep was not dreamless. She dreamt she was a child again playing hide and seek with her parents, becoming frantic when she couldn't find them. Suddenly they appeared, laughing and reaching out to her. With relief she threw herself into their arms, feeling safe once more.

# chapter 7

High on Jeanne's list was finding her grandmother's recipes and family papers and she began her search the next morning. After going through the cottage collecting a hotchpotch of paperwork she piled it all onto the kitchen table.

Then she remembered the attic.

Grabbing a torch she went up the ladder. It was cold and extremely dusty. Shivering, she looked around at the scattered boxes and all the items which represented her family's past. There was an old wooden tailor's dummy – she had forgotten that Gran had made her own clothes; an ancient leather sailor's trunk bearing the initials O.E. Le P. – (Granpa's?); a Singer sewing machine in a solid wooden case and various boxes filled with photo albums, old clothes, pictures and children's toys. There was also stuff from her parents' house that had been considered worth keeping, but she wasn't ready to look through that yet. She found some older boxes filled with assorted papers and notebooks and took them down, one at a time.

Coughing up the disturbed dust, Jeanne washed her hands and brushed off the cobwebs before carrying the boxes into the kitchen. It was becoming cluttered in there and she decided to eliminate all the papers not worth keeping. Grabbing a black sack, she went through old bills and receipts that were no longer relevant; old magazines about fishing her grandfather had accumulated over many years, so well read that they were falling apart; and the parish magazines her gran had kept which looked unread.

Thinking about this, Jeanne realised that she had rarely seen her gran reading anything. She preferred to be doing something she considered useful, like cooking or gardening and was quite dismissive of reading as a leisure activity. She had always tut-tutted when she saw Jeanne with her head buried in a book which, as a teenager, had been most of the time.

'You're not reading again, my girl, are you? You could give me a hand in the garden. The herb beds need weeding and I want some chives, sage and rosemary to make up a remedy for old Mrs Le Prevost who's been poorly. Now, put that book down and out you go!'

'Okay, Gran,' Jeanne replied, reluctantly putting down the P.D. James she'd been reading and went out to the herb bed. She usually enjoyed pottering amongst the herbs and loved their scent on her hands as she picked the bunches her gran had asked for, but she had just come to a particularly gripping part of the thriller and had been loath to break away. She sighed, anticipating the pleasure of getting back to her book later. Going back indoors she was given the rare privilege of helping Gran prepare the tincture for Mrs Le Prevost. Gran's remedies were much sought after by elderly neighbours who preferred them to modern medicines.

Smiling at the memory, Jeanne remained thoughtful for a few more minutes. Books had been, and still were, very important to her but her gran had had a far more limited education. She had also held the traditional view that women were to run the household and raise children and not forge careers. Her daughter-in-law had met with approval by renouncing her job as soon as she had married her son, Owen.

Shaking her head, Jeanne filled the black sack with the unwanted items so that she could start sifting through the boxes from the attic. These yielded the most interesting finds yet – old notebooks with a mix of pasted in and loose pages, neatly written in varied handwriting. They proved to be recipes in English, French and the local dialect, Guernsey French and seemed to cover many years of cooking from both sides of the Channel. Jeanne's heart began to race as she turned the pages. *Wow! What a treasure trove, must go back more than a hundred years!*

For Jeanne, Guernsey French, or patois, and related to the French dialect of Normandy, was equivalent to double-Dutch. It was no longer taught in schools and because most of the island children had been evacuated during the Second World War, there had been little chance to pass it on to the next generation. But the more elderly islanders still used it occasionally among themselves, particularly when they wanted to say something unflattering about the mainlanders or much younger locals. She remembered her gran chatting to her friends in patois and unable to understand a word they were saying. Probably just as well! She smiled to herself, putting the notebooks and loose recipes carefully to one side before looking at the other boxes.

One contained a variety of papers from her father's childhood and youth. After a quick glance, she decided to go through them more thoroughly another time. Even seeing her father's name on the papers made her stomach lurch. The ghosts of the past were not going to lie down quietly. Frowning, she opened another box which had been sealed long ago, full of yellowing, handwritten letters.

Intrigued, she flipped through the envelopes and noticed that none bore any stamps so must have been hand delivered. All were addressed, in the same handwriting, to her grandmother in her maiden name of Ozanne. With mixed feelings, she carefully opened the top letter. *Mm, what are these? Perhaps I shouldn't be reading them. They're private letters belonging to Gran. Looks like a firm hand but the English is poor, can't really make it out.* Turning to the last page she glanced at the signature – 'Wilhelm'.

*A German! Was this written during the German Occupation? That was over sixty years ago when Gran was a young woman. Mm, could Gran have had a secret past? She didn't destroy them so perhaps she meant me to read them one day? Or maybe I'm just trying to excuse my prying!*

Troubled, she paced around the kitchen, deciding to read it properly later.

By now it was late morning and Jeanne made herself a coffee as she flicked through her grandfather's papers. Most of them were old receipts from the Fisherman's Co-operative on the Castle Pier where he sold his catch, bought by the catering industry and housewives wanting fresh fish.

In her mind's eye she saw herself as a little girl sitting in her grandfather's van, intoxicated by the smell of freshly caught fish and so happy that she had been asked to help, that she bounced up and down in excitement.

Granpa, twinkling, turned to her, 'Calm down, m'dear. Not sure the ol' springs can cope with all that bouncin'. Soon be there, eh.'

When they arrived at the wholesalers he gave her a small tray of fish to carry, making her feel important.

'There you are, lass. I'll take the big 'un.'

Jeanne was honour bound not to drop it and she didn't, even though her arms ached. She walked so slowly that her grandfather had to shorten his stride to avoid bumping into her. Reaching the counter, she passed the tray to a smiling man waiting with outstretched arms. After putting down his own much heavier load, Granpa had patted her head and said, 'Good girl. I couldn't have managed without you, eh.' Jeanne had glowed with pride all the way home and couldn't wait to tell her parents how much Granpa had needed her help.

The smell of freshly caught fish that always clung to the van and to her grandfather had remained with her over the years and whenever she went into a fishmongers she was reminded of him, winking at her as she carried that tray.

He had died at sea, still working at seventy. His fishing boat had been caught in a sudden squall and been dashed onto the hidden rocks, notorious in these coastal waters. A strong and capable sailor, he was knocked out and alone. His mate, who should have been with him, was taken ill at the last minute and her grandfather had gone out to collect his lobsters, fetching premium prices at that time.

After his death Jeanne and her mother had spent more and more time at her gran's cottage and less in their own house not far away. Her father, an engineer, worked abroad for weeks at a time so they were happy to be with Gran. A couple of years after Granpa's death her father had secured a job on the island, enabling him to spend all his free time with his family.

Jeanne sighed as she turned over the fragile pieces of paper which still stirred up such vivid images of the past. She didn't want to throw the receipts away but was unsure what use they had, apart from being a link with the past.

As a writer she was conscious that seemingly innocuous documents might have a relevance at some time and she began to toy with the idea of a story or article based on the papers now strewn over the table. Having decided that she needed proper containers and files, she went out and bought a selection from a shop in Cobo.

By the time she had sorted the papers into labelled files she was hungry and cooked herself a light lunch. After clearing away she still had a couple of hours before the builder was due and concentrated on the recipes.

The majority of these were in her grandmother's

handwriting, but she did not recognise those written in French, which looked much older. The paper was almost brown with age and the ink and writing seemed to belong to an earlier era, perhaps the 1800s, she guessed.

Jeanne vaguely remembered being told that her gran's family, from Normandy, had connections to well-known mid-nineteenth century Parisian restaurateurs. They had catered to the gourmands of the city and their food had, according to legend, been of the highest standard. When the couple retired they went to live with their married son in Normandy. It was this couples' daughter and her husband who had moved to Guernsey sometime in the late 1800s or early 1900s, as Jeanne remembered the story.

It was thrilling to think that she might be in possession of the recipes that had originated from those Parisian restaurateurs, possibly written down by their son or granddaughter. Scanning them she hoped that her schoolgirl French would be up to translating them.

She grinned as she read *Daube de Boeuf Provencale* and was able to translate it sufficiently to recognise the recipe that Molly had pinched from her mother, Janet. All the French dishes were of the classical *haute cuisine* style and a complete contrast to the local Guernsey dishes usually favoured by her grandmother. She guessed that the French dishes were cooked on more formal occasions and at times when her grandparents could afford the expensive ingredients required, such as beef and wine, which had to be imported into the island.

The local dishes were based on ingredients more readily and cheaply available, such as fish, shellfish, rabbit, pigeon, chicken and eggs. Jeanne fondly remembered some of Gran's chicken and rabbit dishes and thumbed through the recipes in her handwriting to find them. Written in a mixture of Guernsey French and English made them difficult to follow. She read some of the headings –

*'Bouidrie d'Poulet et Legumes'*, obviously something to do with chicken and vegetables – *'Aën Pâtaï à Lapins'*, rabbit? – *'Enne Jarraïe d'Haricäots'*, probably the famous Guernsey Bean Jar and *'D'Ormés Picquelaï'*, something to do with ormers, a local delicacy, Jeanne guessed. Struggling, she decided to ask Molly for advice on the translations.

As she was flicking through the notebooks, trying to make sense of what her gran had written, the doorbell rang and Jeanne was surprised to find that it was already half past four. She opened the door to greet Martin Brehaut and invited him in. Of medium height, with his dark hair showing flecks of grey, his eyes darted around the kitchen as she led him through.

'Thanks for coming so quickly, Martin, I know how busy you builders are.'

'No problem. Good to see the old cottage again.'

He must have noticed her puzzled expression as he went on, 'About five years ago I did some work on the roof for your grandmother as well as one or two other little jobs she had at the time. Hope the roof's stayed sound since then?' His smile was hesitant.

Hmm, she thought, a shy and honest builder. That's a plus.

'Yes, I think so. Shall we go round and I'll explain what I'd like done?'

Martin nodded and they went from room to room while Jeanne consulted the list Peter had drawn up. He made little comment, just nodded occasionally at appropriate moments. Once upstairs, Martin went up into the attic on his own and was gone so long that Jeanne was concerned that he may have knocked himself out on a low beam. Just as she was about to go up the ladder, his now much greyer head appeared in the hatchway and he joined her on the landing.

'Yes, it's dry, for sure, and the beams are sound. No sign

of dry rot or woodworm.'

Jeanne smiled her relief and they checked the bedrooms, with Martin tapping and knocking on the walls and ceilings as they went round. As she opened the door to the little bedroom she waited for a reaction from him but none came, he just tapped and knocked as before. They went outside for Martin to take a good look at the walls and roof.

'Can see a few tiles that've slipped and the gutter's leaking in places,' he said as he pointed to rusty stains on the walls and down the drainpipe.

'Best to replace the lot with black plastic and get rid of the old iron ones,' he added. Jeanne nodded her agreement and they then inspected the windows and doors, made of weathered wood but still sound. Once they had checked everything off the list Jeanne asked him if he wanted a cup of tea but he shook his head.

'Best get going, Jeanne. Lots to do tonight. I'll work out some figures for you by next week and drop 'em in. Need to talk to my plumber and electrician first, though.' Nodding at the cottage he added, 'Be good to see the old place come alive again. Mrs Le Page was a nice ol' dear but she wasn't as bothered about the cottage as the garden, eh?'

'No, she wasn't, but at least she kept it dry and in one piece.'

Martin nodded and left, bearing his copy of the list of works.

Jeanne decided that she, at least, needed a cup of tea and switched on the kettle. As she stood waiting for it to boil she thought about Martin Brehaut. She liked his quietness and the fact that he hadn't bombarded her with lots of extra work he considered necessary. He had accepted that she only wanted the basic professional work doing and that she would do the finishing touches herself, sourcing her own fittings. He had even offered her his builder's discount on sanitary fittings and tiles – another plus.

After she had finished her tea Jeanne phoned the Ogiers. Peter answered.

'Jeanne, I'm glad you phoned, I'd been wondering how you are. Staying warm?'

'Yes, very warm, thanks. But it sure is a messy job cleaning out those fires every day. Makes you appreciate the wonders of central heating! Martin Brehaut came round today and I was quite impressed with him. I should get his quote by next week and then I'll have to chat up the bank manager.' She paused. 'Is Molly there, Peter? I'd like a quick word if she is.'

Molly came to the phone and Jeanne told her about the papers she had been going through. She mentioned the recipes and the problems with the Guernsey French.

'Do you know anyone who could translate them for me?'

Molly thought for a moment and answered, 'Yes, I do. There's a Mrs Le Maitre who, like us, is a member of *La Societé Guernesiaise* and is fluent in the patois. I could give her a ring and ask her. Is there much to translate?'

'About thirty recipes, I think. But they're all quite short and some are partly in English, too. I'm trying to translate the French recipes which are a bit easier but if I get stuck would you give me a hand? Your French was pretty good if I remember rightly.'

'Yes, of course. I'd love to see the recipes anyway, particularly if they're as good as the *Daube de Boeuf Provencale*. How exciting! Perhaps you could write a cookery book, Jeanne.'

'Mm, perhaps. Hadn't thought of that. Have to see how they turn out in English and if the ingredients are easily available.'

She tingled with her writer's buzz.

'There's something else, Molly. I've found a number of letters written to my grandmother before she was married and they're from a German. Do you know anything about Gran's past, perhaps during the Occupation?'

'No, I don't. Your grandparents were very private people and your father never said anything. Do you think these are love letters then?' Jeanne heard the disbelief in Molly's voice.

'Well, at first glance I certainly think so! The English isn't very good so I'll have to read them more thoroughly to be sure. There's about forty letters so I think they must have been, at the least, very good friends! He was called Wilhelm.'

'Heavens! It certainly sounds as if there was something going on. A number of local women did have German lovers during the Occupation and some even had babies. A few married after the war although I don't think many stayed here. I suppose it would have been awkward for them and any children. Well, I'm all agog now! I love mysteries – hope you'll keep me informed.'

'For sure. Gran didn't start going out with Granpa until after the war as he was in the navy fighting for king and country, so she was a free agent. I guess the tricky bit was his being the enemy. But it might make a good story.'

'Hmm, I can hear the wheels in your writer's brain grinding from here,' Molly laughed. 'The scent of a good story and a delicious meal, what a combination!'

Jeanne laughed. 'Hey, who's getting carried away now! I'll let you know if there's anything to be excited about when I've read a few letters. In the meantime, I'd be glad if you'd talk to Mrs Le Maitre for me.'

They said their goodbyes and Jeanne began to think about what she was making for supper that night, the talk of food having made her hungry. It would be something simple, but the thought of all those mouth-watering recipes prompted her to go through some of them that evening so that she could buy the ingredients for a real feast. I might even invite Peter and Molly, she decided.

By about ten o'clock she was yawning and decided to go up with her book and the very first letter that Wilhelm had written. She found that they had all been dated, starting in July 1943 and ending in February 1945, just a few months before the British liberated the islands. Diving under the duvet she settled down for a glimpse into her grandmother's past and an intriguing sixty year old mystery.

# chapter 8

Springing out of bed the next morning Jeanne ran a bath – a slow process thanks to the rusty pipes – while she went downstairs to make a cup of tea. Back upstairs she perched on the bath sipping slowly as the water reached a suitable depth for immersion. The addition of exotic smelling bath gel made it more inviting, the foam hiding the cracks in the enamel. She enjoyed a good soak as her mind raced in different directions, inspired by Wilhelm's letter, which she now re-read in the bath. It had been a love letter and stirred her romantic soul. Now she was desperate to know what had happened between the two lovers. She read:

*Mein Leibling Jeanne!*

*It was good so to see you last night at the movie theatre. Was the film good, it not was? It was shamed one, that we were not able to seat us together and Griffhande, however it another pleasure was always to be in the same room. I love to see and know your smiling face that you want to be also with me. I have this week the duty at the Gewehreinbettung on the bunker and to see you soon hope. Were we able to meet at 8 o'clock on Friday in the wood near of the bunker, yes? For the walk? I want that my English it improves and is that why I at the writing to you. Bitte, write back to me!*

*Ich liebe dich!*

*Wilhelm*

Ah! They must have known each other a while if Wilhelm's already expressing his love for Gran. If only she knew what Gran had thought about Wilhelm. Oh, it's so frustrating reading a one-sided correspondence.

The recipes she had read through the previous day had spurred her to invite Peter and Molly for dinner on Friday. After her bath she made a quick call to Molly who was happy to accept the invitation to a French supper adding, 'As long as you're sure you've translated the French correctly.'

Jeanne laughed. 'Don't worry. It's very straightforward. I'm not likely to get my *pommes de terres* mixed up with my *pamplemousse.*'

Excited at the thought of cooking and entertaining, she wrote out her shopping list for the ingredients and added candles and candleholders.

They would eat in the kitchen where it was cosy. Jeanne wanted to create a welcoming ambience. As she looked at the room critically she decided that the table might benefit from a crisp white tablecloth to set off her new cutlery and glassware. Gran's blue and yellow china would add the finishing touch. She checked the linen in the airing cupboard and underneath a pile of decidedly threadbare sheets, spotted an Irish linen tablecloth with elaborate cutwork. She shook it out and it was perfect – no stains or holes and still white. Jeanne stroked the cloth, thinking how wonderful it was to use such lovely things. Gran had owned it for years, but it looked rarely used. Digging around again she unearthed matching napkins, also in good condition, though everything needed airing and ironing.

Deciding to have a quick look in the attic for anything that could throw more light on her grandmother's relationship with 'Wilhelm', Jeanne climbed up the ladder, shining the torch ahead of her. She gave the trunk lid a big shove and looked inside. It seemed to be full of old men's clothes. Searching through them she couldn't see anything else except a battered hip flask and a pair of binoculars.

Probably Granpa's..

Closing the trunk, she moved over to the boxes she had glanced at the previous day. The one containing the photo albums looked promising and Jeanne put it aside to take down. Another box contained what seemed to be Gran's clothes. They looked very dated and slim-fitting whereas Gran had been decidedly cuddly in later life. Wondering if they went back to the forties she began to sift through the dresses, skirts and blouses with a reverence befitting such old and personal items.

She was particularly anxious to find anything with pockets and searched right to the bottom of the box. Just as she was admitting defeat, she pulled out one last item, a pretty cream cotton tea dress packed carefully in old wafer-thin tissue paper. As Jeanne shook it free something fell out of the pocket. Picking up the torch she saw it was a small black and white photo of a man in uniform. It wasn't very clear in the torch light so Jeanne re-packed all the clothes and, popping the photo in the box of albums, went back downstairs.

Sitting at the kitchen table she picked up the photo for a closer look. The man was bareheaded with fair hair and wore a soldier's uniform with knee-high leather boots. Jeanne couldn't distinguish any insignia on the uniform but it looked like the ones she had seen as a girl at the German Occupation Museum. Her grandfather had been in the Navy and had had dark hair when young, so she knew it wasn't him. *I can't believe it! I think I've found Wilhelm.* She jumped up and down with excitement.

Calming down, she remembered seeing a magnifying glass in her grandfather's desk. Peering through the glass she could now quite clearly see the German eagle on the sleeve. Jeanne then looked more closely at the man smiling cheerfully at the camera. He had an open, intelligent face and looked young, probably in his early twenties. Mm, he's certainly attractive, she mused. She could see why Gran was drawn to him. He looked anything but a fighting machine and if not for the war, perhaps he would have gone to university and become who knows what. Turning over the photo she saw in small neat writing – '30th May 1943'. No name. Pity. Jeanne was still sure it was Wilhelm as the date fitted in with the letter and hoped to find out more as she read his letters, placing the photo and envelopes in a protective polythene binder.

Jeanne then opened the box of photo albums. Even though there weren't likely to be more photos of Wilhelm, she still wanted to browse through those of her family. The very earliest ones, in sepia, were neatly arranged in an album with white hand-written descriptions beneath each photo, standing out clearly against the charcoal coloured card. The first one was labelled 'Marie-France Dupres and Edward Bougourd, married 12th April 1900'. *Mm, this must have been my French great-great-Grandmother, the granddaughter of the Parisian restaurateurs. How exciting!* The couple looked stiff and ill at ease in their wedding clothes, a high-necked, wasp-waisted dress adorned with lace for her and a heavy wool suit with stiff collar and tie for him. The following photos showed the family of the bride and groom gathered around them, all staring sombrely at the camera.

Next were photos of the new parents with their first child, a boy named Alfred, in long christening robes, and others showing them with their next, and apparently last child, a girl called Jeanette, born in 1902. This would have been her grandmother's mother, who went on to marry, according to the photos, a certain Raymond Ozanne in 1923. *This is great, my family history in pictures. My roots – where I belong.* Jeanne couldn't remember having seen the photos as a girl, making the find that more exciting.

The album was solely devoted to her grandmother's

family and right at the back was the wedding photo of her own parents, which gave her a jolt. She picked up another album, not as well organised, with the photos only labelled sporadically, and seeming to follow the male side of the family, from the Bougourds to the Le Pages. As she flicked through the album Jeanne could see why people wanted to trace their family trees and fill in all the missing details.

Judging by the clothes worn and the backgrounds depicted in the photos, Jeanne guessed that her family had been neither poor nor rich but fairly comfortable by the standards of the times. She knew there was a tradition of fishing on her grandfather's side and a mixture of farming and fishing on her grandmother's.

Island life had precluded university for all but the more wealthy islanders and her father had been the first member of the family to study in England for a degree. It was now very common for youngsters to go away to study and, unfortunately for the islands, many did not want to return after a taste of mainland life and the opportunities available to bright, ambitious graduates. Phil and Natalie Ogier being a case in point. Jeanne bit her lip as she considered her own defection. She'd had pressing reasons to leave (in her mind anyway) and had never contemplated returning to live here but she could see that there might be compensations. The pace of life was still slower than in the UK but the island had become far more cosmopolitan with the dramatic influx of the finance industry. And it was easy to fly to London for the bright lights. She had no real ties to the mainland – apart from her Aunt Kate – and she could work here as well as anywhere else.

She allowed herself to think about what it would really mean to stay, reclaiming her newly discovered roots. *Well, I could write a cookery book as Molly suggested and perhaps I could write an article on the transformation of island life...and a...Hey, at this rate I could keep busy writing articles and books on my family and Guernsey for ages!*

She was still toying with this thought when the phone rang.

'Hi, Jeanne? It's me, Marcus. How are you?'

'I'm fine, thanks. What a surprise. How'd you get my number?'

'From Mr Ogier. I wanted to invite you to the barbecue I mentioned the other day. We're planning on going to Portelet Harbour on Saturday, about four o'clock. Please say you'll come.' His voice was warm and persuasive.

'Yes, I'd love to. Do I have to bring anything?' Jeanne's heart was racing and she was glad that Marcus couldn't see her pink face.

'No, I'll provide the food etc. We're all chipping in with supplies and you'll be pleased to know the men are in charge of the cooking, so you girls can just relax,' he chuckled.

'Sounds even better! How many of us will there be?'

'About eight, I think. There may be some you remember from school.' He paused. 'How's your cottage?'

Jeanne brought him up to date, then he said, 'Well, best get going, got a few people to call now. I'm really looking forward to seeing you on Saturday. Pick you up about a quarter to four, if that's okay?'

'Fine, thanks. Look forward to seeing you then.'

After Marcus had checked her address and said goodbye Jeanne sat for a moment deep in thought. She knew she needed to get out and make friends and she was still attracted to Marcus, but she was also scared about re-joining the human race and particularly meeting people she knew from school. *Ah well, I'll just have to be a big brave girl, I guess. At least they can't eat me.* Amused at the thought she settled down with Maeve Binchy and Robbie Williams for the evening.

Friday dawned bright and clear and as the sun shone

through the thin curtains Jeanne slowly came to. A feeling of well-being flowed through her as she stretched and opened her eyes. The usual mental review of the previous day brought a smile to her face as she recalled the phone call from Marcus. She also remembered that tonight she was due to be the "hostess with the mostest" and the thought propelled her out of bed to run her bath, humming 'Angels' to herself.

After giving the cottage a good clean Jeanne went for a walk before lunch. As she headed up the beach she heard bursts of laughter from groups of children making sandcastles, playing with a Frisbee or a bat and ball. Their laughter was infectious and when a Frisbee headed in her direction she caught it and laughing, spun it back to the grinning boy who had sent it winging towards her. 'Well caught!' he shouted before throwing it back again.

Jeanne played with him for a few more minutes before spotting what looked like the boy's mother coming to check on him and, after a quick wave, she set off back down the beach. Groups of parents had settled themselves against the granite walls edging the sand, sheltered from any wind yet still able to keep track of their offspring. It looked as if some families had grouped together. Typically, she thought, the women were chatting happily with each other, while the men were less sociable, their noses buried in newspapers or books, with an occasional glance to check little Johnny wasn't too close to the water.

Jeanne sighed, wishing she was nine years old again playing on the beach with her own family. Still, she could be a child again on the inside and she ran back along the beach, arms aloft as if she were flying a kite. Catching the eyes of bemused children she laughed, encouraging them to join in. She arrived home feeling exhilarated and ready for anything.

After a quick lunch Jeanne headed up the coast to the

Bridge to buy the food and other necessities for her small dinner party. She decided that if she did put in a new kitchen she'd definitely buy the biggest fridge and freezer she could afford. Then she wouldn't need to go shopping more than once a week. Bliss! Her smile was broad as she drove along the coast, enjoying the sense of belonging, of "coming home". Then, as the unwelcome memory of why she had left Guernsey popped into her head, her smile disappeared. If only the truth behind the fatal accident would emerge she could move on and make a new life for herself. She sighed. *Perhaps I should consider Molly's suggestion of using hypnosis to recover my memory. But that'll have to wait until I've made a decision about the building work and whether or not to stay on the island.*

Before shopping she decided to take a quick stroll round by the harbour and have a look at the new marina which had just been completed. It had always been a busy little port with small boats moored at random but had looked messy at low tide, with the boats balancing precariously on the mud. Now the same small craft were neatly lined up against new pontoons stretching out from the harbour walls. Jeanne admired the ranks of boats buoyant on the high tide. Breathing in the fresh sea air, she passed the warehouses where the marine engineers and boat-builders were based. *Mm, wonder if that's where Muscles hangs out?*

The day was still sunny, with a few scattered clouds, and Jeanne felt good as she drove along, Island FM blaring out of the radio. Even being caught in a tailback behind a small car being driven at exactly 20 mph didn't dent her mood. She was nevertheless relieved when the car turned left at Albecq, allowing her to increase her speed to a dizzy 35 mph.

After unloading her shopping into the kitchen, her first concern was keeping the white wine chilled. This would not have been a problem less than a week ago as the whole house had been freezing. Now the only cold places were the pantry with its marble shelves and the small bedroom which only seemed cold to her. She put the Chablis in an old terracotta pot on the lowest shelf and hoped for the best.

She prepared her starter which also needed to be chilled before serving, placing the stuffed grapefruit shells on another pantry shelf. The wine still felt cold to the touch and Jeanne settled down at the kitchen table to prepare the vegetables for the main course.

Having checked that the range was still going strong, she set the table, twisting the napkins into a stylish shape and setting candles either side of the vase of freesias down the centre of the table. Jeanne smiled with pleasure, hoping that the food would live up to the table setting.

While the casserole was simmering on the hob she went upstairs to freshen up and changed into a more dressy long black linen skirt and red T-shirt. Fishing around in the small jewellery box she'd brought with her, she found some pretty gold hoop earrings and a plain gold chain. She peered into the small bedroom mirror to admire the effect.

After uncorking the Bordeaux, giving it time to breathe, she set out a selection of cheese on a plate in the pantry. As she went into the sitting room and switched on the stereo the doorbell rang.

'Hi, welcome to my humble abode!' Jeanne smiled at them, giving them each a hug.

The meal was a success and Jeanne was happy to receive compliments on both the food and the way the cottage had improved. She had served *Pamplemousse au Crabe* as the starter and *Agneau Champvallon* for the main course. The lamb so tender it fell off the bone.

Molly said that Mrs Le Maitre would be happy to do the translations for her but would like to keep copies and Jeanne was happy to agree. She lived near Portelet Harbour so Jeanne could pop them round the next day.

As her guests were leaving, Molly asked, 'Would you like to come round for dinner on Sunday? There's a good drama on TV so you can catch up with some culture.'

'Thanks, I'd love to. And, er, would you mind if I bring my washing round as well?'

They left, laughing. Jeanne went into the kitchen and filled the sink with hot, soapy water and, Marigolds to the fore, she waded through the pots as Dido sang out from the CD player.

In bed by eleven o'clock she was ready for a few pages of Joanna Trollope, having finished the Maeve Binchy. She was pleased with her first attempt at entertaining and the success of her food. Good on yer, Great-great-grandma, she thought, with a grin. Obviously, old recipes (and cooks) never die. Even though she'd enjoyed the evening, she would really like to have friends her own age, to talk about the more youthful topics of films, the latest fashions and music, rather than builders and cooking. Fond of Molly and Peter as she was, Jeanne was glad that the next day she would be spending time with people her own age.

Thinking about the barbecue reminded her that she would be seeing Marcus again and she started to think about why he had invited her. *I got the impression he didn't have a girlfriend. Was he attracted to me? Or just needed someone to tag along with? After all, he thinks I'm only here for a little while so I wouldn't be looking for a relationship. Perhaps he just thinks I'd like to meet old friends? If he is looking for a relationship would I be interested? No way! It's too soon…Not sure I even like men much at the moment and I don't even know what to do about the cottage. And I haven't decided if I **want** to live here – it'll mean facing those blasted demons if I do!*

# chapter 9

Jeanne's biggest decision the next morning was what to wear for the barbecue. Deciding against shorts – legs too pale and it might be cold later – she settled on a slim-fitting pair of black, low slung jeans with a blue V-necked cotton top which emphasised her figure and the colour of her eyes. She wasn't trying to attract anyone, she told herself. Definitely not. Decision made, she threw on her usual, decidedly grubby jeans and a clean T-shirt before having a quick breakfast and two cups of coffee.

Going through her gran's notebook of recipes, she ticked those that needed to be translated from the local patois and put the book in a plastic bag with a note to Mrs Le Maitre. She then started on her translation of the French recipes, taking a break for lunch.

Later Jeanne spent about an hour wrestling with the last of the French recipes and when a mal de tête threatened to develop, she went into the garden for some fresh air. The prospect of seeing the garden being improved next week helped to lift the tension evoked by the intense concentration. She pottered about, idly pulling up weeds, even though the gardeners would be doing some heavy digging in a couple of days. At the top of the orchard stood a grand old oak tree in pride of place, the very tree which had given its name to the cottage and which she had loved to climb as a child. Jeanne hauled herself up to where the branches formed a natural seat. As she sat gazing down at the orchard, she pictured herself as a child again.

She was about eight, skinny, with long dark hair tied

back in a ponytail and running amongst the trees crying out 'You can't catch me!' to her father who, handicapped by a blindfold, kept stumbling into the trees. Jeanne darted around, teasing him. 'Come on, Daddy, you're not trying very hard,' she laughed at the tall, brown haired man who was nearly on his knees.

'I give up, you win – again!' he groaned, before collapsing in a heap and pulling off the blindfold, revealing bright blue eyes. She rushed towards her father and threw her small arms around him – or rather his leg which was all she could manage. He laughed down at her and pulled her up, tickling her until she screamed for mercy.

She shook her head at the memory and allowed herself to focus on the far-reaching vista spread before her. From this sheltered vantage point she could see Vazon Bay to her right and Perelle Bay to her left, noting that the tide was low and the sea calm. Good, perfect for the barbecue. Glancing at her watch she realised it was time to change and scrambled down inelegantly, landing with a bump.

Fifteen minutes later she had changed and was just spraying on perfume when the doorbell rang.

'Hi, Jeanne. Hey, you smell nice!' Marcus grinned as he gave her a kiss on both cheeks. Holding her arms, he added, 'and you look great too.'

'Thanks.' She felt flustered, from the last-minute rush, she reassured herself.

'Ready?'

'Yep. I'll just grab my things. I've got to drop something in at a house in Rocquaine, if that's okay?'

'No problem. We've plenty of time.'

Marcus waited until she had locked up and then opened the passenger door of his two-seater sports car for her. Very nice, she thought, glad that she was wearing trousers and not a short skirt. She had never mastered the art of getting in and out of a low slung car with any degree of decorum, while wearing a skirt. Perhaps she'd better start practising, she smiled to herself.

Marcus said little as he drove down the coast, except to confirm there would be eight at the barbecue. Jeanne enjoyed the novelty of being driven by someone else. She was able to admire the view of fields and hills to her left and the low-lying craggy coastline to her right.

'Which road do we want at Rocquaine?'

'Route du Coudre, just before the Cup and Saucer,' she replied, referring to Fort Grey, an old Napoleonic Fort, now a nautical museum and shaped like an upside-down cup on a saucer. As they pulled in to the road Jeanne had to check the names of the houses – numbers were rarely used on the island – pointing to a stone cottage on the left.

'Won't be long,' she said, before popping the notebook through the letterbox.

He drove back to the main road, turning left towards Pleinmont, the furthermost corner to the south-west of the island.

'I've had a builder round this week, to give me a quote for the work that needs doing.'

'So you've decided to do it up after all?'

'I'm waiting for the quote before making a final decision. But I'm slowly coming round to the idea.'

'So I guess that would mean you staying here for some time, then?' he asked, an edge to his voice.

'Mm. Several months, at least, I suppose,' she replied, thinking he sounded a bit odd.

By this time they had reached the parking area just before Portelet Harbour and Marcus opened the door for Jeanne before retrieving two cool boxes and a picnic hamper from the boot.

'You've brought loads! I should have brought something.' Jeanne was dismayed.

'Don't be silly. There's not that much, but you can give me a hand carrying it if you're feeling guilty.' He laughed at her.

Jeanne took hold of the picnic hamper and they walked along to the slipway leading to the beach. As they went down she saw two couples standing together, focused on a large portable barbecue secured amongst sheltering rocks, while surrounded by bags and boxes.

'Hi guys!' Marcus called out as they approached the group, who turned round and smiled.

'This is Jeanne who used to live here but has been in England for years. I'll introduce you – Scott and Colette, Tim and Rachel.'

As they shook hands and exchanged greetings, almost simultaneously, Jeanne and Rachel said, 'I know you, don't I?' and they both burst out laughing. They had been in the same class at school.

'It's been so long, Jeanne. How've you been? It was so awful about your mum and dad...' Rachel's voice was sympathetic, putting Jeanne at ease as she told her what she had been doing over the years.

'Now I have to decide what to do about the cottage and I'm not sure if I'll be staying here long.'

'Well, I hope you do stay. It's great to see a familiar face as a lot of our year have settled in the UK. After uni I came back here to teach and I love it.' Rachel's face lit up as she spoke.

'That's great. How are your family? I seem to remember there were a lot of you?'

Rachel laughed. 'Yes, I'm one of five – three boys, two girls. Fancy you remembering. Everyone's well, my parents are still growers and enjoying being grandparents.'

Jeanne raised her eyebrows and Rachel grinned and said, 'No, not me! Not yet. Tim and I are engaged and getting married in October, at half-term.' Rachel turned and smiled at Tim, who had been standing by quietly as the girls chatted.

'Congratulations, both of you. Are you a local lad, Tim? I don't remember you from school.'

'Oh yes. I'm a Guern, for sure. I went to the college but as I'm a bit older than you, our paths may not have crossed.'

Tim was dark with brown eyes and a shy smile but when he looked at Rachel he looked the confident fiancé, Jeanne noticed wistfully. While she had been talking to Tim and Rachel, another couple had arrived and Marcus came up to her and said, 'Come and meet Nick and Sue. They're late as usual.'

Jeanne turned round and gasped, 'Muscles!'

'Sorry? What did you say?' Nick asked, looked nonplussed.

'Mussels! I mean…all those crates of mussels, stacked there on the beach. I've, er, only just noticed them,' Jeanne stammered, embarrassed as she recognised Muscles from the ferry.

'Oh, yes. I see. They're farmed here, you know. Anyway, I'm Nick and this is Sue.' He was standing by the leggy blonde from her class at school.

'Hi. I'm Jeanne. We were at school together, weren't we, Sue?'

'Yes, I thought I recognised you. How are you?'

They exchanged their news, Jeanne learning that Sue hadn't gone to university and was now a legal secretary. While they chatted, the men were lighting the barbecue and the smell of smoke began drifting towards them. The girls formed a separate group and Jeanne introduced herself properly to Colette.

'Were you at the grammar school as well?'

'Yes, but I'm a bit younger than you girls. So you wouldn't have noticed me, little squirt that I was!' Colette laughed. She was still small and dark with blue eyes that looked familiar and an attractive, elfin face.

Jeanne asked, 'So, what sort of work do you do?'

'I'm a chef. A pretty humble one, I'm afraid, at the St Pierre Park Hotel. My dream is to have my own restaurant one day, just like every other chef in Guernsey.'

For its size there was a disproportionately large number of restaurants in Guernsey, it being possible to visit a different one every week for a year without repetition.

'I wish you luck on that one, Colette. It must be such hard work and the hours are awful. Doesn't your boyfriend mind?' Jeanne nodded towards Scott, standing with the other men.

'He works in a hotel himself so he's used to the long hours. It's unusual for us both to be free at the same time on a weekend, so this is a treat. And it's great to see the men cooking for a change,' she giggled.

The other girls agreed that the men seemed to think it was macho for them to be in charge of a barbecue, but not of a domestic kitchen.

Marcus came up with beers from the cool box and offered them round.

'How're you getting on, Jeanne? You all seem to be chatting easily enough.' He slid his arm around her waist.

'Fine, thanks. I remember Rachel and Sue from school, which helps. Will the food take long? All this talking is making us hungry.'

'About fifteen minutes, I should think. Just relax and enjoy yourself.' He squeezed her waist gently before going off to re-join the other chefs. Jeanne did feel relaxed. She was enjoying the company, the sun warming her face and the beer soothing away the last remaining threads of tension.

'Didn't you used to go out with Marcus when you were at school?' Jeanne asked Sue.

'Oh, that was so long ago now! It was never anything

serious. I left the Grammar after doing my GCSEs and we drifted apart. Do you like him, then?' Sue grinned at Jeanne.

'I don't really know him very well. But he seems nice. He invited me to join him today but we haven't had a chance to talk much yet. Have you been going out with Nick long?'

'Oh, we're not a couple! Not that I'd mind if we were,' she added, *sotto voce*. 'I first met him at Colette's house ages ago and he picks me up when we gather as a group. We live near each other, you see.'

Jeanne frowned and Sue added, 'Oh, you probably don't know – Nick and Colette are brother and sister, though he's several years older than her.'

'I see. It's hard to imagine – she's so small and he's so… much bigger!' Jeanne was surprised, but, thinking about it, they did share the same colouring and their eyes were the same deep blue.

Before the conversation could continue Scott shouted that the food was ready. The girls went to sort out the plates and cutlery and Colette offered everyone some of the fantastic looking salad she had made.

It was difficult to talk much when chewing overcooked steak and charred, but tasty, sausages so the conversation became more sporadic. Jeanne really appreciated the effort the others had made to feed her, and also to make her feel welcome. The only slight fly in the ointment was the unexpected meeting with Nick or "Muscles" as she'd christened him. Her inadvertent wit had saved an awkward moment, but really it had been a bit embarrassing and she wasn't sure if he had recognised her. Recalling what had happened in the café, she didn't think many men would like to be reminded of a time when they were being yelled at in public. Equally, she didn't want to be reminded of their meeting on the ferry.

Marcus came to sit by her and asked, 'Okay? Enjoying yourself?'

'Yes, thanks. Everyone's being very nice and the food's not bad either.'

Marcus nodded. 'I've known virtually everyone for years and we've had a lot of fun together. You know what a small world Guernsey is!' He gave her his crinkly smile.

Jeanne felt herself going pink – *damn those hormones!* 'Nick seems older than the rest of us. You wouldn't have met him at school, would you?'

'No. He's about thirty-six or thirty-seven I think. Only met him through Scott. Seems okay, if a bit serious.'

More beer and food was passed round and there was much joshing and laughing. Jeanne noticed that Nick seemed quiet and looked a bit bored. *Perhaps he'd rather be working on Mr Evans' boat than sitting around on a beach eating cremated food…*As if he'd read her mind he looked up and for a moment their eyes met. He frowned, shook his head and looked as if he was about to say something when Scott interrupted. 'How about a spot of Frisbee, everyone?'

The suggestion was generally well received though some had to be chivvied with cries of, 'You need some exercise or you'll fall asleep!' The plates were collected up and they gathered together on a flat stretch of sand. Forming a circle, the Frisbee was sent at random, causing much laughter when the wrong person made a dive for it. Jeanne was standing between Mark and Nick and at one point both she and Nick dived for the Frisbee, colliding with some force.

'Oomph,' she cried.

'Are you all right?' he asked as he picked her up.

'Yes, fine, thanks. No bones broken this time!' She rubbed her arms.

'Have we met before? Only there's something familiar about you. I can't think…' he frowned.

Jeanne was saved from replying by a shout of, 'Hurry up,

you two, get back to your places as the light's going to fade soon.'

They moved apart and the game continued without any further contact between them. Jeanne could still feel the touch of his arms as he picked her up. The feeling had been like an electric shock and she was still stunned.

After a few more minutes of flying Frisbees it was decided to call it a day. The sun was sinking lower in the sky and the debris from the barbecue still had to be cleared. A happy group worked quickly to restore order on the beach and within minutes there were no visible signs of anyone having been there.

As they loaded up their cars, goodbyes were called out and Jeanne exchanged telephone numbers with the other girls, agreeing they would arrange a 'girls only' night out soon.

Marcus opened the car door for her and she eased herself into the narrow seat.

'Well, you seemed to enjoy yourself, Jeanne. Glad you came?'

'Yes, very glad, thanks. And you?'

'Oh, yes. Always like getting together with the lads.' He swung the car round to go back up the coast.

A short while later he pulled in to the driveway of Le Petit Chêne and after he had switched off the engine Jeanne asked, 'Would you like to come in for a drink?'

'Yeah, great.'

As she put the kettle on he looked around.

'Doesn't look like this has been touched for years. You'll need a new kitchen, for starters.'

'Oh, yes, for sure. Also a new bathroom, cloakroom, complete re-wiring, central heating and lots more besides. At least it's sound and a good size – four bedrooms. Tea or coffee?'

'Coffee, please, white and two sugars.'

'Shall I show you around the cottage? It's too dark to see the garden now.'

She handed him his coffee and picking up her own mug she led the way around, starting with the sitting room. Marcus didn't say much as they walked round and seemed to notice nothing wrong with the small bedroom.

They made their way back to the kitchen and Jeanne asked, 'What do you think?'

'Not bad. With a ton of money spent on it, could be great. Really for a family, though. Be a bit big for you on your own, won't it?'

'Suppose so. I'm not sure if I'll live here yet, I just want to see if it's feasible to renovate first. So, where do you live?'

'I've got a flat in town, overlooking the QEII marina. I only moved in last year, when they were finished. Very hi-tech and fantastic views, I can even keep an eye on my boat as an added bonus.'

'Oh…so you're a boating man. What kind – motor or sail?' Jeanne twisted her hair.

'Motor, a Sunseeker, twenty-seven foot. Now the weather's improving I hope to get out in her soon. Perhaps you'd like to come out with me?' At the look on her face he quickly added, 'Sorry, Jeanne, I forgot. I guess you haven't been on a boat for a while?'

'No, not since the…accident. Except for the ferry, of course. Perhaps one day, but not yet.'

'I heard you didn't remember anything that happened that night. Is that, er, true?' He asked, shifting from one foot to another.

'No, I didn't. But I've had nightmares which could be flashbacks. I may still remember it all one day though.' She shivered.

'Right. Well let's hope that it helps, if you do,' he frowned and Jeanne thought he seemed a bit nervous. Unlike the Marcus she remembered. His expression cleared and he added, 'How about coming out for a meal with me – just the two of us, this time? One night next week – Friday or Saturday suit you?'

'Sure, love to. How about Friday?'

'Great. I'll ring you when I've booked somewhere and confirm a time. I'd better get going now. Thanks for the coffee.'

'No problem. Thanks for inviting me today. I had a great time.'

Marcus took her face in his hands and kissed her firmly on the lips. As he drew back Jeanne smiled at him.

'Bye for now, see you next week,' he called as he got into his car. Jeanne waved and  shut the door with a sigh. How come if she'd fancied Marcus all those years ago and still did,  she hadn't felt anything when he kissed her? She couldn't work it out. All she knew was that her whole body had responded when Nick had touched her on the beach and although he was attractive, in a brooding sort of way, she wasn't really interested in him. No way. It was Marcus she had a date with and that couldn't lead to anything serious. She still wasn't ready for that, even if she did hang around Guernsey for a while. Realising she'd been mulling over this very question only the previous evening without result, Jeanne gave in and grabbed a bottle of wine. Might as well try in *vino veritas*.

# chapter 10

On waking the next day Jeanne groaned as she realised that instead of insight, the wine she'd drunk had just given her a hangover. A couple of cups of strong coffee and some paracetamol helped her to contemplate the day ahead with some degree of enthusiasm. With the sun pouring through the kitchen windows she thought it would do her good to drive up to L'Ancresse in the north of the island, home of some beautiful sandy beaches and bays and great for hangover-clearing walks.

She parked at Pembroke with L'Ancresse beach stretching out ahead of her. Assorted groups of walkers strode purposefully round the bay. A light, northerly breeze ruffled her hair but the air was mild and Jeanne set off towards the far side and the forts. Numerous on the island, they were erected when Britain was at war with Napoleon and afraid of invasion. Guernsey and the other Channel Islands were particularly vulnerable, being so close to the French coast, and the forts had been the first line of defence, as well as the then mighty British Navy. Jeanne strode along the headland, nodding and exchanging greetings with other walkers.

As she turned back later her stomach was rumbling so made for the kiosk to buy a sandwich and a hot drink, feeling glad to sit down for a few minutes and people watch. The beach was quite busy with what looked to be a mixture of holidaymakers and locals, either sitting determinedly on bright beach towels in spite of the breeze or playing beach games. As she surveyed the laughing faces it was becoming increasingly difficult for her to envisage returning to her old life in England. The sea was in her blood and she was now making friends in Guernsey, or more correctly, rekindling old connections. The thought of having dinner with Marcus was cheering, too. Although not ready for a new relationship, it would be nice to have some fun.

Lost in these thoughts she did not notice the mobile ringing. Only the glares from a nearby couple alerted her it was her own disrupting the peace.

'Hi, it's Rachel. Have I called at a bad time?'

'No, not at all. I'm out for a walk and was completely lost in thought. How are you?'

'Fine, thanks. Good day yesterday, wasn't it? I've been talking to Sue and Colette and we're planning to go to the cinema on Wednesday. It's a chick-flick so the boys won't want to go. We thought we'd have a meal afterwards in the brasserie. What do you think?'

'Love to come, thanks. Is it still at Beau Sejour?'

'No, it's at the Mallard Cinema, near the airport. I can pick you up as it's on my way. Say seven o'clock?'

'Fine. Look forward to seeing you all then. Bye.'

*Great, my social life's positively blooming.* She beamed as she stood up. It was time to make tracks as there was still the length of the bay between her and the car. The breeze was becoming stronger as Jeanne walked briskly along the firm sand, whipping her long hair around her face.

By the time she reached her car she felt as if she had run a marathon, not just had a walk. It was time to get fit, ready for all the gardening that would soon be beckoning, she decided, before pointing the car south towards home.

After a refreshing soak in a hot bath Jeanne dressed quickly and collected her bag of washing, a bottle of wine and the file of French/English recipes for Molly to check.

As Molly opened the door Jeanne thrust the wine at her saying, 'In payment for my supper and the use of your washing machine.'

Molly laughed and gave her a quick hug before leading the way to the kitchen where Peter was in the midst of vegetable preparation.

'Hello, Jeanne. Had a good weekend?' he asked, waving a peeler in one hand and a carrot in the other.

'Great, thanks. And you?'

'Very pleasant. Nice and relaxing.' He smiled.

After loading up the machine in the utility room Jeanne returned to the kitchen and showed Molly the recipes. She started flicking through them.

'Looks to me as if you've done a pretty good job of translating them. I'll read through properly in a day or two. I can see some very interesting dishes here: *Escargots de Bourgogne, Cousinette, Calamares a là Provencale, Grenouilles au Riz, Clamart Purée, Topinambours au Daube* for a start. I feel hungry just thinking about them! By the way, it's *le poulet rôti* tonight, or roast chicken for the uneducated!'

Jeanne and Molly set the table in the dining room leaving Peter in charge in the kitchen. While they were on their own Molly asked Jeanne if she'd read any of the letters yet.

'Yes, the first one, written in July 1943. It's definitely a love letter as it starts *'Mein Leibling Jeanne'* and ends with *'Ich liebe Dich'*. Pretty conclusive evidence, wouldn't you say?'

'Yes, it is. He certainly sounds smitten at least. When do the letters end?'

'February '45. It's likely he would have been rounded up with the other Germans by the British liberating forces a few months later. I haven't found anything else from him at a later date and I went back into the attic to check. But I did find what I think is his picture!' Jeanne announced triumphantly, handing over the photo.

'My word. You're really enjoying playing the detective,

aren't you? Let me have a good look.' Molly studied the photo for a moment before handing it back. 'He looks a kind man as well as handsome. Not at all like a vicious conqueror.'

'Agreed. I'll read some more of the letters to get a feel for what was happening between them. I think they must have met up quite often but, by the look of it, he only wrote about every three weeks. It must have been difficult to keep it a secret.'

'From what I've read and heard about the Occupation, it wasn't as bad as it was in France, where the female "horizontal collaborators" were viciously treated by their fellow countrymen. I'm sure it was very much disapproved of here but at least the women didn't risk getting their hair shaved off and being tarred and feathered!'

'But the islanders must have resented the Germans?'

'Oh, they did, but the resistance was usually low key. If you disobeyed the rules you could be imprisoned or worse. The biggest concern was always the lack of food.'

Molly paused as she collected wine glasses from a cabinet.

'Anyone who could grow their own food, like your grandmother's family, was slightly better off. The men could still fish too, within limits.'

'What did the Germans eat?'

'Initially they got supplies from France but these dwindled once the Allies started winning. Towards the end it was the Germans who were starving while the islanders received Red Cross parcels.' Molly looked up and added, with a grin, 'Perhaps Wilhelm only pursued your Gran for the food she slipped him!'

Jeanne laughed. Was it really only cupboard love, after all? She didn't really think so, but it was an amusing thought.

Peter came through the archway demanding to know

what was so funny and Molly replied that she would tell him later.

As they ate their chicken Jeanne told them about the barbecue.

'Are you seeing Marcus again?' Molly asked, eyebrows raised.

'Is a girl not allowed any secrets?' Jeanne protested, laughing. She mentioned the date on Friday and also that she was meeting up with the girls on Wednesday.

'It certainly hasn't taken you long to get your foot in the door, has it?' Peter remarked.

'It's the overpowering charm, works every time!' she said, enjoying her new-found popularity.

Once the programme finished at ten o'clock, Jeanne drove home with her clean washing and was soon cosily tucked up in bed with Joanna Trollope.

At 8.30 the next morning Jim Le Prevost and his lad Carl were unloading their tools from a pickup in the drive. Jeanne went out to say good morning and confirm what was to be achieved that day.

After checking that her little team was happy, Jeanne knew that her only role from now on was to provide cups of tea at strategic intervals. Before the first cups were required she drove off to the cemetery, buying flowers from a hedge-stall en route.

As she approached her parents' grave she saw that her earlier flowers were beginning to fade. Jeanne substituted the new for the old and as she tidied up had a quick chat with her parents, telling them of the progress she had made that week. She felt totally calm and enjoyed the peace of the setting, feeling that her parents were close by, watching and listening.

Minutes later she walked the few yards to her grandparents' grave and talked to her gran about the recipes, saying what an exciting find it had been for her. *Better not mention the love letters– must spare Granpa's feelings!* The time passed quickly and Jeanne collected up the old flowers and said goodbye to her family.

She smiled inwardly at the thought of the possible reaction of anyone watching and hearing her.

'You know, there's a mad woman goes up to them graves and talks to those dead souls as if 'em still alive. Should be locked up in the Castel Hospital, she should!' She didn't think she was mad but she did get a great deal of comfort from her commune with her parents and grandparents, even if it was a bit one-sided.

She had never given much thought to what happened after death but lately had been attracted to the belief that souls do live on, in another dimension perhaps, and that maybe they could see us even if we couldn't see them. One of her favourite films was Ghost and she cried buckets every time she saw it. She so wanted the girl to see her dead lover, so desperate to talk to her and warn her of imminent danger.

By the time these thoughts had flowed through her mind Jeanne was back at her car. As she put the rubbish in the boot she noticed a man wearing a dog collar coming towards her from the direction of the church.

'Good morning. How do you do? I'm John Ayres, the vicar of this parish, as you can probably tell from the way I dress.' His eyes twinkled at her as he reached out and shook her hand.

'Morning, Vicar. Nice to meet you. I've just been putting flowers on some graves.' Her heart raced – had he been watching her talking? How embarrassing!

He nodded. 'Yes, I saw you. Am I right in thinking that you're Jeanne and that it's your parents and grandparents who are buried there?' He indicated the graves she had just left.

'Yes, but how do you know my name?'

'You won't remember, but I conducted the service for your parents and I had the honour to do the same for your grandmother recently. I'm so glad to see you here. How have you been?' The vicar's face was kindly, like that of a benevolent old uncle and Jeanne could imagine many a grieving soul being comforted by him. He must be pushing seventy, she thought, and witnessed so much sorrow over the years.

'Not too bad, Vicar. I've only been back just over a week and I'm at Gran's cottage. She left it to me and I came back to see what needed doing.'

John Ayres smiled and replied, 'It's wonderful to see you back here, after all these years and you've put some really lovely flowers on the graves. They've always looked so neglected, though your grandmother came up as much as she could, you know.'

He hesitated before continuing, 'I'm a great believer in being able to talk through one's problems with someone and if at any time you felt the need to unburden yourself, I'd be happy to listen.' Jeanne saw the compassion in his face and again wondered if he had seen her pouring out her soul a few minutes ago.

'Thank you, Vicar. I'll remember that. Maybe I'll take you up on that offer one day. That's if I do stay on the island.'

'Oh, I think there's very little doubt that you will stay here now, don't you?' His brown eyes looked into hers and she felt almost mesmerised by him. Oddly enough she wanted to believe him.

'Perhaps. I'll keep you posted on that. Now, I'd better get back as I've two thirsty gardeners waiting for their next dose of tea.'

They shook hands again and Jeanne went off feeling that she'd made another friend, albeit a much older one. But a friend is a friend, she thought, as she drove home.

Jim and Carl were just setting aside their spades and picking up their lunch boxes when Jeanne arrived in a flurry of gravel and put the kettle on. They had made good progress that first morning and the beds looked a lot tidier without all the dead remnants of previous seasons. Jeanne made appropriate noises of satisfaction at their efforts as she handed them their tea and went back inside to make herself some lunch.

After she had cleared away and checked that all was well with her men, she made a phone call.

'Hi, Freya. It's me, Jeanne. How are you?'

'Jeanne! What a surprise. I'm fine, thanks. But where are you? Last time we spoke you said you might be going over to Guernsey. So tell me, girl, what are you up to?'

Freya, a friend from university, used to be a junior editor for one of the magazines Jeanne wrote for but had since made it up the ladder to become an editor for a publishing company. One of the few people she had kept in touch with, partly because of their business connections, but mainly because they'd always been such good mates. They would meet up occasionally in London where Freya was based. Jeanne brought her up to speed with her life as concisely as possible, before coming to the crunch.

'I've got a proposal for a book which I'd like to bounce off you, if that's okay. Non-fiction, a sort of cookery book cum wartime romance, with French undertones.'

'Sounds intriguing. Tell me more.'

Jeanne then explained about the collection of old recipes and the love letters and her idea for writing a book which incorporated the former with a kind of family history, but focussing on the love story of two young protagonists, her gran and Wilhelm. 'A sort of *Country Diary of an Edwardian Lady,* but different,' as Jeanne put it.

Freya seemed taken with the idea, firing a few questions at Jeanne before she said, 'Okay. Go ahead and prepare a thorough outline with lists of the illustrations that you could provide. Then ask your agent to send it to me and I'll happily submit it to my senior editor. At least I know you can write!'

They chatted for a few more minutes before saying their goodbyes. After she'd put down the phone it hit Jeanne that she had possibly committed herself to something she had never previously contemplated – writing a complete book. It would involve a lot of work if the publishers gave her the go-ahead, meaning extensive research before she even started writing. For a moment the whole idea seemed too daunting and she was tempted to ring Freya back and say that she'd changed her mind. But the thought of looking like a prat and walking away from a potential breakthrough into mainstream publishing that most writers only dream of, stopped her. The underlying reason for making the proposal was to provide a way to finance the work on the cottage, she reminded herself.

Taking a deep breath she did what she usually did in times of crisis – put the kettle on and made everyone a cup of tea.

# chapter 11

The gardeners had made good progress on Monday and the flower beds and vegetable patch looked neat and healthy with freshly-turned rich brown soil and a subdued display of late spring flowers and vegetables. What a difference a day makes – was that from a song? – thought Jeanne as she made her inspection on Tuesday morning.

The palms and bamboo were still majestically in situ and the general outline of the wonderful garden it had always been was slowly emerging. That morning Jim was in charge of weeding and digging over the herb beds. Carl, meanwhile, was happily setting up one of the machines so beloved by those not quite so keen on the effort of digging – a powerful mower.

Grey, heavy clouds hung low over the island and they all hoped that the rain would hold off or possibly move over to Jersey and out of harm's way. For centuries there had been a semi-friendly rivalry between the two largest islands, illustrated by their pet names for each other – crapauds (toads) for the Jersey islanders and donkeys for those in Guernsey. Interbreeding happened, naturally, and Jeanne couldn't help feeling sorry for the resultant offspring – fancy being half toad and half donkey!

With the workers set on their day's path Jeanne settled down in the kitchen with her notebook and folders. She began by setting down ideas for the book which she could expand upon later. Thinking it might be interesting to start with the French side of the family she made a note to research their genealogy, back to the Parisian restaurateurs. The book would then focus on her grandmother's Guernsey family, leading up to the Second World War and

Occupation. However, the core of the book would be the recipes – the lavish dishes from nineteenth century Paris and the bucolic food of nineteenth and early twentieth century Guernsey.

The letters would be pivotal to the story and Jeanne had looked at a few more the previous evening. Keeping them in chronological order, she made notes from the letters so that she could write a précis of their contents. In themselves they were not very exciting – just Wilhelm's expressions of pleasure at his meetings with her gran and arranging further assignations. She had worked out from various descriptions in the letters that the bunker where he was often on duty must be the one nearby in a large private garden. Known to have had a gun emplacement on top it was quite high up and well placed to fire at enemy (British!) aircraft. The bunker had provided accommodation for the soldiers while off duty.

Wilhelm would have spent a lot of time in the area when he was on watch there but so far it wasn't clear where he worked at other times. The biggest concentrations of troops had been at the airport and in Town around the harbour. Jeanne made a list of sources she wanted to research, planning to visit the library that afternoon.

By lunch time she had made copious notes and could begin to visualise the form the book would take. The rain had held off and the clouds seemed to be breaking up as she went out to the men with their tea. The herb garden looked much neater but Jim had had to cull some herbs, leaving gaps like missing teeth which Jeanne itched to fill.

Later she went off to St Peter Port armed with her list of books needed. It occurred to her that this would be the first time she'd been there since the day of her arrival and she was yet to explore it properly. There wouldn't be much time today as she wanted to get back before Jim left, but after parking on the Crown Pier, she looked around to see what, if any, changes there had been.

Some of the shops were new and she spotted smart boutiques and wine bars lining the way to the Guille-Alles Library. She gasped when she emerged from Commercial Arcade and turned right into Market Street, shocked by the sight of scaffolding covering the old market opposite the library. The assistant on the library desk informed her that major renovation was in progress and that the old market would not be returning. Upset by the thought, she headed to the Local History section for her books. She loved libraries, at one time considering becoming a librarian, but the desire to write had won and she had never regretted her decision.

After leaving with her pile of books, she popped into Boots for some toiletries and treated herself to some new make-up, guaranteed to make her skin look 'dewy fresh and youthful'. Got to give nature a helping hand, she thought, splashing out on a lipstick as well.

Driving out of town was slow as The Grange was clogged with traffic and Jeanne had time to admire the Queen Anne and Georgian houses that lined the main road. This elegant part of Town used to house wealthy British and French families, drawn here in the late eighteenth and early nineteenth centuries. Guernsey's wealth at that time was built on the legalised piracy sanctioned by the Crown in the seventeenth century. Nowadays the finance industry brought money to the island.

Jeanne arrived home in time to make mid-afternoon tea for everyone and drank her own surrounded by books. She browsed through one about the Occupation, sticking in post-its for reference. Jim popped in to say goodbye, rubbing his hands through his hair – a bad move, as they were thick with soil.

'Should finish tomorrow, for sure. It's taking shape, it is,' he said, looking pleased.

'Great. But I'm not sure I can manage to keep the grass in the orchard tidy myself. Could Carl come round, say fortnightly, to keep it in order?'

Jim agreed to that and they tidied up their tools and drove off. The phone rang as she shut the door.

'Hi, Jeanne, it's me, Marcus. How are you?'

'Fine. And you?'

'I'm good. Slaving away over a hot computer, but mustn't grumble,' he laughed. 'I've booked us in at eight o'clock at Nello's on Friday. I'll pick you up at seven thirty, shall I?'

Jeanne was impressed. Da Nello's was one of the top restaurants on the island and had been a favourite of her parents although she had never been.

'Sounds lovely. But are you sure you don't mind coming out all this way for me? I could get a taxi.'

'No, of course I'll fetch you. How are things with you?'

They chatted for a few minutes before ringing off. Jeanne's first thought was what on earth was she going to wear? Throwing open the wardrobe doors she scanned her meagre supply of clothes hanging forlornly on the rail. Most of her stuff was still at Kate's and there was nothing here suitable for posh restaurants, far from her mind when she packed. She had planned to stay only a few weeks while the cottage was put up for sale. As she stood by the wardrobe she felt overwhelmed by her loss – her grandmother and her baby – and she let out an involuntary moan. The pain was still there, still raw, even though she was not so conscious of it. But lurking just below the surface, ready to ambush her at any time.

Jeanne was lost in her grief, her fingers twisting her hair when she heard an engine running in the lane and brisk footsteps in the drive. Pushing away the hurtful memories she went downstairs as an envelope was pushed through the letterbox and the footsteps retreated. Opening it she saw the heading 'Martin Brehaut, General Builder'. Ah, his quote.

She sat in the kitchen to read the figures and as she scanned them was just aware of a sea of numbers and turned to the bottom of the next page to find the total. Oh blow, it's quite a bit more than I'd hoped. Slumped in the chair doing her sums, Jeanne succumbed to doubts. Perhaps it really wasn't a good idea, all this renovation business and she should call it quits and sell without any hassle. Reminding herself that she didn't have any valuations yet, she called the estate agent who had sold her parents' house and arranged for a Mr Dorey to call round the following afternoon. Feeling that she had done enough that day, Jeanne gave herself a break and after supper settled down with her novel, a glass of wine and Coldplay.

Next morning the clouds still hovered and there was an odd spot of light rain but insufficient to stop Jim and Carl in their tracks. While they pitted their brawn against the hedges and grass, Jeanne pitted her brains against the internet as she searched for ways to trace her family in France. She made less progress than the gardeners but by late morning she had narrowed down the choice of resources. At this stage she only wanted to know that she could obtain all the information needed. The outline for the book was taking shape now and copious notes were filling her notebook.

She continued to work after lunch and just before four o'clock she went to see Jim and Carl as they loaded the pickup.

'It all looks wonderful, thank you both. You've worked so hard. I'm sure Gran will be smiling on you!'

Jim scratched his head and grinned.

'Well, Jeanne, your gran must've worked very hard over the years. You can see how well thought out it all was. Been a pleasure to get it straight for you – and we both appreciated all the tea.'

The men climbed into the pickup and, with cheerful waves, drove off.

Mm, at least the garden's looking lovely. Should help the estate agent come up with a good figure! She had a few minutes to freshen up and tidy the kitchen before the doorbell rang.

A young man dressed in a sharp suit stood on the step, carrying a clipboard and folders.

'Miss Le Page? Matthew Dorey. How do you do?' He gave her a warm smile and they shook hands.

'Please come in.'

She led the way into the kitchen saying, 'I need to decide whether or not it's worth modernising the cottage before selling. I've recently inherited it and have talked to a builder about costs based on this list.'

Jeanne passed him a copy and he quickly looked through it.

'You seem to have covered everything. But the final value would also be affected by the quality of the finish, particularly the kitchen and bathrooms. Are you going for high quality fittings and tiles etc?'

'Oh, yes, I should think so. Shall I take you round?'

As they walked Matthew made notes and the occasional comment about "original features present". As they went into the garden his eyes opened wide.

'This is brilliant! I never expected it to be as big as this! Does that orchard belong to the cottage as well?'

'Yes and the reason it all looks so good is that the gardeners have just finished working on it.'

'You do realise that you've probably got a potential building plot there, don't you?' he said, pointing to the orchard.

'That may be. But I'm not interested in building there.

I'd prefer it to stay with the cottage.'

'You might not, but if someone else was to buy it they could sell off the orchard as a building plot, getting at least £200,000 for it.'

Jeanne gasped. 'You're joking! I had no idea land was so expensive here! Can you give me a valuation with the orchard just as it is?'

'Sure. Let me have a wander round again.'

Jeanne left him to look around and waited in the kitchen.

Coming back, Matthew said, 'Basically, it's got great potential. A good property in a very popular area, there would be no problem selling it, either as it is now or when modernised. In its current state I'd value it at about £350,000 and after modernisation I'd expect to market it for £450,000 or more.'

Jeanne gulped.

'I…I don't know what to say! I was thinking about half of that!'

'I take it that you've not been back in Guernsey long?'

'No, not long. I was away about fifteen years. So I guess I'm a bit out of touch with house prices. Guernsey must be about as expensive as London,' she stammered.

'Nearly. It's the shortage of building land which keeps the prices buoyant, of course. You're sitting on a little gold mine here, if you don't mind my saying so,' he looked around the kitchen as he spoke. 'And that's the value without planning permission for building, of course,' he added.

Jeanne nodded numbly.

'Well, thanks for coming round, Matthew and for your helpful and, er, illuminating advice. I'll get back to you when I've decided what to do.'

'Sure, no problem. We'd love to market the property for you whenever you decide to sell. I've given you a bit of a shock.' He grinned as he handed her his card.

'You could say that! Thanks again, anyway.' Jeanne closed the door with a deep sigh. *I need a drink!* She reached for the bottle of wine opened the previous night and poured a small glass, sitting at the kitchen table while she tried to clear her head.

If those figures were accurate she would more than cover her costs if she did the renovation work so it would make financial sense to go ahead if she could raise the money. Looks like a visit to the bank manager is called for. Deep in thought she lost track of time until she suddenly remembered that she was going out with the girls that night and it was now nearly six thirty.

Jeanne dashed upstairs and put on black jeans and a red top. She added some jewellery and applied her new make-up. Mm, not bad. She was barely downstairs when the doorbell rang and Rachel stood on the doorstep, a cheerful smile lighting up her face.

'Hi! Say, I think your cottage is awesome! Sort of thing Tim and I would love. And the garden looks huge, ideal for barbecues. I'm so jealous! Ready?'

Jeanne nodded, and grabbing her jacket and bag, shut the door behind them.

As they drove off, Jeanne asked Rachel if she knew what cottages like hers would sell for.

Rachel confirmed the agent's figures adding, 'Way out of our price range, I'm afraid. Why, you're not selling are you?'

'No, just wondering. I hadn't realised how expensive housing is here.'

'It's awful. We're both earning good money but we only managed to buy a small modern house in Cobo. Ideally, we'd love an old cottage like yours but they're always much dearer and harder to find. Still, at least we do have our own home and it's big enough for a family,' she grinned at

Jeanne.

The film, a story of romantic adventures and misadventures, had the girls giggling along with the rest of the audience, and they were in merry mood as they ate their meal afterwards. Later, the farewells were warm, with a promise to repeat the experience soon. Rachel and Jeanne hummed a tune from the movie as they drove home.

'I really enjoyed this evening. Thanks for inviting me, Rachel. It's been a long time since I laughed so much.'

'Glad you came. Can't have you sitting at home on your own, staring at the walls, can we?' Rachel smiled. Jeanne had admitted to having no television.

It didn't take long for Rachel to negotiate the winding roads back to Le Petit Chêne and Jeanne was ready for bed soon after she was dropped off. As she lay, waiting for sleep to overcome her, she recalled the exciting developments of that day. The film had also triggered thoughts of romance. She found herself re-living the early days of her relationship with Andy. She had been so sure that he was The One – they had fitted so well together, sharing much in common, including their love of travel and books. The attraction had been instant and mutual and Andy had asked her to move in within a matter of months. Initially all had been wonderful. Andy had been attentive and only too happy to help with the household chores.

Jeanne remembered their laughter as she had cooked their first disastrous meal, so inedible that Andy had ordered a Chinese takeaway. She sighed. *Where had it all gone wrong? Was I so wrapped up in what I wanted that I lost sight of Andy's needs? My wish for a family wasn't what he wanted. At least not at that time when I was…*Her stomach clenched at the memory. Tears threatened but she brushed them away, determined not to feel maudlin after such a fun evening. The film had reminded her that love and happiness could be found even after the painful end of an affair. At least that's the way it happened in films! Her thoughts drifted towards Marcus and their imminent date.

Her heart was still fragile and the loss of the baby made it even harder for her to contemplate a speedy recovery. She knew that time would help. The passing of the months and years had eased the gnawing pain of her parents' deaths. But Gran's death had brought back some of that pain. Then she had lost Andy *and* the baby! No, she told herself, it would be a while before her heart would be fully healed but maybe, just maybe, Marcus might be the one to start that healing process. That thought, together with the memory of the great evening with the girls, helped her drift off to sleep.

# chapter 12

By mid-morning on Thursday Jeanne had arranged an appointment at the St Peter Port branch of her bank for that afternoon. She then spent time preparing figures of income and expenditure on her laptop. Although it appeared she had a valuable asset in the cottage, she wasn't sure if her irregular income would be considered sufficient for a loan.

After downing a quick cup of coffee Jeanne set out to buy herbs at a nursery recommended by Jim, wanting to fill the gaps in the revived beds. She also bought a couple of potted geraniums for the kitchen which could go outside once the builders arrived, together with books on herbs and basic gardening. She was now fully equipped to put the finishing touches to her gran's legacy. A quick lunch and she made a start on planting out, managing to finish the herb garden before going in to clean up and change.

Wearing a long black skirt, T-shirt and linen jacket, Jeanne drove into town and found a long-term parking space. She had reasoned that she might want to do some shopping after visiting the bank.

The appointment went smoothly and the young woman assured Jeanne that it should be possible to have a short-term loan or even a mortgage. The cottage was considered to be excellent security for the comparatively small loan required. She came out bearing a folder full of forms and figures and the need to make a decision.

*Right, I need a coffee.* With this in mind she headed up Smith Street to the leather chaired café which had offered her much needed sustenance on her return to the island.

The same cheerful waitress was on duty and Jeanne again succumbed to the sales pitch of 'non-fattening' scrummy chocolate cake. Why not, surely working in the garden will burn off ooh, say, at least one mouthful!

It was restful to sit and do nothing for a few minutes and Jeanne's mind went back to the last time she had been there, nearly two weeks earlier. *Mm, guess I've moved on quite a bit. Certainly not as lonely and there's so much I can do now. Create a beautiful home, continue to earn an income from writing and perhaps even see my book published. Carry on building up a circle of friends. Maybe even find love – eventually. Nice! Then maybe have children to complete the happy family.* A shadow crossed her face. Perhaps one day…

She left the café and headed for the shops. Time for a little retail therapy. She wanted something really nice for Nello's and explored the High Street until she came to a small boutique. It wasn't long before she found exactly what she wanted; a short, silky skirt and a sleeveless top with just enough sparkly decoration to add some glamour. As she came out of the shop she thought – shoes! She remembered the shoe shop near the harbour selling shoes to die for at a reasonable price and set off in search of the perfect glitzy sandals.

It was nearly six o'clock by the time she arrived home and, after dumping everything on the kitchen table, she called the Ogiers to ask if she could pop round for a chat later. Molly said that was fine.

After supper Jeanne collected up the papers she needed and walked round to her friends.

'Hi, Molly. Thanks for letting me come round. Hope I'm not intruding?'

'No, of course not. Glad to be of help. Come into the sitting room where Peter's been buried in the papers long enough. Would you like a drink?'

When they were all comfortable and nursing glasses of

wine, Jeanne explained why she was there.

'I really need help to decide what to do about a bank loan and hoped that you'll be able to offer some guidance.'

She explained about the valuation and the bank proposals.

'I need to be sure that it's cost effective to carry out the renovation as I'll need to borrow some of the money, at least in the short term. I've already had the quote from the builder.' She handed over all the papers from the bank and builder and added, grinning, 'Oh, and by the way, I may have a publisher interested in my book proposal so, with a bit of luck, I might be earning a nice advance!'

Peter and Molly looked at each other for a moment.

'You've been busy this week, haven't you? I admire your enterprise! I think Molly and I had better look through the figures before we say any more, all right?'

Jeanne sat quietly sipping her wine while the others, heads together, pored over the paperwork.

Finally Molly looked up and said, 'I think the crucial question is, do you want to stay in the cottage once the work's completed?'

Jeanne hesitated for a moment before answering.

'Yes, I *do* want to stay there. I've begun to realise how much I love Guernsey and there's nothing for me in England, apart from Kate, bless her. But it's quite a large house and I can't help wondering if I should buy something smaller and cheaper to run, like a modern flat,' she replied, pulling a face.

'I see. Don't worry about running the cottage just now. You know you could always sell at a good price. You need to be where your heart is, Jeanne. And from what Peter and I have seen, that's the cottage.'

Jeanne's shoulders dropped in relief. It was as if she'd received permission to follow what her heart was telling her to do.

'Okay. So if I stay in the cottage, which is the better loan?'

Peter replied, 'If you can afford the mortgage payments for at least the next year, then that would be the better choice as the interest and monthly payments are much lower. Remember you can claim tax relief which also helps. You might even be able to pay off a chunk if your book's a bestseller!' He laughed. 'I take it you're not going to apply for planning permission for the orchard?'

She shook her head. 'No, I'd have Gran turning in her grave! I'm sure I can manage without that.'

'On paper, at least, that's right. And in the future if you do go back to England, you'll be quite a wealthy young woman.'

Jeanne laughed. 'Never thought I'd ever hear that! Right, a mortgage it is, then.'

Just before Molly topped up their glasses she fetched the French recipes and handed them to Jeanne.

'Only one or two errors. You did a good job and they're such interesting dishes, aren't they? They'll look wonderful in your book.'

Jeanne mentioned that she was off to Nello's on Friday and Molly admitted that it was one of her favourites, giving Peter a meaningful look which he seemed not to notice.

Back home Jeanne went up to bed with her book. After switching off the light she lay still until she realised, with a jolt, just how much it did mean to her to stay in the cottage on this special island. Though the boat accident and her parents' terrible deaths had been traumatic for her, it had happened a long time ago. At sixteen she had been little more than a child. It had been a child's response to the pain to run away and perhaps she'd been wrong, she conceded. Although she had been very lucky with Kate and her unstinting support, she realised how much she had missed by not being at her grandmother's side all those years. They had both suffered as a result. *I've been so immature! Poor Gran. To have lost all her family in one fell swoop. And she didn't try to stop me, just wished me well, telling me to work hard at school and follow my parents to university. Oh, Gran!* Tears pricked her eyes. *I'm so, so sorry.*

Jeanne brushed away the tears as the thoughts whirled through her mind. In spite of her sorrow over her past mistakes, she felt more peaceful as sleep finally claimed her.


On Friday morning she rang Martin Brehaut and told him she was happy to accept his quote, asking when he'd be free to start and how long the work would take.

Martin was quiet for a while before answering. 'Should be able to start by late June and I reckon it's about two months' work, unless we hit any snags.'

'Fine. Can you book me in, please, and keep me posted as to a definite start date? I'll be getting rid of most of the furniture which will make life easier for you.'

'That'll help, thanks. I'll be in touch.'

Another decision made. Jeanne then filled in the mortgage application ready for posting later. Needing a break from mental activity, she went into the garden to start planting the beds with the bulbs rescued by the gardeners. The sun had returned after a couple of days' absence and she enjoyed the fresh air and getting her hands dirty with soil. It was therapeutic and calming and the rest of the morning flashed by.

After lunch she settled down to work on the outline of the book before typing up the translated French recipes. By late afternoon she was glad to break off to go and run a bath.

The new clothes slid on with a delicious whisper and the make-up worked its magic once again. A spray of perfume, earrings and a delicate little necklace and she was ready. Jeanne picked up a pretty faded velvet jacket to slip over the top and went down to the kitchen to wait. She poured a glass of water and paced around the kitchen, taking small sips, nervous at the thought of her first date for some years. *Come on, girl! You're a grown woman and he's only a man, for heaven's sake!* She had just managed to calm her breathing when, exactly at seven thirty Marcus's car crunched over the gravel. Jeanne went out to meet him.

'Hi! I'll just lock the door.'

Marcus climbed out of the car and, after giving her a lingering kiss, held open the passenger door. She carefully sat on the seat and, as she'd seen it done in films, swung her legs into the car in a reasonably smooth movement.

Marcus slipped into his seat and turning to her, said, 'You look great. Très chic!'

'Merci, monsieur! You don't look so bad yourself.'

He wore dark cotton chinos and a crisp blue open-neck shirt with the cuffs turned back. The car was soon filled with the heady mix of Calvin Klein and Armani.

The walk from the Crown Pier to Nello's in the Lower Pollet took just a few minutes and Jeanne was soon ushered into a seat in the bar by an attentive Marcus. He told the waiter he had a table booked in the name of Davidson while Jeanne gazed around, admiring the marble floor tiles, elegant tables and seating, set against an expanse of exposed stone walls. She felt as if she'd been wafted off to Italy, particularly when a charming wine waiter asked what the Signorina wanted to drink.

'A Bellini, please.'

Marcus ordered a lager and they studied their menus while they waited.

'There's always great fresh fish here. And I'd suggest you save some space for a pudding as they're all delicious,' Marcus said, stroking her arm.

Their drinks arrived and they clinked glasses in a salute. Mm, heavenly, Jeanne thought as she sipped the chilled cocktail and the Maitre D' bustled off with their order.

110

'Now, tell me what you've been up to.'

She told him about the garden and that she had chosen a builder. She didn't mention the book or the mortgage, feeling it was too soon to share such personal matters with him.

'It's going to be quite a busy and noisy few months for you, with builders crashing about. Think you'll cope?'

'I'll have to. But it will be worth it, I'm sure. With the garden looking great I'm spurred on to do the same with the cottage. Now, that's enough of me, what have you been doing?'

Marcus shrugged off the week as just the usual work-dominated days with the occasional evening out for a drink with mates. Apparently he worked very long hours but this was par for the course if he wanted to rise through the ranks in finance.

'But now it's the weekend and I can relax for a few days. So let's start by enjoying our first evening together,' he said warmly, squeezing her hand.

The waiter arrived to show them through the restaurant to a corner table. He pulled out the table for Jeanne and Marcus took the facing chair. She glanced around, admiring the conservatory reached by a flight of stairs and the tasteful décor of the main room. The candlelit tables were slowly filling up.

'This is so lovely. An Italian grotto tucked away from the hustle and bustle of Town. It's even better than I expected. Of course, when I lived here I was too young to appreciate good restaurants and was more into fast food. I'm a little more sophisticated these days.'

'I still like fast food occasionally myself but it certainly doesn't compare to this,' he replied as their starters arrived, presented with a typical Italian flourish – the waving of a giant peppermill.

'Right, now I want to know everything about you since

you left. Where did you go to university?'

'Bristol, where I read English. I then went on to do a journalism course before getting a job in a local newspaper as a trainee reporter. I lived in a shared house until I met Andy. About that time I also started submitting stories to magazines and, wonder of wonders, some were published!' She smiled at the memory. 'It was so exciting to see my name in print as my reports in the local paper were never attributed to me, I was far too junior. Eventually I decided to bite the bullet and become a full-time freelance and although it's been a bit scary at times, I've no regrets.'

'What happened with this Andy?'

Jeanne's stomach tightened as she remembered. 'Oh, we just drifted apart. You know how it is. And I went back to stay with my aunt before coming here. Now, it's your turn, what have you been doing over the years?'

'Well, I went to the LSE and studied Accounting and Finance. Then I took a gap year and travelled around Australia and the Far East before coming back to work for my father in his accountancy firm. I found working with him a bit, er, restricting,' he grinned ruefully. 'So I applied to a trust company who were more than ready to appreciate my talents.' He finished with a big smile.

'Mm, didn't your family come over here when you were quite young?'

'Yes, Dad was offered the chance to join a practice here so we came over when I was ten. He was originally here on a housing licence but now we're all counted as local. Although not as local as you, naturally.' He reached out and touched her arm as his pale blue eyes swept over her.

Jeanne flushed slightly under his gaze and said, 'I can't remember whether or not you have any brothers or sisters.'

'Just one brother, Dan, who's a few years older than me. He runs a successful antiques business in town and has fingers in various pies,' he frowned, as if the thought of his brother was distasteful in some way.

Jeanne noticed and asked, 'Don't you two get on?'

'Not really. We just have different lifestyles, I guess. But let's not talk about my brother. How's your monkfish?'

'Delicious. As is everything. It'll be a struggle to keep space for a dessert.'

'You'll just have to do your best.'

After a break while they chatted about the changes on the island, they decided to order desserts and when they arrived Marcus said, 'A few of us are meeting up for a drink on Sunday morning at Cobo and the more energetic of us will go surfing later. Would you like to join us? You'd be welcome to come surfing too, if you'd like.'

Jeanne had not swum out of her depth since the accident and the thought of surfing made her heart beat faster.

'I'd love to join you all for a drink but not the surfing. I've never tried it but I'm not sure it would be for me. At least not yet. What time?'

'About eleven thirty, at the Rockmount. Good. Now, how about some coffee?'

As they were drinking it, Marcus reached out and put his hand over hers.

'I really like you, Jeanne. I've enjoyed this evening and would love to see you again. How about you?'

His eyes focussed intently on hers and she heard herself say, 'Yes, I'd like to see you again, too,' smiling at him as she took in his fair hair flopping over his forehead Hugh Grant style and his sexy smile.

'Great! Perhaps one night next week? If you're not too busy with the girls, that is.' Jeanne had told him about their fun night out.

She shook her head. 'Nothing's planned at the moment. So that would be fine.'

They agreed that he would let her know on Sunday which evening would be best for him. He settled the bill, brushing aside Jeanne's offer to pay her share and as they left Jeanne was presented with a red rose by the Maitre D' – a well-established ritual at Da Nello's, Marcus said. Jeanne appreciated the romantic touch and Marcus laid his arm possessively around her shoulders as he guided her back to the car.

As he was unlocking the car door Jeanne caught sight of Herm, a dark shape dotted with twinkling lights on the horizon. Suddenly she began to shake and her breathing quickened. She had to fight hard to clamp down the rising feeling of panic.

'You cold, Jeanne? You're shaking!'

Making a supreme effort, not wanting Marcus to know the truth, she took a deep breath.

'Yes, I…I did feel cold for a minute. But I'll be fine. Can we have the heater on?'

'Sure. We'll soon have you warmed up, no problem.'

The moon was a full pale yellow disc in the dark sky and the stars became more visible as they left the lights of Town behind. With the roof down and the heater on full blast Jeanne felt calmer as they drove across the island. She was thankful that Marcus hadn't realised what was happening. If this carries on she'd have to do something about it, she decided.

Marcus pulled into her drive and switched off the engine. Undoing their seat belts he turned towards her and, pulling her close, kissed her firmly on the lips. The kiss seemed to go on forever, until he eventually pulled back and, stroking her hair away from her face, murmured, 'Any chance of a coffee?'

She hesitated before replying, guessing it wasn't only coffee he wanted. 'Perhaps another time. I…I'm not sure.' It was just too soon…

For a moment he looked sulky, then seemed to rally and smiling, replied, 'Okay, got the message. See you on

Sunday, then.'

Jeanne smiled uncertainly and got out of the car unaided and waved as he drove off. She let herself in and went straight upstairs, suddenly feeling very tired. It had been a lovely evening, and if Marcus didn't rush her, she would enjoy being with him. Though there were still no fireworks when he kissed her. *Mm, maybe it'll take time. The ol' hormones are still all over the place and my life's been turned upside down. And getting panic attacks doesn't help! Just have to wait and see. There's no rush, no rush at all.*

# chapter 13

Sunday morning dawned bright and clear, with just enough breeze to satisfy the surfers. Jeanne parked at the rear of the pub in Cobo and spotted the familiar faces outside at the front.

'Hi, Jeanne, glad you could come. What would you like to drink?' called Marcus as he waved her over to them.

'A lager, please. How are you?' In reply Marcus gave her a kiss before going indoors to buy her a drink. She sat down next to Rachel saying hello to her, Tim, Scott, Sue and Nick. Scott explained that Colette had to work.

Marcus returned with her drink and they all carried on talking, enjoying the warm spring sunshine and watching the waves turn into white surf on the golden sands.

'So, how did it go on Friday?' Rachel asked when Marcus was deep in conversation with Scott.

'Okay, thanks. It's a lovely restaurant, isn't it? And the company wasn't bad either!'

'Seeing each other again, are we?' Rachel asked, eyebrows raised.

'Yes, this week sometime. You and Tim been out lately?'

'We went to the local Chinese last night, which was a nice change. We're restricting ourselves on eating out 'cos we're saving up for the wedding. Still, all work and no play!' She laughed.

Sue leaned over to ask what they were laughing at and Rachel said that it was just about the need to go out and enjoy themselves.

'God, you're so right! Apart from going out with you girls and the barbecue, I haven't been out for ages. Anyone fancy the cinema this week?'

Jeanne nodded. 'Sure. What about you, Rachel?'

'The cinema, yes. But I can't manage a meal as well – cost-cutting exercise as I was saying earlier.' She turned round. 'Scott – is Colette free one evening this week, do you know?'

'Think she's off on Thursday, when I'll be working.'

Rachel agreed to ring Colette later and would get back to the others. Marcus sat down next to Jeanne, putting his arm round her shoulders.

'How about Wednesday evening for a meal? Fancy the Indian at L'Eree?'

'I'd like that, thanks. Fan of Indian food are you?'

'I like all kinds – Indian, Italian, French, Greek, Chinese, whatever. And you can get them all here, without a passport and having to fly.' Marcus grinned at her, giving her arm a squeeze. 'Pick you up at eight o'clock, okay?'

Jeanne nodded and he went off to buy a round of drinks. She found herself next to Nick.

'Do you get out much, Nick?'

'Not a lot. Much too busy at work.'

'Oh, right. What exactly is it that you do?'

Nick's bored expression changed and there was a light in his eyes as he replied, 'I'm a boat builder by profession but these days I do mostly renovation and re-fitting.'

'That must be interesting. So you're your own boss?'

'Yep. Which means the buck stops with me. And I've a big job on at the moment which is giving me a few headaches, I can tell you,' he sighed.

'Burning the midnight oil and all that,' Jeanne smiled.

'Unfortunately. Colette's always trying to get me to chill out and have fun but it's been difficult.'

'I take it you're a surfer?'

'Sure am. I love anything to do with the water – surfboarding, windsurfing, boating and fishing. The sea's in my blood, I guess. My father was in the boat business and his father was a fisherman.'

'My grandfather was a fisherman, too. They probably knew each other. Is your father still in the business?'

His face clouded. 'No, he died a few years ago, just after he'd retired. And Mum died while I was still a boy. Cancer.'

'Oh, that's awful! I know what it's like to lose your parents too soon,' Jeanne's face creased with sympathy.

Nick nodded. Then, after looking at her closely he said, 'You know, there's something familiar about you...'

He was interrupted as Marcus arrived with the drinks, sitting down between them. The conversation turned to surfing and Jeanne was left to her thoughts for a few moments.

She was warming a little to Nick, in spite of his detachment and abruptness. She could empathise with the loss of his parents and it provided a sort of link. Even his seriousness was admirable given that he had a business to run and 'horrible' clients like Mr Evans to deal with, she decided. It didn't look like his main motivation was money either, given the state of his battered jeep parked next to Marcus's swish sports car. Perhaps he wasn't hung up on material possessions in the way Marcus was. She didn't admire the fact that Marcus's only ambition seemed to be to make as much money as possible. Maybe that's why she was finding it so hard to feel close to him?

'Hey, Jeanne! Where were you? Miles away by the look on your face.' Marcus punched her arm playfully.

'Sorry. Was just thinking about...something. Did I miss anything?'

'Only us surfers saying it was time to hit the waves. What're your plans?'

'I don't know. Haven't thought about it.'

Rachel chipped in. 'Why don't you come round to our place? I'll be on my own while Tim's surfing and we can have a snack.'

'Love to, thanks.'

Sue was surfing with the men and they said their goodbyes to go and collect their boards and wetsuits.

After a pleasant lunch with Rachel Jeanne drove out of Cobo. She could see the group surfing the waves and wondered if she should try it sometime. But she needed to feel safe in the sea, difficult since her near drowning. Since the accident she had only swum in calm, tropical waters and never out of her depth. If she stayed in Guernsey she needed to conquer her fear or miss out on a lot of island activities, including boating. She sighed. There was still so much to resolve. Reminding herself that she had become stronger over the past two weeks, Jeanne cheered up. Anything was possible.

On Monday morning Jeanne was immersed in brochures collected from a bathroom specialist recommended by Martin, when the phone rang. It was Mrs Le Maitre, advising her that the translations were ready.

Jeanne drove down the coast to Rocquaine with a sense of anticipation. The ingredients of the book were coming together and she would soon be able to complete the outline for the publisher. She rang the doorbell and a smartly dressed, elderly lady opened the door and shook her hand.

'You must be Jeanne. Please do come in and I will fetch the recipes.'

Jeanne stepped into the hall of the cottage and was admiring the paintings of local scenes on the walls when Mrs Le Maitre returned, bearing the notebook and a sheaf of papers.

'What wonderful pictures you have. Is that a Caparne?'

'Yes, it is and we are lucky to have both a Toplis and a Naftel,' she pointed to two watercolours. 'My husband and I added to our collection over the years when funds allowed. I'm rather obsessed with anything to do with the islands – the history, art, language and, of course, food. Do you share my obsession, Jeanne?'

She laughed. 'I don't think I'm obsessed, no. But I do find it fascinating and intend to learn more now that I'm back. I'm ashamed by my lack of knowledge to be honest. Writing this book is a good start and I hope to be a much better cook as well by the time it's finished.'

Smiling at her, Mrs Le Maitre handed over the bundle. 'I've typed up the translations on my late husband's typewriter and made a carbon copy for myself. Hope they're legible enough for you?'

'They look fine. Thanks again. Hope you enjoy trying them out.'

'I certainly will. And if you need any further assistance in the future, please do not hesitate to ask me. I look forward to reading your book.'

'I'll make sure you get a copy if it's published, don't worry.'

They shook hands and Jeanne gave a final wave as she drove off. The old lady had been charming and Jeanne really appreciated the work she had done for her. She decided to spend the rest of the afternoon working on the book, leaving the bathrooms for another day.

By Tuesday morning Jeanne had a visual picture of her book and the final pieces of the jigsaw would be photos and images from the past. Mrs Le Maitre had been right. The old Guernsey dishes were unusual and could still be re-created today as all of the ingredients were available locally, although some were now more scarce and expensive than they had been when the recipes were written. Crab, lobster and oysters had been relatively cheap in the 1800s but were now considered luxury foods. This was in contrast to the French *haute cuisine* dishes which had been based on the then more expensive ingredients such as beef, wine, *foie gras*, duck and cream.

Jeanne had also researched what food had been available to the islanders during the Occupation. She thought that a section on the privations endured at that time would add an extra dimension to a book which was essentially about food, but also forbidden love. With this in mind she set out her findings:

*Initially there had been a glut of tomatoes as they could no longer be exported and the poor housewives must have been demented trying to think of different ways of serving them. The excess were dried and used as cattle feed.*

*Early on there was also a good supply of eggs but this diminished over the years as chickens were killed, while potatoes remained a staple part of the diet. Islanders who grew their own vegetables occasionally had to fight off others trying to steal them. There was a case where a German soldier stole some potatoes from an islander's garden and the grower was so determined to stop any more being taken that he dug up the rest of his crop and buried them under his kitchen floor. He then reported the theft of all his potatoes to the local authorities who in turn complained to the Commanding Officer. Theft was severely punished. Although soldiers were not allowed to steal food from the locals, bartering did take place, usually in the form of swapping food for tobacco.*

*Any excess food not needed by the grower had to be sold to the Controlling Committee which set up food distribution and communal kitchens around the island. Bread rationing began in 1941 and meat had been rationed even earlier. By the end of the war the islanders' diet was severely restricted to a few vegetables, occasional fish, rabbit or eggs and bramble tea instead of the real thing.*

Jeanne had never fully comprehended how difficult it must have been for her grandmother and all islanders at that time. It was a real eye opener reading first-hand accounts and she was humbled by what she learnt. Thoughtful, she polished up her outline and typed a covering letter to her agent before walking up the road to the post box. Right, she thought, on the way back, better get on with planning new bathrooms and a kitchen. Everything took so long to arrive on the island that the sooner she ordered the sanitary fittings and tiles, the better.

But when she added up the total cost of the fittings Jeanne's stomach lurched. It was more than she had budgeted, but knew it was important not to skimp if she wanted to get a good price for the cottage if obliged to sell. She really hoped that wouldn't happen but...And she still had to choose tiles and a kitchen! Martin had given her the names of tile companies and a kitchen supplier and Jeanne drove off on the next part of her quest.

Her first port of call was a tile merchant in town and Jeanne fell in love with some limestone and marble look-alike tiles in ceramic which were both beautiful and inexpensive. As she browsed for ideas for the kitchen she spotted some hand-glazed tiles in gorgeous colours which were stunning but expensive. Mm, she'd better wait until she saw what the kitchen costs, as at this rate she'd be broke before she started.

The kitchen showroom was at The Bridge and Jeanne drove up from the town, along Les Banques. Herm came into view and initially Jeanne was fine but when she stopped at traffic lights and glanced at the island she was suddenly overwhelmed by such a strong feeling of panic that she had to grip the steering wheel hard.

She struggled to breathe. Closing her eyes she had a blurred vision of something white – a speedboat? – heading towards her parents' boat at speed. It was night with a clear sky and she could see the full moon guiding their boat back to St Peter Port from Herm. Odd images flashed in and out of her mind – her father seemed to be shouting at someone in the other boat – her mother knocked off her feet as their boat was hit broadside on – her father calling to Jeanne. Then – nothing, just blackness.

# chapter 14

Jeanne came to, her breathing still erratic, disturbed by the blaring of a car horn punched repeatedly from behind. Shaking her head, she moved forward, quickly pulling in at the side of the road as the angry motorist shot past, mouthing something at her. Shaking, she replayed the scene in her mind. *God, that felt so real! Was that what happened? And that white boat was definitely going at some speed. Must have been drunk, like the police said.*

A few moments later and her breathing returned to normal. She stopped shaking and set off to the Bridge, parking near the café.

Feeling in need of something to revive her shattered nerves, she went in. It looked full and she was beginning to despair of finding a table when she spotted an arm waving at her from the back of the room. Nick.

'Hi, Jeanne. Thought it was you. Care to join me? It's pretty crowded today, I'm afraid.' Nick smiled at her and Jeanne sank with a sigh into the chair opposite.

'Thanks, if you don't mind, Nick. I…I need to eat but I think I need a drink first,' she stammered.

'Why, you're as white as a sheet! What's the matter?'

'Just had a bit of a shock. I'll be fine in a minute. Could you get me a glass of red wine, please?'

He fetched the wine and Jeanne took a grateful gulp.

'Now, tell me what's happened.' Nick looked at her intently and she felt compelled to tell him about the flashback.

'You poor girl! It must be so awful re-living it like that. How're you feeling now?' he asked gently.

'Better, thanks. I think it's worse 'cos I wasn't expecting

it. Took me by surprise, although there've been other…incidents since I came back.' She still felt as if the blood had drained from her face and bit her lip before continuing, 'I'd been thinking of having therapy to, maybe, sort it out for good. After what's happened I'll arrange it as soon as I can. Then no more flashbacks.'

He nodded. 'Sounds a good idea. You need professional help with something like this. I bet you're still afraid of boats and the sea?'

'Yep. And I want to cure myself of that fear. I used to love boats,' she added, remembering, with a pang, the happy times they had spent as a family on their little cruiser.

'As a fully paid-up member of the boat-loving fraternity I can sympathise with you. But for the moment, the most pressing thing is lunch. I can recommend the fish soup – it's fantastic,' he said, reaching out and covering her hand with his. It felt good, as if he was draining all the fear away. She found herself smiling.

'Soup it is then. And I think I'll have a ham and tomato sandwich to go with it.'

The waiter came over and took Jeanne's order. Nick had already eaten and was drinking a coffee.

'So, where were you heading when all this happened?'

'A kitchen showroom recommended by my builder.'

'What sort of kitchen are you after?'

'Farmhouse with a modern take. The cottage is old but I don't want the proverbial *olde-worlde* look. Something a bit more contemporary.'

'Sounds great. And where's your cottage?'

Jeanne told him and also what she was planning to do with it and then mentioned her gran's pride and joy, the garden.

'Ideal for barbecues then!' Nick grinned at her.

'That's funny, Rachel said the same. But once the builders are in it's…wait a minute! I've had an idea. I could have a barbecue before the builders start.' Jeanne thought for a moment and then said, 'Do you think everyone would be free this weekend?'

Nick shrugged. 'No idea. But we've not arranged to go surfing so it's possible. Sunday afternoon might suit everyone, I think. And Colette mentioned she will be free in the afternoon. Shall I ask around?'

'Please. And everyone could bring friends if they like, then I'll get to know even more of the friendly natives,' she grinned at Nick. After reflection she added, 'There is one, rather big problem, though.'

'And what's that?'

'I don't have a barbecue!'

Nick laughed. 'Minor problem! Scott can bring the portable one we used on the beach.' As he drank his coffee and Jeanne ate her soup an odd expression flitted across his face.

'It was here, wasn't it? Here, where I've seen you before?'

'Ye...s. You had that horrible man with you,' admitted Jeanne, worried that he'd now feel uncomfortable in her presence, knowing she'd witnessed his embarrassment.

Nick nodded, looking grim. *Oh dear, he'll probably just go now and avoid me like the plague.*

Then a slow smile spread over his face and his eyes were definitely laughing when he said, 'That wasn't one of my best business meetings, was it? I had to stop myself telling that 'horrible man' exactly what I thought of him. Once his darned boat is finished and I've cashed his, admittedly large, cheque, I might just let rip!'

Jeanne relaxed and smiled back.

'Good for you! But it's awful being bullied by people you're working for, isn't it? I've had some quite nasty editors to deal with in my time and when I first started as a journalist there were a couple of times when I was reduced to tears.'

'At least I wasn't that bad! Ah, sorry, was that patronising?'

'No, don't be daft. How could a big, strong successful businessman like you patronise a small, weak female like me?'

They both burst out laughing and Jeanne felt all the earlier upset and tension ease away.

'Hey, our first meeting was actually on the ferry, wasn't it? You crashed into me as if you were drunk.'

She shook her head, no longer laughing.

'I wasn't drunk, I was having a panic attack, looking at Herm.'

'Oh, sorry. Well, at least I've been more supportive this time.' He gripped her hand and she replied, with a smile, 'Yes, very supportive.'

'Look, much as I enjoy your company, I really must get back to the grindstone. Can't have you a witness to another shouting match, can we?' His eyes were still laughing, she noticed, wishing that he didn't have to go.

'Give me your phone number, Jeanne, and I'll let you know about the barbecue. Are you seeing Marcus this week?'

Jeanne nodded. 'Yes, tomorrow night. I'll ask him about the weekend then. Did you know we girls are out on Thursday evening?'

'Colette did say something about it. Enjoy yourselves. Right, I'm off. Hope to see you on Sunday, okay?'

Jeanne smiled as he left and then concentrated on her food. The soup had been delicious and she wondered if it was a local recipe. She chewed the last bit of the sandwich deep in thought. Part of her regretted confiding in Nick about the flashback even though he had been so nice. He now knew her weakness, making her vulnerable, in her eyes, at least. Another part of her was glad someone helped her when she was so upset and she had enjoyed his company. And now she'd agreed to a barbecue! Must be mad. She shook her head at the thought and the waiter, hovering nearby, asked if everything was all right.

'Fine, thanks. Can I have my bill, please?'

Sitting there in the café she recalled the images that had flashed in her head, unbidden, on the way there. She had not previously remembered the other boat but 'seeing' it in her mind's eye had made it very real. It's no good, she'd have to remember more, then the police could track down who had been at the wheel...

Leaving the café, still feeling unsettled, she walked to the kitchen showroom. After a quick look round and admiring the displays, she arranged for a designer to come and measure up on Friday morning. She left bearing yet more glossy brochures.

Late that afternoon Jeanne arrived at Molly's bearing flowers and a laundry bag. Molly thanked her for them but insisted it was not necessary to buy her anything.

'It's no big deal having you use the machine. It would be a lot worse if Natalie was still at home. If she wore anything for five minutes it went in the wash. But you don't have much at all,' Molly said.

'That's because I've been living in grubby jeans most of the time. But now my social life is improving I may be round more often,' Jeanne grinned at Molly as they loaded the washing machine.

'Right, now that's on, how about a cup of tea while you tell me all about this great social life of yours.'

They sat in the kitchen drinking tea while Jeanne brought her up to date.

'It all sounds lovely, Jeanne. And how's the outline for the book coming on?'

Molly listened intently as she talked.

'Everything's coming together really well for you. I'm so pleased. It's about time that your life turned the corner.' Molly hesitated for a moment and then said, 'But there's something else isn't there? Perhaps not quite as positive?'

Jeanne sighed and, looking up at Molly's concerned face, said, 'Yes, I had a flashback today and it was very…upsetting. So,' she took a deep breath, 'I've decided that I do want to use hypnosis, if you're still happy to help me.'

'Of course I am. It's the least I can do to help, assuming I can. We don't know yet how well it will work as you've buried the memories for so long. I'd start slowly, using hypnosis to relax you for a few sessions first. Then if you're receptive, we can begin the regression therapy. How does that sound?'

Jeanne nodded. 'Okay. As long as I don't fall to pieces as I've got so much going on at the moment.'

'Of course, I understand, my dear. But if we take it a step at a time, you're not likely to fall apart, I promise. And all my clients so far have remained intact!'

'Good! How about if we start next week? I'll keep my social diary a bit clearer just in case I do become a gibbering wreck.'

Molly smiled. 'That's fine by me. Let me check my own diary so I don't double book you with that multiple personality I'm seeing at the moment. Might just add to the already high level of confusion.'

She returned a moment later with her diary and they settled on three o'clock the following Monday. Although Molly usually worked in a clinic she suggested that it would be less stressful if they met at her home. 'Peter won't be home until after five so we won't be disturbed. All right?'

'Sure. Thanks, Molly. Oh, by the way, I'm planning a barbecue at home next Sunday afternoon and hope that the group I've met will come. Would you and Peter like to join us? I'm assuming Peter doesn't mind mixing with his old students.'

'I think he could deal with a load of his old students without any problem at all. He'd enjoy the flattery. We'd love to come. What time do you want us?'

'I don't know yet as it's not confirmed. So I'll give you a ring by Saturday with the details.'

Jeanne went to check the washing and as she waited for the machine to finish its final spin, Molly came up and said, 'Might as well bring your washing when you come for the hypnosis. Then we're solving two problems at once,' she said, grinning.

Jeanne scooped up her wet clothes into the bag and hugged Molly before setting off back to Le Petit Chêne. This was obviously commitment day, she mused. First, she'd committed herself to hosting a barbecue and then to sessions of hypnosis. She could only hope that both were steps in the right direction, but a flicker of doubt still hovered around the idea of unearthing her buried memories. She had a feeling that she would find out things that she'd rather not know. Things that would have been better left buried and undisturbed for good.

# chapter 15

In the post on Wednesday there was a letter from her bank. Opening it she was pleased to see that her mortgage had been approved. Reading further she was informed of the need to attend Court in two weeks' time to sign for the Bond on her cottage. Relief surged through her as the window shopping was proving very expensive to date and now she could order the sanitary fittings.

Nick had phoned the previous evening to say that the others could all make that Sunday and he'd already checked that the weather forecast was favourable. Everyone was going to contribute to the food and drink so Jeanne didn't have to worry about feeding the proverbial five thousand.

When he asked her how she was feeling she told him that she was much better and had arranged to see a therapist.

'Good. We don't want to have to keep plying you with alcohol every now and then, do we?' he teased.

Jeanne laughed. 'No problem with the alcohol, I just don't want any more flashbacks.'

After putting down the phone Jeanne hummed to herself with pleasure. *Never thought that within a few weeks of being back I'd be a vibrant part of the local social scene.* She smiled to herself.

That afternoon Jeanne went for a long walk on the beach, beginning to fill up thanks to the hotter days. Now June, summer was showing her very warm, sunny side to the world, or at least to this little twenty-five square mile corner of it. The sea sparkled under the sun's rays but not many people were venturing into its chilly embrace. A few small children paddled, chaperoned by bored looking parents with their trousers or skirts tucked up out of harm's way. Farther out, surfers encased in wetsuits rode the waves.

Wonderful, for those who had no fear of the sea, Jeanne thought, with a slight shiver. Still, with Molly's help she might soon be frolicking about in the surf herself, just as she did when she was younger. Images of her teenage self, splashing in the sea with her friends came floating in and she remembered how much fun it had been. Sighing, she carried on walking briskly up the beach and, after another half hour, turned back, accompanied by groups of sea gulls. They swooped up and down, looking for picnic scraps, calling to each other with a high pitched shriek whenever they hit gold.

Back at the cottage she had plenty of time for a leisurely bath before changing for her evening out with Marcus. With the rise in temperature outside, the cottage felt much warmer and needed little heating. The sitting room, in particular, got plenty of sun during the day and felt pleasantly warm at night.

Acknowledging the arrival of summer, Jeanne chose a bright patterned cotton skirt with a toning plain top. The time spent outdoors had produced the healthy glow of a light tan and it was good to know how much better she looked than on her arrival. She was also feeling so much better.

Marcus arrived promptly at eight looking relaxed in jeans and a short sleeved shirt.

'Hi. Hmm, you've caught the sun and I like it.' He stroked her face before kissing her.

'I'd better do some serious sunbathing and start soaking up the compliments as well as the sun,' she replied, grinning.

With the roof down Marcus drove along the coast away

from the red and gold rays of the slowly setting sun. A light breeze blew Jeanne's hair out behind her. It was only a few minutes' drive to L'Eree and Marcus parked at the back of the restaurant. Although it was right opposite the sea, unfortunately there were no views once inside but the Indian décor created its own ambience.

Marcus ordered drinks as they studied the menu and discussed their favourite Indian dishes.

'I prefer the milder ones like korma, pasanda or tandoori,' Jeanne remarked.

'Yeh, they're okay, but real men eat real curries like vindaloo or jalfrezi!' he replied, beating his chest with his fists, Tarzan style.

Jeanne laughed and they agreed that he would order a vindaloo and she a korma after a shared starter of lamb tikka and onion bhaji. While they waited for the food they chatted about the few days since they'd met and it seemed that Marcus was as busy as ever. Jeanne told him that she was now ordering fittings for the cottage and then mentioned the barbecue and asked if he could come.

'Of course. I'm looking forward to seeing this garden I've heard so much about. And perhaps we could play hide and seek in the orchard!' he teased.

Jeanne retorted, 'I'm afraid fruit trees have very small trunks. No chance of hiding behind any of them. And you'll have to behave yourself as Peter Ogier is coming.'

'Oh no!' he feigned a look of horror which was quickly replaced by a smile. 'He was always such a nice old stick that we wouldn't want to upset him, anyway. Any other old codgers coming?'

'Hey, don't be so disrespectful of my friends! And remember we'll all be 'old codgers' one day.'

The service was particularly quick and it didn't seem long until it was time for desserts. They both chose Indian pistachio flavoured ice cream and it slipped down a treat after the curries. When the waiter asked if they'd like coffee Jeanne said yes as she didn't want to offer Marcus coffee at home. He'd been very tactile during the meal and he might want more than a good night kiss. Perhaps it was time for honesty.

'Marcus, you know I told you that I'd recently split up with my boyfriend?'

He nodded.

'Well, what I didn't tell you is that I became pregnant by him and I…I had a miscarriage some weeks ago. So I'm still dealing with a lot of emotional stuff and that's why I don't want to rush into a new relationship. I wanted you to know that it's not personal,' she smiled uncertainly.

'Oh, I'm so sorry. It must have been rotten for you.' He reached out and held her hands. 'Don't worry. I admit I'd like us to be more than friends but I can see that this isn't good timing at the moment. Can we still see each other?' Again the lop-sided grin worked its charm.

'Sure we can. I won't be in Purdah for ever! And thanks for dinner. I really enjoyed it.'

'So did I. By the way, are you, er, getting nightmares still? Only you mentioned them last time and I don't like to think of you getting upset,' he asked, fidgeting with a teaspoon.

'No, I've not had any nightmares lately, but I did have a flashback the other day.' Her eyes lost focus as she remembered.

His hand jerked and the spoon went flying. After he picked it up, he reached to squeeze her hand, looking worried. 'Let's…hope you won't get any more. I want you to enjoy yourself now you're back here.'

Jeanne nodded and the waiter arrived with the bill.

The air was cooler as they strolled back to the car and Marcus put the heater on as they drove back to her cottage. When they arrived he gave her a kiss as they exchanged good nights.

'See you on Sunday!' he called as he drove off and Jeanne went upstairs to curl up with her book. How long before I'm ready to share my bed with a man instead, she wondered, with a heavy sigh.

A low rumble, followed by a sound resembling a motorbike doing wheelies woke Jeanne the next morning. What on earth! Still drowsy, she reached for her dressing gown and peered out of the window but couldn't see what was causing the noise, definitely coming from the garden. Garden – lawnmower! Of course – it was Thursday, the day Carl was due for the fortnightly trim. Glancing at her alarm clock Jeanne saw it was ten past eight.

Downstairs in the kitchen she thought it lucky Carl was here just before the barbecue. At least the garden would look immaculate for her guests, compensating for the current state of the cottage.

After clearing away the breakfast things she spread out the kitchen brochures and browsed for ideas. She became so absorbed in drawing a rough plan of the kitchen that it took a few moments to register the ringing of the phone, competing as it was against the even louder noise outside.

'Hello, Jeanne speaking.'

'Hey, thought you were out – it's me, Freya.'

'Sorry, didn't hear the phone. Did you get the outline from my agent?'

'Yes, that's why I'm phoning. I loved it and my boss is just as fascinated as I am. The upshot is she's going to present it at the next editorial meeting on Monday morning. There'll be a vote but my boss's views carry a lot of weight. So, it's looking good! I'm so excited for you and I'm convinced it'll make a great book.'

Jeanne felt her heart hammering away in her chest and had to take a few deep breaths before replying.

'That's great, Freya, thanks. Sounds like you've done some pretty good PR for me. When will I know whether you're going ahead and would there be an advance if you do publish?'

'Officially, your agent won't hear till the end of next week but I'll know immediately so I'll ring you, probably about lunchtime. So make sure you hear the phone ringing!' Freya laughed and then continued, 'There'd certainly be an advance and if we go all out on the marketing, aiming for high sales, then it could be generous. But that's not my province, that's where my boss and the accountants come in.'

'Uh huh. Could 'generous' be enough to help renovate my cottage, d'you think?'

Freya chuckled. 'Depends if you're going in for gold taps, a Jacuzzi and a swimming pool, girl! If you're being more modest, then yes, it certainly could. Don't panic, I'll be rooting for you. And I'll also tell them how photogenic you are and what a draw you'll be at book signings.'

It was Jeanne's turn to laugh and she said, through her laughter, 'Okay, don't let's get too carried away now. But I promise you this, Freya, if I do get a contract and the deal's a good one, I'll treat you to a slap up night out in London with all the trimmings.'

'I'll hold you to that, never fear. Now must go, lots of other authors to talk to, egos to massage, etc. etc. Byee.'

Jeanne replaced the receiver and went back to the kitchen and sat down heavily on her chair. Although she had good vibes about the book she knew how few were ever accepted by publishers and the odds had been against her. But it looked promising and she now had to get through the next four days without thinking about it. Definitely not easy as she tried to focus on her proposed kitchen.

Remembering that Carl would be needing his usual cuppa, Jeanne broke off from the kitchen plans and made tea for him and coffee for herself.

'How's it going, Carl?' she asked, handing him his mug.

'Ta. Won't take too long, I reckon. Another hour should see me finished, miss. You've got the beds looking good, you have. Those herbs are coming on a treat, they are.' Carl nodded towards the herb garden, looking well established with the new plants firmly bedded in.

Jeanne left him to his tea break and returned to her plans, sipping her coffee for caffeine-induced inspiration. It seemed to work because an hour later she was pleased with the rough plan she had sketched out.

While she had been playing with her ideas she had decided that, if possible, she'd like to knock a doorway through to the dining room from the kitchen. Making a note in her building file, she wondered how many more bright ideas she'd have before the work began and whether or not she could afford them.

Rachel rang the bell at seven thirty and they set off for the cinema.

'We're looking forward to your barbecue on Sunday,' she said. 'Hope you didn't think I was putting pressure on you to have one when I said you had the ideal garden?'

'No, not at all. I just realised that I might as well have one sooner rather than later. If it's a success we could have more through the summer, providing the builders don't make a mess outside. As you rightly pointed out, I do have plenty of room.' She giggled. 'We can think of it as a sort of house warming party without actually being in the house!'

They arrived at the cinema shortly before Colette and Sue and they went through to watch the comedy they had chosen.

An hour and a half later they were still laughing at the misadventures of the hapless hero as they walked out.

'Fancy a quick drink in the bar, anyone?' asked Sue.

Minutes later they were seated at a table nursing their

drinks. A pleasant half hour passed as they discussed their week and how great it was that summer had arrived.

'Should be T-shirts and shorts on Sunday,' Rachel remarked. 'Trouble is, my legs are so white that I look like I'm balancing on inverted milk bottles!' They laughed and shared their own dislike of pale legs on display. All of them admitted to cheating with fake tan until the real thing became established and there was talk of checking their bathroom cabinets for supplies when they got home.

Hugs were shared and they split off to their cars. On arriving at Le Petit Chêne Jeanne invited Rachel in for a coffee, but she said she needed an early night in order to face year five the next day.

'They're lovely really, but so draining. I don't know where they get their energy from. You can give me a guided tour of the cottage on Sunday. Night.'

Rachel backed out of the drive as Jeanne went inside, switching on lights and drawing curtains.

She wasn't at all tired and settled down with a hot drink, Joanna Trollope (nearly finished) and Kylie to while away an hour or so before going up to bed.

The thought of the crucial editorial meeting on Monday kept her awake for a while. It was a bit like having a job interview without actually being there in person. Would her words be persuasive enough to convince the editors that she was a star in the making? Or would they decide she was just another talentless wannabe?

# chapter 16

After shopping for the barbecue on Saturday Jeanne drove down to one of her favourite spots, Moulin Huet, to walk along the cliffs for a couple of hours.

The perfume of wild flowers mingled with the tang of the sea as she gazed down on the idyllic bay, sheltered by the cliffs, with its soft, golden sand and rock pools. Seagulls wheeled over her head and their raucous calls were the only sound on the cliff path. She sat on one of the benches to drink in the sights and smells, admiring the view that had so captivated Renoir that he had painted over a dozen pictures of it. Enjoying the peace of the cliffs reminded her of what she had missed about Guernsey and knew it was the right decision to stay. Whatever life now had in store for her. Getting up to walk back to the car, the name of another Guernsey-loving Frenchman popped into her head, Victor Hugo. After being expelled from Paris, he had settled in St Peter Port for many years, and Jeanne idly wondered if he had been a valued customer of her family's restaurant in Paris at one time. If she could prove that he was, what a boost that would give her book. Ah, such are the imaginings of writers, she thought, shaking her head as she arrived at the car.

While out shopping she had bought some garden chairs and a sunbed. Once home she flopped on the bed for the remaining hours of sun to boost her tan. After all, she needed to be ready for more compliments.

The weather on Sunday morning was just as forecast. A hazy start followed by a clear sky and temperatures reaching into the twenties. Jeanne had woken feeling a bit stiff from her hike on the cliffs and enjoyed a long soak with the bath salts "guaranteed to melt away all tension and strains". They must have worked their magic because she hopped out of the bath more easily than she'd climbed in. The sun beckoned so it wasn't a hard decision to chill out for the morning, putting her new sunbed to good use.

Soon after 2.30 Scott and a friend turned up with the barbecue.

'Hi, Jeanne. This is Jonathan, another old Grammarian. Nick said we could bring along new faces.'

'For sure, the more the merrier. Good to meet you, Jonathan. Sorry to ask as soon as you've arrived but could you two carry out the kitchen table, please?'

Once the table and barbecue were set up on the lawn Jeanne thanked them, adding, 'I'll buy a proper garden table next time so you won't need to flex your muscles again.'

Scott grinned. 'No problem. But I think we've earned a beer before the others get here.'

They placed a cool box full of beer under the shade of the table and opened some cans as they chatted.

'Weren't you in the year above me, Jonathan? In the same class as Marcus?' Jeanne had vague memories of a lanky boy with dark, straggly hair, who scowled a lot.

'Afraid so. I was one of those who put the fear of God into the younger ones. Or so we thought.'

'And who are you terrorising now?' she grinned at him.

'My patients, of course. I'm a doctor now and everyone's scared of the doctor, aren't they?'

She and Scott laughed at the unlikely scenario of anyone being afraid of Jonathan who looked like the gentle, caring man he was and, according to Scott, had his patients eating out of his hand.

The sound of cars arriving filtered through to them and Jeanne went to the front and showed her guests where to park up the lane before directing back to the garden. When

Peter arrived with Molly he was greeted enthusiastically by his former pupils. After much exaggerated politeness on their part Peter said, laughing, 'Okay, there's no need to go overboard. Let's assume you're all mature adults now and we can be on first name terms. Otherwise I'll feel as old as the hills!'

The garden seemed to fill up quickly as people carried through cool boxes and the clink of bottles marked their passage to the table, soon awash with various meats, salad, drinks, plates and cutlery. Everyone grabbed a beer or poured wine into the plastic cups Jeanne had provided and the men took charge of the barbecue, now alight and warming up nicely.

Marcus gave Jeanne a hug and kiss on arrival and then joined the other chefs. Nick arrived with Sue, late as usual, and after a quick 'Hi, how are you?' he too had drifted off. Jeanne stepped over to say hello to Molly and Peter, who had finally escaped from his ex-students.

'I must say, I'm impressed with what you and the gardeners have achieved, Jeanne. It's just as it was when your gran was around,' Peter remarked.

'Thanks. But I've not finished yet, I've got plans for some changes, money permitting, naturally.' She described her ideas for a pergola and patio and Molly was particularly enthusiastic, making suggestions for the planting which had to include, she insisted, passion flower, honeysuckle and vines. After an animated discussion of the pros and cons of materials and plants, Jeanne excused herself and went off in search of Rachel. She found her in a laughing huddle with Sue and Colette.

'Hi, girls. Anyone fancy a tour of the cottage?'

'We've been waiting for you to ask,' said Rachel as they followed her inside. Nick must have been watching them as he came up and asked if he could join the tour. Jeanne explained the planned changes as they went from room to room.

She was intrigued that, once again, no-one commented on the chill of the small bedroom, the only remark being one of envy from Rachel concerning the intended en suite bathroom.

Colette was particularly envious of the size of the kitchen.

'Our flat's kitchen is miniscule. And yours will be lovely once it's finished. Perhaps, one day…' she sighed.

'Well, I live in a tiny flat at The Bridge but I like small spaces. Not so much to clean,' said Sue. 'But I do think you've got a great place here, Jeanne. Good luck to you. You'll need it once those builders start ripping it about!'

Jeanne nodded. 'That's not something I'm looking forward to. I'll have to set up a barbecue in the garden for cooking and sling a hammock between the trees in the orchard for sleeping.'

'You could put a tent up in the garden. Think of it as an extended camping holiday,' joked Rachel.

They were standing in the kitchen and Nick was poring over the rough plans Jeanne and the designer had drawn up.

'This isn't bad. What materials are you using for the units?'

'Painted MDF in a Shaker style and probably a mixture of granite and oak for the worktops. I want a warm, contemporary look. I guess you're more used to making compact wood galleys?'

'Yes I am, but some boats are spacious enough to have a large and luxurious galley, especially if we use the best hardwoods. Which reminds me, you'll be interested to know that we finished Mr Evans's boat on time, and the cheque's been banked,' he grinned at Jeanne.

'That's great! Now you can tell him to get stuffed and you'll be able to relax a bit.'

'What's this? How did you know what Nick was

working on?' Sue looked accusingly at Jeanne.

Nick explained about the meeting in the café and Sue seemed satisfied. But she still gave Jeanne a hard look as they went outside. *Oh dear, bet she thinks I'm after Nick as well and she's jealous.*

The aroma of grilled meat and fish wafted towards them, setting taste buds tingling. Jeanne was relieved that Peter was keeping tabs on the cooking. Hopefully, there'd be no cremated offerings today.

The food was ready shortly afterwards and the choice of chicken, fish or steak, served with salad, was soon being served up to enthusiastic cries from the hungry partygoers. Once the food had disappeared into the now full stomachs everyone spread out, either on the lawn or in the orchard. Time to give in to the combined soporific effects of sun, alcohol and good food.

Marcus and Jeanne stretched out in the orchard and he flung his arm across her body and quickly succumbed to a doze. She was trying to stay awake, feeling duty bound as the hostess to be alert to her guests' needs, but the sun's warm caress was winning. She made herself focus on the party, concluding it had been a success. Several new faces had appeared and it felt good to be offering hospitality to so many.

She and Andy had not been great socialisers, and as Jeanne looked back she realised, with a shock, that it had been Andy who had resisted having friends round, not her. Thinking about it now, she could see he had been more of a loner and she had subdued her own more gregarious personality to suit him. Well, she was her own person now and free to have as many friends and parties as she wanted, she told herself, feeling empowered by her new life.

Jeanne sat up, dislodging Marcus's arm and he stirred, opened his sleepy eyes and grinned at her.

'Hey, it feels so good just lying here, do we have to

move?'

'You don't, but I thought I'd make some tea or coffee for those that want some. Care to give me a hand?'

He shook himself and answered, 'I'm yours to command, O Mighty One. Lead on.'

Giggling, Jeanne made her way to the kitchen and Marcus asked the slowly stirring bodies who wanted teas or coffees. As he passed on the numbers to her, she had a sudden inspiration.

'Marcus, you mentioned the other day that your brother Dan is an antiques dealer. I've got some furniture I want to sell before the builders arrive. Do you think he'd be interested in buying it?'

He frowned. 'He might be. Just furniture?'

'Yes, I'll show you after we've handed out the drinks.'

They returned inside and Jeanne showed Marcus the items on her list.

'I think it's the sort of stuff he sells so I'll give him a ring. But you might get more money from an auction, you know.'

'I realise that, but it would be less hassle if Dan bought it all. If there's anything he doesn't want, I could still send it to auction.'

'Okay. I'll get him to ring you and insist he pays you a good price.'

Jeanne smiled her thanks and they went outside to mingle. As she looked around she caught Nick looking at her and she flushed at the intensity of his gaze. *Why's he staring at me? Have I got something on my face? A zit?* She cautiously touched her face. Nick seemed to realise he had been staring and turned away to talk to Jonathan. She glanced round, thankful to see Marcus deep in conversation with Tim.

'You seem to have another admirer,' Molly said, coming up to Jeanne.

'Oh, I…I don't think so. He was probably just staring into space when I came into his line of vision,' she replied, wondering how much Molly had seen.

'Have it your own way. But I certainly don't think he's indifferent to you. And he is rather attractive, isn't he?' Molly said admiringly.

'Molly! Behave yourself. Remember you're a happily married woman with two grown up children,' Jeanne said, trying to sound shocked and disapproving.

Smiling sweetly Molly said, 'Doesn't mean I have to stop window shopping, does it? Peter's certainly enjoyed a little of that today, all those shorts and long legs!'

Jeanne laughed and agreed that there was no harm in window shopping, no harm at all.

It was a still, hot morning as Jeanne walked through the cemetery with fresh flowers. As she put some on her parents' grave she told them about staying on in Guernsey and living in the cottage. And that she was hoping to have a book published, although she was yet to write it. She smiled as she pictured her parents' pleasure and pride in her news and went off to her grandparents' grave.

'Gran, you'll be so pleased to know that I'm staying here and I'm going to, er, renew the plumbing and wiring so that the cottage is brought up to date. I promise not to spoil it, just make it more comfortable to live in. Your garden's looking great and I've planted more herbs and…' Jeanne chatted on, really wanting her gran to know that life was definitely on the up for her.

As she headed back to the car Reverend Ayres came from the direction of the church.

'Morning, Vicar. I think it's going to be hot again today, don't you?'

'Yes, it is. I envy you being able to dress more casually,' he said, glancing at her T-shirt and shorts.

'I'm dressed for a little gardening later. By the way, I've decided to stay on here and be a proper Guern.' She looked at him expectantly.

'That's good news, Jeanne. I'm so glad and I'm sure your family would be pleased,' he said, nodding towards the graves.

'Oh, does that mean you saw me talking to them?' Jeanne felt her mouth open in dismay.

'Actually, I did. But don't worry, I don't think you're mad. If you are, then so are a lot of my parishioners! It's quite normal to want to converse with those we've lost, you know. And remember we talk to God in our prayers and yet we've never met Him and we can't see Him.' His eyes twinkled at her and Jeanne felt reassured that she wasn't alone in her need to 'talk' to her lost family.

'Thanks, Vicar. I didn't fancy being dragged off to the Castel, particularly as I've got so much to do. I'd better get going now, but I'll probably see you again soon. Bye.'

'Goodbye, Jeanne. God Bless.'

She drove back to the cottage trying hard not to dwell on the promised phone call from Freya. But it was like being told 'don't think about a pink elephant' – it was the first thing that came into one's mind. Her stomach was permanently in clench mode and she'd made more trips to the loo that morning than she cared to remember. She could really do with Molly's soothing, hypnotic voice now, she thought, taking a few deep breaths.

Back at Le Petit Chêne she busied herself in the garden, picking up the odd bits of detritus missed in the tidy up after the barbecue. They had finally called it a day about eight o'clock and everyone had happily helped in the clean-up operation. Jeanne had promised to hold another one before the end of summer and there had been a warm exchange of hugs and kisses as the group dispersed. Even Nick, not known for expressions of affection, had given

Jeanne a hug and a firm kiss on both cheeks. She had responded with her own kiss, breathing in the citrus tang of his aftershave. Her legs had felt a little weak in the few seconds of the embrace and she would have been happy to stay there a while longer. But Marcus had come up and Nick backed away, enabling Marcus to place a passionate kiss on her lips.

Recalling that moment now, Jeanne realised that physically she had responded more to Nick than to Marcus and she was troubled by this. After all, Nick came across as a loner, not even tempted by the lovely Sue. And she wasn't interested in a relationship herself at the moment, was she? Jeanne sighed and was saved from further soul searching by the strident ring of the telephone.

Glancing at her watch she saw it was not even twelve o'clock so unlikely to be Freya, but even so her stomach did a flip as she answered.

'Is that Jeanne Le Page? Dan Davidson. My brother asked me to call you. About some furniture?'

'Yes, Dan, thanks for phoning. Did Marcus tell you what I've got for sale?'

'He did, but I'm not sure if I'd be interested until I see it. When can I come round?'

'Would tomorrow morning be all right?'

'Eleven would suit me. What's the address?'

Jeanne gave him the details and then replaced the phone. Dan had sounded quite different to Marcus, abrupt and with no charm at all. Perhaps that's why they don't get on, she thought, like chalk and cheese.

Determined to keep busy and hoping to up the buying price, Jeanne dug out the wax polish and started on the furniture in the sitting room. The wood positively glowed by the time she'd finished, reflecting the glow on her face from all the elbow grease. She had just rubbed in a coat of wax on the dining table when the phone rang. This time her stomach did a complete somersault and backwards flip as she went to answer it. She knew it was Freya, with news that might well change her life. Her hand was shaking as she picked up the phone.

'Hi, Jeanne speaking.'

# chapter 17

'Hi, it's me, Freya. I've just come out of the meeting. Are you sitting comfortably?'

'Just grabbing a chair. Okay, fire away.' Jeanne's heart pounded in unison with the somersaulting stomach.

'Well, my friend, the powers that be really liked your proposal and are keen to publish. So what do you say to joining the ranks of our successful authors?'

Jeanne's stomach finally calmed down and she let out a long breath. Wow! She was going to have a book published! Even though it wasn't written yet – small point, really. She might be famous, make a lot of money…

'Hey, are you there? You haven't gone and had a heart attack, have you? Just when I need you!'

'No, my heart's still beating, though it's a bit erratic at the moment. I'm just gobsmacked. It's all happened so quickly.'

Freya chuckled, 'You're right there. Most writers would have to wait months for a decision, assuming they could get through to a publisher in the first place. They liked your fresh approach with the background of a love story and the Occupation, and anything to do with food seems to be flavour of the month, if you'll excuse the pun. By the way, they also liked the proposed title, *Recipes for Love.*'

'So, the fact that you and I are old friends didn't play any part?' Jeanne laughed.

'We…ll, let's just say it smoothed the way a bit. But it's your idea, your book which

has secured the deal, so you can be proud of yourself, girl. I'm happy to have been of service. And I haven't forgotten the offer of a *splendido* night out as my reward.'

'Fair enough. As long as it's a good deal, remember. Has anything been said about that?'

'No figures were mooted. We have to get our publishing costs confirmed first once the format's been chosen. My boss will contact your agent so that a contract can be negotiated. What did she think of it?'

'Sally rang to say she really liked it, too, and if you didn't make me an offer she had another publisher in mind. So I do have a Plan B to keep you on your toes.'

'I don't think you'll need it. There was a definite buzz of excitement round the table this morning so I'm sure we'll come up with a good deal. The big question is how long is it going to take you to write the book? I think we'd like to publish next year, certainly in time for the Christmas market, always a boost for sales.'

Jeanne did a mental review of what she'd planned to include in the book before answering. 'That should be possible. The priority is making sure all the recipes work with modern oven temperatures etc. But I've got someone in mind to help with that.'

'Sounds like you're as efficient as ever, girl. It'll take a couple of weeks before the contract's sorted so don't go ordering that swimming pool yet will you?' Freya's throaty laugh echoed down the line.

'Don't worry. Remember I'm sensible as well as efficient. Or at least that's what I tell myself! So, shall I phone you or will you phone me?'

'Let's say whoever knows the details first, shall we? I want to know when to buy my new party frock! Talk to you soon. Byee.'

Jeanne sat still for a long while, her mind racing along various avenues. Even though she didn't know the financial value of the contract yet, just publishing her first book would be rewarding enough. Her writing career was heading in a different direction than she'd visualised when turning freelance. Her head buzzed with ideas for future books. Perhaps she could write an historical novel, based in the islands? Or France? Her research for the current book might prove invaluable.

The flow of adrenaline finally prompted Jeanne to move and she remembered the furniture that needed polishing. Right, first things first, she said to herself. Polishing comes before writing bestsellers as it might help raise some much needed cash now.

Once all the various pieces were gleaming she had time for a quick lunch and a call to Kate with the good news, before her meeting with Molly.

Her aunt was overjoyed. 'Darling, I'm so proud of you. It's what I always hoped would happen. But how are you going to write with all that building work going on?'

'Ah, fair comment. Perhaps I could ask Molly if I can work at her place. I'm sure I'll sort something out. And that reminds me, I must get off to Molly's soon for my first session of hypnosis. I'll ring again soon.'

'Good luck with the session, my dear. I so want you to be able to put the past behind you. Take care.'

Jeanne had a quick wash and change of clothes and although she felt cleaner and cooler she was not much calmer as she set off to Molly's, experiencing a mix of emotions, including anxiety about the hypnosis.

Molly gave her a keen look as she shepherded her through to the study at the back.

'Right, it's as plain as the nose on my face that you're bursting with something and I think it's something good. Do you want to share it with me or are you just going to hold on until you burst?'

Jeanne grinned. 'There's no hiding anything from you, is there? If you must know, the publishers like my book and they'll shortly be discussing a contract with my agent.'

'Oh, Jeanne, that's wonderful news. No wonder you're so excited! I can see I'll have my work cut out getting you to relax today. Are you going to be rich?' Molly asked, giving Jeanne a hug.

'I doubt it. But I won't know how much money's involved for a couple of weeks. So, I definitely need to learn to relax or I'll be bouncing off the ceiling!' she chuckled.

'Right, we'd better get started then, hadn't we? Make yourself comfortable in the recliner. Good. How does that feel?'

'Fine, thanks. Wouldn't mind one of these myself.'

'Now, I'll just explain what I'll be doing and what we hope to achieve before I begin. Hypnosis is a natural state of deep relaxation which we all go through as we fall asleep and come back through as we wake up. It's best described as that lovely, dreamy state we gently wake up to. And it's definitely not mumbo jumbo!'

'I never thought it was. Can't imagine you as a witch doctor – you're not fierce enough.'

Molly smiled wryly. 'Believe me, when I first started using hypnosis, many moons ago, there were people here who certainly thought I must be a witch or something equally nefarious. But, let's continue. I want to emphasise that hypnosis is natural, like meditation or yoga, but without the contortions. All right so far?'

'Yes, that sounds fine.'

'Right. Now basically I do not hypnotise you, you hypnotise yourself. It's as if I'm reading from a book of instructions and you're carrying them out. So all hypnosis is self-hypnosis and if you respond well enough I'll teach you how to do it for yourself. Which I think you'll find pretty useful by the sound of things!'

'You're right there! But will it take me a long time to practise?'

'Only about three or four minutes, once you've got the

hang of it. So you'll still have plenty of time to write bestsellers and organise property renovations, never fear. But today I want to concentrate on helping you to relax here. We can use hypnosis to help change the pattern of thinking, by using positive suggestions to help you see things differently. I use this technique a lot to overcome fears and phobias and it should help with your fear of the sea and boats. And, as I've already explained, we can use hypnosis to unearth the buried memories that are still causing you problems. Even before we uncover exactly what did happen that night you could begin to feel more relaxed about swimming or going out in a boat. How does that sound?'

'I'd be really happy if you could help me with that fear. In some ways that's been more of a problem than the lost memory.'

'Of course. This may take a few sessions, but I would hope you'd feel the benefit after about three. And then we'll focus on recovering that lost memory. Now, I shall talk to you in a soothing manner, guiding you into a relaxed state. I call it a verbal massage and it's very pleasant. Once you're physically and mentally relaxed I'll come in with those positive suggestions. Any questions so far?'

'No, all sounds very clear.'

Molly then proceeded to talk in a slow measured manner and Jeanne felt herself drifting into a dreamlike state. After what felt like five minutes, Molly asked her to open her eyes.

'So, how was that?'

'It was lovely. I could hear what you were saying but it was as if you were far away and I was floating somewhere else. When you asked me to picture myself in a favourite place I immediately went back to when I was a child, with my family at Moulin Huet, having a picnic.'

Jeanne smiled at the memory and for a moment felt as if

she was still that small, innocent and happy child.

'Good. And are you relaxed now?'

'Sure am. I'm impressed. I didn't really think I'd react like that at all.' Jeanne's voice sounded dreamy and, as she glanced at the clock, was surprised to see twenty minutes had elapsed.

'I'm pleased because this means you're receptive and we're more likely to get the desired result. Shall we meet next Monday at the same time?'

'Yes, no problem. I'll look forward to it, thanks.'

'I think it's time to put the kettle on now, don't you?'

They decamped to the kitchen and over a cup of tea and the requisite slices of gâche, Jeanne went into more detail about Freya's phone call. Molly seemed as excited as if it was her own publishing debut and insisted that Jeanne come round for dinner the following evening so they could celebrate properly.

As she was getting up to leave Jeanne remembered the favour she had to ask.

'Molly, when the builders move in it's going to get incredibly noisy and I need to work on my book. Is there any chance of my working here during the day, a few days a week?'

Molly frowned. 'There shouldn't be a problem until mid-July, but after that we've got first my sister and her family and then Peter's cousins coming over for most of the summer, making it difficult. I'm so sorry, you know we'd love to help,'

'Not to worry. I'd appreciate the weeks you're free and I'll sort something else out for later, I'm sure.'

Jeanne left the cottage still relaxed and uplifted and almost floated home. Now no longer afraid of hypnosis she had every confidence in Molly's ability to steer her into a safe harbour and retrieve her buried memories. She must stop being so fearful of new experiences, she told herself as she arrived home.

Later that evening Jeanne was more successful with the second favour she had to ask.

'Hi, Colette. It's me, Jeanne. Is this a good time to talk?'

'Yes, no problem. Something up?'

'No, I've actually had some good news and I'd be glad of your help.'

Jeanne explained about her book and the recipes that she needed checking out, revising the cooking instructions to ensure they were more appropriate to the present day rather than the nineteenth century.

'Gosh, that sounds so exciting, Jeanne, and I'd love to help, but I don't get a lot of free time. Not sure when I could do it.'

'I've thought of that. Are you due any holiday or could you take unpaid leave and I'd pay you the going rate for your time? That way you wouldn't be out of pocket and of course you'd be acknowledged in the book, and possibly the hotel too, if we needed to twist their arms. Free publicity and all that.'

'I'd rather take unpaid leave and keep my holiday for when Scott's free. I'll ask my boss for a couple of weeks off and explain why. I'm sure he'll be supportive. Will I have a sous chef? For the donkey work?' Colette giggled.

'You'll have to make do with me, I'm afraid. I'll buy all the ingredients and help with basic preparation, if I don't get in your way. But will your kitchen be big enough for both of us?'

'Hardly. But I could ask Nick if we could use his. He's hardly ever there and it's super equipped, Helen saw to that.'

'Who's Helen?'

'Sorry, forgot you've not been back here long. Helen was Nick's fiancée until about two years ago, when she suddenly upped sticks and ran off with some guy she'd met at work. She and Nick had been together for years and were planning to marry the month after she left. He was pretty heartbroken, as you can imagine, and has hardly been out with anyone since. Don't think he trusts women very much and you can hardly blame him, can you?'

Jeanne was shocked.

'Poor Nick! Is that why he doesn't seem to respond to Sue's advances? He's just off women?'

'I'm not sure he even notices how keen she is. She's managed to get him to partner her a couple of times to work dos but it hasn't led to anything. Mind you, I've noticed that he seems a bit more relaxed these days so perhaps she's worn him down.' Colette chuckled. She then added, 'Mustn't keep you gossiping. You've got a book to write!'

'Thanks for reminding me. You work out the kitchen scenario once you've sweet talked your boss and let me know. I think it could be a lot of fun, as well as hard work. Talk soon.'

Well, well, well, Jeanne thought, absorbing the news about Nick. She could imagine his pain when Helen ran off, jilting him almost at the altar. On a small island like Guernsey, the news would have spread like wildfire and he wasn't the sort of man to accept pity from others, no matter how well-meaning. She felt a surge of sympathy towards him but knew that there was nothing she could do. Still, she admitted to herself that she was glad he and Sue were not yet an item though, of course, it wasn't anything to do with her, was it? With a deep sigh she brought herself back to her own problems, selling her furniture being the most immediate one.

The next morning Jeanne heard from the builder that he was free to start a week from the following Monday, giving her just under two weeks to get organised. And she hadn't even ordered the kitchen! Well, if she could sell the furniture to Dan that would at least solve one problem. The calmness induced by the hypnosis was still very much in evidence and Jeanne sat down to work out exactly what needed to be done in the next two weeks, feeling more in control than she had for months.

Dan turned up just after eleven and Jeanne gave a start when she opened the door. He was tall and fair like Marcus but more heavily built and marked with a pale jagged scar on his left cheek, white against the tanned, lived in face. Glancing down at his big hands as he took one of hers in his, she could imagine him throttling someone quite easily and gulped.

He gave her a hard stare with the blue eyes so like Marcus's, but yet so different.

'Morning. Shall we get straight down to business? Busy day,' he said abruptly.

'Er, yes. Please come in,' she said, leading him into the sitting room. He examined the cupboard and tables critically but made no comment, his face inscrutable. She then showed him the dining room and bedroom furniture, excluding the main bedroom. She needed something to sleep in.

Everything was thoroughly looked over before they returned downstairs.

'It's all solid, well made stuff and there's no sign of woodworm. So I'm prepared to make you an offer for the lot,' Dan said before naming a figure which, though not large, was certainly not to be sneezed at. As she led the way into the kitchen in order to offer him a coffee, Dan noticed the dresser.

'Is this for sale as well? I'd certainly be interested in buying it. A Le Mesurier, isn't it?' He looked animated for the first time since his arrival.

'I'm afraid it's not for sale but you're right, it's a Le

157

Mesurier. It's my favourite piece and has sentimental value for me.'

'We'd be talking thousands if you were to sell,' he said, looking covetously at the dresser.

'It's still not for sale. But thanks for your interest and I'm happy to accept your offer on the other furniture.' She was feeling increasingly uncomfortable as he ran his hand over the dresser, and was relieved when he refused any coffee.

'I'll bring my van tomorrow, if that's all right? And I pay in cash.' He looked around the shabby kitchen. 'You staying on here, then?'

'Yes, the builders are starting soon, which is why I'm having a clear out.'

'Aren't you the girl whose parents died in that boating accident some years ago?'

Again that intense stare unnerved her.

'Yes, I am.'

'I heard that you didn't remember what happened.'

'No, I didn't. The doctors called it traumatic amnesia.'

'Sometimes it's best not to remember bad things that happen. What you don't know can't hurt you. Isn't that right?'

'Suppose so.' She shifted her feet. 'If we've finished, Dan, there are things I have to do.'

Nodding, he confirmed he'd be back on Wednesday about twelve and left a relieved Jeanne to make a much needed cup of coffee for herself.

What was it that had made her so edgy with Dan? she wondered, sipping her coffee. He hadn't actually been threatening in his behaviour, just abrupt to the point of rudeness, but somehow there was an air of menace…She shivered. It was almost impossible to think of him as Marcus's brother in spite of some physical similarity.

This thought prompted her to phone him.

'Hi, it's me. Am I interrupting anything important?'

'No, not at all. I'm off to lunch in a minute. And it's always good to hear from you,' Marcus said warmly.

'I thought I'd let you know that Dan's been round and has agreed to buy all the furniture I'm selling. So that's a relief.'

'What's he paying you?'

Jeanne told him and he seemed to think it was fair, though not overgenerous.

'Still, he didn't rip you off so I'm glad about that.'

'I couldn't help noticing the scar on his face. Has he had an accident?'

He laughed shortly. 'No, he got in a fight when he was seventeen and high on drugs and someone cut him with a broken bottle. He was in Morocco with some mates and didn't get decent medical help so the wound failed to heal properly, leaving that nasty scar. Dan didn't seem too bothered, made him look like the tough guy he wanted to be. Hey! You don't fancy him do you?'

'Oh, no, definitely not. Don't be silly! To be honest, I found him a bit rude. But please don't tell him or he might back out of the deal.'

'No worries on that score, we hardly speak. Now, how about coming out to dinner with me on Friday? We could go to Christie's. Might be warm enough to sit out on the balcony.'

'Lovely, thanks. Bye for now.'

Jeanne was thoughtful after her call to Marcus. She now realised why she had felt the way she had with Dan. It wasn't just the scar that had unnerved her. It had been his eyes. Although not an expert on drug use, she had seen the signs at university. She was convinced that Dan was still a drug user and, with his history, he was definitely not to be trusted. She'd prefer not to have anything more to do with him. It was a relief to know that she wouldn't have to, once he'd paid for the furniture.

## chapter 18

The next few days passed quickly and the furniture had been duly collected by Dan and his assistant without any mishap. Jeanne had kept out of their way as much as possible and Dan barely acknowledged her, which was a relief. It had been very satisfying to pocket the wad of cash he thrust at her once all had been loaded up and she made tracks to the bank as soon they left.

The celebratory meal with the Ogiers had been a chance to relax and Peter had generously opened a bottle of champagne.

'It's not every day we get a chance to dine with a famous author!' had been his comment and even though they all knew that fame might still evade her, it was a happy thought and Jeanne was warmed by their generosity.

She made the most of the quiet time left before the builders descended, working on the book for several hours a day. She pored over library books and surfed the internet for background information, putting in motion a search for details of her ancestors, the Parisian restaurateurs. After coming across UK websites used for tracing family trees, she found similar ones in France, albeit in French. *Naturellement!* Not her strong point! She heaved a sigh as she scanned the pages of one such website, wishing she had paid more attention in her French classes at school. Her starting point was her great-great-grandmother from Normandy and after finding some possible connections she printed off the pages to discuss with Molly.

If the worst came to the worst she could always pop over to France, specifically Paris, for a more hands on approach. It would provide extra colour to her story if she could see where her family had lived and worked. And there was always Le Shopping – subject to a generous advance, of course.

On Thursday she received the quote and detailed plan for the proposed kitchen. Jeanne loved the design. The warm, buttermilk painted units would make the kitchen look light and bright without losing the homely look of the cottage – perfect with the oak and granite worktops. Colette would definitely be jealous. The price was less perfect, being on the high side of her budget. Still, as the estate agent had said, quality counts, so she lost no time in confirming her order before settling down to work.

On Friday morning Colette phoned.

'Hi, Jeanne. I finally managed to talk to my boss last night and he's agreed to let me have two weeks unpaid leave from the end of June. Luckily no-one's off just then. And Nick's happy to let us use his kitchen with the proviso that he gets to eat the fruits of our labours. All right with you?'

'Yes, sure. And it's good that Nick will be our official taster as he's likely to be more objective than us. By the way, where does he live?'

'At Bordeaux and it was our parents' cottage. Nick moved in after Dad died, although it was left to both of us, it made sense for Nick to buy me out, being so close to his business.'

'Well, it'll be handy for the supermarket at The Bridge when I do the mountain of shopping we'll need. Bit of a trek from here, mind. Have we got to promote the hotel as recompense for depriving them of their up and coming chef?'

'Let's just say that they wouldn't be averse to some free publicity, but they're not making it a condition of my leave. Oh, could I have a look at the recipes now so that I know what to expect?'

'Sure, good idea. I'll print off copies and have them ready later today. I could pop them in to you as I'm in town tonight with Marcus.'

All the recipes were now on the computer in English and easy to print off. The original handwritten recipes were safely stored in plastic folders and one of Jeanne's ideas was to incorporate a few facsimiles of the originals in the book. She also planned to include photos of her grandmother, great-great-grandmother and anyone older she could trace, as well as the one of Wilhelm.

After a day spent researching, Jeanne was looking forward to an evening out with Marcus. As she changed into a linen skirt and a white top she asked herself what she was going to do about their friendship. He had made it clear he was pretty keen on her, but she had yet to feel a 'spark'. If the chemistry wasn't there now, would it ever be? From her own, admittedly limited, experience, there was usually a connection pretty early on. Although she had never been to bed with a man on the first date, there'd been times when it had been very hard to say no. With Andy, she'd lasted until the third date and she could still remember the frantic tearing at each other's clothes before they fell naked and entwined into bed.

The erotic memory stirred her body with the old feelings of desire, dormant for so long. Oh my God, she groaned, guess the hormones are back on form! But the image that was uppermost in her mind was not that of Marcus or Andy, but of Nick. She shook herself. *I think my brain's got its wires crossed. Why am I not feeling like that with Marcus? He's good looking and charming and I used to fancy him rotten.* She sighed and decided that if there was no spark for her within the next couple of weeks then she'd stop seeing him. It wasn't fair to string him along, after all.

Later that evening they were on the balcony at Christie's enjoying the warm, balmy air as they waited for their first course to arrive. As soon as Jeanne had mentioned that she was going to have a book published, Marcus had insisted on ordering champagne as an aperitif.

'At this rate I shall be permanently awash with champagne,' she laughed as they clinked glasses. 'Peter opened a bottle the other night and I haven't even signed a contract yet.'

'Just be positive. I'm sure it'll all work out. After all, you've got the letter from the publishers to prove good intent.'

A letter from her agent, Sally Coulson, had arrived that morning and confirmed that negotiations were in progress.

'True, so when I do get a contract I guess there'll have to be more champagne.' She smiled at Marcus.

'If you're going to be rich then you'll have to pay for it,' he joked.

'Oh, I won't be rich. But it would be nice to get a big, fat advance,' she giggled, intoxicated by the bubbles.

'And where are you and Colette going to cook up those delicious dishes?'

'Nick's kindly agreed we can use his kitchen as he's hardly ever there.'

'I see. Not sure if I like the idea of your spending time at Nick's. I think he fancies you,' Marcus said, scowling.

'Oh, I don't think he does. And I'm not likely to see much of him as I'm only helping Colette with the donkey work. I'll be in and out, really.'

As both Molly and Marcus had now said the same thing, perhaps Nick did fancy her, she thought, her stomach contracting. She was lost in her thoughts for a moment and when she looked up she noticed that Marcus still looked sullen.

Jeanne sought to lighten the atmosphere between them and eventually he cheered up. By the time their coffee arrived he was laughing at a joke she'd heard.

As he dropped her back home Jeanne was subdued as they kissed – he with some passion and she with less enthusiasm.

'I'm sorry for making a fuss earlier about Nick. But I think I'm falling in love with you and I don't want to think of you spending time with another man,' Marcus said. He was still holding her face between his hands and as she looked into his eyes they seemed to change and become those of his brother.

She blinked and the eyes were his own again. It startled her.

'Please, Marcus. It's too soon to talk of love. We hardly know each other and I'm not sure what I feel for you. And I don't want to be told who I may or may not see!'

She was beginning to feel angry about his possessiveness and she slipped out of the car before he could reply.

Going straight upstairs she was relieved to hear his car pull out of the drive. With a shock she found her hands were shaking. Once she was in bed and trying to sleep all Jeanne saw were eyes – Marcus's turning into Dan's and then back again. Her sleep was restless with vivid dreams full of staring, baleful blue eyes.

The following week was to be a solitary interlude for Jeanne. She told her friends she wouldn't be going out, what with preparing for the builders and working on the book, but planned to stay in touch by phone. Colette said she couldn't wait to start work on the recipes, particularly the French ones. She thought that her two weeks would be enough to try out at least the oven based recipes. Others could be incorporated into her normal home cooking schedule.

'It just means that we'll be eating a strange mixture for a while, but I don't think Scott will mind. He's used to my experimenting on him!' she laughed.

Marcus rang at the weekend to apologise again and she was quite cool towards him.

'Let's just take a break for the moment, Marcus. I've got a lot on my plate just now so if you want to ring me next weekend I'll see how I feel then, okay?'

'If that's what you want. I hope you have a good week and miss me as much as I'll miss you. Take care,' he said, his tone sulky.

It was a relief to Jeanne to put Marcus on hold and concentrate on more practical matters. She had not proved to be very successful in the emotional stakes in the past and wanted to get it right this time.

On Monday she took flowers to the graves before going off to her appointment with Molly. The session went well and she felt even more relaxed than she had the first time. Molly taught her the self-hypnosis technique and she agreed to practise it religiously each day. If nothing else, it helped her stay focussed on her work and the pile of notes grew steadily.

Sally phoned about the publishing contract.

'We've only really touched base so far. But I hope to receive the main deal points in the next few days. They're proposing a high-quality hardback backed up with extensive marketing for maximum sales. The key figure is the advance which has yet to be confirmed so I'll get back to you on that. Happy so far?'

'Yes, fine. I'm sure I can rely on your impressive negotiating skills. Once the contract's ready I'll pop over to London and you can take me out to lunch to celebrate. That's the tradition, isn't it?' Jeanne chuckled.

'Might manage a burger and chips. See you soon.'

Jeanne had done very little work through Sally as yet, barely earning a cup of coffee, let alone a meal. But if this contract was as good as Sally expected then the lunch was likely to be, if not at The Ritz, at least at a decent restaurant, she hoped.

By Sunday Jeanne was fed up of her own company and was actually looking forward to the builders arriving the next day, in spite of the disruption they would bring. She knew her life would be turned upside down but at least things would be happening and within a couple of months she would have a home to be proud of. Assuming nothing went wrong.

# chapter 19

By nine o'clock on Monday morning Jeanne felt as if she'd been transported to a war zone. A large skip had taken over the drive and anything she had designated as rubbish was being thrown into it, at some cost to her eardrums. Elsewhere drills and crowbars were in full use and she could both hear and feel her house disintegrating around her. Once everything was on track with the builders she planned to go off to Molly's to work in peace and quiet.

Martin had arrived with his plumber, electrician and labourer in tow and had wasted no time in working out a plan of action.

'Once the place is clear we'll concentrate on the new central heating and the electrics. We'll have to cut off the present supply in a couple of weeks or so. Afraid there'll be no water at some stage too. By then you might want to move out as it'll be a bit uncomfortable,' Martin said dryly.

'Oh, I see. How long will I need to be out?'

'A week or two. And there'd be times when you might not want to be here during the day as well. To be honest, we'd get on much quicker if you're not living here. No need to worry about power and plumbing or to keep clearing up, see. And all the floors upstairs have to come up.'

Jeanne nodded, wondering where she could go. Molly couldn't help and it was likely that anyone with a spare bedroom in Guernsey in summer had a list of relatives and friends eager to visit. Even if she could find a room in a guest house or hotel it would be very expensive and she didn't want to spend hundreds of pounds on a room if she could avoid it. There was always a new problem, she sighed, loading up her car with her laptop, printer and files.

She let herself in and headed for the study which Molly had said she could use. Her priority was sifting through Wilhelm's letters to learn more about his relationship with her gran.

By 1944 Wilhelm's English had improved considerably and his letters were easier to read. A letter dated April 1944 proved to be a revelation:

*My darling Jeanne*

*I feel myself so honoured your love and trust earned to have. I know doubtless that you my heart have and I yours have. I have slept not with a woman before and after the last night my heart is with love for you and joy that you have given me, full. I hope that for you also it special and joyful was?*

*I want the rest of my life in your arms to spend, where I belong. I want to love you and from all harm to protect. When this senseless war over is, will we the world as man and wife face.*

*I can hardly wait, for you again, my darling, to see. But will try, patient to be. Until next week, at our usual place.*

*All my love*
*Wilhelm*

Oh, my God they were lovers! How exciting! But dangerous, too as they were enemies. Jeanne felt a rush of sympathy for them both. Wilhelm sounded more passionate, more sure of himself and of their mutual love. What had happened to prevent them becoming man and wife as Wilhelm had so confidently predicted? The question drove her on to read more letters and the next couple were full of similar expressions of Wilhelm's feelings. There was a letter, dated July 1944, which left Jeanne so shocked that she had to make herself a cup of coffee before sitting down to read it again. It wasn't true! It just wasn't true!

Jeanne sat staring into space, the colour drained from her face, when she heard Molly pottering about in the kitchen. Then a knock on the study door announced Molly's entrance.

'What on earth's the matter, Jeanne?' Molly cried.

She said, 'Read that,' and thrust the letter from Wilhelm at her. Jeanne knew the contents by heart.

*My darling Jeanne*

*Such news! How wonderful! I know it a secret we have to keep but I want from the tops of the roofs to shout. You our Baby are going to have! I am going a father to be. My dearest wish is that we were free to marry and have a home together, our little family.*

*I know not how we will manage after our Baby has been born, but we will, somehow. This War cannot go on much longer and I know that we Germans will probably lose. Now it goes badly for us.*

*But when the War is ended, if I am allowed to stay here, we will marry, my love. If I am not welcome here, and I would understand why, then we could to another land go where I might be accepted. We will work out things, never fear, mein liebling!*

*I want to cherish you and our Child. I hope that enough to eat, you have, you your strength will need in these next months. You must stop bringing food to me and must eat it yourself. I will manage, I am strong! We will meet again next week, my darling.*

*All my love,*
*Wilhelm*


'Gran had his baby! And we never knew. What happened to it? Oh, Molly, I'm so shocked, I just don't know what to think!'

'Nor do I. But perhaps you'll find out more when you've read the other letters. And there's always a possibility that your gran had a miscarriage which would explain why this is news to you.'

Jeanne was stricken.

'Oh, my dear! I'm sorry! I don't want to upset you even more.' Molly reached out and touched her arm.

She shook her head. 'It's not your fault, Molly. Don't worry. I just keep thinking of Gran, so young and burdened with such a big secret. I expect she had to keep it from her family, too. How did she feel when she realised she was pregnant? Happy? Scared? Angry? Wilhelm seemed happy enough but his letter doesn't show what Gran felt. And she might have hidden her true feelings from him. He loved her so much! Here's another letter I read earlier,' she said, handing Molly the letter written in April.

'I see what you mean, Wilhelm sounds a lovely man. I wonder if it will be possible to find out what happened to him?'

'I'd love to try. I feel I need to know, not necessarily for the book but for me, personally. But I don't even know his surname,' she sighed.

'There must have been a list of the soldiers stationed here and then rounded up by the liberating forces. That could be a starting point. But is tracing Wilhelm a priority just now? Make some enquiries by all means, but perhaps the focus now ought to be on the rest of the book so that you don't get behind schedule. After all, you don't want to be in trouble with your, hopefully, generous publishers, do you?'

Jeanne managed a weak smile and promised to prioritise her research.

'Do you feel up to our session now? Or shall we re-schedule?' Molly asked, gently.

'It'll probably do me some good now. Calm me down. I'll just clear the decks a bit.'

After Jeanne had tidied up her papers she and Molly settled down for their session. A much calmer and more relaxed Jeanne opened her eyes twenty minutes later.

'That was good! And I noticed you included suggestions about my fear of the sea and boats. I could actually imagine myself on a boat without feeling terrified. So that's progress! But it's not the same as physically going on a boat, is it?'

'No, that's true. But once your mind accepts that you feel relaxed about it the actuality will be easier, too. I'll keep reinforcing the message to build up your confidence. Now, let's have some tea.

Jeanne piled her belongings into the car and arrived home in time to find the builders packing up. According to Martin it had been a constructive day but as Jeanne looked around she would have said it had been more destructive. And the dust was everywhere! She quickly vacuumed up the worst so the main rooms were habitable, but it was dispiriting to sit amongst the mayhem. To cheer herself up she played a favourite CD, a compilation of 90s music, as she typed up the day's notes.

A couple of hours later, Jeanne went out for a long walk on the beach followed by some impromptu weeding in the herb bed. The fragrance of roses and honeysuckle hung in the air and as she brushed against the herbs they released their own heady scents. Rosemary and thyme were her particular favourites and she picked some for her evening meal, leaving her fingers impregnated with their perfume. The beauty and scents of her garden, together with the tang of the salt-laden sea air flowing in from the beach, combined to compensate for the apparent destruction of her home. It would only be temporary, she reasoned, and perhaps she should spend more time outdoors to make the most of the summer. Even Rachel's jokey idea of a tent in the garden was beginning to look tempting if nothing else turned up.

The next few days followed a pattern, with Jeanne either spending a few hours at Molly's or going to the library for research after a site meeting with Martin. She also spent time at the Greffe, the office where all births, marriages and deaths were registered, tracing her family's records to fill in some gaps. Her knowledge of the Occupation was increasing daily and she had made enquiries about tracing Wilhelm, but was warned it could take time. A manifest had been made of all German personnel but there were procedures to follow to gain access. In the meantime it occurred to Jeanne that if any of her gran's friends were still alive they may be able to shed some light on the affair. This thought was so promising that Jeanne was impatient to ask Molly if she knew of any such women.

'Yes, your gran did have some friends who were still alive when she died. Three attended the funeral but one was pretty frail, as I remember. Let me think.' Molly's face creased up in concentration.

'There was Mrs Ozanne, from Perelle. And Mrs Robins from Vazon. And I believe the frail lady was Mrs Thompson who lived in a nursing home in town. I think they had been friends for years. I can't say if that included the Occupation, but it's possible. Years ago Guernsey was like a big village and everyone seemed to know everyone else. The old ladies were all widows, I remember, and I think Mrs Ozanne still lived in her own cottage. Is this any help?'

'Yes, that's great, thanks. I'll see if I can track them down.'

Jeanne didn't have time to start her enquiries as early the next day she got a phone call from her agent, asking her to come over to London.

'Why, what's happened, Sally?'

'I've just received the draft contract from the publishers and it would be better if we went through it together, face to face. Can you come over tomorrow?'

'I'll check the flights and get back to you. Does this mean you know the advance figure?' Jeanne's heart was racing and she was sure all this tension wasn't good for her blood pressure.

'Ah, yes, a figure has been included in the terms. But remember, we have to be happy with everything before we accept. That's why I need to see you.'

Jeanne didn't know why Sally was being so evasive, was this good news or bad?

'I'll ring you back when I've booked a flight. Bye.'

She got onto the airline and booked a seat to Gatwick for the following morning.

When she rang back Sally suggested that Jeanne met her at the office, just off Piccadilly, at twelve and they would then go out to lunch, she promised. But she didn't say where. Jeanne hoped that the contract warranted somewhere more salubrious than a burger café.

Then she rang Freya.

'Hi, it's me, Jeanne. Have you heard anything about my contract? Sally's received a copy but she's not telling me the details till we meet tomorrow.'

'Sorry, haven't heard anything, my boss would deal with that. But if Sally wants to see you I'd say that was good news, wouldn't you? Are you staying over for the weekend?'

The next day being Friday Jeanne had booked an open return flight just in case. The thought of a weekend in London was very tempting.

'Guess I could.'

'You'd be welcome to stay with me, if you don't mind the sofa bed. Rob's away this weekend visiting his parents so you can take me out for the super-duper evening you promised me!'

Rob was Freya's boyfriend and although they did not live together they were usually inseparable.

'Thanks, I'd love to stay with you. And we'll definitely go out, whatever happens with the contract. I need to let my hair down a bit. Do you want to book a table somewhere? Whatever's your favourite these days. And we can fit in a club afterwards.'

After they'd rung off Jeanne checked that everything was all right with Martin. She gave him her mobile number in case he needed to reach her before going off to Molly's.

The rest of the day passed in a blur as she attempted to concentrate on the book while her mind kept wandering off to the coming meeting with Sally. She could only hope that Freya was right and that it was good news that Sally wanted to meet before giving her the details. When Molly arrived home from work she was as optimistic as Freya had been and wished Jeanne good luck.

'And you have to ring me as soon as you can. I don't want to be on tenterhooks all weekend!'

Jeanne had not been back home long when the phone rang.

'Hi, Jeanne, it's me. How are you?'

'Oh, Marcus. Okay, thanks. Just about to start packing,

actually as I'm off to London tomorrow for the weekend. Got a meeting with my agent to discuss the contract.'

'I see. That's good news, then. If you'd let me know, I could have come over with you and we could have hit the town.' Marcus sounded hurt.

'I'm staying with Freya and I'd promised to take her out as a thank you for her help. Thanks for the offer, though.'

Jeanne wasn't sure how to react to him. They hadn't seen each other for two weeks and had hardly spoken on the phone and yet he wanted to go away with her. It surprised her to realise that she would enjoy a weekend with Freya more than with Marcus. That presumably said a lot about her feelings for him, she thought ruefully.

'So, is it a big celebration in London? Are you being paid a fortune?' Marcus asked, a little more warmly.

'I don't know yet. That's what Sally wants to discuss. But I plan to enjoy myself, regardless.'

'I'll ring you when you get back, then. Have a great weekend.'

After her supper Jeanne packed her case. Her smartest outfit was the one she'd worn to Nello's so that was packed along with casual wear for the inevitable shopping trip. As she had no idea where Sally was taking her she decided on her black linen skirt, a smart cotton top and the washed velvet jacket, which should take her most places, she reasoned.

It was difficult for her to get off to sleep but finally, after some tossing and turning, she drifted off. When she awoke the next morning her stomach was clenched with tension and Jeanne needed to practise her self-hypnosis to calm down before she headed off to the airport and her appointment. She was also practising all the positive thinking that Molly had taught her but, just to be on the safe side, she crossed her fingers as the plane took off.

# chapter 20

By the time Jeanne had humped her weekend case up the three flights of stairs to Sally's office in Sackville Street, she was so breathless that she struggled to announce herself to the P.A.

The girl took pity on her saying, 'You must be Jeanne Le Page. Why don't you sit down and I'll get you a glass of water before I tell Sally you're here.'

Jeanne sank gratefully into the squashy chair which immediately swallowed her up, making her wonder if she'd get out of it again without a hoist. Sipping her water she questioned why Sally insisted on staying in an office without a lift. It was a good address and very central but if she moved just a bit further from the action it would surely be possible to rent an office on the first floor, or at least one with a lift, for a similar rent. She consoled herself with the thought that at least it would be easier taking her case down the stairs.

By the time her breathing was reasonably normal Sally came through and, after a welcome hug, led her into the office. Low-ceilinged but spacious, it was painted white giving an impression of airiness. Her battered partners' desk was covered in piles of manuscripts and assorted papers. Sally was dressed in a smart suit, leading Jeanne to think lunch was unlikely to be at McDonalds, and she smiled inwardly.

'It's lovely to see you again, Jeanne. Must be what – two years? And it looks as if living in Guernsey suits you, you're positively blooming!' Sally smiled warmly.

'Yes, it does, the sea air is wonderful after all those years in the Midlands.'

Sally nodded and opened the file in front of her.

'Hope you didn't mind dragging yourself away from all that ozone, but it's a fairly complex contract and I wanted to make sure you fully understood all the implications. As you haven't actually written the book yet the publishers have included clauses to cover stage payments of the advance which are dependent on your producing a satisfactory MS at an agreed time. In other words, if you produced a load of rubbish they would want their money back!' she laughed.

'Well, I hope to do better than that and I can hardly mess up the recipes! So, may I ask what advance they're offering?'

Sally smiled broadly and answered, 'It's actually very generous for a first time author. £20,000 in total, spread over three stage payments.'

Jeanne gasped, '£20,000! I never expected as much as that! You're absolutely sure that's the right amount?'

Sally was amused. 'I can read, you know. But see for yourself,' she said, pushing the contract over the desk.

Jeanne's eyes swam as she looked at the words and figures dancing before her. After blinking a few times, she read the magic clause:

The Publisher shall pay to the Author or to her duly *authorised representative an advance of £20,000 against all the Author's earnings under this Agreement payable as follows:*

a) *£8,000 within 30 days of the signing hereof*

b) *£6,000 within 30 days of the Acceptance by the Publisher of the MS of the Work and as is later provided*

c) *£6,000 within 30 days of publication of the Work and as is later provided*

Jeanne looked up at Sally and grinned as she said, 'Where do I sign?'

Sally laughed. 'Hold on, I want to cover all the main points with you first.'

They spent the next hour going through the contract paragraph by paragraph and Jeanne's head began to spin. Sally, totally professional, had already earmarked some clauses for change, which she felt should be no problem. She also explained about the royalties and translation rights. By the time they had covered most things Jeanne was in dire need of a drink and something to eat. Sally was obviously a mind reader.

'Right, that's enough for now. Let's go celebrate, shall we?'

Leaving her case in the office, Jeanne followed Sally downstairs and out towards Piccadilly.

'We can walk, it's just down the road. I've booked us into Greens. Hope you won't miss your burger!'

Jeanne was very happy at the choice. She had not been there herself but Freya had once said she loved it. Judging by Sally's reception by the Maitre D' it seemed that she was a regular and popular customer. There was a hug for Sally and a welcoming smile for Jeanne as they were ushered to a spacious corner table and fussed over in a way to which Jeanne could easily become accustomed.

Before she had a chance to get properly settled a bottle of Veuve Clicquot arrived in a silver ice bucket and two glasses were poured with due ceremony.

'Santé! Here's to *Recipes for Love*. May this be the first of many successful books!' cried Sally as they clinked glasses.

'Thanks, Sally.' Jeanne was exhilarated and the champagne went straight to her head, making her giggly.

'I'd better eat soon or I might disgrace myself and get barred for life,' she grinned at Sally.

'Don't worry. They've seen it all before. The staff are used to my bringing up and coming writers here to celebrate their first contracts. And they'll be particularly interested in your book, with its focus on food. Right, let's order, shall we?'

The delicious meal soaked up the champagne so that Jeanne, although slightly squiffy, behaved herself, and welcomed a large cup of coffee, presented with chocolate creams.

Three flights of stairs seemed less steep when you were floating on air, Jeanne thought as they arrived back at the office. Once they had tied up the remaining points she was free to leave and Sally promised to send her the contract to sign as soon as the publisher returned the amended copy.

'Should only take a few days. Just get it back to me by return and I'll chase up the first payment. Now, have a great time with your friend and call me when you're next in London.'

Jeanne made her way, gingerly, down the stairs with her case. Once outside she phoned Freya.

'Hi, it's me. Guess what? I'm being paid £20,000! Is that reason to celebrate or not?'

'Sure is. My boss told me this morning but I wanted you to hear it from Sally. We can sure push the boat out, now! How did your lunch go?'

Jeanne told her about Greens and the champagne and Freya chuckled.

'Thought you sounded a bit merry! It's just as well I've booked us to go out tomorrow night and not tonight. You may need to take it a bit easy this evening, girl. How about coming to my office now and after I've sobered you up I'll introduce you to my boss, who'll be your editor. And it might be better to get a taxi in your condition!' She rang off, still laughing.

Ensconced in Freya's office, Jeanne drank all the coffee put in front of her and began to feel more compos mentis. Her intoxication wasn't just from the alcohol but the sheer joy of being paid a large sum of money for her book. It would go a long way towards paying for the work on the cottage, she mused. Once Freya was happy that Jeanne was presentable she took her along to her boss, Louise Williams. Louise was delighted to meet her and they spent some time getting to know each other.

'I'm really looking forward to working with you, Jeanne, and would like to think that this is the start of a long and rewarding relationship. Now, I think it's time that Freya took you off and showed you the sights. Hope to see you again soon.'

Freya was only too happy to finish a bit earlier than usual and they took the Tube to Covent Garden where Freya had a third floor one bedroom flat in a side street off Long Acre. The flat was tiny, but it did have the advantage of a lift and was well placed for the theatres and restaurants of the area.

'I thought we could go out for a quiet meal tonight at a local bistro. We can take in a film as well, if you like,' Freya suggested as they sprawled on the sofa.

They decided on a film and enjoyed a quiet, but happy evening out, catching up on each other's lives over dinner. Jeanne was still full from lunch and chose the lightest choice on the menu and drank only a couple of glasses of wine. They walked home, arm in arm, chatting contentedly. By the time the sofa bed was made up they were both yawning and Jeanne fell asleep immediately, images of giant fifty pound notes pervading her dreams.

Saturday was designated for shopping and they didn't have far to go to find enticing boutiques. In a generous mood, Jeanne not only bought herself several items but treated Freya to a new dress.

'Jeanne, you shouldn't have! Paying for a night out was the deal, not a new outfit as well,' Freya said, taken aback by her friend's generosity.

'Nonsense, I might not have got my contract without your help. Now, we can both dress up in our new glad rags and London won't know what hit it when we finally venture out – after we've put our feet up first, of course!'

That evening the two girls arrived at an upmarket fish restaurant, and the waiters were like bees to nectar as they hovered around, solicitously helping them into their leather seats.

Freya laughed, 'I don't get this attention when I'm with Rob! I guess it's the sight of two gorgeous girls on the loose that sets their testosterone soaring!'

Jeanne giggled. 'It's great, isn't it?'

The evening was rounded off with a visit to a small night club in Covent Garden. They were soon invited to dance and happy to oblige. Even though her partner was attractive, in a Brad Pitt sort of way, Jeanne wasn't interested in getting to know him better and found her thoughts wandering to Nick. What would he be doing on a Saturday night in Guernsey? Having a drink with the lads, possibly. Or perhaps Sue had finally persuaded him to go out on a date? Not a pleasant thought. But why should it bother her? Not wanting to go there, Jeanne smiled at her partner and carried on dancing.

On Sunday morning Freya suggested they chill out by having a coffee first, followed by a late lunch in a local wine bar. Weaving their way through the jugglers and mime artists vying for attention, they settled for a café offering live jazz.

'Mm, Freya, I'd like your advice on something. Can you play Agony Aunt for a while?'

'Sure. I think a couple of brain cells are functioning now. Fire away.'

Jeanne told her about Marcus and her feelings, or rather lack of them, toward him.

Freya's eyes crinkled up in amusement. 'Hello! It's a no-brainer, girl. Stop seeing him! It's obvious you don't love him and any initial attraction seems to have evaporated. I'm sure you know this yourself. So what's stopping you ending it?'

'I don't know. I guess I've been scared of ending up on my own. And after Andy... well, let's say my self-confidence took a big dive. Marcus boosted me up again. But you're right, it won't work between us, I can see that now. I was just trying to force it to work, based on a schoolgirl crush,' she grinned.

'Jeanne, my girl, I'm sure there must be loads of men who will fancy you. Look at last night! You certainly could have scored if you'd wanted to! Isn't there anyone in Guernsey who gives you the eye and melts your insides?' she asked, head cocked to one side.

She flushed. 'Well, yes there is someone who I'm told fancies me but he hasn't said anything yet. Might be 'cos he's gone off women a bit. But I do find him attractive, I guess.'

Freya demanded to know more and Jeanne found herself describing her various encounters with Nick and finished up by telling her about the planned use of his kitchen.

'Aha! This will be your chance, girl. Flutter the old eye lashes as you serve up an irresistible meal. You know what they say about the way to a man's heart, don't you?' She looked at Jeanne thoughtfully, before adding, 'I've got good vibes about this Nick. I expect to be kept posted with all the gory details. Please don't bother sparing my blushes, I'm a big girl now!'

They both laughed and after leaving the café sauntered around the shops and stalls before stopping at a jewellery stall displaying delicate necklaces of semi-precious stones on gold chains. Jeanne fell in love with a heart shaped rose quartz pendant with matching earrings and, with a little encouragement from Freya, bought them.

'Rose quartz for love, eh?' Freya grinned and then

ducked as Jeanne aimed a mock punch at her.

Later that afternoon Jeanne had finally managed to squeeze her new purchases into her case and Freya went with her to flag down a taxi.

'It's been a great weekend. We must do it again sometime. Preferably when my liver's in remission! And thanks for paying for everything, you were more than generous. Now, all you have to do is write that bestseller and snare that dishy man. Not too much to ask, is it?' she said, giving Jeanne a hug.

'I'll do my best. On both counts!' Jeanne waved goodbye as the taxi headed off towards Victoria. She sank back into her seat, a mix of emotions flowing through her –sadness at saying goodbye to Freya, excitement at her book deal and anticipation at what lay ahead for her in Guernsey. Would she indeed 'snare that dishy man'? Did he even want to be snared? She sighed as she remembered Colette telling her how hurt Nick had been when Helen left him. He might not want to risk heartbreak again, she thought. And nor did she – once was enough in a lifetime.

# chapter 21

The builders had continued to make progress, in their eyes anyway, although all Jeanne could see were holes in the walls and ceilings, wires hanging down everywhere and pipes force-fed around the skirting boards downstairs. It was a shame there were solid floors downstairs, she sighed, sympathising with her grandmother's views on the ugliness of central heating. She was impressed that the plumber was hiding his pipes as much as possible and at least the radiators were slim and stylish.

Once she had caught up with Martin, Jeanne was glad to escape – floorboards were coming up that day and with her poor sense of balance she didn't fancy tottering along the joists. After her visit to the cemetery Jeanne went off to The Bridge for some shopping and then, feeling the need to be with people, popped into the café for lunch. If she was at all honest with herself she rather hoped that Nick would be there but in that she was disappointed.

She had not long been at a table and was trying to decide what to order when a voice disturbed her thoughts.

'Hi, Jeanne. Long time no see. May I join you?'

'Nick! Of course you can. How're things? Any nice, wealthy clients on board?'

'Business is picking up, thanks. In fact I've just negotiated an order to fit out a brand new boat that'll keep us pretty busy for a while. And the client is definitely much nicer than Mr Evans!' His smile was so broad that his whole face lit up and Jeanne felt warmed by his obvious happiness. *Mm, he's really very attractive when he smiles. Quite fanciable!* She felt a little frisson of desire and had to take a deep breath before replying.

'That's wonderful news. It must be exciting to work on a brand new boat and I'm so pleased for you. I've had some good news too,' she said and told him about the book contract.

'Well done! It looks like we both have something to celebrate. Shall we go mad and have a bottle of wine with our meal?'

The waiter took their order, returning promptly with a bottle of white wine.

'Here's to success! And to better times ahead,' he said, clinking glasses.

As their food arrived she told him about her weekend in London and that she hoped to go over more often in the future.

'Yes, London offers a great culture buzz and when I'm over on business I try to catch a play or two and wander around the museums. But like you, I prefer it in small doses. I'd get withdrawal symptoms if I was away from Guernsey for long,' he said, his eyes locked on hers.

Jeanne felt she was being drawn into his gaze and had to force herself to continue the conversation, asking about his favourite plays. After a few minutes of comparing notes Nick asked how things were going at the cottage.

'Oh, it looks awful! I have to get out during the day – it's so noisy and dirty. And I'll need to move out altogether soon as there'll be no water or electricity. You don't know of a cheap B & B do you?'

'No, I don't, I'm afraid. Not sure that there's such a thing here. Certainly not in high season.' He looked thoughtful. 'I may have an alternative suggestion to make.'

Jeanne looked at him warily. He wasn't going to confound her belief in him and suggest she stay at his place, was he? She had to admit it would have its obvious attractions but...

He must have noticed her expression and smiled. 'It's

okay, I'm not going to make an indecent proposal!'

She wasn't sure whether to be relieved or not.

He continued, 'It's all above board. Literally, as it happens, that's why I hesitated to suggest it. I could offer you sanctuary for as long as you need – on a boat...' her face must have registered her alarm as he carried on quickly, 'moored at Beaucette Marina and most definitely not going out to sea. I only bought it a few weeks ago and it needs some work but it's completely habitable. It came with a six months paid-up mooring so I'm leaving it there until the winter. If you remember it's the only marina on the island where live-aboard is allowed and there are some massive yachts there to prove it.'

He chuckled and went on, 'I hasten to add that *La Belle Élise* is not one of those but a modest twenty-six foot motor cruiser. She has a good sized berth, working head with a shower and a well-fitted out galley. She's even connected up to mains electricity. Anyway, I do understand if you're not keen but it could solve your problem,' he said, with a warm smile.

Jeanne was still taken aback.

'I...don't know what to say. You know how I feel about boats. But, as it happens, I've been having some hypnosis and I think it's making a difference. And if it's moored...Look, I'm going for a session this afternoon and I could ask Molly what she thinks. If she's happy for me to try, perhaps I could come and have a look at it?'

Nick nodded and was just about to say something when Jeanne's mobile rang.

'Oh, hi Martin. Anything wrong?'

'No, but we've found something under the floor in that there small bedroom. The plumber was getting ready to lay his pipes but this, er, bundle is in the way. Would you be able to pop along and take a look? Don't want to touch anything.'

'Thanks for letting me know. I'm just finishing my lunch at The Bridge so won't be long.'

Wondering what on earth the 'bundle' could be, she explained to Nick what had happened.

As they stood outside the café Nick gave her a quick hug.

'Let me know about the boat and I'd be interested to know what's under those floorboards. Perhaps it's the family fortune!'

She laughed. 'Not much chance of that! But I'll call you later and let you know, don't worry.'

Jeanne was met by Martin at the cottage and he took her upstairs to what had been the small bedroom. Most of the floor boards were up and pipes snaked around the edges. Martin pointed to what appeared to be a bundle of rags squeezed between the joists in the middle before leaving to direct operations downstairs.

She had to tread carefully as she slowly inched her way across the joists. There was a piece of wood lying nearby and she grabbed it to kneel on as she got close enough to pick up the bundle. It still looked like rags, grey and dusty. She grinned at the thought that it was unlikely to be 'the family fortune' as, lifting it up, it didn't feel very heavy. Unless it was wads of paper money, she thought. Slowly she unwrapped the layers, crying out as she stared at the mummified remains of a baby.

# chapter 22

It didn't seem long before the house was full of police officers taking statements from the builders and poking around upstairs. A doctor had arrived with the police and as he turned round Jeanne cried out 'Jonathan! What are you doing here?'

'Hello, Jeanne. I'm the duty doctor for the station today and as I was already there I was asked to come along. How awful for you! Are you all right? Need anything for the shock?' he asked gently.

She shook her head. 'No, I'll be fine, thanks. It was a terrible shock but I'm calmer now. Just had a cup of tea. Have you…seen it, yet?'

'Yes, just quickly. There will be a post mortem by the pathologist, of course, but it looks to me like a full term baby, probably still-born. And it's been there so long that the dry, cool air under the floor must have mummified it.'

'Could it have been there sixty years?' Jeanne asked, her heart racing.

'I guess so. But I'm no expert on these things. Why? Do you know something about what happened?' he asked, looking puzzled.

Before Jeanne could explain the inspector came up and said he would like to ask her a few questions. He was very kind and she told him all she knew about the possible parentage of the baby.

'I've recently discovered that my grandmother was in love with a German soldier during the Occupation and…and that she became pregnant by him. But I don't know that she actually gave birth.'

'Well, if it was still-born that could certainly explain why it was buried under the floor and not properly in a graveyard. Would have meant a lot of questions for your grandmother. Very sad,' he sighed. 'It doesn't look as if a crime has been committed but we will have to wait for the results of the post mortem to confirm that the baby died naturally. And there will have to be an Inquest too, I'm afraid. The body's being taken to the hospital now and we can leave you alone. But that room is a potential crime scene and is out of bounds until we've got the results through. I'll try to rush through the autopsy so we don't hold up the building work too much. Be in touch when I've got some news.'

Jeanne nodded and turned around in time to see a small body bag being carried outside. Jonathan came up and put his arms around her as she blinked away the tears.

'I have to get back but I don't like leaving you like this. Is there somewhere you could go? I don't think you should stay here tonight.'

'I'm supposed to be at Molly's for a…a session now and I'll ask her if I can stay there. Thanks, Jonathan. I'll catch up later.'

It was agreed the men should finish work for the day and as everyone filed out Jeanne quickly phoned Molly to see if she could still come round as she was late.

'And can I stay with you tonight, please? I'll explain when I see you.' This was fine by Molly, and Jeanne packed up a few things before locking the door and driving down to find much needed peace and quiet.

Over a cup of strong tea Jeanne poured out all that had happened to a stunned and for once, speechless Molly. Jeanne cried as she described seeing the tiny body, conscious that the pitiful sight had undoubtedly rekindled the grief for her own lost baby.

'It must have been so awful for Gran! She must have been desperate to have buried her baby under the floor like that. Always knowing it was there. What a burden to carry! If only she'd told someone and been able to have a proper burial,' Jeanne said, shaking her head in sorrow.

Molly took her hand. 'At least now, when all the formalities are over, the baby can be buried with your gran. They'll be reunited and at peace.'

A thought struck her. 'You always said there was something odd about that bedroom, didn't you? It was much colder, but only to you. This must be why.'

Jeanne nodded. 'Yes, that makes sense. I must have been sensitive to the vibes in some way. Gran's pain, I suppose. In a way, it's a relief to know that's what caused it and that I wasn't just imagining it. Do you think that if something awful happened in a place then people can sense it?'

Molly looked thoughtful.

'Personally, I've always felt that places, like people, can hang onto memories, particularly ones that are traumatic. Like 'place ghosts' that haunt the place where they died suddenly and violently, leaving unfinished business. But not everyone's sensitive to them. You seem to be, and probably also responding to genetic memory. As you've experienced a lot of personal trauma you're more likely to tune into someone else's pain. Particularly the pain of a common loss,' Molly said, squeezing her hand.

Jeanne nodded.

'So, perhaps the atmosphere in that room will be all right now for me. I was too shocked to notice today so I'll check it out when I'm allowed back in.'

She became lost in her thoughts for a while and Molly pottered about, clearing away the cups.

Jeanne came to and said, 'Molly, I mentioned to Nick that I would have to move out of the cottage for a while and he offered me the use of a boat at Beaucette. Do you think it's too soon for me to be on a boat?'

'Hmm, it's hard to know, but you did say the idea of

being on one wasn't as scary now. It could boost your confidence and as it's moored you'll be totally safe. The first step before going out to sea,' she paused. 'I think it's worth a try as you could just walk off if you're uncomfortable.'

'True. And it would solve my housing problem! Any chance of a quick session now? To help me deal with everything that's happening.'

'Of course. All this has rather overtaken the excitement of your contract, hasn't it? Peter and I were thrilled when you phoned and told us, and we were planning to take you out for a meal to celebrate. But that will have to wait. It's time for calm now,' she smiled at Jeanne and they headed off to the study. The strain of the day finally caught up with her and she went to bed soon after dinner.


The next morning she phoned Nick.

'Jeanne! So glad you phoned. I've just heard a rumour that a baby's body was found in a house in Perelle. I was worried about you. If I'd known what you'd have to face I'd have gone back with you to the cottage.'

He sounded so concerned that she felt guilty for not having phoned earlier.

'Yes, it…was a baby's body. And I was so stressed out by it all that I forgot to phone you. Sorry.' She told him the story of her gran and Wilhelm and that she was now at Molly's for a few days.

'The police have stopped the building work until they receive the results of the autopsy. Should only be a few days. As long as the death was natural the builders can move back in. But I don't feel I can face it right now.'

'No, I can understand that. What a terrible thing to have happened! Your poor grandmother.' His deep voice was so full of warmth that she felt soothed.

'I managed to have some more hypnosis yesterday and Molly thinks I could cope with staying on a boat, as it's safely in the marina. So could I have a look at it?

'Sure, whenever you're ready.'

'Thanks. I'll ring you when things are calmer. Bye.'


Three days later Jeanne was sitting in Molly's study opening the file containing Wilhelm's letters. She felt ready to read all the remaining ones, hoping to find clues as to what had happened between him and her gran. And their baby.

She had just started reading when her mobile rang.

'Hi, Jeanne, it's me. Thought I'd check how you are as it's been a while since we spoke.'

'Oh, hi Marcus. Not been too great, actually.' She told him about the baby.

'Blimey! Your family's certainly not boring is it?' he chuckled and she flushed with anger. How dare he! It wasn't funny, it was very sad.

'Look Marcus, it's been very upsetting and I don't appreciate your levity. I'm busy and I see no point in continuing this conversation. Goodbye.'

Before she could cut him off he interrupted. 'Hey, I'm sorry if I've upset you. I didn't realise you'd take it so personally. And you haven't told me how it went with your agent.'

She told him about the contract and he whistled appreciatively.

'Wow! That's great news, I'm pleased for you. How about we go out to celebrate sometime this week? And I'll make it up to you for that crass remark. Please say yes,' he begged her.

'No, thanks, Marcus. I'm not sure it's a good idea for us to see each other at the moment. I really am busy and have a lot on my plate just now. Bye.'

This time she disconnected him before he could say any more. She knew she should tell him face to face that she no longer wanted to go out with him but was not feeling strong enough just now. She'd deal with it later. Still feeling annoyed and upset, she made herself some coffee before settling down with the letters again. They were disappointing with no real news in them. Loving and passionate as ever, Wilhelm was clearly still over the moon about becoming a father and there was more talk of the war coming to an end. He had so many plans that Jeanne gulped and wiped away a tear as she read his joyful words. There was nothing to suggest that Gran had grown cooler toward him. They still met up regularly but apparently only for a few moments each time. The final letter, dated 15th February 1945 was heart-breaking.

*Yesterday so good it was to see you. My Valentine you truly are! The card you to me gave I will treasure - may not meet until after our Baby is born - take care - let us pray your parents us forgive - they will surely their Grandchild love - pity your mother in hospital is - many are sick now...*

Jeanne couldn't stop the tears as she read it again and again and it was only the noise of her mobile ringing that made her stop and blow her nose.

'Hello, Miss Le Page. Inspector Ferguson here. Just to let you know the results of the post mortem. Are you still there?' he asked into the silence.

Jeanne took a deep breath and said, 'Sorry, Inspector. Please go on.'

'It seems you were right. The baby, a girl by the way, was born a couple of weeks before full term and was still-born. The umbilical cord was still around its neck. There's no suspicion of any criminal act. The consultant pathologist also thinks that the baby was born during the war as it was wrapped in a piece of Red Cross blanket issued to the islanders in the final winter of the Occupation. But further tests will confirm that. Are you all right?' he asked, as Jeanne let out a gasp.

'Yes, yes, I…I'm fine.'

'Right. I know this must be difficult for you. At the Inquest the magistrate will want to confirm the baby's identity before giving permission for burial. We will need sight of the letters you mentioned and, ideally, we need to match your DNA with that of the baby. If we can show that she was related to you then I think that would satisfy the magistrate. Technically, you're next of kin,' he said gravely.

'Oh! I hadn't thought of that! But you're right, unless Wilhelm is still alive, of course.'

'Hmm, if he is alive and we could trace him, then that would provide conclusive evidence. But under the circumstances the proof of a connection between you and the child should be sufficient. May I ask you to provide us with a DNA sample? If you could pop into the station sometime today and bring those letters along, I'd be grateful.'

'Yes, of course, but I'll need the letters back.'

'No problem. We'll take copies of the relevant ones to keep on file. By the way, the builders can return to the cottage. It's no longer a crime scene. I'll catch up with you later.'

Jeanne stared at the letters in front of her for some time after switching off her phone. The pieces of the jigsaw were slowly fitting together but there was still one piece missing. *Oh, Wilhelm, what happened to you? And are you alive – or dead?*

# chapter 23

After the phone call from the inspector, Jeanne made a few calls. The first was to Martin with the green light on the building work and he offered to return with his men after lunch. The next was to Nick and they arranged to meet at Beaucette Marina that afternoon.

The third call was to Reverend Ayres.

'Morning, Vicar. I need your help please, if you're not too busy.'

Jeanne arrived at the marina on the north-east coast just before two o'clock. She parked near The Marina Restaurant, handily placed for boat owners wanting a break from cooking in their galleys. It was strange to be there after so many years. The boats moored on the pontoons looked much bigger and flashier than the ones she remembered seeing as a girl. As she was gazing at the largest yacht thinking that it looked like a floating palace, Nick drove up in his jeep.

'Beautiful, isn't she? Way, way out of my league! But I think you'll agree that *La Belle Élise* isn't bad for her size.'

He gave her a quick hug before leading her down to the main access ramp then turned right towards the furthest pontoon, near the harbour entrance. The marina had been formed from a disused gravel pit and the steep sides provided protection from the elements. It was a perfectly still day and the boats barely stirred in the water.

'Well, just looking at the boats feels okay which I couldn't have said a few weeks ago. I used to love going out with my parents on their small cruiser and fishing with my grandfather on his dory. I know the sea's in my blood – I just need to feel safe again.'

'Let's hope my boat proves the turning point, then – here she is,' he said, pointing to the last boat along the pontoon. Moored in splendid isolation from any others, Jeanne was able to have a good look at her.

'She's a Fairline Sun Fury, just over twenty-six foot, built about ten years ago. I want to do a complete refit and overhaul the engines but basically she's in reasonable condition for her age.'

Nodding, Jeanne said, 'She's quite attractive with those stripes on the hull and that bow looks long enough for sunbathing.'

'Typical woman! You'll be pleased to know there's a sunbathing mat supplied for just that purpose. Ready to go aboard?' he asked, watching Jeanne's expression.

'Aye, aye captain,' she grinned at him.

*La Belle Élise* was moored astern and they climbed in to the aft cockpit after Nick had removed the cover. Steps led down to the galley which, although compact, was equipped with a sink, fridge, oven, hob and a grill.

'I'm impressed! Dad's boat was pretty basic compared to this,' Jeanne remarked as she moved forward into the main cabin area composed of banquette seating around a central table. Nick showed her the head, with a loo and shower and then the second cabin with two berths.

'So, what's the reaction?'

'Mm, I like the boat, for sure. And I think I could live on board for a while – as long as she doesn't move! Thank you, Nick, I'd like to accept your offer of sanctuary.' She smiled and then as a thought struck her, added, 'Ah, but I forgot to ask about rent, didn't I?'

Nick shook his head, 'Don't be daft, I don't want rent. I want to help you out – mind you, as you're about to become wealthy perhaps I should charge you!'

'Hey, I haven't had any money yet and it will be spread

out over months of work when I do get it. But I'll happily pay for my electricity – I don't want you to be out of pocket.'

Nick locked up the cabin and as they returned to the car park he explained about the facilities available which included a launderette, hot showers and WCs. As they stood by the cars Jeanne told him about the inspector's phone call and the final letter from Wilhelm.

'It's all looking pretty conclusive, isn't it? Are you hoping to find out what happened to Wilhelm?'

'Yes, I want to talk to old friends of Gran if I can trace them,' she twisted her hair. 'I'm off to the police now for the DNA swab and I'm hoping that the Inquest can be held soon. I just want to bury that poor baby as soon as I can.'

Nick hugged her. 'Of course, and if there's anything I can do to help, please call me.' He paused a moment, searching her face before adding, 'Unless you'd rather call Marcus?'

'Marcus and I are not really talking at the moment. So I'd prefer to phone you, if that's okay.'

'Oh, I see. Well, anytime, just shout.'

They parted and drove off, Nick to the Bridge and his workshop and Jeanne to the police station in Town. A female officer quickly took the swab from the inside of her cheek and when she handed over the letters promised to return them promptly.

Back at the cottage the builders had been and gone. When she checked the small bedroom, she saw that Ed must have finished laying his pipes as most of the floorboards had been replaced. After a look around at the other rooms Jeanne headed for the kitchen and put the kettle on in readiness for her visitor.

About four thirty the doorbell rang.

'Good afternoon, Jeanne. I was pleased you called.'

Reverend Ayres smiled at her as he grasped her outstretched hand.

'Hello, Vicar. I'm so glad you're here. Please come in.'

She led him into the kitchen, the only room relatively untouched by chaos.

'Would you like some tea before we go upstairs?' she asked, beginning to feel a little nervous.

'I'd rather have some afterwards, if you don't mind. We might both appreciate it more then.'

'Okay, I'll lead the way.'

Jeanne opened the door to the small bedroom and they walked in.

'So, this is where the body was found?' he asked and Jeanne nodded and pointed to the area now boarded.

'I don't feel cold, as you described, but I do feel that something isn't right. Maybe traces of energy from your grandmother's suffering – that's what we need to disperse. Do you have any cushions? I'm afraid my old knees don't bend like they used to.'

Jeanne fetched some cushions from the sitting room and after the vicar lit the candle he'd brought with him they both kneeled while he prayed out loud. It wasn't a prayer that she recognised but it seemed to be seeking solace for the spirits of both the baby and her grandmother. The vicar's voice resonated reassuringly around the small room. Jeanne could have sworn that the candle flame grew bigger and brighter as he prayed. Finally he asked her to join with him in the Lord's Prayer and by the time they'd finished, tears were pricking at her eyes. In spite of this she was suffused with a tremendous feeling of calm and release.

'Thanks, Vicar. That...that was lovely. I can already sense a change in here, can you?'

'Yes, something has changed, my dear, the pain has gone at long last. I'm so gratified you sought my help. And I'm ready for that cup of tea now!' His eyes crinkled as he smiled.

While they were drinking their tea Jeanne told him about the post mortem result and the DNA test she had undertaken.

'I'm technically the only living relative of the baby but I don't know if Wilhelm is still alive and I'd dearly like to find him,' she said. Pausing for another sip, she went on, 'My friend Molly has told me that some of Gran's friends attended her funeral. I'd like to talk to them and see if they know anything about Wilhelm. Would you know who they are?'

He pursed his lips. 'I know two of them who were at the funeral, Mrs Ozanne and Mrs Robins who are both my parishioners. Would you like me to talk to them? Discreetly of course. I'd simply ask if they knew your grandmother during the Occupation as you're researching your family history. Would that be all right?'

'Oh, Vicar, that's great! And your story's true as I'm writing a book about my family. I'd be happy to go and see them if they'd agree. You really are God sent, aren't you?' she smiled at the vicar, who started chuckling.

'What a lovely compliment! Let's hope I can 'come up with the goods' as the saying goes. Now, before I set off on my mission, have you given any thought to the burial of that poor baby?'

'Yes, I have. I'd love you to conduct a service for her and I rather hoped she could be buried with her mother. Would that be allowed?' she asked anxiously.

'I don't see why not. It's slightly out of the ordinary but…' he shrugged and smiled at Jeanne, 'I think we can call this an exceptional case, and although it won't be a conventional funeral I can offer a service of burial which should be acceptable to all. We can discuss it again after the inquest. Now, I'd better get going. I'll be in touch.'

Jeanne showed him out, feeling excited that she might

be a step nearer to tracing Wilhelm. To reassure herself she went up to the little bedroom and opened the door to find – nothing. No chill, no feelings of unease. Just a perfectly ordinary empty room.

After a lot of thought Jeanne realised that it would be better all round if she moved out of the cottage now, staying first with the Ogiers and then on the boat.

Martin was visibly relieved when she explained her plan the next day, promising to allow her back as soon as he could. She was to keep in touch and make frequent site visits. Once she'd transferred her incoming calls to her mobile Jeanne set off back to Molly's with her cases. The rest of that morning she made good progress with her French research having been guided by Molly on how to understand the websites. Just before lunchtime she made a big breakthrough. Tracing back through the generations, she'd finally found the Parisian restaurateurs. As their names, Louis and Hortense Bonnet, appeared on the screen she let out a whoop of joy. *Wow! I've done it! I've found them. But, boy, it wasn't easy! If only my French had been stronger. Still, I've got there and perhaps I can still justify a trip to Paris for some extra colour. Might even be able to trace the original restaurant! And I could afford Le Shopping once my advance arrives!*

On this happy note Jeanne decided she deserved a treat now and took herself off to a café along the coast specialising in fresh fish. In need some exercise she then set off for a walk on the beach at Rocquaine, filling her lungs with the salty air as the hot sun caressed her skin. It wasn't exactly as peaceful as she'd have liked as the raucous cries of seagulls pierced the sky overhead, attracted by the detritus from the fishing boats now safely back in the bay. As she was heading back to her car to escape their racket her mobile rang.

'Hello, Jeanne. John Ayres here, is it a good time to talk?'

'Yes, fine, Vicar. Have you got some news for me?'

'Well, it's looking promising. I saw Mrs Ozanne this morning and she confirmed that she and your grandmother had been friends since school and were close all through the war, living near each other as they did. She would be happy for you to visit her for a chat and I'll give you her telephone number. You'll find her as bright as a button and, like most old people, would thoroughly enjoy talking about the past. I haven't contacted Mrs Robins yet, thought I'd see how you get on with Mrs Ozanne. I wish you luck!'

'Thanks, Vicar. I really appreciate your help and I'll let you know how it goes.'

Jeanne made a note of the telephone number and was so impatient to see the old lady that she rang her straight away. Mrs Ozanne sounded a little frail but spoke clearly, suggesting that she called in for tea about four thirty.

As Jeanne switched off her phone she noticed her hand was shaking.

This could be it, she told herself, the adrenalin pumping through her body. This could be the last piece of the jigsaw. The answer to the mystery. What *had* happened to Wilhelm?

# chapter 24

Jeanne found it hard to settle back at Molly's, willing the afternoon to move on. Eventually it was time to go and she gathered together the remaining letters, Wilhelm's photo and her notepad and pen. Mrs Ozanne lived ten minutes' walk away and she set off, the papers tucked in a file under her arm. On the way she bought a bunch of freesias from a roadside hedge-stall. The cottage was a smaller version of her own, semi-detached with a pretty little garden in front.

The door was opened by a white haired lady bent awkwardly over a stick. Her brown eyes still possessed a spark and regarded her with keen interest.

'Jeanne, please come in. I've been looking forward to seeing you since the vicar called round this morning. Oh, are those for me? How lovely, thank you. We'll go through to the garden, shall we?'

She led the way along a narrow, dark hall leading to the back door which stood open. Jeanne followed her into the sunlit garden and gasped. 'Oh, this is lovely, Mrs Ozanne! It's like a miniature version of Gran's garden!'

The old lady chuckled, 'Where do you think I got the ideas from? Your grandmother was always round here telling me what I should plant, she was. Now, sit you down and let me have a good look at you.'

Jeanne sat on the cushioned garden chair pulled up to a small table laden with afternoon tea. Mrs Ozanne lowered herself carefully into a matching chair before giving Jeanne a thorough inspection.

'I would have known you anywhere. You're your father's child, for sure, with your grandfather's eyes. But you inherited your mother's hair.' She sighed. ''Twas not right, them all dying so young. Even your grandfather had a few good years left in him. Broke Jeanne's heart, it did. She had more than her share of pain, for sure.' She gazed at her friend's granddaughter and added softly, 'But so have you, m'dear, so have you. Do you remember me at all?'

She had to be honest. 'I'm afraid not. Would I have met you at Gran's?'

'Yes, I saw you there as a little girl with your mother, more than once. Of course I was a lot younger and livelier then,' she said, looking at her stick with disdain. 'Your gran and I used to pop round each other's cottages regular like. We were widowed within a year of each other so were glad of the company. Then my legs started playing up so I was stuck here.' Mrs Ozanne sighed, tapping her stick. She seemed to wander off for a moment.

Jeanne cleared her throat.

'Now,' the old lady went on, becoming brisk, 'can you pour the tea for us, please? I take two sugars even though doctor tells me I shouldn't,' she chuckled.

Jeanne passed her a cup of tea and offered her the plate piled up with the ubiquitous buttered Gâche. Jeanne helped herself to a slice, not really hungry, but wanting to be polite.

'And I was at your parents' funeral, but I doubt if you knew what was going on, you were still so shocked.'

'Oh, I'm sorry if I was…'

'There's no need to be sorry, gal. You were very distressed, and rightly so. You were white as a sheet, you were. You just clung onto your gran as if you'd fall over if you let go. Mind, you'd been in the hospital for ten days so you were still weak.' She reached over and patted Jeanne's arm.

'I…I don't remember anything about the funeral. Or what happened before…The doctors told me my mind had just shut down. As a sort of self-defence,' Jeanne replied, twisting her hair round her finger.

Mrs Ozanne nodded.

'That can be a good thing sometimes. But it's a pity whoever killed your parents wasn't caught and punished.'

'Well, they might be soon. I'm starting to remember a bit and I'm having hypnosis to boost my memory. So perhaps I'll know who did it. If I can recognise them, of course.'

'That'd be grand. But you didn't come here to talk to me about your accident, did you now?' She cocked her head.

'No. I'm hoping you'll be able to help me with a rather, er, delicate matter regarding Gran. I believe that during the Occupation she became friendly with a…German soldier called Wilhelm. Did you know about their friendship?' Jeanne bit her lip, trying to remain calm.

The old lady regarded Jeanne intently before answering.

'How did you know about Wilhem?'

'I found some letters from him to Gran in the attic. It would seem they were,' she coughed, 'lovers. So you did know about him?' her voice rose in excitement.

Mrs Ozanne nodded. 'Yes, I knew about him. Met him, too.'

'Oh! Is this him?' Jeanne showed her the photo.

'Yes, that's Wilhelm all right. Good looking lad he was. And a real gentleman, not like some of them other soldiers we had here. 'Twas obvious he hated being a soldier, but o'course he had no choice. And he thought the world of Jeanne. He even learnt English so that they could talk together.' She paused and sipped her tea.

Jeanne twisted her hair again.

'How did they meet?'

'He was based in Perelle most of the time, at a gun emplacement on a bunker. They met when Jeanne was out for a walk in the lanes nearby. She tripped and twisted her ankle and Wilhelm found her, unable to move she was. He strapped up her ankle and gave her painkillers from the bunker's medical supplies. Although they couldn't understand each other, I think 'twas love at first sight,' she sighed and took another sip.

'Sounds very romantic! But it must have been very difficult for them to keep their meetings a secret,' Jeanne said, leaning forward.

'Yes, it was. But they were very careful and her parents never knew. I was the only one Jeanne confided in, see. I sometimes took messages for 'em. I liked him and saw how happy she was. They were right for each other – or would've been if they weren't enemies!' Her face clouded over.

Jeanne, although reluctant to stir up painful memories, was anxious to know more.

'Was it very bad? In the Occupation?' she asked gently.

The old lady gazed at Jeanne and nodded. 'Wasn't good, that's for sure. Worst was the lack o' food. We were always hungry, but eventually just got used to it. That last year was the worst, when we couldn't get supplies from France. We were all starving, soldiers an' islanders alike. People were eating cats, dogs, rats. Anything just to stay alive. And that winter was so cold, worst I'd known.' She looked up at Jeanne and went on, her eyes clouding at the painful memory. 'You have to remember, we had no power, nothing at all for heat, light, cooking. Many people got taken ill and ended up in hospital. Like your gran's ma. She was real bad, she was. But she got better.' Mrs Ozanne sipped the last of her tea and remained quiet.

'I've read that you finally got help from the Red Cross,' Jeanne prompted.

Mrs Ozanne smiled. 'Yes, and were we glad! That Red Cross ship Vega it was called, arrived in St Peter Port and they started unloading thousands of parcels, enough for everyone. But not the Germans, o'course. They still had no food, poor souls. But we had tinned food, tea, chocolate and even cigarettes. And clothes for the children. And warm blankets! By then we knew the Allies were winning, that Jerry was finished. We hadn't always known what was happening out there, in the rest o' the world. Our radios were confiscated most o' the time. We'd been cut off from everything.'

She seemed lost in thought again but then brightened and said, 'But we survived and life's been good since then, so mustn't complain.'

Jeanne could only admire the old lady's spirit and she could see why she and her gran had been such good friends, they were from the same mould.

'Mrs Ozanne, did you, er, know that Gran got pregnant?'

She nodded. 'Thought this would be what you wanted to talk about. It's that baby's body that's been found, isn't it?'

'Yes. It was under a bedroom floor. I think it was Gran's.'

'Was her baby, yes.' Mrs Ozanne's face twisted, as if she were in pain. 'It came early...I was meant to be with her...but it was sudden like...I couldn't get there in time, couldn't help. The cord was round the baby's neck, if only I'd been there she may have lived. 'It was my fault...I was too late!' Tears glistened in her eyes and Jeanne reached out and held her hand.

'You mustn't blame yourself. No-one was to blame. It...it happens. But where were Gran's parents?'

The old lady blew her nose on a lace trimmed handkerchief before answering.

'Her father was out fishing and her mother was in the hospital with a fever, like I said. So she was on her own. When the pains started she sent a lad to fetch me, but I was out and by the time I got the message it was too late. I found Jeanne lying there, exhausted and the baby was blue, didn't draw breath.' She stopped, her hands shaking.

Jeanne was trying to hold back her tears.

Mrs Ozanne continued, 'I helped clean up Jeanne and we decided to bury the baby under the floor. Couldn't think what else to do and she was past caring. And there wasn't much time, her father was due back any minute.'

Jeanne cleared her throat. 'How did she hide her pregnancy? Surely she was quite big at the end?'

'It was winter when she began to show and because o' the cold we all wore lots o' layers. Jeanne just looked like anyone else with baggy tops and trousers. Was too cold for skirts. 'Tis possible her mother guessed but she never said anything. And by the time she came out o' hospital it was all over.'

Jeanne braced herself for the next and most important question.

'I need to know, Mrs Ozanne, what happened to Wilhelm? Why didn't he and Gran get married?'

The old lady looked surprised at the question and then understanding seemed to dawn on her.

'O'course, you wouldn't know, would you? Poor lad was dead – killed in an explosion. An accident, they said, at the airport, where he'd been sent on duty. Some other soldiers were injured as well but poor Wilhelm was killed outright.'

'Oh no! How awful! But when did this happen?'

'The day before Jeanne went into labour. That's why the baby came early. It was the shock, you see. Shock from hearing the man she loved was dead.'

# chapter 25

By half past nine on Thursday morning Jeanne had completed the Bond on her cottage, just in time to make a stage payment to Martin on Friday.

As she came out of the Royal Court into the bright summer sunshine she was tempted to play hooky and disappear to the beach for the day. But, on reflection, she decided to take time off at the weekend instead and see if Rachel could join her. She'd love a good girls' gossip after all the trauma of the past couple of weeks.

All was proceeding well at the cottage after the enforced delay and Jeanne collected her post and disappeared to Molly's. Amongst the usual bills and circulars was a letter from Sally, attaching an amended contract. The publishers had agreed to Sally's changes and Jeanne was happy to sign and return it immediately. I'm being showered with money today, she thought, smiling happily, as she dialled her aunt's number. They had only spoken briefly after the baby's body was found.

'Jeanne, lovely to hear from you. How are you coping? Have things quietened down?' Kate asked, concerned.

'Not exactly. Been an interesting few days, actually.' She went on to describe her visit to Mrs Ozanne.

There was a moment's silence at the other end of the phone.

'I see. Do you feel it's helped to have talked to the old lady?'

'Oh, yes. It was sad to hear what Gran went through and Wilhelm's death must have been awful. But at least now there are no unknowns and it was good to have heard it all from someone so close to Gran. I now know how she felt about everything, not just Wilhelm. She loved him and hoped they'd marry and was so excited about the baby. Scared too of course.' Jeanne paused and took a deep breath.

'Gran was always strong and knew she'd cope. But it seems Wilhelm's death knocked the stuffing out of her. I think she wished she'd died with her baby. According to Mrs Ozanne she was depressed for months afterwards. It was only the arrival of the Liberating Forces which shook her out of it.'

'I'm not surprised she was depressed! She'd experienced such tragedy, and so young. She was only about twenty, wasn't she?'

'Yes. And only Mrs Ozanne knew the whole story. She's a lovely lady and I plan to keep in touch. The interesting thing is she married the nephew of Gran's father so we're related by marriage. Her memory's fantastic and she said Gran had chosen the names William for a boy and Marie for a girl. And that Wilhelm's surname was Schmidt. He was well liked among the locals, considering he was an enemy occupier. Apparently he helped out whenever he could, particularly with the elderly. People were genuinely saddened by his death.'

'Are you going to include the story about the baby in the book?'

'I'm not going to mention the pregnancy or the baby, although locals may guess now the...that Marie's body's been found. I will mention Wilhelm's death as it's relevant as well as poignant. It explains why they didn't marry, which is important. Even though I'm not mentioning Granpa in the book I did find out from Mrs Ozanne that Gran was really in love with him and they were very happy together, which was always my impression, too. They met a year after the war ended and married a few months later. So she did find happiness in the end,' Jeanne said, with a satisfied sigh.

'Are we up to date now?'

Jeanne told her about the signing of the contract and the loan from the bank, finishing the call on a happier note.

Although Saturday had been dull with a scattered shower or two, Sunday was a typical summer's day of clear sky and hot sun and Jeanne picked up Rachel just before noon. Tim was surfing with the others and Rachel was glad of some company and the excuse to sunbathe. They each brought a picnic to share and Jeanne had packed a bottle of white wine in the cool box. Settling themselves on the beach in Ladies Bay, they stripped down to their bikinis.

'This is the life! I never seem to have time to really enjoy a day on the beach. I've always got something else I should be doing – like housework or marking homework!' Rachel said as she stretched out, luxuriating in the sun.

'I know what you mean. It can be difficult to just let go, but I'm determined to enjoy this summer. My first seaside summer for fifteen years!' Jeanne replied, slathering on the sun cream.

'How are things? Haven't spoken to you for what seems like ages.'

'Well, you'd better make yourself comfortable as I've a lot to report.' By the time Jeanne had covered all that had happened, Rachel's first words were, 'I need a drink!'

Jeanne opened the bottle of wine and poured generous measures into plastic glasses.

'You know something, Jeanne Le Page? You're a dark horse, you are. You look absolutely normal on the outside – but, boy, it's all bubbling away inside, isn't it? I think it's fantastic about your book, I really do. I know I'd never be able to buckle down to write the way you do. And under such circumstances! I'd have been on tranquillisers by now,' said Rachel, taking a large gulp of wine. In a more serious tone, she added, 'Do you know when the inquest is to be held?'

'No, but I expect to hear tomorrow. They're just waiting for the DNA results. And now that I've Mrs Ozanne as a witness it should be an open and shut case. If I can arrange for the burial to be outside school hours, would you come along? I'd like as many friends with me as possible.'

'No problem. It's all so sad and I'd be happy to offer some moral support. I noticed that you haven't mentioned Marcus at all. What's going on in that department?' Rachel said, lifting her eyebrows.

'Oh, not a lot. I don't feel it's going to work out between us, although he's quite keen. I just find him a bit, well, shallow.'

Rachel nodded. 'He is a bit. He's nice enough but there's not much substance. Very hooked on money, just like the rest of his family.'

'Oh, you know the Davidsons, do you?'

'They live near my parents in a very posh house, but they've never mixed much with us poor Guerns. You could tell that the father was very ambitious as he was always throwing parties for the Open Market brigade, to which us *hoi polloi* weren't invited. He cultivated the wealthy for his accountancy practice. A mix of Rollers and Mercs often cluttered up their drive. I guess Marcus was brought up to feel he had to succeed and add to the family fortune.'

'But what about Dan, his older brother? He didn't go into a profession.'

Rachel grimaced. 'Dan! The black sheep of the family. But he likes money, for sure. He's always been a wheeler and dealer and there was even talk about him being into drug trafficking years ago. But I don't think he got caught and it was hushed up.'

'A drug dealer! God, that's scary. You know, I met him recently when he bought my old furniture. I felt really uncomfortable with him and I'm sure he's on drugs.'

'Could be. But he's managed to stay out of reach of the law all these years. You're not going to do any more business with him, are you? He's bad news.'

'Oh no, don't worry. Once was enough! And even though Marcus is nothing like him I don't think we'll be going out anymore. Could that cause a problem with our meeting as a group?'

'These things happen. If you can part on friendly terms it should be all right. You…weren't lovers were you?'

'That's a very personal question to ask, Miss Mahy! But no, we weren't as I wasn't ready yet after…you know. So that should make it easier to remain polite. I'm happy to see him in a group situation, just not one to one.' Jeanne paused, twisting her hair. 'You don't know how things are with Sue and Nick do you? Only Colette seemed to think that Sue might be wearing down his defences.'

Rachel shook her head and turned over onto her stomach. 'I haven't seen or heard from them since your barbecue. I think Nick was due to go surfing today with the others but I don't know about Sue. I don't think they're very well matched so I doubt they'll ever be a couple. I'd have thought Sue was more Marcus's type than Nick's, wouldn't you?'

Jeanne was glad that Rachel couldn't see her face flush.

'Marcus and Sue were certainly close at school. But I'm not sure what Nick's type would be.'

'I could see him going for someone a little more mature – in outlook I mean, not age. He strikes me as being a bit deep and he'd be an ideal family man. I had my nephews with me once and he was great with them, so natural. Just like Tim, who'll make a wonderful father one day,' Rachel said dreamily.

'Hey, hang on a minute. You two haven't walked down the aisle yet! Give him time to get his breath back from the long march!' Jeanne cried, flicking sand at Rachel's back.

They ended up laughing and as they unpacked their picnic Rachel regaled Jeanne with a humorous version of the rather less exciting life she'd led the past few weeks.

Jeanne was nervous as she drove up to Bordeaux on Monday morning. It was going to be very strange being in Nick's cottage and she wasn't sure how she'd react if he was around. There was an intimacy about spending time in someone's home and using their things, especially kitchen utensils chosen by an ex-fiancée.

She went slowly up Rue Robin and finally found his detached granite cottage, La Tonnelle, on the right. Colette's Mini was already parked in the spacious drive but there was no sign of Nick's jeep. Not sure whether or not to be relieved, she unloaded her files and laptop and rang the bell.

'Hi, Jeanne. Good timing, I was just writing my initial shopping list. Hey, let me help you with those,' Colette said, relieving Jeanne of some of the files.

The cottage was similar in size to Le Petit Chêne but had a very different feel to it. From the outside it was a traditional Guernsey cottage, but it had been radically modernised internally and was now open-plan. Jeanne did not think it looked right, a bit too stark for her taste – an expanse of white with wooden floors and beams. Colette led her into the large clinical kitchen which appeared to be the result of two rooms being knocked into one and the stainless steel units gleamed under the bright lights.

Colette caught Jeanne's eye and said, grinning, 'I know what you're thinking and I agree with you. I'm used to professional kitchens at work but I like those in houses to be more homely. Unfortunately, when Helen moved in she persuaded Nick to make all these changes and by the time they'd been completed she'd moved out again. He's not too keen on it either, but he's not here very much, so puts up with it. Still, at least we've got a well-equipped kitchen to spur us on! Now, let's have some tea while we finish the shopping list and I can check if you're happy with my work plan.'

They worked companionably, sitting at the granite-topped island unit.

'I think you've got it all worked out, Colette. It makes sense to start with the complicated French dishes so that we can see if any are going to be unsuitable for modern lifestyles. We'll leave out any recipes that could be too difficult, either to source ingredients or to make, or that wouldn't be to modern taste. I want people to enjoy these dishes, not find them exhausting or unpalatable. Do you agree?'

Colette nodded. 'Yes, totally. *Haute Cuisine* can be very off-putting these days as traditionally it was very rich and I'd like to tone that down. But I don't think you need worry too much about these here, I can tell they'll be great. As I can't start the cooking without food shall we go shopping together? We've got a huge fridge here and we can stock up for a few days, no problem. You'll have to make a trip to the market for fish at some point, that's all.'

After they had returned with the biggest load of shopping Jeanne had ever bought, the preparation began in earnest. Jeanne was allocated the vegetables, watched over by a critical Colette, in charge of the more complicated meat preparation and desserts.

The day passed very pleasantly and Jeanne even found time to work on her laptop for an hour or so. Colette aimed to make two each of starters, main courses and desserts each day but making smaller quantities than those suggested. Some of the recipes catered for ten people and rather than feeding the street, it was decided to cook for four, giving them all a chance to taste the results. Scott was roped in as another guinea pig with Nick.

Late that afternoon, as they were clearing up the kitchen, Jeanne received a call from Inspector Ferguson.

'Thought you'd like to know that the DNA test results are through. They confirm that there's a genetic link between you and the baby so we should be able to hold the inquest this week.'

Jeanne told him about Mrs Ozanne and her account of what had happened sixty years ago.

'That's very helpful. Makes it conclusive. Have you asked her about giving us a statement? We wouldn't expect her to attend Court.'

'Yes, I thought you'd want one and she's fine about it. Although talking to me brought back a lot of sad memories for her, I think she's quite enjoying all the attention. I'll give you her number.'

They left it that the inspector would phone her when the date was fixed for the inquest.

During the morning Colette had said she knew about the baby from Nick so Jeanne had told her about meeting Mrs Ozanne.

Colette, being a little younger, was still an incurable romantic and thought the whole story was wonderful, even if it was sad. 'Your gran sounds quite something. She could probably have run a fantastic restaurant,' Colette said as she made choux pastry. 'You must be very proud of her,' she added, glancing up at Jeanne who was carefully slicing vegetables with an extremely sharp knife.

'Oh, I am. She's been an inspiration to me over the years. But she was content with her domestic way of life. It was all she'd known and she wasn't at all materialistic. Finding those letters and talking to Mrs Ozanne has given me so much more insight into what she was really like. I've seen a side of her I never knew existed. I'm even more proud of her now. I just wish I'd known all this when she was still alive,' she sighed.

'Hey, come on! Don't get maudlin! If you start crying you'll make the veg too salty!'

Jeanne ducked as a tea towel was hurled her way.

'Okay, okay, boss! I'm glad I've only got to work with you for two weeks. Wouldn't want to be your assistant at the hotel!' Jeanne laughed.

After the phone call they finished clearing up and Colette served the food. This included *Poulardes à La Godard* for a main course and for dessert *Paris-Brest* and *Meringue à la Reine.*

'This all looks wonderful! The French weren't bothered about their waistlines were they?' Jeanne remarked, suddenly feeling peckish.

'These are light compared to some of the dishes. They loved sauces and lots of cream in the nineteenth century, a bit too much for my taste. Nowadays we can substitute less fattening ingredients like yogurt or low fat crème fraîche. But I'm still worried we're all going to put on weight these next few weeks. Definitely be a strict diet after this lot!'

Nick arrived as they were dividing the food into portions.

'Hey, you've been busy. What a feast! I can see I'm going to enjoy having you two in my kitchen,' he grinned at them both.

'Don't get too used to it, big bruv, it's only for two weeks then it's back to baked beans on toast for you,' Colette said, giving him a playful punch. She added, 'Why don't you and Jeanne eat together? I'm nearly finished and I'll take my goody bags home with me. Then you can tell Jeanne what you really think of the food – and we want the truth, mind!'

'That's a great idea. Are you happy to join me? Or do you have to dash off?' Nick's smile was warm and inviting.

Jeanne couldn't think of a reason to say no though she wasn't sure how she'd survive such intimacy with this warm and friendly version of Nick, without giving away how attractive she found him. She was also worried that Sue might turn up and that would surely mean trouble.

# chapter 26

Sue did not arrive and Jeanne forced herself to relax. They sampled each of the choices for the different courses and Jeanne wrote down both her own and Nick's comments. So far, so good, as the food was as tasty as it looked. Colette had worked out the modern oven temperatures to perfection.

When they had cleared away the dirty plates and sealed up the leftovers Nick made some coffee with the fanciest espresso machine Jeanne had ever seen.

'Trying to emulate James Bond, are you?' she said, arching her eyebrows.

'Hell no. It was chosen by someone else. They had to have the best of everything and this was top of the range. On the plus side it does make fantastic coffee. But it took me ages to work out how to operate all the bells and whistles!'

They had eaten at the kitchen table and continued to sit there with their coffee, relaxed and replete after their meal.

'So, any more news since I last saw you?'

'The DNA test proved a good match and the inquest is likely to be later this week, meaning we might have the burial on Saturday. Oh! I haven't told you about Mrs Ozanne, have I?' He shook his head. She told him about the illuminating meeting with the old lady and he listened attentively.

'Well, that's all good. Now you know what happened you can finish the story. Anything else?'

'I signed the contract on Thursday so am now waiting impatiently for my first cheque.'

'Great news! You have had a busy week, haven't you?

Surprised you find time to write. We'll have to celebrate properly when you do get your money,' he said, his face breaking into a smile.

Jeanne's stomach flipped over. Did he mean taking her out somewhere? Would it be a date? She thought it safer to change the subject.

'Have you started work on that new boat yet?'

'The hull's being made in England and will be shipped over to us to in a week or two. It's literally a skeleton so we'll have plenty to do when it arrives. But we're still finishing off smaller contracts at the moment, so keeping busy,' he paused. 'Are you still happy about moving onto the boat next week?'

'Yes, I think so. I haven't managed much hypnosis lately but I'm feeling more confident. Guess there's a way to go before I'll be free of the worst of the fear.'

'Any more flashbacks?'

'No, not since that day I met you in the café. And with everything else that's been happening I haven't really given them much thought. But it's another mystery to solve before I can truly get on with my life,' she said wistfully.

'So, what do you see yourself doing with the rest of your life?' Nick asked, his deep blue eyes locked onto hers.

'Well…I want to settle down here properly. Finish the cottage, build up my social life and focus on my career as a writer. Once I've finished this book I plan to start another, possibly fiction this time, I'm not sure,' she answered, a little fazed by his question. *Why's he looking at me like that? And his questions are getting a bit personal. That's not supposed to happen!*

'Don't you want to settle down with someone? Have a family?'

Jeanne frowned. 'Yes, one day. But I've only recently come out of a long-term relationship and I had a…a miscarriage a few months ago.'

'I'm so sorry. I didn't know, forgive me. I just thought as you'd been going out with Marcus…'

'That wasn't a proper relationship. More a friendship, really. But when the right man comes along, I'd be prepared to give him fair consideration,' she smiled. 'And what about you? Do you want to marry and have a family?' She felt herself tense.

Nick was thoughtful. 'I'm not against marriage and children. But it would have to be someone very special for me to make that commitment. I came close once, but it didn't work out. Like you, I'm biding my time. Seems we've got something in common with our failed relationships, haven't we?' he said, pulling a face.

'Mm, yes. Look, I'd better get going. Got to make the hazardous journey down the west coast remember. Perhaps I'll see you tomorrow,' she said, standing up, feeling a sudden desire to leave, even though part of her wanted to stay.

'There's a reasonable chance of that, seeing that I live here,' he said, amused.

She stood in the kitchen, hopping from foot to foot, wondering whether to just say goodbye and leave when Nick came over and gave her a hug.

'Thanks for a great meal and great company. Can we eat together tomorrow night as well?'

'I…I'm not sure if Molly's planned anything. I'll let you know. Glad you enjoyed the food.' As she turned to go Nick kissed her cheek.

'Take care. Watch out for dangers on the road home,' he said, grinning.

Jeanne smiled and mumbled goodnight before going out to her car. As she drove down the 'dangerous' road she realised that any danger lay closer to home. In the cottage she'd just left there was a man she was in grave danger of falling in love with.

The next couple of days passed quickly. Jeanne and Colette produced more delights in Nick's kitchen and in the evenings he and Jeanne ate the various courses as they chatted. She had not wanted to lie and pretend she was expected at Molly's and, for some reason, Molly had actually encouraged her to stay and eat with Nick. Is she trying to push us together? Jeanne wondered. The only thing which marred the otherwise enjoyable meals together was the spectre of Sue bursting in on them.

On Tuesday the inspector had phoned to say that the inquest was fixed for eleven o'clock on Thursday and he saw no reason why the body could not be released for burial. Jeanne phoned Reverend Ayres and he agreed to conduct a service at nine thirty on Saturday, well before a wedding booked for that day.

Jeanne then phoned Mrs Ozanne with the news and it was arranged that Jeanne would collect her on the way to the church. Nick, Colette, Rachel, Molly and Peter were also going to attend and when Jeanne mentioned it to Martin he said he'd like to pay his respects too.

'I knew your grandmother a bit, remember, and I found that poor baby o' hers. I'd be honoured to be there,' he said gravely. Jeanne was very touched and had to blink away a tear.

The inquest was straightforward and Jeanne did not have to say anything. The magistrate outlined the circumstances of the finding of the body before saying there was sufficient evidence to identify the remains as that of the stillborn child of Jeanne Ozanne, born on February 19th 1945. The whole procedure lasted about fifteen minutes and once again Jeanne found herself outside the Royal Court.

As she stood on the steps trying to shake off the feeling of sadness which had overtaken her, she was joined by the inspector.

'You must be glad that's over, Jeanne. I understand a burial's been arranged for Saturday?'

'Yes, Inspector. It will be a relief to lay little Marie to rest properly. And I'd like to thank you for the way you handled the investigation. You were very understanding,' she smiled at him.

He looked uncomfortable, as if not used to being thanked by a member of the public.

'Thank you. I just do my best and it was a sad business, that baby. But I understand it's not the only mystery in your family,' he said, giving her a jolt. 'As yet no-one's been traced in connection with the death of your parents and I don't like unsolved cases. I didn't move here until a few years ago and I've inherited the case from my predecessor. You were the only witness, I believe?'

She nodded. 'Apparently. I was knocked out at some point and suffered amnesia, but I've been getting flashbacks and am having hypnosis to help recover my memory.'

The inspector's face lit up. 'What do you remember so far?'

Jeanne told him about the white boat which looked like a speedboat and what she saw happen to her mother.

'This could prove quite a breakthrough. I'll get the file out and see how it fits. You will let me know as soon as you remember anything else, won't you?'

'Of course! I want this solved even more than you do. It's haunted me for the past fifteen years and I want to see it laid to rest, just like Marie. I'm really pleased that you're in charge, Inspector. I have every confidence in you,' she said warmly.

The inspector cleared his throat. 'Right, I'll wait to hear from you, then. And if I discover anything I'll let you know immediately,' he said, before going off towards the nearby police headquarters.

Jeanne was thoughtful as she drove up to Bordeaux. She believed the meeting with the Inspector was significant – perhaps a sign that the remaining mystery in her life would soon be solved. She sincerely hoped so.

By Friday afternoon Jeanne was beginning to be sick of the sight of food in all its shapes and textures. She could not understand why anyone would want to devote their working life to preparing and cooking food for the masses. But Colette was in her element and made it clear she was enjoying herself.

'You know, Jeanne, this has been great. It's so different to working in the hotel kitchen where I get orders shouted at me all day long. This week has made me more determined than ever to have my own restaurant one day.'

'Well, you're certainly a great cook. Every dish you've made has been delicious and beautifully presented. If I had the money I'd set you up in business myself.'

Colette replied, cheekily, 'You'll have to write another book and collect an even bigger advance then you could do just that!'

They both laughed and carried on with the seemingly endless preparation. Jeanne had meant what she said but knew it was expensive to set up a restaurant locally, thanks to the high cost of living in Guernsey. Colette was so bubbly as well as hard working that she had a good chance of success. There must be some way, Jeanne thought, as she continued chopping.

Colette took pity on her a few minutes later and declared that it was time for a break and Jeanne was free to escape to her beloved computer. They sat drinking tea, thankful that the day's meal was now cooking in the oven and they could relax.

'I was wondering if Sue and Nick had become an item yet. After all, she's been pursuing him for a while now.'

'Oh, I know she has but Nick was never interested in a relationship with her. He was happy to be just friends, helped to balance the numbers in the group. But I've heard that she's now met someone who appreciates her obvious charms!' she grinned.

'I'm so pleased for her. That's great.' *For me too.*

She went off to work in the sitting room while Colette carried on happily in the kitchen, humming along to the pop music erupting from the radio.

As Jeanne drove home that evening she was glad that Nick had been busy and not able to join her for dinner. Now that she knew he was still single she felt more unsure of herself than when she thought he might be unavailable. They were both free to pursue a relationship and much as she fancied him she was still scared. She sighed as she pulled into Molly's drive. Was she getting close to 'snaring that dishy man' as Freya put it, or did he just see her as a friend? Was she even ready for a relationship? After all, she'd been telling everyone, including herself, that she wasn't. She just didn't know.

A little later Jeanne was watching a particularly gripping drama on television with Peter and Molly when her mobile rang. She went into the kitchen to answer it and found, to her dismay, that it was Marcus.

'Hi Jeanne. How are you?'

'Okay, thanks. And you?'

'Fine. But I've missed you. I really want us to be friends again. Please could we make a fresh start? I know I've handled things badly and I'm sorry. I'd like to explain how I feel properly. Can I come round and see you?'

'It's not a good time as I'm about to move tomorrow.'

'But where are you going? Why are you leaving the Ogiers'?' His voice grew louder and she felt angry.

'I have to leave as Molly has visitors arriving so I'm going to stay on a...a friend's boat until I can return to the cottage.'

'A boat! But you're scared of boats, you told me that! How can you bear to stay on a boat?'

'I'm not as scared now as I've been having hypnosis to help. Now, Marcus, I really have to go. I'll call you sometime.' She switched off her mobile and took a few deep breaths, feeling angry – angry with Marcus for pursuing her like that and angry with herself for saying more than she'd intended. Not wanting him to know about the boat, but at least he didn't know whose it was. She squared her shoulders, took another deep breath and went back to the fictional drama playing out on the screen in front of her. Not a patch on her own real one, she thought wryly.

Saturday dawned hot and sunny. A day more suited to weddings than the burial of a tiny infant who hadn't had a chance to live, Jeanne reflected as she arrived at the church with Mrs Ozanne. Other cars pulled up and the small group gathered together, exchanging muted greetings before making their way inside. It felt so cold in the church after the heat of the sun that the women, in light summer dresses or separates, shivered while the men were glad of their jackets. Reverend Ayres was waiting to welcome them with his warm, sympathetic smile and firm handshake.

They walked down the nave towards the altar and Jeanne gasped as she saw the tiny white coffin on a small white covered stand. The white signified the innocence of a child and for a moment her legs trembled. Images of the little body of Marie mingled with that of the imagined, even tinier foetus from her own miscarriage. It was only Nick's hand holding her elbow firmly which kept her steady.

It was a simple service, reserved for stillborn and neonatal deaths with a short address from the vicar to be followed by a hymn. Jeanne had chosen 'All Things Bright and Beautiful'. Reverend Ayres stood at the side of the coffin and in his deep, resonant voice referred to the sad circumstances surrounding Marie's birth and lack of life. Although brief it was beautifully phrased and Jeanne felt comforted that he had also conducted the funerals for both her parents and grandmother.

The singing of the hymn, so well-loved by children, lifted the spirits of the small congregation and although they were few, the sound they produced resounded around the church.

It was a shock going out into the sunshine again. Eyes blinked and sunglasses were dug out of bags or pockets. The vicar led the way to the grave which had been dug out, exposing old Mrs Le Page's coffin. Peter had volunteered to carry the small coffin and he now gently placed it by the side of the larger one. It was not much bigger than a shoe box and looked so tiny in the grave.

The vicar intoned the appropriate prayers and the assembled group made their due responses. It was over in minutes and Jeanne placed a bunch of freesias in the grave before moving away.

Back at the lychgate Reverend Ayres shook hands with the mourners and had a particularly long chat with Mrs Ozanne. Jeanne had noticed her crying silently in the church. She was still dabbing at her eyes as the vicar spoke to her. Jeanne felt so sorry for the old lady who had convinced herself that Marie's death had been her fault.

At last she moved away and Jeanne approached him.

'That was a really moving service, Vicar. Just what I'd hoped for. I'm sure Gran will truly rest in peace now.'

He nodded solemnly. 'There's no doubt about that, Jeanne. No doubt at all. Now, you just take care of yourself and I look forward to seeing you here again when you bring

226

your lovely flowers. God Bless.'

The group made their way to the parked cars and after hugs and goodbyes had been exchanged Jeanne helped Mrs Ozanne into her car. After dropping her back home Jeanne was to return to Molly's to start packing, once again. It was time to move on. She had to prove to herself that she had really conquered her fear of boats in order to live on one for several weeks. She must be mad! Just then she caught Nick's eye and it came to her that what was helping her beat this fear, apart from the hypnosis, was that Nick, so big, strong and reliable, would be there for her. She only had to call him.

# chapter 27

It was late afternoon before Jeanne made her way to Beaucette Marina and her temporary life afloat. Molly and Peter had insisted that she joined them for lunch and, in need of cheer after the funeral, she was pleased to accept. They had eaten at Crabby Jacks, a lively restaurant at Vazon, and it was great to relax under a giant umbrella while tucking into a good meal.

It felt strange to know she was on her own again and Jeanne had to admit to herself that it had been great to be cosseted by the Ogiers. But now it was time now to recover her independence, she thought, parking close to the main access ramp to unload the car.

She had only a couple of bags but one was heavy, filled with files and her laptop, and was struggling with it when Nick arrived. He lifted it out of the boot easily with one hand.

'Hey, let me help. I'll carry these down to the boat while you park,' he said.

By the time she reached *La Belle Élise* Nick was on board with her luggage.

'Right, I'd better show you how everything works. The gas cylinder's here, and should last for weeks,' he said, pointing to a cupboard in the galley. He then showed her how to work the electric supply and the heads.

'See this valve? You flick it over to pump water in to flush and then flick it back again when you've finished. Don't leave it on as water will continue to pump in. And you've got hot water for a shower. Any problems, either give me a shout or you can use the marina facilities if it's urgent. But everything was working fine when I last checked. Any questions?'

'I don't think so. Just a bit nervous of coming free of the moorings and floating out to sea,' she said, with a shudder.

Nick laughed. 'There's no chance of that happening, don't worry. You're perfectly safe here. But if you're concerned about anything, anything at all, just call. I don't want you to be scared on your own,' he said, gently stroking the hair off her face.

A flick of desire flowed through her at his touch. 'I'm not scared! A bit nervous, that's all. I'll be fine. There's no need for you to worry about me,' she said, not quite truthfully.

Nick frowned. 'But I do worry about you after all that's happened and I don't want you to go on having a tough time. You deserve so much better. To prove my good intentions I'd like to take you out to dinner tonight at the Marina Restaurant.'

'Oh, Nick, I'd have loved to accept but I've just gorged myself at Crabby's. Perhaps another time?'

'Okay, how about tomorrow lunchtime? You should have your appetite back by then,' he grinned.

'Yes, I'd like that, thanks. I'll have a long walk first to work up an even bigger appetite 'cos I hear the food's very good!' she teased.

'Don't make the walk too long, I'd be embarrassed if you asked for seconds! Shall we say one thirty? I'll book it now, and you can settle in. Here's the keys. Hope you sleep well tonight,' he said as he kissed her lightly on the cheek.

'Thanks. See you tomorrow.'

After he'd gone Jeanne dreamily unpacked her possessions. Nick was being so caring and his touch certainly did things to her! It dawned on her that there was a kind of electricity between them that she'd not experienced before, even with Andy. She wondered if he had felt it too and tried not to daydream as she put her clothes away in a locker and the odds and ends in the cupboard. It would be so nice to stop living out of a suitcase and return to her cottage, surrounded by all her possessions, most of which were still at Aunt Kate's. Never really suited to the life of a gypsy, she feared she was fast becoming one.

Waking up on the boat felt strange. Even though it was firmly moored there was a slight rocking motion and the compactness verged on the claustrophobic. As Jeanne stretched her arms she felt as if in a womb – a beige coloured womb, mind you – a womb that had held and rocked her gently into a deep, dreamless sleep. The previous night she had felt nervous about closing her eyes in the bunk but must have drifted off almost at once and it was now after nine o'clock.

The shower proved to be little more than a warm trickle, and as she soaped her body Jeanne pictured the powerful shower shortly to be installed in her cottage. It will be worth the wait, she told herself, as the water slowly rinsed away the lather. After dressing in shorts and T-shirt she sat in the cockpit with the awning rolled back and ate her breakfast.

Now it was time for the long walk she'd promised to make and Jeanne strode out along the headland as far as L'Ancresse Bay. The sun's heat bore down and she felt the sweat trickle down her neck and between her breasts. The sea sparkled and looked so tempting that for a moment she wished she'd brought her bathers. A few braver souls than her were already swimming and the excited cries of children hung on the air as they splashed about in the water.

Back at the boat she ran a shower and stood impatiently as the water trickled over her and then changed into a cotton skirt and sleeveless top smart enough for Sunday lunch. A mirror on the back of the locker guided her in the application of eye shadow, mascara and lip gloss. She combed her hair and with a quick spray of perfume she was ready. Making herself comfortable in the cockpit she began reading a book by Rosie Thomas.

So engrossed was she that she lost track of time and was startled by a laughing voice saying, 'So I've been stood up for a book, have I?'

'Nick! I'm sorry, am I late?'

He stepped aboard and kissed her lightly on the cheek before replying, 'No, we've got five minutes. Shall we go?'

Jeanne locked up and Nick helped her off the boat and led the way along the narrow pontoon. As she followed him she ran an appreciative eye over his toned physique set off by linen slacks and a crisp white short sleeved shirt which also emphasised his tan. His walk was the confident stride of a man who felt good about himself and was totally at ease around water.

As they arrived at the top of the main ramp he reached out and held her arm until they entered the restaurant.

The Maitre D' welcomed Nick warmly. 'Signor Mauger! How good to see you again. Your table is ready or would you prefer to have an aperitif outside?' He smiled at Jeanne. 'Signorina,' he said, with a slight bow.

'We'll have a drink outside first, thanks, Giovanni. Two Kir Royales, please.'

Jeanne raised her eyebrows and Nick said, 'Thought we could celebrate your signing of the contract.'

They were ushered to a small iron table on the patio and Nick helped Jeanne into a chair and his fingers lightly brushed her arm as he waited for her to settle. Her body tingled in response and for a moment she fantasised about the pair of them stripping off each other's clothes and making love in the cabin. The image was so strong and pleasurable that the heat rose in her face and she noticed Nick looking at her oddly.

'Are you all right? You're looking a bit flushed. If you're

too hot we could go inside,' he said, solicitously.

Jeanne took a deep breath and said, 'I'm fine, thanks. Probably caught the sun while I was walking, but I'd like to stay out here. The view's fantastic.' Calm down, girl, she told herself. Don't get carried away, he's just being friendly.

Their aperitifs arrived and as they clinked glasses Nick said, 'To fame and fortune!'

As Jeanne sipped her drink she began to relax. The view was, indeed, wonderful. Not only was she able to drink in the attractions of Nick, but as she was facing the marina she was able to admire the boats, from huge ocean-going yachts to small cruisers like *La Belle Élise*.

He cut into her reverie by asking how she had slept.

'Like a baby. I'd never slept on a boat before and didn't know what to expect. But I loved the slight rocking motion and with the peace and quiet here I felt so safe,' she smiled contentedly at him and he touched her hand.

'I'm glad. That's what I want you to feel – safe. I've always loved being out at sea and sailed the Med several times, sleeping on board for weeks at a stretch. Perhaps when your confidence returns you'd like to come with me to Sark. We could stay on board at night and enjoy the island during the day.'

Jeanne bit her lip and Nick added, quickly, 'But that doesn't have to be for ages, don't worry. I don't want to rush you.'

Her concern was not only about going to sea on a small boat but being in such close proximity with Nick. But she couldn't tell him that!

Instead she replied, 'I guess I'm still a bit of a scaredy-cat. But thanks for the offer. As soon as I feel ready to take the plunge, I'll let you know. I'm sure you're a very good sailor.'

'You'd be in safe hands with me, for sure. I know these waters like the back of my hand. Now, I don't know about you, but I'm starving. Can we choose some food before I disgrace myself and eat all those peanuts?'

Jeanne giggled and the knot in her stomach uncoiled. They made their choice from the menu and moved inside when the waiter collected them.

She wasn't sure if Nick had been sensitive to her unease earlier but, for whatever reason, he steered the conversation away from anything intimate. It was fascinating to hear about the trips he'd made, particularly to the Mediterranean. He was much more travelled than she was, making her envious of his confidence and experience.

'My favourite trips were to the Greek Islands. I took a year off after college and went crewing for British yacht owners. Some of the islands were barely touched by tourism then and the sight of the brilliant white buildings and incredible blue roofs was magical. The Cyclades were particularly popular with yachties and we regularly went to Paros, Naxos and Mykonos. I also remember Delos, the fabled birthplace of Apollo, as something special. You can still see the temples and impressive mosaics,' he sighed. 'There are times when I wish I could just take six months off and go sailing round those islands again.'

Jeanne's eyes shone. 'It sounds wonderful, Nick. I've always wanted to go to the Greek Islands but having to use ferries put me off. I'm fascinated by ancient Greece and its mythology and Apollo's birthplace has to be special. Perhaps one day I'll be able to see for myself.'

Nick opened his mouth to say something then seemed to change his mind.

'How about some coffee?' he asked a moment later.

'Please, I'd like a cappuccino.'

They lingered over their coffee and it was only after a discreet cough from one of the waiters that they realised they were the only diners left.

He took her hand as they walked slowly in the direction

of the access ramp.

'Thanks, Nick. That was lovely. And you've obviously been there before,' she said, smiling at him.

'Glad you enjoyed it. It's one of my favourites. Have to admit I'm a bit lazy where cooking for myself is concerned. It's easier to go out.'

'You're well catered for next week, anyway. Colette will be performing wonders in that wasted kitchen of yours.'

'I'm looking forward to it. And I'm hoping that you'll join me?'

'Yes, don't see why not. But I'd like to get back to the boat before it gets dark.'

'I shall make sure that Cinderella leaves well before midnight, never fear. And thanks for being with me. I really enjoy your company, Jeanne, and I'd like us to get to know each other better. But I don't want to rush you into anything.' He turned to face her, putting his hands on her shoulders and she gazed up into his eyes, which reflected the blue of the water.

'I enjoy being with you, too and it'd be great to spend more time together. Won't be difficult, what with my working in your house during the day and living on your boat at night!'

He laughed.

'Right, yes. Good. I'll look forward to dinner tomorrow.' He then kissed her lingeringly on her mouth, gently parting her lips with his tongue. Jeanne felt her body respond and could have stayed locked in his kiss forever, but Nick pulled back slowly and said, huskily, 'Bye for now.'

Jeanne nodded numbly and watched him stride back to his jeep. She went down the ramp and along the pontoon in a daze. *What a kiss! He must fancy me to kiss like that!* Incapable of doing much else, she changed into shorts and stretched out on the mat on the bow, daydreaming about strong arms and soft kisses.

The next few days were a pleasant antidote to all the drama of the previous couple of weeks. Even though Jeanne was not enjoying the food preparation as much, she did enjoy Colette's company and the monotony of chopping up food was relieved by the odd foray to buy fish and shellfish. She wondered if Colette had sensed here waning enthusiasm as she encouraged her to spend more time on her book whenever possible.

Jeanne's session on Monday with Molly provided another boost to her confidence with boats. Thanks to their progress, Molly had said that the following week she might use regression therapy to focus on the accident. Jeanne felt both nervous and excited at the thought and shared her feelings with Nick as they tasted some of the day's offerings on Tuesday, *Calamares a la Provencale.*

'I can see why you'd still feel nervous. But I'm sure Molly's stressed that you'll be remembering something that's already happened and you survived. You know you will be all right. So there's nothing to be afraid of. What you might remember, more importantly, are details of the white boat and who was on board. With luck you'll be to give the police a good enough description to track them down. And that's what you want, isn't it?' Nick said, gently.

Jeanne smiled her relief. 'Yes, that's exactly what I want. Thanks for putting it in perspective for me. I'll be fine. As you said, I'm still here!'

The evenings with Nick had gone well, he'd been attentive and entertaining and at all times the gentleman. He kissed her goodnight when she left but they were only light caresses of her lips. Secretly she'd have enjoyed more passionate kisses but she did appreciate his forbearance – for both of them. It looked as if he didn't want to frighten her away but was slowly, tenderly reeling her into his arms. And it felt good, she smiled to herself, it felt very good indeed.

# chapter 28

It was with mixed feelings that Jeanne helped Colette with the final touches to the food on Friday afternoon. Colette's leave was over and the cooking of the Guernsey dishes would take place in her own time, in her flat. They had worked through a large number of recipes over the past two weeks and all received top marks from the tasters.

Although Jeanne was glad to be free of the cooking she was going to miss Colette and spending time with Nick. The boat was a bit too claustrophobic to spend all day on it and she planned to spend more time in the library.

That final evening, Colette was joining Nick and Jeanne for the meal and the girls decorated the dining table as if for a celebration. Jeanne had bought wine to complement the food and they were both feeling pleased with their combined efforts.

'It's such a shame Scott has to work, he'd have appreciated a proper sit-down meal instead of a tray perched on his lap,' Colette said, fiddling with the *Hors D'Oeuvre*.

'At least he knows you're safely with your brother and not entertaining some strange man,' grinned Jeanne.

Colette threw her a sly look. 'I might be safe, but are you? Seems to me I'll be playing gooseberry this evening.'

Jeanne flushed. 'Don't know what you mean! Nick and I are just friends. Nothing's happened between us, honest.'

'Yet! But if I know my brother, and I should do, he's got the hots for you, all right. I don't think you'll be able to play Miss Innocent for too much longer!' Colette smirked.

'Mm, well, I guess we do hit it off. But neither of us wants to rush things. We've both been hurt too much before to make another mistake.'

'Don't get me wrong. I think it'd be great if you two become an item. I can see how well you get on and I think you'd be good for him. And I hope he'd be good for you, too. He's a really nice guy who got a bit prickly after he was dumped but I've noticed how much happier he's been since you came on the scene. And just think, one day we could be sisters!'

Jeanne threw a napkin she was folding at Colette who burst into a fit of giggles. It was infectious and Jeanne was soon joining in until they were both on the verge of collapse. They fell, laughing, into chairs and that's how Nick found them.

'Anyone care to share the joke?' he said, standing over them like a teacher with naughty schoolchildren.

This just prompted another fit of giggles and Nick stood there, rolling his eyes.

'Is it something in the food? Some new ingredient you're testing? Or have you already started on the wine?'

The girls managed to pull themselves together and insisted that they had not touched a drop.

'Just a female joke, that's all. You wouldn't understand, bruv. Now, why don't you go and freshen up while we finish off here?' suggested Colette, waving Nick off in the direction of the stairs.

'Okay, okay. I'll be back in fifteen minutes. Perhaps you'll have calmed down by then,' he said dryly.

Colette and Jeanne just grinned at each other and hurried to finish off serving the starters, a mixed *Hors D'Oeuvre* and *Escargots de Bourgogne*. The main courses were *Turbot Dugléré* and *Morue Gourmet*, much lighter than some of the meat dishes they had been eating earlier that week. The puddings were less healthy, *Clafouti Limousin* and *Coeurs à la Crème*, but they wanted their last meal to end in style.

When Nick returned to the kitchen he was met by a

candle-lit table set with the starters, and the girls looking very summery without their cooking aprons.

'I almost feel that I should be wearing a jacket and tie,' he said, putting his arms around their shoulders. 'And what more could a man want than to wine and dine with his two favourite women?' he grinned.

Colette rolled her eyes and ushered him to his seat.

The meal was fun, the food delicious and the Chablis a perfect accompaniment. They were all in good spirits by the time they started to clear away and Nick looked fondly at Colette and Jeanne.

'This has been quite an experience, girls. I've not eaten so well and for so long before. Colette, you've surpassed yourself. And the sous chef wasn't bad either,' he said, catching Jeanne's eye.

'That's very kind of you, bruv. But, although, in all modesty, I must agree with you that I'm a great chef, I have to give credit where it's due. And that's to those recipes of Jeanne's. Some of them were truly inspired and I've thoroughly enjoyed recreating them. When I open my own restaurant I'd be happy to serve such food to my diners.'

'We'll definitely be your first customers when you open your doors!' Nick said.

Jeanne noticed the term 'we' and her heart fluttered. If he's looking that far ahead he must think we're going to be a couple, she thought. Hope he's right!

The weekend was a time of peace and reflection for Jeanne, free from her kitchen duties. Some of the time she spent collating all the details of the recipes Colette had worked on. It was difficult to concentrate for long in the heat of the cabin and she went out to the cockpit at regular intervals for air. She concluded that it would be more sensible to work in the early evening and relax more in the heat of the day.

She and Nick had agreed to forgo eating out for a while

to give their stomachs a chance to recover after the barrage of gourmet meals. They planned to stay in touch by meeting up at the café on The Bridge for a coffee or light lunch a couple of times a week.

On Monday morning Jeanne went off to the cottage to check on Martin's progress and was delighted to see that destruction had given way to construction. The plasterer was due to start that week, a sign that the work was progressing apace. Martin was cheerful.

'It's saving us at least two weeks with your being out o' the cottage, Jeanne. May even be able to let you back in here in a couple o' weeks,' he grinned. 'Are the kitchen people still coming next week?'

'Yes, they phoned to say they'd be here next Monday. Are you ready to take out the old range and cupboards?'

Martin nodded. 'I've got a couple o' lads coming in to dismantle the range this week. If you could pack up your pots and pans we can start on the cupboards.'

Jeanne emptied the cupboards and the dresser and the labourer carried the boxes up to the attic for safekeeping. Her home was slowly emptying of everything from her past and she felt a pang as she looked around. It may have been shabby and a bit uncomfortable but it was her family's heritage and Jeanne felt guilty about what could be seen as a desecration of that legacy. Her only consolation was that the cottage would retain its charm and character with its uneven floors and slightly ill-fitting windows. It was just going to lose its dodgy plumbing and winter chill, she reminded herself.

One aspect that she felt particularly proud of was the exposed beams. The black paint had been sandblasted off to reveal the original golden brown oak underneath and the rooms looked lighter and warmer, leaving Jeanne feeling that, on balance, her efforts at transformation were beneficial.

By the time she had finished changing the flowers on the graves it was nearly three and Jeanne set off to Molly's for her therapy session. Still a little nervous, in spite of Nick's reassurance, but she had complete faith in Molly's professionalism.

'Hello, Jeanne. Had a good week?' asked Molly as she gave her a quick hug.

'Yes, thanks. Progress all round,' Jeanne smiled.

'Good. We might as well get started then.'

When Jeanne was settled in the recliner Molly explained how the session would proceed.

'When you're relaxed I'll reinforce the positive suggestions I've been using in the sessions. Then I'll ask your subconscious mind to take you back in time to the day of the accident. My questions will help you remember and you'll be able to answer while still in an hypnotic state. You may not see everything clearly this first time. Some people say it's as if they're seeing things through a fog so don't worry if that happens. We can always repeat the session. All right?'

Jeanne nodded and managed a tight smile. 'Sure, let's get going.'

Molly spent a few minutes talking Jeanne into a deep relaxed state, and she found herself letting go as Molly continued with her 'ego-boosting routine'.

'Now, Jeanne, I want your subconscious mind to help you go back in time, back in time. To the evening of Sunday, 6th August 1989. I repeat, the evening of Sunday, 6th August 1989. You are in your father's boat *JayJay* with your parents and have been to Herm for the day and are now on the way home to Guernsey, to St Peter Port. Can you see yourselves in the boat, Jeanne?'

'Yes. Dad's at the steering wheel and Mum and I are in the cockpit, in the stern. Mum's standing up, near the rail and I'm sitting down.' Jeanne's voice was quiet but clear.

'Good. Do you know what time it is?'

'About ten, I think. It's dark and we're late coming back, we don't usually come back so late. But Mum and Dad were delayed, I don't know why. Dad's cross about something and wants to get home quickly.'

'Right. Can you tell me what happens next?'

Jeanne shifted slightly in the chair and she frowned, still with her eyes closed.

'Um, we're about half-way back. We've been the only boat around till now but I can see another boat behind us, coming from Herm I suppose. It's white. Looks like a speedboat. Seems to be doing a few knots. Dad's seen it now. He calls to Mum. It sounds like "It's them!" I think.' Again Jeanne stirred and she felt anxious.

'It's all right, Jeanne. Take your time. Can you see who's in the boat?'

'I...I...think there's two...two men. Yes, definitely two.'

'Can you describe them to me?'

'I can see fair hair. Both have fair hair. And they're tall. Seem tall in the boat. The one steering looks young. Both look young. But their faces are a bit blurred. It's so dark,' she whispered.

'That's good, Jeanne. What happens next?'

'They seem to be heading for us. Dad's shouting at them – but they keep coming. We're near some rocks. Dad pulls the wheel but we're still too close to the rocks. The boat's hit us!' Jeanne gasped, writhing in the chair. 'To starboard and the boat shudders. Mum's losing her balance, staggers. We hit the rocks and Mum staggers again, looks dizzy. I think she's hit her head, she's trying to hold onto the rail. Oh no! the boat's hitting us again –capsizing – Mum's falling over the rail – Dad yells at me – "take the wheel" – he goes toward Mum – Oh, I can't see them!' Jeanne cried out, thrashing about in the chair.

'It's all right, Jeanne. It's all right. I want you to leave that time now. It's time to come back to the present. I'm going to bring you back to the present and there will be no part of you left behind in the past.'

Jeanne became aware of Molly's voice guiding her back from that night and the memory of what happened, telling her to open her eyes.

She blinked, her eyes unfocussed, as Molly handed her a glass of water.

'Here, Jeanne, take some deep breaths and drink this.'

She felt washed out but began to feel calmer after drinking the water and her eyes regained focus.

'How do you feel?' Molly asked gently.

'I've felt better! But I guess I'm okay. It was like watching an old film. Some bits were clearer than others.' Jeanne shuddered.

'You did really well, my dear. I know how hard this must have been for you, but you've already remembered so much. I'm sure you'll be able to recollect more but I thought you'd had enough for today. You remember what you saw?'

She nodded. 'Yes and how I felt. But I'm calmer now. I guess it was the younger me's emotions I was experiencing.'

'Yes, for a while you were a teenager again. And it must have been a terrible experience for you. Now, I think we both need some tea, or would you prefer something stronger?'

Jeanne managed a grin. 'I'll settle for the tea, thanks. Don't want to get done for drink driving on top of everything else!'

Before Jeanne left Molly's she phoned Inspector Ferguson and arranged for him meet her at the boat. She also phoned Nick to ask if they could meet up that evening and he suggested she came round to his place.

The inspector listened attentively to all that Jeanne had to say, asking questions and making notes as they talked. His face was sombre as he got up to go.

'This is a great help, Jeanne. I couldn't find anything in the file that gave me any clues at all but what you've just told me puts a very different complexion on the affair. Rest assured, I'll bring those responsible to justice. It's now my number one priority. What bothers me is your being here on your own. You sure you're all right?' he said, looking askance at the boat.

'I'll be fine, Inspector. Really. It's good therapy for me to be staying on the boat and my friend lives nearby.'

'Well, if you say so. I'd better get off, lots to do, now. I'll keep in touch.'

A while later Jeanne locked up the boat and drove off to La Tonnelle.

'Hi! Good to see you. And you look like you need a hug.' Nick greeted her at the door and took her in his arms. She breathed in his smell – a mixture of citrusy aftershave and freshly cut wood. It felt so good to be in his arms and they kissed before he led her into the sitting room.

'Red wine okay? Or would you prefer something else?'

'That's fine, thanks.'

After Nick had poured out two glasses he sat next to her on the sofa and, taking hold of her hand, said, 'Right, now tell me all about it.'

Jeanne repeated what she'd told Inspector Ferguson – what she'd remembered under hypnosis. She had been quite calm with the inspector earlier but for some reason she was finding it harder to tell Nick. It may have been the combined effect of the wine and his loving sympathy but she was almost in tears as she finished.

'You know, the biggest shock was that I got the strong impression those men in the boat were *deliberately* steering towards us – they *wanted* to crash into us – wanted to kill us!' As she clung onto his arm all her pain and anguish flooded through her body. She added, brokenly, 'So it wouldn't have been the drunken accident we'd supposed but...but...*murder!*

# chapter 29

Nick had wanted Jeanne to stay at his cottage that night but she had resisted, feeling she had to face her fears. The cottage possessed a couple of spare bedrooms so there was no pressure to share his bed. He had argued long and hard and only gave up when she reminded him that she could phone at any time and he was less than five minutes away by car.

'It's not as if I'm in any danger, Nick. Hardly anyone knows that my memory's returning and I still couldn't describe those men in the boat. I promise that if and when I can identify them I will make sure I'm somewhere safe. But for the moment that's not an issue. I have to learn to be less fearful!' she said firmly.

After a restless night on the boat Jeanne regretted her stubbornness. She had tossed and turned for hours and when she finally succumbed to sleep her dreams were vivid and disturbing. In the last one she was being chased by faceless monsters towards the edge of a cliff and just as she was about to fall over the edge she woke up, bathed in sweat.

The next few nights she slept a little better and by the end of the week her sleep was restful once more. During the day she divided her time between the boat and the library and made occasional trips to a beach to relax. She met Nick in the café a couple of times and they planned to go out for a meal on Saturday evening.

'Do you like Thai food? I'll book a table at Sawatdi if you do.'

'Yes. Haven't eaten Thai for ages. Certainly make a

change from French!'

'That's what I thought. I'll pick you up at eight and we'll have a drink somewhere first.'

It was hot and sticky on Saturday and Jeanne was finding the humidity in the boat uncomfortable. The sky was not the clear blue she was accustomed to and grey clouds were edging their way over the island. In the evening she changed into her coolest cotton dress, wanting to avoid the stuck-on clothes look. Not at all sexy, she smiled to herself.

'Hey, you look nice and fresh. And you smell delicious!' Nick said as he kissed her tenderly on the lips.

'Thank you, kind sir. But in this heat I'm not sure I'll stay cool and fresh for long,' she replied, savouring the touch of his lips on hers. He tasted of minty toothpaste and wore the citrus aftershave that suited him so well. She thought he looked very sexy in his loose-fitting linen shirt and trousers.

As they drove to Town he said, 'There's a storm forecast to hit us tomorrow. That's why it's so heavy today. It's expected to arrive late tomorrow evening so you'll need to batten down the hatches. Can you manage the awning on your own?'

Jeanne nodded. 'Yep, no problem. I'll make sure I get it fixed in good time. My poor garden will be glad of the rain so I'm pleased we're finally going to get some. As long as the sun shines again on Monday. Need to keep working on the tan!'

Nick glanced sideways at her and grinned. 'Looks pretty good to me now. Don't overdo it and go all wrinkly on me, will you?'

'No fear! I'm being sensible and using SPF 20 and avoiding the midday sun, unlike the proverbial mad dogs and Englishmen. Where are we going for a drink?'

'The new bar in the Pollet. Have you been there?'

'No, I haven't. Good, I'm slowly making my way round the bars and restaurants of the island. Another year or two and I'll have them all sussed!'

Nick parked the jeep on the Crown pier and they walked along the Esplanade and into North Plantation. He guided her into the lower entrance of the bistro and then up the stairs to an intimate bar with leather club chairs around the tables.

'This is nice! Guernsey's becoming very sophisticated these days,' she said as Nick pulled out a chair for her.

'Well, we 'ave to compete with them ol' crapauds, for sure,' he replied in an exaggerated local accent which set Jeanne off into giggles.

Changing back to his usual, urbane voice he asked her what she wanted to drink and went to the bar, returning with a glass of white wine for her and a lager for himself.

Jeanne relaxed into the chair, enjoying the air conditioned comfort of the room. For the first time that day she felt cool.

When they had finished their drinks they retraced their steps down to the North plantation and headed towards the restaurant.

They were greeted by a waitress dressed in traditional Thai costume and led to their table. It was warmer in here and Jeanne asked for iced water with her white wine and chose the milder dishes to avoid the lobster look.

As they started chatting Nick mentioned that the glass fibre hull of the new boat was about to arrive and Jeanne caught his sense of excitement.

'Your work sounds so interesting, Nick. I'd love to see round your workshop some time. I'm fascinated to see how you get so much into such a small space.'

'I'd be happy to give you a guided tour and will let you know when's a good time, perhaps after the hull has arrived. And how are things in the book world?'

'Great. I'm much more in tune with the food aspect of the book since I helped Colette with the recipes. It's made it more real. As soon as I'm back in my cottage with a fully functioning kitchen I plan to start cooking the Guernsey dishes.'

'And will I be invited round as a taster this time?' he asked, his head on one side.

'There's a slight possibility that I'll need a guinea pig. I'll let you know,' she teased. The thought of Nick sitting in her brand new kitchen while she served the food made her flush and she kept her head down to hide her face. She found herself imagining what might happen after the meal and was mentally climbing the stairs, arm in arm with Nick, when the waitress arrived with the food.

Jeanne enjoyed the unusual, delicate flavours of the food and the exotic setting. Towards the end of the meal she found the heat enervating and even outside the air still felt clammy, causing her hair to stick to her scalp. In the jeep she was so overcome with tiredness that she found it impossible to stifle her yawns.

Nick glanced at her and said, sympathetically, 'It's the heat, it drains everyone's energy. I hate to admit it, but I'm feeling tired as well. Perhaps we should both have an early night. I've got a lot of work to catch up on tomorrow. I was going to invite myself in for a coffee but...'

Her heart beat faster. *So he wants us to get closer! Great! If only I weren't so wiped out. But I can wait a bit longer...*

'Another time. Once the storm's passed and we're both full of energy again, I'd be happy to invite you round. Perhaps Monday night?'

'Great.'

'I'll look forward to it,' she said, with a lingering look.

Returning her look he said, softly, 'So shall I!'

Jeanne woke up late on Sunday and although she had slept

soundly, felt tired and drained. It had been so hot that she had stripped to her pants and thrown off all the coverings. Feeling in need of a decent shower she walked to the shower block and came back refreshed and energised. Any sun was completely hidden behind a mass of black clouds bruising the sky.

Too restless to stay cooped up in the boat she decided to check on the cottage, not having been there for a couple of days. After re-attaching the awning and checking that the moorings were securely fixed, she drove down to Perelle. It was strange entering the cottage with no-one else there and the quiet was almost unnerving after the cacophony of noise that usually accompanied her visits. Glad to find it cool inside she entered the kitchen and gasped. It was completely empty – the range and cupboards had been stripped out and the dresser and table moved temporarily into the dining room.

Thinking the space looked enormous, Jeanne wandered around. The doorway had been knocked through to the dining room and an old door matching the others was already in situ. The utility room – the old larder – was stacked with appliances waiting to be connected. A new oil fired range was to be delivered the following day in time for the kitchen fitters.

All the first fix wiring and plumbing was complete and by the end of the week she hoped to have a functioning kitchen. She checked the rest of the ground floor and was particularly pleased with the cloakroom. The suite was plumbed in and the walls tiled half-way round as she had designed. Both the wall and floor tiles were limestone, providing a touch of luxury. The soft Etruscan Red that Jeanne had chosen for the rest of the walls gave the room warmth, definitely more welcoming than that awful green her grandparents had used.

Upstairs also showed much improvement with the main

bathroom fitted and partly tiled while in the en suite only the shower was in place. A spacious walk-in model with a powerful jet system she couldn't wait to try out. Won't be long now, she hoped. Waiting to be fixed to the wall was a giant ladder radiator guaranteed to provide plenty of heat, wiping out the memory of the cold room it had been. At least to her.

Jeanne reckoned that at this rate the plumbing would be finished in just over a week and she would be a big step closer to moving back in. The bedrooms had only needed re-wiring and fitting with radiators and this was now finished. All that remained was decorating which she planned to do herself, one room at a time. She had chosen soft neutrals for the bedrooms and sitting room with a splash of warm terracotta in the dining room where she now made herself a cup of coffee in the temporary kitchen set up by the builders.

Going outside she made herself comfortable, sipping her coffee as she savoured the peace of the now lovely garden. Finishing her drink, she pottered; dead-heading and weeding until the heat became too much. She had just gone inside for a glass of water when her mobile rang.

'Hi, Jeanne. Please don't hang up on me. I need to talk to you. Will you give me a few minutes, please?'

'Oh, Marcus. All right, I'm listening,' Jeanne sighed. She was no longer angry and, strengthened by Nick's support decided to humour him. She knew how painful it was to love someone who didn't love you and felt Marcus deserved some sympathy.

'I'm sorry for the way I've been. I realise that you don't feel for me the way I feel for you. I guess I'll just have to accept that's not likely to change. But I hate us not being friends and would like us to meet for a drink.' He paused and Jeanne heard him take a deep breath. 'If we're to see each other as part of the group it would be easier for us both if we could be friendly. So, what do you say? Can we have a drink for old time's sake?'

He sounded so contrite and Jeanne had to agree that it would make sense to patch things up a bit.

'I suppose so. As long as you promise not to come onto me.'

'I promise. How about this evening?

'Oh, oh all right. When and where?'

'Let's say eight thirty. At The Doghouse in the Rohais?'

'Okay. I'll see you later.'

Jeanne was left feeling slightly unsure of herself. It was all right in theory agreeing to see Marcus face to face but she wasn't sure how it would go in practice. She certainly wouldn't have instigated such a meeting, but if it meant so much to him…Ah well, she mused, can't do any harm and I won't need to stay long.

After spending a further couple of hours at the cottage she returned, with reluctance, to the boat. The evening air was charged with electricity and she could hear the rumble of thunder in the distance. Not a great time to be going out, she thought, as she changed. It was clear the storm was well on the way and it promised to be a wet night.

She drove to Town and parked behind the bar. Walking towards the entrance she could hear what sounded like live music and was pleased that she might not have to make polite conversation after all. The music would provide the entertainment.

As she walked in she spotted Marcus at a small table nursing a pint. He looked up as she approached and jumped to his feet.

'Hi, Jeanne. I'm really glad you came. Wasn't sure if you would, to be honest. Thought you might've been fobbing me off,' he said, with a tentative smile.

'I always keep my word, Marcus. How are you?'

As Jeanne sat down she looked at him closely in the dim light of the bar and was shocked at what she saw. His hair was unwashed and unkempt and he did not appear to have shaved for days. He looked pale and tired. Surely this wasn't all down to her? Pushing down a twinge of guilt, she hoped not.

'I…I'm fine. Just a bit tired as I've been working long hours lately and can't sleep in this heat. Look, let me get you a drink.'

He went off and she looked turned around to watch the trio playing in the corner. She liked the music though it seemed a tad loud for the small space. From the enthusiastic applause she gathered they were a regular fixture.

Marcus came back with a glass of white wine for her and another beer for himself. She took an appreciative sip.

'Thanks. So, you've been working hard? You do look pretty tired.'

Marcus ran his fingers through his hair making it even messier.

'Yep. There's been a bit of a panic on lately. But things should get back to normal soon. What about you? You're looking great. Positively glowing! Things going well?' he asked, gazing at her with bloodshot eyes.

'Apart from the upset over the baby's body, everything's been fine, thanks. I've been busy writing the book,' Jeanne replied, feeling uncomfortable under his gaze. She didn't want him to know about Nick, worried that it might provoke him. She had a feeling he'd been drinking heavily even though his speech wasn't slurred.

Marcus nodded. 'I saw the report of the inquest in the paper. And I heard that you'd had a funeral. I'm sorry I made fun of what had happened. It was uncalled for. And I'm glad that you're doing well with the book. Have you had your money yet?'

'No, but it's on the way.'

There was a lull in the conversation as he stared into his beer and Jeanne was relieved when the band struck up another song. Marcus remained lost in thought so she just focussed on the music. The lead singer, a diminutive blonde in jeans and a skimpy top, had a powerful voice. Jeanne found herself tapping her foot to the catchy beat and for a while forgot where she was.

'Hello, Marcus. Fancy seeing you here,' said a familiar voice and Jeanne turned round to find herself being stared at by Dan.

'I see you've got your friend with you. Hello, Jeanne. How's the building work going?' he said, his face expressionless.

'Fine, thanks. I hope to move back in soon.'

Jeanne noticed Marcus looking at his brother with an odd expression on his face: a mix of fear and awe. She was taken aback. Marcus was usually so confident, almost too much so. In his brother's presence he became somehow diminished.

'Let me get you both a drink. Same again?' Dan said, pointing at their nearly empty glasses.

They nodded and he disappeared to the bar.

Marcus looked apologetic. 'Sorry about Dan. As I told you, we don't really get on but it wouldn't look good to snub him.'

'It's okay. Not your fault. Perhaps he won't stay long,' she said hopefully.

Dan returned with their drinks and Jeanne's wish was granted as only a few minutes later he took his leave of them, muttering that he had someone to meet.

Jeanne let out a sigh of relief and Marcus seemed to perk up, becoming more chatty.

'You never really told me much about your weekend in London. What did you end up doing?'

She felt on safer ground and was quite happy to describe

both her meeting with the agent and the good time she'd had with Freya. Time passed quickly and it was with a shock that she saw it was nearly ten o'clock.

'I'd better get going as I don't want to be late tonight with the storm about to break. Thanks for the drink. I guess we can still be friends,' she said, smiling.

He stood up and kissed her lightly on the cheek before saying, 'Thanks again for coming, Jeanne. I appreciate it. I expect we'll see each other around. Take care.'

She went back to her car relieved to find that so far the rain had held off. Twenty minutes later she was back at the marina and as she was preparing to board *La Belle Élise* the first drops of rain fell. Flashes of forked lightning lit up the horizon and the rumble of thunder was getting closer. She had taken her torch which was just as well as it was pitch black and judging by the lack of lights on the neighbouring boats everyone else was either already in bed or out. Since her arrival she had hardly seen anyone on the other boats and for the first time she wished for company.

By the time the cabin was unlocked she felt desperately tired, even worse than the previous night. It must be this heat, she thought drowsily. And perhaps the wine. She almost fell into the bunk and was immediately asleep.

Several hours later Jeanne stirred after waking from a bad dream, feeling afraid with her heart racing. In the dream she was in a sinking boat which had been hit by another, and she was drowning. Reaching groggily for the light switch she cried out. Something was wrong, the boat was listing and she could hear water sloshing about. As she swung her legs over the edge of the bunk her head swam and she felt dizzy. Putting her feet down gingerly she found herself standing in water.

'Oh my God!' she cried. 'The boat's sinking!' She struggled to keep her footing as waves of nausea overwhelmed her as she grabbed her clothes and the torch before stumbling towards the door. The water was a few inches deep and the boat was rocking from side to side but she finally made it and after a struggle managed to pull it open. She crawled up the steps and into the cockpit.

Here it was dry but she could hear the rain lashing down on the awning and through the clear plastic window caught flashes of lightning overhead. Gingerly she lifted up part of the awning and screamed. The boat was no longer moored safely on the pontoon but was drifting, battered by the wind and rain, towards the rocky harbour entrance and the open sea.

# chapter 30

Panic began to engulf Jeanne as she fought to clear her head while dizziness and nausea kept sweeping over her. Nick, she must ring Nick! She stumbled back down into the cabin to find her phone. It was a while before she could remember where it was. The previous evening was a blur and she struggled to think what she had done on returning to the boat.

Handbag! She rummaged around on the bunk and found it under the bedclothes and dialled Nick's number. It rang and rang and Jeanne was just about to give up in despair when his groggy voice answered.

'Izzat you, Jeanne? Whassa matter?'

'Oh, Nick! Thank goodness. The boat's adrift – it's going out to sea – and – and she's sinking! There – there's water in the cabin!' She was now crying with terror.

Nick came to as if he'd been slapped. 'Okay. Hold on, I'm on my way and I'll get help. Wait in the cockpit.' He cut off the call and Jeanne was left shaking but hopeful. Nick wouldn't let her drown. As she looked around the cabin she saw her laptop and files. She couldn't lose them! Disobeying Nick's command to stay in the cockpit she began to slowly transfer the computer and the files up the steps and into the relative safety of the cockpit. It was slow and difficult because the boat kept shifting and she was still dizzy, finding it hard to carry anything and remain upright at the same time.

She was crawling up the steps with a box file when she heard a shout – 'Ahoy there! Jeanne – can you hear me?'

She scrambled into the cockpit and opened the awning. Two men in a dinghy were heading towards her and she could just make out one was Nick.

'Yes, I...I can hear you. Wh...what do you want me to do?'

'Just stay there for the moment. We're going to attach a rope for a tow. You're quite safe, she's not that low in the water. Just hang on!' Nick shouted.

She thought she might as well bring up the other files while she waited. There was no way she would leave them on the boat once she was rescued. The men's voices mingled with the sound of the rain as they made fast the rope.

'Okay, Jeanne. We're going to start towing now. Won't be long. Better if you sit down.'

She sat on the bench seat and felt the boat lurch as the dinghy started to pull away. It must have a powerful outboard, Jeanne thought, as it took the strain. *Le Belle Élise* was only metres away from the nearest pontoon and slowly the boats inched back towards safety.

There was a bump and the boat rocked for a moment and then steadied. The awning was thrown back and Nick jumped down into the cockpit. Jeanne staggered into his arms and burst into tears.

'Hey, it's all right. You're safe, darling, you're safe. Hush, now, hush,' he said gently as he held her tight. Jeanne felt his fingers brush the hair back off her tear streaked face before  guiding her to the side of the boat and then onto the pontoon. The other man reached out to give her a hand and threw a waterproof cape around her shoulders.

'All right, miss? You've had a nasty experience, you have. We'll soon have you in the warm and dry.'

Jeanne nodded numbly, still in shock. She saw Nick's head appear in the cockpit and called out to him, 'Nick, my laptop and files. Please don't leave them!'

'Don't worry. I'll make sure everything's safe. I've just

got to stop the water coming in and might be a while. Mike, could you please take Jeanne up to the office? And if you've got any brandy or something, for the shock?'

'No problem. Come on, miss, let's get you out of this rain. Nick knows what he's doing, he'll be along directly.'

As Mike guided her steadily along the pontoon Jeanne saw lights on in a couple of boats and voices called out to ask what was going on.

'It's all right, folks. A boat lost its moorings but it's safe now. You can go back to sleep,' Mike answered and within moments all was darkness again. The rain ricocheted off the boats with a sharp staccato and lightning lit up the sky overhead. She was glad of the hooded cape as she stumbled up the office steps.

Mike unlocked the door and helped her into a chair. He then disappeared into another room and came back with a tumbler containing what must have been at least a double measure of brandy.

'Here, miss. This'll make you feel better,' he proffered the glass, shifting from one foot to another.

'Th…thanks,' Jeanne murmured and took a cautious sip. The fiery liquid caught the back of her throat and she gasped. The brandy's fire spread through her body and began to settle her groaning stomach.

'Will you be all right now? I'd best see if Nick needs a hand.'

'Of course. I can manage.'

He quickly left the office and she sat huddled in a chair taking small sips of brandy. She groaned. What a night! And how on earth did the boat become adrift and start taking in water? The questions swirled around her befuddled brain. Nothing made sense to her. And she couldn't understand why she felt so dizzy and sick. Her head was like cotton wool and when she tried to remember what had happened the previous day everything was a blur.

Sometime later, as she was on the verge of losing consciousness, the sound of heavy footsteps outside startled her awake and for a moment she thought that danger was still stalking her. Her heart was hammering in her chest when, to her great relief, Mike entered, followed closely by Nick. They were carrying her boxes of files and Nick also had her laptop. After putting everything down Nick went over to her and she stood up shakily as he threw his arms around her.

'Well, you sure gave me a fright, young lady. I've never been so scared in my life as when you phoned to say the boat was sinking! But you're safe now,' he said, stroking her hair.

'But what happened? How did the boat come loose? And why all the water?'

'The sea cock had given way, I don't know why. And the valve in the heads was set to the pump position. I've managed to fix it temporarily so at least no more water can come in. As for the moorings – they couldn't have come loose on their own,' Nick's jaw tightened as he added, 'We'll talk about it later. You need to get to bed, you look all in. And you should see a doctor. I'm taking you home, okay?'

She nodded, too horrified by the implication of what he'd just said to say anything herself. If Nick was right, then it meant someone had just tried to kill her!

# chapter 31

It was midday before Jeanne opened her eyes and again felt that disorientation of not knowing where she was. Realisation dawned that this was Nick's bedroom and she was in his bed. She vaguely remembered asking him if she could sleep with him as she didn't want to be alone. He had been happy to oblige, even managing a joke about neither of them being in a fit state for seduction and they were both quite safe.

Nick had called a doctor and he had carefully examined Jeanne while she told him about the dizziness and nausea. He had taken a blood sample before leaving, telling her to rest, before going out of the room to talk to Nick.

As the memories began to surface Jeanne could feel her heart racing at the thought that she had been close to dying at sea for the second time in her life. She was beginning to feel scared at being on her own when the door opened and Nick came in bearing a tray with orange juice, coffee and toast.

His eyes lit up when he saw that she was conscious.

'Hi, glad you're awake. Hadn't wanted to disturb you before but I'm afraid you're going to have a visitor in an hour or so. How are you feeling?'

'A bit groggy still and I'm so thirsty, I could drink gallons. Who's the unwanted visitor?' she asked, drowsily.

'Your old friend Inspector Ferguson. He wants to talk to you about last night. But if you're not up to it I can put him off a bit longer.'

'No, it's all right. Though I think I'd better be out of your bed and dressed!' she managed a faint smile.

'When you've had your breakfast would you manage a

shower? Might make you feel better.'

'I'd love one, if I can stand up without feeling dizzy. Mm, this coffee's good. A snazzy machine special is it?'

He grinned and said, 'Of course! No instant rubbish in this house. I'll leave you to eat in peace. I've got a couple of calls to make and I'll be back in a jiffy.'

'Shouldn't you be at work?' she asked, puzzled.

'I should be, but as the boss I took a unilateral decision to stay home and take care of my, er, guest. I'm running things from here today, hence the phone calls.'

Jeanne sat up nibbling the toast and drinking her coffee and began to feel a little better – at least physically. Her stomach seemed happy to be fed and watered and when she had finished she pushed the tray to one side and slowly swung her legs over the edge of the bed. Taking a deep breath she put her weight on her feet and levered herself upright.

'Hey! You were supposed to wait for me,' Nick said as he came in and strode quickly to her side.

She glanced up at him and said, 'I'm all right. I'd like to try and walk on my own.' She carefully took a few steps away from the bed and although she felt a bit unsteady, she took a few more before returning and sitting on the edge of the bed.

'See? That was okay, wasn't it? I think I could manage a shower now.'

'It's just through here,' he said, pointing to a door. As he led the way Jeanne had a thought.

'What's happened to all my things on the boat?'

'I brought back your files and laptop last night, or rather early this morning. And I grabbed some of your clothes which are downstairs. The rest are still on board but perfectly safe. I'll bring up your clothes while you're having your shower. But don't you think you should stay in bed? The doctor did tell me you needed to rest for as long as

261

possible.'

'I'd rather get up but I don't think I'll be fit for much. Could you please show me how this amazing looking shower works?'

Nick went through the settings with her, setting out fresh towels before leaving her alone.

The shower was as powerful as it looked and Jeanne allowed the jets to play over her body, easing the tension from her aching muscles. She had caught sight of herself in the bathroom mirror and was horrified to see her hair, normally her pride and glory, looking like a bunch of rats' tails and she washed it back into shape.

After wrapping herself in a giant fluffy towel she stepped back into the bedroom. Her clothes were laid out on the bed and for a moment she felt embarrassed at the thought of Nick collecting up her bras and knickers with her other clothes. On reflection, she couldn't remember how she had got out of her wet clothes and into Nick's pyjama top the previous night. Oh well, she thought, it's too late to worry about that now. She noticed that he had also left her a hairdryer – he was obviously well versed in the needs of women.

She had finished dressing and was about to dry her hair when Nick knocked on the door. She called him in and he just popped his head around the door.

'Are you feeling all right? Didn't like to leave you for too long.'

'Fine, thanks. Is the inspector here?'

'No, he's due in about ten minutes. Just take your time, he can wait. We'll be in the kitchen when you're ready.'

'Okay.'

Fifteen minutes later her hair was dry and combed into shape and Jeanne was ready to go downstairs to re-live a night she would rather forget.

She found the inspector and another policeman sitting at the kitchen table with Nick, drinking coffee.

They stood up as she entered and Nick quickly pulled out a chair for her.

The inspector looked sombre as he introduced his sergeant to Jeanne and then continued.

'Jeanne, I'm sorry to bother you when you should be resting but, as you've probably realised, it was no accident that happened last night. Looks like someone tried to kill you and we've got to find them quickly in case they try again.'

She gasped. 'You think someone could try again? I don't understand, who wants to kill me?'

'The same folk as killed your parents, most like. This latest incident proves to me that your parents' deaths were no accident but deliberate, just as you were beginning to suspect yourself. They need to stop you remembering enough to identify them. I'm afraid there's no nice way of saying this, but if someone's already killed two people they're not likely to worry about killing a third,' he said, watching her carefully.

Nick was sitting next to Jeanne and he reached out and held her hand as she struggled to come to terms with the inspector's words.

'So, you're absolutely sure that someone planned to…to kill me last night?' she said eventually.

'Yes, we're sure about that. The blood test confirmed the doctor's suspicions. You'd been drugged and were not meant to wake up till it was too late.'

'Drugged! So that's why I felt so awful. But how, when?'

'That's what I need you to tell me. Where were you yesterday and who did you see?'

Jeanne's head was still not completely clear and she had to think hard for a moment.

'I went to the cottage for a few hours and was on my

own the whole time. Then I went back to the boat and later I changed to go out. Oh! Now I remember! Marcus had phoned me and asked me to meet him...'

Nick cut in sharply, 'Marcus? You didn't tell me. I thought you two had fallen out?'

'We did. But he said he wanted to apologise and wanted us to be friends. I didn't want to see him but wanted to keep the peace for the sake of the group. I didn't think it would hurt to have a drink with him,' she said, upset. She didn't want Nick to get the wrong idea about her seeing Marcus.

Nick squeezed her hand and said, more gently, 'I understand, don't worry.'

The inspector had been watching them, drumming his fingers on the table.

'Please, Jeanne. Tell me who this Marcus character is and what happened.'

She turned to face him and continued.

'His name's Marcus Davidson. I knew him at school and met him again soon after I came back in the spring. We went out together a few times and then we fell out. Anyway, I met him at The Doghouse on Sunday evening about eight thirty and had a drink with him. He looked awful – he's usually very smart – said he'd been working late and not sleeping. Then his brother turned up and bought us another drink. He left soon after and I left about ten and returned to the boat.'

'Marcus's brother, is he Dan Davidson, the antiques dealer?' the inspector asked as he and his sergeant exchanged glances.

'Yes, I'd met him before, at my cottage. He bought my old furniture from me. He...he gave me the creeps. I think he's on drugs. Oh! drugs!' Jeanne's hands flew to her face.

Nick looked horrified. 'I didn't know you knew Dan. He's bad news, isn't he, Inspector?'

The inspector nodded. 'He's not someone to get on the

wrong side of, that's for sure.   Been trying to nail him for years but…Can you excuse us for a minute?' He beckoned to his sergeant and they went outside for a few moments and the inspector came back alone.

Jeanne looked from Nick to the inspector and cried, 'I can't believe that Marcus would try to kill me! He…he said he loved me! And I'm sure he meant it. Perhaps he didn't know anything about it – it was all Dan's doing.'

'Well, maybe he did, maybe he didn't. But at the very least he's played a part in what happened, I'm sure of that. We'll need to talk to him as well as his brother.' He coughed. 'Getting back to what you told me about your parents' deaths. There were two fair haired men in that other boat, you thought. Could they have been the Davidsons?'

'I…I don't know. Their faces were a blur, as I said. They did seem young, which they would have been back then. But I knew Marcus at school! I would have recognised him.' She was feeling queasy at the dreadful thought.

'That's true. You would have recognised him if you'd not bumped your head and suffered the amnesia. They would have known that. Has Marcus ever said anything to you about the accident?'

Jeanne had to think, which was difficult with all the conflicting emotions threatening to engulf her.

'Mm, yes. A few times, actually. He specifically mentioned the amnesia quite early on.' The nausea was getting worse.

'And did he know you were using hypnosis to recover your memory?'

'No, I don't…Oh, no! I blurted it out when he phoned recently. Oh my God!' she covered her face with her hands and cried.

Nick put his arm around her shoulders and looked inquiringly at the inspector.

'We're bringing them in for questioning, sir. We'll need to examine the boat, see if we can find any trace of whoever tampered with it.'

As the inspector got up to leave, Jeanne lifted her wet face and whispered, 'What I don't understand is why they would have wanted to kill my parents. What possible reason could there have been? And why didn't they kill me then as well?'

'I can only guess why they killed your parents. But I suspect that it's because they may have seen something they shouldn't have. That may come out later. As to why they didn't kill you, I'm not sure they knew you were on the boat as well. Or the other possibility is that they had to make a run for it. They might have seen the boat coming out of the harbour, the one that found you a bit later. These questions and a load of others are still to be answered. And there's always a chance these men are innocent. But the evidence is building up.'

Jeanne walked unsteadily with Nick to show the inspector to the front door and dimly noticed the sergeant sitting in the police car, talking rapidly on the phone. As he saw the inspector he got out and said something in his ear. Inspector Ferguson then turned to Nick and said something which Jeanne did not hear but caused a look of alarm to flash across his face. Oh no! What's wrong now?

Nick returned and put his arm round her as he led her gently back inside.

'They've got Marcus in custody but haven't been able to find Dan yet. The inspector assures me that it's only a matter of time before he's caught even though he's probably left Guernsey but, to be on the safe side it's better if you stay indoors. And not alone.'

Jeanne paled, releasing a soft moan. Please God, don't let him be on the island!

# chapter 32

The next few hours passed in a blur. Jeanne slept sporadically and Nick appeared with drinks and food when she woke up. Late that afternoon Molly arrived.

Nick showed her into the bedroom, telling Jeanne he would be downstairs if she needed anything.

Molly sat on the bed, reaching out to give her a hug.

'Oh, my dear. What an awful experience. How are you feeling now?' Concern was etched into her face.

Jeanne grimaced. 'So-so. It's all been a bit of a nightmare, really. It was bad enough thinking it was a horrible accident, but when I realised that someone had tried to kill me...and Marcus may have helped them!' She shuddered and Molly held her tight.

'Yes, what a shock that was! And all those years we thought your parents' deaths were an accident and now to find they'd been murdered! It's hard to take in. These things just don't happen in Guernsey. And Peter is, as you can imagine, devastated. He can't believe that Marcus could be involved in such a terrible crime. I think he feels responsible.'

'Oh no, he mustn't feel that. Whatever Marcus has or hasn't done, Peter couldn't have changed it. It's that Dan who's been a bad influence on Marcus, I'm sure.' She sighed, twisting her hair. 'It just makes me ask who can I trust? If I misjudged Marcus I could misjudge anyone.'

'It's natural to feel wary of people at the moment but I'm sure you'll be able to get things in perspective soon. And Nick has been wonderful, a real life-saver.'

'Yes, he has hasn't he? But he's feeling bad about suggesting I stay on the boat and blames himself for putting me in danger. But I guess none of us are thinking straight at the moment.'

'Probably not. And you're still under the influence of the drugs. Has the doctor been round again?'

'Yes, he was here a little while ago. Apparently I should be clear by morning and able to get back to normal, whatever normal is!'

'Normal is being with people you love and who love you. And knowing that soon you'll be back in your lovely home, finishing your bestseller. You're surrounded by normal,' Molly smiled.

Jeanne looked at Molly and grinned.

'Thanks. Perhaps one day I'll be wise like you.'

'When you're old and grey, you mean. We don't seem to be very wise while we're still young. By the way, I popped into the cottage before coming here, just to see that all was well. The kitchen fitters arrived today and, although it looked like they'd taken over the whole house, things were taking shape. I told Martin you weren't well and he said to tell you not to worry, everything's on schedule.'

'That's good. I can't wait to move back in. Not that Nick's not looking after me, it's just that...' she lowered her eyes, twisting her hair into a tangle.

'Does this mean you two are a proper couple now?'

She looked up and felt the flush on her cheeks.

'I guess so. Though nothing's actually happened yet, which is why it could be awkward being here for long.'

'Nonsense! Just let things take their course. I know you don't want to rush things, Jeanne, but don't be too slow either. From what I've seen, you two are made for each other. And if I were in your shoes I'd make sure he didn't get away!' Molly's eyes twinkled.

Jeanne laughed. 'Honestly, Molly, you're incorrigible! I wonder if Peter knows what sort of woman he's married to!'

'Oh, he knows all right. That's why we're still together – we know how to keep each other happy. Now, I've probably tired you out and Nick will be cross. So I'd better love you and leave you. I'll ring tomorrow and see how you are – oh, and Peter sends his love.'

Molly kissed her as she left.

She was right, I do feel tired, Jeanne thought as she snuggled under the duvet. Then remembered what Molly had said about not letting Nick get away. A smile spread across her face as she thought he might find it difficult, seeing as how he was trapped with her in his bed.

It was a very different Jeanne who woke up on Tuesday. All the sluggishness and nausea had gone and she felt alert and surprisingly strong. It wasn't just that the drugs were no longer in her system – she was in love. And it seemed that Nick was in love with her. As she stretched out in the bed a lovely, warm glow spread through her body and her face wore the satisfied look of the cat who had licked the cream.

Nick was downstairs preparing breakfast and she allowed herself the luxury of reliving the events of the previous night.

During the early evening she had dozed but later on had felt more alert and Nick had brought up a portable stereo and some CDs for her to sort through. She chose an album of love songs.

'I like your taste, Nick. Do you spend much time listening to music?'

'Yep. I find it helps me unwind after a busy day. Now, do you want to be left on your own? Or would you like some company?'

His look was so warm and tender and what with the gravelly voice on the CD crooning 'Tonight's the Night', she found herself melting.

'I…I'd like some company, please.'

'Good, haven't had much chance to be with you today, at least not while you've been awake,' he said as he settled himself on the bed next to her. She was propped up on pillows and he put his arm around her shoulders.

'Feeling better?' he asked, studying her face, which she knew was still pale.

'Much better, thanks. I don't think I've actually thanked you for saving my life, have I? Will a kiss be sufficient reward?' She moved her face closer to his.

'It might. Shall we see?'

He used his free hand to stroke her hair back off her face and then bent his head so that his lips pressed on hers. She opened her mouth to accept his gently probing tongue. Desire shot through her and she put her arms around his neck. Gently Nick pushed her back, easing her body down in the bed before sliding down to lay beside her. Their eager hands explored each other's bodies and Jeanne helped him to ease off his jeans and T-shirt. Expertly he stripped off her top and panties before removing his boxers.

Lying entwined she admired his naked body. It was hard and muscled next to her soft curves and for a moment she felt vulnerable and afraid. His strong, capable hands cupped her breasts as he softly kissed them. She moaned with mounting excitement.

'Oh, please, make love to me – now!' she cried out as his fingers moved down to stroke her belly and inner thighs.

'With the greatest of pleasure,' he murmured.

As she clung to him he made love to her passionately but tenderly for what seemed like hours. They finally fell apart sated and exhausted and went to sleep curled up in each other's arms.

The delicious memory of their love-making was still being replayed in Jeanne's mind when Nick pushed open the bedroom door and walked in with a loaded tray. He was wearing a bath robe and a big grin.

'Good morning, darling. Ready for breakfast?' he said as he put the tray on the bed. Set for two and with a single rose in a glass vase.

'Oh, Nick. You're just an old romantic at heart aren't you?'

'Hey! Not so much of the old! I will admit to being a bit of a romantic, but only in exceptional circumstances,' he said as he leant over and kissed her.

'This is nice. Breakfast before or after?' she asked slyly.

'Brazen hussy! I think breakfast first or I won't have any strength to meet your insatiable demands.'

An hour later they were both showered and dressed and in the kitchen when she asked if he was going in to work.

'I can't leave you here on your own.'

Jeanne frowned. 'Does that mean that the police still haven't caught Dan?'

'Afraid not. But they don't think he's here. In his shoes I would've gone by now, probably to France by boat. But I'd never forgive myself if anything happened to you so I don't want to take any unnecessary risks.' He reached out and held her for a moment.

'Okay, I don't want to take any chances either. I'll just have to hope that Dan's picked up soon. But why don't I come with you to the workshop? I'd love to see it and I can sit in a corner, quietly reading, while you work. I won't be in the way, promise,' she smiled innocently.

Nick looked at her thoughtfully.

'I'm not sure about you not being in the way, you'll certainly be a distraction. But I don't seem to have much choice, do I? Just don't give me any of those 'come to bed' looks,' he said, giving her a quick kiss.

'Aye, aye sir! Shall we go?'

It only took a few minutes to drive to The Bridge and Nick's workshop on North Side. Jeanne tried not to feel nervous but the thought that Dan might still be around was scary – very scary. She was relieved when they arrived safely and Nick walked with her inside.

It was noisier than she'd imagined. Four men were working at benches and the sound of sawing and hammering was played out against a background of Island FM. Four faces looked up and grinned at Nick as he went over to them for what looked like an animated discussion.

Jeanne gazed around at the stacks of handsome hardwoods waiting to be transformed into flooring, galley kitchens and storage cupboards. Rolls of expensive looking cloth and leather for upholstery and boxes of brass fittings were piled alongside. Nearby were partly finished wooden skeletons which she guessed would ultimately be beautifully upholstered seating on some lucky owner's boat. In spite of her own pretty disastrous relationship with boats she could admire the craftsmanship. Nick joined her.

'So, what do you think?' he asked.

'I'm impressed. The men must be very skilled and from what I can see, the finished products will be quite something. You must be proud of what you do here.'

'Yes, I suppose I am. My father built up a damned good business and a couple of the lads here worked for him for years. So I've been very lucky. Let me introduce you to the talented workforce!'

Taking her arm he went over to the workbenches. The men, varying in age from their twenties to sixties, nodded shyly at Jeanne as they were introduced and, as she was turning away she glimpsed the youngest one making a thumbs up sign to Nick, which he acknowledged with a grin.

He took her outside to show her the boats waiting to be fitted and explained that the new hull was arriving the following day. He frowned.

'I shall have to be here when it's delivered so either you'll have to come with me or we'll find another solution. Now, do you mind sitting quietly with your book in my office while I do some work?'

They exchanged lingering glances and as Jeanne collected her book from the jeep Nick gave her a playful slap on the bottom. She grinned and wiggled her hips provocatively as she walked back to the office. Sitting down to read she couldn't help smiling to herself.  All that fantastic sex had gone to her head and she couldn't wait for tonight.


They left the workshop about six and as they turned into the drive of La Tonnelle, Nick swore softly. 'Shit! I think we were followed. Stay here a moment.'

He got out of the jeep and quickly unlocked the front door, beckoning Jeanne to come in. She ran into the cottage and he said, after shutting the door, 'Wait here and don't open the door to anyone, okay? I'm going to see who's in that car parked down the road. I'll go out the back and come up behind them.'

'Nick, please be careful! Perhaps you should call the police,' Jeanne's stomach clenched with anxiety.

'It's okay. Won't be long, promise.'

He went out of the back door and all Jeanne could do was wait.


Although it seemed like forever, it was in fact only minutes later when she heard the key in the door and the sound of voices.

She went warily into the hall and saw Nick ushering in the sergeant she'd met the previous day.

Nick was looking relieved.

'I didn't know it, but Inspector Ferguson has been

keeping watch on us since yesterday, so we're quite safe.'

Jeanne let out a long sigh. Her vivid imagination had conjured up all kinds of scenarios, none of them pleasant.

'Would you like a cup of tea, sergeant?'

'No thanks, miss. I go off duty soon, but don't worry, there's another officer taking over from me.'

'Has there been any news about Dan Davidson?' she asked, twisting her hair.

The sergeant shook his head. 'Not that I've heard, miss. But the British police and Interpol are on full alert. It can't be long now before he's apprehended. And his brother's made a statement and is co-operating fully with us.'

'Does that mean he's confessed?' Nick chipped in.

'Not exactly, sir. He claims he didn't know what his brother planned to do. But he has, er, admitted being on the boat that killed Miss Le Page's parents.'

Jeanne gasped and Nick gripped her hand.

'Well, must be off. Good evening to you both,' the sergeant said as he headed for the front door.

'Are you all right?' Nick asked gently, wrapping his arms around Jeanne, who stood like a frozen statue.

She buried her head in his chest and her voice was muffled as she answered.

'Now Marcus has admitted being on that speedboat then I should soon learn, after waiting fifteen years, why my parents were killed. Why they were so horribly murdered.'

# chapter 33

Early on Wednesday morning Nick and Jeanne were rushing to get ready. There would be no lazy lie-in with breakfast in bed today. He had to be at the yard for the delivery of the boat and Jeanne was going with him. She was secretly looking forward to being part of the excitement. There was no way she could focus on her writing at that time, feeling her life was on hold until Dan was safely in custody.

An air of anticipation hung over the workshop and the men smiled broadly as Nick and Jeanne arrived. She settled herself in the office with her book while the men continued their work and Nick made some phone calls.

When the huge transporter pulled into the yard everyone dashed outside to help. After many shouted directions from Nick and the lads and much manoeuvring on the part of the driver, the trailer was finally in position ready for the hull to be winched off. It was fascinating to watch and Jeanne cheered with the others when it was at last on its blocks, waiting to be transformed into a luxurious gin palace by the assembled craftsmen.

Her heart swelled with pride and love as she watched Nick organise his team. He was modest about his business but she guessed he must have worked very hard in order to compete with the big boys in the boating world.

As she joined the others returning inside, her mobile rang. It was Inspector Ferguson.

'Morning, Jeanne. How are you feeling now?'

'Much better, thanks, Inspector. Are you phoning to tell me you've got Dan?' her breathing quickened as she hung on his reply.

'No, sorry, I'm not. But I'm sure it won't be long now. I'm actually ringing about Marcus. He'd like to talk to you, if you'd agree to see him.'

She gasped. 'Oh, no!'

'Don't worry, there'd be someone with you at all times and anyway I'm convinced he doesn't want to harm you. What do you think?'

'I don't know. It depends what he's got to say. I don't want to listen to a load of self-pitying excuses, that's for sure!' she exclaimed.

'It seems he wants to tell you what happened fifteen years ago. He's admitted he was on the speedboat but hasn't given us any more details, saying he said he wanted you to be there, to hear it from him and not some third party. It's an unusual request and normally it wouldn't be considered, but these are extraordinary circumstances. If you could bear it, then it would be the way for us all to learn what really happened.'

This was what she had waited for. This was what had haunted her dreams for so long. But could she sit facing Marcus while he told her what she was also afraid to hear? Her mind raced with these thoughts until, with a sigh, she realised that there was only one possible answer.

'All right, I'll come.'

She heard him let out a long breath.

'Good, you're being very brave, Jeanne. I'll ask your, er, shadow, to bring you to the station in an hour, if that's convenient?'

Switching off the phone she looked up to see Nick watching her and with a heavy heart told him about the coming meeting.

Although Nick was concerned about her facing Marcus, he agreed it was the best way for Jeanne to find out the truth and finally lay the ghosts. The policeman arrived at the agreed time and they drove in silence to the station.

'Jeanne. Thanks for coming. Shall we go straight in?' Inspector Ferguson shook her hand warmly and then, with his hand on her arm, guided her down a corridor to an interview room. Before they went in he turned to Jeanne, saying, 'You might be shocked at the way Marcus looks. He's hardly slept since he's been here and hasn't eaten much either. I'm having him checked by a doctor once we've finished. It's possible he's on the verge of a mental collapse. But he's quite lucid and not at all violent,' he added reassuringly.

'Hello, Marcus. I was told you wanted to see me,' Jeanne said, taking in the unkempt figure hunched over the table in front of her.

At the sound of her voice he looked up and she had to stifle a gasp at the sight of his bloodshot eyes framed by dark shadows.

'Jeanne! I wasn't sure you'd come, even though they told me you would.' He paused, staring at her. 'I suppose it's a daft question in the circumstances, but how are you?' He looked so concerned and so defeated, so unlike the cheerful, generous man she had known that Jeanne almost felt sorry for him. Then she remembered why she was there.

'I'm all right, considering what I've just gone through! But I don't want to talk about me. I want to know what happened to my parents!'

He winced at the hardness of her voice. Looking her in the eye he said, 'I owe it to you to tell you the truth, even though you'll probably hate me even more once you know.'

The inspector cut in to say that from now on what Marcus said would be recorded and transcribed as a statement for him to sign. Marcus nodded his agreement and the machine was switched on.

Marcus began.

'Dan and I had gone over to Herm that Sunday to pick up a supply of drugs that had been dropped off earlier. I wasn't directly involved in the deal – I didn't take drugs myself and was still at school, remember – but Dan...persuaded me to go with him as cover. He thought it would look less suspicious if he was with a schoolboy,' Marcus gave a hollow laugh.

'He knew the police were keeping an eye on him in Guernsey so he used Herm as the pick-up point. The drugs were brought over from France. So we went over that evening and moored some way up from Rosaire Steps. The drugs were in a sealed waterproof container attached to a marker and all we had to do was haul it in.' He paused to drink from the glass of water in front of him.

Jeanne sat immobile, but her mind was racing as she remembered the time Marcus had seemed on edge when she mentioned staying in Guernsey – when she told him about the flashbacks – having hypnosis. It all made horrible sense.

'Normally we'd have waited till it was dark but the tides were wrong that night and anyway the light was already. So we thought we'd be safe.'

His bloodshot eyes fixed on Jeanne as he continued.

'Just as we were pulling up the container Dan noticed a couple walking along the cliff path towards the harbour. They must have noticed us and stopped. I suggested to Dan that we leave it but he was determined not to and said they probably wouldn't realise what was going on. So we hauled it up. Then we noticed that the man had a pair of binoculars and he was training them on us and the container. We both panicked and Dan completely flipped. If we'd stayed calm, acted as if there wasn't a problem, maybe things would have been different.'

He groaned and ran his hands through his now very dirty, fair hair.

'I tried to calm him down but it was no use. He was high on drugs and booze and just kept waving his arms about and shouting. The man on the cliff must have sussed that we were doing something illegal and grabbed the woman's arm and they started running along the path. It took me ages to get Dan to calm down even a bit and then he started up the engine and headed towards the harbour. We saw them get into a small cabin cruiser. It looked like they were going to head off to Guernsey and we waited, just out of sight.'

He took another sip of water.

'I swear to you Jeanne, I didn't know what Dan was planning to do. I thought we'd make a run for it after they'd got out of sight. We could have dumped the drugs and there'd have been no proof of anything illegal. But Dan was...not thinking straight. Neither of us recognised your parents and we didn't know you were on board until...until later.'

Jeanne's heart was pounding as her memory of that fatal boat ride from Herm was stirred. She remembered that initially she'd been in the cabin. They'd had a picnic on the beach and she was putting things away in the storage area while her parents had gone off for a quick walk.

Marcus's voice cut across her thoughts.

'Dan gave the other boat a good start and then went after them. When I realised he was chasing them rather than staying clear, I asked what the hell he was doing. He didn't answer, just increased the revs and narrowed the gap. As we got closer the man saw us and started waving his arms and shouting, but Dan kept on.'

Marcus dropped his head in his hands and shuddered. Jeanne sat as if in a trance, which to some extent she was. Marcus's voice was having an hypnotic effect on her and the lost memories continued to surface as he spoke.

Inspector Ferguson sat, impassive, his eyes fixed on Marcus.

After a few moments Marcus raised his head and she could see the tears in his eyes.

'Dan aimed our boat straight at their starboard side. To port were some visible rocks and I guess he wanted them to...to...smash onto them. We...we hit them and I saw the woman stumble and hit her head. We hit them again, and again the woman fell. The man shouted and went to her but...but the boat was keeling over to port and she...she fell overboard. He jumped in after her. Then we saw a girl take the wheel.'

Again Marcus looked directly at Jeanne, whose eyes were filling with unchecked tears.

'I couldn't see you clearly, it was dark. I could just tell it was a young girl. I called to Dan to help but he just laughed crazily and pulled alongside, to port near the rocks. We saw the man – your father – trying to hold onto the...your mother. Dan grabbed our mooring hook and for a moment I thought he was trying to give your father something to hold onto. But he...he...hit him on the head a couple of times. The man let go of the woman and...and...she disappeared. Then the man seemed to lose his strength and he...he disappeared as well,' his voice was now little more than a whisper.

Jeanne was now crying uncontrollably and the inspector switched off the recorder before opening the door and calling for someone to bring a glass of water. He then sat by Jeanne, his hand on her heaving shoulder.

Marcus was slumped forward, his head in his hands.

The water arrived and Jeanne blew her nose before taking a sip.

'Couldn't you have stopped him, Marcus? Couldn't you have saved them?' she cried.

He raised his head and flinched as he must have seen the pain in her face.

'It all happened so fast! He was like a madman! He kept pushing me away when I tried to hold him back. I even thought of jumping in but at that moment we caught sight of the lights of a boat in the distance, coming out of St Peter Port. Dan revved the engine and sped off. It looked like you'd lost your balance as when we left you were lying down in the cockpit.'

'Yes, I remember now. After Dad went to…to…help Mum I tried to hold the boat steady but…but she was holed on the rocks. A wave hit us and I stumbled. I guess that's when I hit my head, as the next thing I remember is waking up in hospital.'

Inspector Ferguson, who had switched on the recorder after the water had arrived, interrupted. 'So where did you go when you left the damaged boat, Mr Davidson?' His voice was icy.

'We headed up to Bordeaux. Dan thought it would be too risky to go into St Peter Port. We beached the boat and then Dan went off to phone a friend who had a trailer and he came and picked us up. He was one of Dan's partners in crime and didn't ask any questions. We hid the boat in a lock-up. She only had a dented prow and Dan got that fixed some time later. The…the rocks had done the most damage to the other boat.'

For a moment all was quiet in the cheerless room. Each seemed lost in their own thoughts. Jeanne felt completely drained. It had been a horrible replay of that night's horror and she just wanted to curl up in bed and grieve for her parents, again.

Inspector Ferguson touched her arm and asked, 'Do you want to go now, Jeanne? Or have you any more questions before we call it a day?'

She shook herself out of her reverie and said, 'I'd like to know what Marcus thought would happen last Sunday when he asked to meet me.'

Marcus looked up and she witnessed various emotions chasing across his face. Sorrow, despair, self-disgust and, oddly, love. She shivered.

'I don't know what I thought. Dan just said he wanted to see us together and although I thought it was odd, I wondered if he was going to make some sort of confession.' He laughed harshly. 'What a fool I was! As if Dan would have gone willingly to prison – and for life!'

He reached out and grabbed Jeanne's hand.

'I swear to you, Jeanne, I would never have knowingly helped him to kill you! I love you! God help me, I love you!'

He fell forward onto the table.

The inspector opened the door and asked a policeman to come in. He then switched off the recorder and, holding Jeanne by the arm, led her out of the room and along to his office.

After settling her into a chair he phoned for a doctor to look in on Marcus before bringing her a cup of tea.

'Here, drink this. Wish I'd got something stronger to offer but it's frowned on by the bosses,' he said, with a wry grin.

Jeanne took a grateful sip of the over-sweet tea and she too wished that it was something stronger.

They were both quiet for a few moments.

'Are you going to be all right, Jeanne? Or would you like to see the doctor?'

She shook her head.

'I'll be fine, Inspector. It's safe to assume I'm no longer suffering from traumatic amnesia! My memory's completely returned. Horrible as it was listening to Marcus, I'm glad I now know what happened and why. My parents were just unlucky. They were in the wrong place at the wrong time.' She shuddered.

He nodded.

'It's more or less what I thought must have happened. I'm not surprised drugs were involved,' he said gravely. Then he sighed and went on. 'Although I understand it doesn't take away the pain of your loss, I hope that now you know what happened you can move on. You've shown a lot of courage, Jeanne, and I hope that you now find happiness.' He cleared his throat.

She was touched. 'Thank you. That's exactly what I'm hoping to find. Happiness at long last.'

Jeanne stood up to leave and as the inspector went to open the door the sergeant burst in and blurted out, 'Sorry to interrupt, sir. But we've just had news of a reported sighting of Dan Davidson.'

# chapter 34

Jeanne waited in the inspector's office while he shot off with the sergeant. They'd rushed away without giving her any details so she still didn't know where Dan had been sighted and if indeed it was really him. She prayed that he wasn't still in Guernsey. Marcus's chilling description of the way Dan had deliberately mown down her parents had brought home to her how dangerous he actually was. It seemed likely he was mentally ill, not surprising after years of drug addiction, she thought, pacing around the room and twisting her hair into tight spirals.

Her nerves were stretched tight when, about twenty minutes later, Inspector Ferguson returned.

He was smiling.

'It's good news, Jeanne. Davidson was sighted near Toulouse, probably heading for Spain and then North Africa. According to Marcus he has an apartment in Marrakech, as well as a home in Caen. We advised the French police of this and they were watching out for him. Anyway, we've just heard that he's been picked up on the auto-route and is now in custody. He'll be sent back here under armed guard as soon as the formalities are completed.'

By the time he had finished Jeanne's relief was written over her face.

'Oh, thank God! I've been feeling so scared at the thought of him still free to try again. He's evil!' she shuddered.

'Well, if he isn't, he comes close. We'll make sure he goes away for a very, very long time.'

'You do have enough evidence? There's no chance of his

getting off, is there?' she asked, still anxious.

'His brother's testimony is pretty damning and we're following up some leads that may provide more evidence. And we can link him to the attempt on your life. He carelessly dropped some keys on *La Belle Élise* and we've found a witness who saw him on the boat and is positive they could identify him. So, Jeanne, I think it's safe to say you can relax. Now, I'll arrange for someone to take you home.'

Jeanne asked to be dropped off at the boatyard and it wasn't long before she was pouring out all that had happened to Nick. He was saddened by the story of her parents' deaths but cheered by the news that Dan was safely in police custody.

'If you're up to it, I'll take you out to dinner tonight. The inspector's right, darling. It's time to move on and build your new life. And I hope to be a part of that life,' he said, holding her hands.

'I think there's a very good chance of that,' she said softly. 'A very good chance indeed.'

They had a quick, belated lunch at home and Nick then returned to work while she headed off to her own cottage. Her mind was still in turmoil as she grappled with the events of the morning. Would her life ever get back to normal? And what was normal, anyway? She sighed. Molly's version sounded great, but she didn't feel quite there, yet.

Le Petit Chêne was overrun with men. As she walked into the hall she spotted workmen in the sitting room and kitchen and Martin in discussion with the plumber at the top of the stairs. He waved her to come up.

'You're better now? Mrs Ogier said you were ill.'

'Yes, I'm a lot better now, thanks Martin. I'm dying to know what you've all been up to. Can you show me, please?'

Everything looked to be nearly finished and Jeanne was pleased with what she saw.

Downstairs she found the two kitchen fitters half-buried in base carcasses.  Looking at the units already in place she was amazed at how many there were. Even though she had designed the layout that had not prepared her for the reality. There was a mass of storage and the range cooker looked resplendent next to the butler sink. The fitters said they hoped to be finished by the end of the week. The worktop next to the sink would need to be measured for the granite to be ordered. The tiler would return once the worktop was in place, meaning the kitchen wouldn't be completely finished for about two weeks, but would be functioning sooner.

She wandered into the other rooms, greeting the plasterer finishing off the sitting room. After a final word with Martin she set off to buy flowers. She was overdue at the graves and it seemed imperative for her to go today.

As she walked from the car she saw Reverend Ayres coming out of the church and he came across to join her.

'Hello, Jeanne. This isn't your usual day. Been busy have you?' he smiled warmly at her.

'You could say that! Shall we sit down and I'll tell you what's been going on, Vicar?'

They sat on a nearby bench while Jeanne gave him the gist of what had kept her away that week and his face expressed his horror.

'So, as you can see, it's been quite a week. And now I need to have one of my chats with my parents,' she grinned sheepishly.

'Of course. I'll leave you in peace.'

'I don't know about peace! It'll all be in the papers now. My family seems to hit the headlines a lot these days,' she said sadly.

Reverend Ayres squeezed her arm.

'It will, as always, be a seven day wonder. And there'll be a lot of sympathy for you, my dear. As with your grandmother, your parents can now truly rest in peace. I shall include you and your family in my prayers. Now, I'll leave you to have your chat. God Bless.'

As he walked away Jeanne felt blessed indeed. She had helped Gran to be reunited with her lost baby and she had, admittedly rather unwillingly, been the means of bringing her parents' killers to justice. As she knelt at the grave she took a deep breath before beginning her story.

Before returning to La Tonnelle Jeanne dropped into Molly's to bring her up to date. She stayed just long enough to have a cup of tea and left a very relieved Molly, to drive to Bordeaux.

Once back she rang Aunt Kate. She had avoided phoning before, not wanting to worry her. It was not easy to tell Kate that her beloved sister had been murdered and that she, Jeanne, had, for the second time, come close to being killed. Her aunt tried gamely to hold back the tears as they talked. Feeling guilty, Jeanne agreed to go over for a visit as soon as things settled down. She needed to collect the rest of her belongings, anyway. As she put down the phone she wondered if she could persuade Nick to go with her and meet the one close remaining member of her family. It would do them both good to get off the island for a few days.

They enjoyed a quiet Indian meal at The Bridge that night and all the anxiety and fear of the last few days began to diminish, eased by the spicy food and chilled Indian beer. Jeanne even found herself giggling at something Nick said and when she went to the Ladies and glanced at herself in the mirror she saw the sparkle was back in her eyes.

It was still quite early when they returned home and Nick made them each a coffee before they sat curled up together on the sofa, listening to music. Less than an hour later Jeanne began to yawn and Nick murmured, 'Come on, time for bed. I think you could do with some of my special therapy.'

She peeped up at him.

'Oh, yes. And what's that exactly?'

'Come upstairs and you'll find out!' he said, kissing her enticingly on the lips.

'Mm, might just do that!'

They were no sooner in the bedroom than Nick pushed her gently onto the bed and began to remove her clothes, tantalisingly slowly. His fingers brushed her skin and desire shot through her body. He then pulled off his shirt, kissing her expectant and yearning body as he stripped. Finally, they were lying skin to skin and her excitement mounted to an almost unbearable pitch. They kissed hungrily, their love-making becoming more urgent. Nick slid inside her and she gasped. Intense pleasure flowed through her body, washing away all the horror and anxiety of the day and a while later they collapsed in each other's arms and fell quickly asleep.

Thursday morning saw a revitalised Jeanne busy at her computer, working with renewed enthusiasm on her book. It was if the heavy load she had been carrying for fifteen years had now been shaken off and she felt invigorated. Being in love helped, too. Heady stuff! Her fingers flew over the keyboard and she wrote more in a morning than she had achieved in days before what she thought of as her 'rebirth'. Another spur to creativity was the cheque from her agent which had been in her post at Le Petit Chêne. She was feeling rich and after a very satisfying day's work went off to buy fillet steaks for their supper that night.

By the weekend the couple had established a daily routine which suited them both. Jeanne worked on her book during the day and Nick came home for a light lunch. He was back in the evening in time to help with supper and Jeanne was pleasantly surprised at how good a cook he was, despite his protestations to the contrary.

On Saturday she suggested they both go to Le Petit Chêne as Nick had not visited for some weeks. It was such a glorious day that Jeanne packed a picnic for them to eat in the garden.

Nick was impressed with the changes made and seemed particularly pleased that the original character had been retained. Upstairs the old wooden floors had been stripped, sanded and wax polished and downstairs old reclaimed oak flooring had been laid over the cold flagstones, except in the kitchen which was to have been fitted with honey-coloured terracotta tiles.

'You've got great taste, Jeanne. But I should know that by now, shouldn't I?' he said, with a cheeky smile.

Jeanne grinned. 'I've always thought I had good taste where property's concerned. But my taste in men has been, until now, decidedly dodgy. Now, I'm dying to see the kitchen.'

All the units were in place with the doors and drawer fronts fitted. A bright blue Smeg fridge-freezer stood proudly against one wall and the range cooker gleamed under the spotlights. Her gran's dresser was back in place, awaiting the final touch of the blue and yellow china.

'Wow! This is great! A lot more user friendly than mine. What colour scheme are you using in here?'

Jeanne showed him the paint sample card with a sunny yellow marked off and samples of toning hand finished tiles that would form the splash-back. He nodded approvingly and checked out the utility room where the laundry equipment was now fitted under a laminated worktop and sink unit.

The plasterer had finished and just a few areas were still drying out. In the summer's heat the walls would be ready for painting within the week. The en suite shower was now working and Jeanne took great pleasure switching on the various taps.

'That shower looks awesome! I look forward to trying it out,' Nick said as they stood hand in hand in the transformed room.

'Ah, well now. You'll need to be invited, won't you?'

He looked at her seriously before replying. 'Perhaps we should discuss that over lunch.'

Not sure how to respond she led the way through to the master bedroom. This was completely bare as the old furniture had gone and her clothes and bedding were stored in the attic. The walls had been re-plastered, a blank canvas waiting for Jeanne's personal touch.

'Looks like you need some furniture,' Nick said, waving his arms around the empty space.

'I know. I don't have anything so it means a lot of shopping before I move back in, something I'm quite good at. The most essential item is the bed, of course.' She shot him a provocative look.

Nick cleared his throat.

'So, when are you planning on moving back?'

'Martin reckons they'll be out in a week now. The kitchen will take a bit longer but that's not a problem so I could move back next weekend. I want to start painting as soon as possible.'

He frowned. 'There's a lot of work for just one person. And what are you going to do about wardrobes and other storage?'

'I'll have to buy them. It would have been nicer to have fitted units but they're so expensive.'

He nodded. 'Yep they are, thanks to the high cost of labour. Now, how about we continue our talk over lunch? I've built up quite an appetite.'

Nick carried the cool box while Jeanne spread out a rug on the grass. Her patio and pergola were under construction but not ready for use. As soon as they were, she planned to buy the furniture needed for proper *alfresco* dining. After they'd filled their plates with salad and a selection of cooked meats and cheeses, Nick opened the bottle of chilled white wine.

'Santé!'

They sipped their wine and began to eat. She was aware that Nick had something on his mind and wasn't sure if it was good or bad. *Do I ask him outright or do I sit and stew while he waits to tell me?* Deciding to take the initiative she asked, 'Is there something you want to discuss?'

'Yes, there is. I think we should talk about where we go from here.'

'You mean after lunch?' she replied, all innocence.

'No, you idiot! You know very well what I mean. You've said you want to move back here in a week's time which is fair enough. It's your home and I can see you're longing to get back and finish it. And it's a credit to you, it really is. But I think you've underestimated how much there is still to be done and I don't want you wearing yourself out. It's about time you relaxed and had some fun. So, I'd like to offer my services.'

Jeanne grinned and raised her eyebrows.

'Not those kind of services! Even though they are certainly available anytime madam requires them. I meant painting walls and building wardrobes. The deadlines have eased at work now so I could cut down my hours a little in order to help you. But I do have an ulterior motive.'

'Ah! And what's that?' She bit her lip. It sounded ominous.

'I'd like to spend more time with you and if you're here and I'm up in Bordeaux that won't be so easy. I thought that if I moved in with you while we were finishing off the cottage that would solve the problem. I'd get to see a lot more of you and you'd get your cottage finished more quickly. So, what do you think?'

Think? She wanted to shout for joy! He wanted to be with her. That sounded good to her and she'd be glad of the help. And other…'services'.

'I'd love it. But when two people do up a place together it can really strain the relationship. Do you think ours is strong enough to cope?'

He looked at her so intensely that she caught her breath.

'I think so, don't you?' he said at last, stroking her face.

'Mm, yes. But what happens when we finish the cottage? Will you move back to Bordeaux?'

'That depends on you. If you want me to stay here with you, I will.'

'But what about La Tonnelle? Don't you want to live there? It's your family home.'

He shook his head.

'It hasn't felt right being there since Dad died. And after Helen's renovation…well! It's lost its soul. I'm thinking of selling it and using the money to back Colette with her restaurant. What do you think?'

'I think it's a fantastic idea!' Jeanne was excited. 'Colette's bound to be a success and she can use all my family recipes. Might even boost my book sales!'

A thought struck her.

'But if you sell your home, you'll have nowhere to live except here with me, will you? Are you sure that's what you want? I don't want you to be here just 'cos you're homeless,' she said, half joking.

'Well, I'd quite like some security of tenure, naturally. Wouldn't want to think I could be thrown out at any moment!'

He stroked her hair from her face and kissed her gently on the lips before murmuring in her ear, 'If we were married I'd feel happier.'

Jeanne's eyes opened wide and she felt her stomach flip over as she took in what he'd said.

'You're asking me to marry you?' she whispered.

'Yes, I guess I am. I'd like you to be my wife and the mother of the many children I hope to have.'

As she opened her mouth in protest he laughed and put his fingers over her lips, saying, 'Well, perhaps two children would be enough. So, what do you say, Miss Le Page?'

'I say yes, Mr Mauger. Yes please!'

'Great! I'd say that was reason to celebrate, wouldn't you?'

'And what exactly do you have in mind for this celebration,' she replied, feeling her insides melting as Nick's hands slipped inside her top.

'Oh, I'm sure we can think of something, don't you?' he murmured, his hands encircling her breasts.

'I, er, guess so.' She closed her eyes and allowed herself to enjoy what promised to be quite a celebration.

# chapter 35

The next few days passed in a blissful haze for Jeanne. She made excited phone calls to Kate and Freya, the latter letting out such a screech that Jeanne had to hold the phone away from her ear.

'The dishy man's proposed! Oh, my God! That's brilliant news, girl. I'm so, so happy for you. You weren't by any chance wearing that lovely rose quartz were you?'

Jeanne's fingers instinctively touched the pendant round her neck and smiled.

'Yep, I've been wearing it for a few days now. Perhaps it's my lucky charm.'

'Looks like it. So, when's the wedding going to be?'

'Oh, there's no rush. Perhaps next year. We want to see how we cope with living together while we finish off the cottage. Just in case!'

It was true there was no hurry. They both wanted to make absolutely sure that this time round they had chosen the right partners. As for Jeanne, it had only been a few months since the break-up with Andy and the loss of her baby. At least Nick had made it clear how much he wanted a family and she could now give free reign to her dreams of playing with their children in the garden of Le Petit Chêne. Jeanne hugged that picture to herself as she made a site visit before going on to take flowers to the graves.

She had just parked her car when Reverend Ayres approached.

'Good morning, Jeanne. How are you this fine day?'

'Very well thanks, Vicar. In fact I've got some news for you,' she smiled.

The Vicar expressed his delight at the engagement and

said he hoped to have the honour of marrying them when they'd set a date.

'Oh, I'd love that! It would be so good to have a happy family occasion celebrated here at long last.'

'Yes – completing the circle, as I believe both your parents and grandparents were married here.'

Jeanne nodded and they chatted for a few more moments before going their separate ways.

'Mum and Dad, I've got something wonderful to tell you!'

Kneeling by their grave her heart was filled with love, but sorrow still lurked on the edge. As she spoke she thought of not just what she had gained, the love of a wonderful man, but the loss of her loving and would-be proud parents. She felt so sad that her mother wouldn't be at the wedding, wearing a posh frock and big hat, the beautiful mother of the bride. Her dad would not be walking her proudly down the aisle as he'd always envisaged. Wiping away the tears falling on the freesias, Jeanne consoled herself with the thought that as the wedding would be at St Saviours, her parents and grandparents would be nearby. Surely they'd be wishing them both well. Come on, girl, get it together, she told herself, as she went over to her grandparents' grave.

Molly and Peter were over the moon when Jeanne and Nick popped in on Monday evening, and insisted on opening a bottle of champagne. They had delayed calling round as Molly's visitors had not left until that morning and they'd not wanted to intrude. Peter, no longer feeling guilty about Marcus, made clear his approval of Nick and the two men had soon drifted off into the garden, deep in a discussion about boats and fishing.

'Molly, I need your help with a problem,' Jeanne said as they sat in the kitchen finishing off their champagne.

'Of course. Oh, you're not still having nightmares, are you?' Molly looked worried.

'Oh no, nothing like that. It's just that I feel there's still some unfinished business between Marcus and I. He was so keen for us to be a couple, told me he loved me and everything. But he knew he'd helped kill my parents! Not willingly, I know. But what was he thinking would happen if and when I regained my memory? And been able to identify him?' Jeanne said, twisting her hair tightly round her fingers.

Molly frowned.

'I see what you mean. He wouldn't have been able to relax, ever. Strange. Perhaps subconsciously he wanted to be found out. It must have been a terrible burden to carry all these years.'

'Yes. Maybe that's why he was so materialistic – trying to blot out his guilt.' Jeanne took a deep breath.

'Do you think I should see him again? Ask him to his face?'

Molly looked concerned.

'I don't know if that's wise. You might stir things up for yourself again, just when your life's coming together. Whatever he'd thought about what might happen has no bearing on either the present or the future. I think he's a very confused and unhappy young man who didn't plan to fall in love with you, but did and hadn't thought through the consequences. He may well have found that it was just as painful to be with you as not. Can't you just let it go, Jeanne? Accept that not even Marcus may have known how he was going to handle the future if you'd become a couple?'

Jeanne sighed and her fingers released the tangled hair.

'You're right. I have to, I guess. After all, there's a lot going on in my life now.'

Just then the men came back and Jeanne's heart

contracted as she gazed at Nick. She really was a very lucky girl, she thought. Molly was right. No point in raking up the mud with Marcus when she could just enjoy being loved by Nick.

She was happy living with him in his house but could hardly wait to move back into her cottage. She had to curb her impatience, however, as Nick had pointed out that it would be better to wait until at least some of the rooms were painted and they had a fitted wardrobe in their bedroom. Agreeing, reluctantly, that this made sense, she turned her energy into painting the rooms downstairs while Nick started work on the units for the master bedroom. She loved his designs and told him so.

'Aren't I lucky to have a clever carpenter at my beck and call.'

'Hey! I'm not just a carpenter, you know. And who said I was at your beck and call?' Nick grabbed her and they rolled over in a mock fight, both laughing as they mercilessly tickled each other.

Calming down they went back to checking through their To Do list.

'I definitely don't want stuffy furniture. I'd like squashy leather sofas, a modern light oak dining table with leather, high back chairs and, most importantly, a big, bouncy bed,' Jeanne said and fluttered her eyelashes in an exaggerated fashion before getting a fit of giggles.

'Sounds great. I particularly like the sound of the bed,' Nick grinned as he pulled her close.

'I think we'd better go shopping, then, Mr Mauger.'

'Yes, Miss Le Page, I think we should!'

Three weeks later they moved in and were holding a barbecue to celebrate. Summer was nearly over but the weather remained warm and sunny and the garden was a delight to the eyes. The pergola looked as if it had been there for years, crafted in weathered timber and encircled with young shoots of Russian vine, honeysuckle and passionflower creeping up the posts. By the following summer there would be an umbrella of foliage to offer shade to diners as they relaxed around the large teak table. This was now groaning under the weight of the food prepared to feed the guests invited to the celebration.

Jeanne linked her arm with Nick's as they strolled around, checking that nothing had been forgotten. Colette had generously offered to help with the catering as her moving in present to the couple.

'It certainly won't be *haute cuisine*, just good ol' hearty food to feed the troops,' she said. 'I'll even provide desserts now we've got the use of that fantastic Smeg.'

They had only moved in a few days previously but, apart from some unpacked boxes of books, the cottage was looking as if they had been settled there for months. Colette was busy putting the finishing touches to her food as the guests began to arrive. As they mingled in the garden, Nick introduced Jeanne to those of his friends and family she hadn't met. Her left hand sported a sapphire and diamond engagement ring, which flashed in the sunlight as she waved at her friends.

Peter was to be Head Chef in charge of the barbecue, with Jonathan and Scott as his sous chefs. Scott had started heating up the large gas fired grill but Peter and Molly were missing. Jeanne was just wondering where they'd got to when they arrived. They were not alone.

'Kate! Oh, my God! What a surprise!' She rushed at her aunt and flung her arms round her. 'But how, where...?'

Kate laughed. 'When you told me about the party I felt I just couldn't miss it but wanted to surprise you. Peter and Molly have just collected me from the airport and they've kindly offered to let me stay with them. I didn't want to intrude on you in your new home. You're probably not ready for guests yet.'

Jeanne was so excited that she could barely introduce Kate to Nick so he shook her hand warmly and introduced himself.

'Welcome, Kate. I've heard so much about you and we were planning to come over soon so you could give me the once over,' he grinned.

Kate smiled. 'I think you can take it that you have my approval. I've never seen Jeanne look so happy!'

Indeed, Jeanne was grinning from ear to ear as if intoxicated. She felt as if she could burst, with love and pride. Love for the people closest to her and pride for the beautiful home she had created. As she linked hands with Nick she could have sworn she heard Gran chuckle and whisper, 'There you are, my girl. Home at last!'

# glossary

| | |
|---|---|
| Le Petit Chéne | Chéne is patois for oak tree |
| The Bridge | The area around St Sampson's harbour in the NE of the island |
| Bordeaux | The area around Bordeaux harbour just north of the Bridge |
| L'Ancresse | A beach and bay in the Parish of Vale, in the north of the island |
| The Castel | The hospital for mentally ill patients |
| Hedge-stalls | A long established local tradition for selling fruit, flowers and vegetables by the wayside, usually home-grown |
| Open Market | There is a two-tier system of housing on the island – Local and Open. Anyone can buy or rent an Open Market property (usually much more expensive than Local) but only locals or those living under a work-related licence can live in Local Market property. |
| Crapauds | The local name for Jerseymen meaning toads |
| Island FM | A local commercial radio station |
| La Societé Guernesiaise | The local society dedicated to protecting Guernsey tradition, including the Guernsey-French dialect |
| Caparne, Naftel | |

and Toplis | Well- respected local artists whose works have become much sought after

Bathers | Swimsuits

# recipes

Bouidrie d'Poulet et Legumes – Boiled Chicken Dinner

1 boiling chicken (2.5-3 kilos)
  drawn and trussed
Lemon juice
2 sliced onions
240-500g carrots
1 teaspoon salt

1.5 kilos potatoes
4 rashers of bacon
rosemary and parsley
black pepper

Rub the chicken with lemon juice and put into a pan of boiling water with the onions, rosemary, parsley, pepper and salt. Simmer gently for 1½ hours, removing any surface scum which rises. Add the prepared vegetables and simmer for a further 30 minutes, or till all is tender. Remove the bird from the pan and garnish with fried bacon rashers and a little chopped parsley.

Aën Pâtaï à Lapins – Rabbit Pie

1 or 2 young rabbits

240g beef steak
120g sausage meat
2 onions
240g mushrooms
30g butter
1 bouquet garni
Sage and nutmeg

freshly ground black
pepper
salt
stock
1 glass red wine
240g flour
120g butter
cold water to mix

Soak the rabbits in cold water for 1½ hours, then wipe dry and joint them. Skin the sausage meat and, using floured hands, make up into meat balls. Cut the beef steak into cubes, and prepare the onions and mushrooms. Arrange in a well-buttered pie dish and add the herbs and seasoning. Cover with a thick stock and a glass of red wine. Make up the pastry and close the pie, using any surplus to decorate the top. Bake in a hot oven (220°C or Gas Mark 7) for 15 minutes and then in a moderate oven (180°C or Gas Mark 4) for a further 1½ hours. Cover the pastry with cabbage leaves or tin foil when it begins to brown.

Enne Jarraïe d'Haricaöts – Guernsey Bean Jar

| | |
|---|---|
| 1 pig's trotter or piece of shin beef | 1 litre thick stock |
| 500g small pearl haricot beans | parsley, thyme and sage |
| 240g onions | salt and pepper |
| 240g carrots | 1 bay leaf |

Soak the beans in water overnight and drain the following day. Put them into a casserole with the meat, sliced onions, carrots and seasoning. Pour in the stock, cover with a lid, and cook in a slow to moderate oven (150-170°C or Gas Mark 2-3) for about 7 hours, till all is tender. Top up with water or stock when necessary and check the seasoning before serving.

D'Ormés Picquelaï – Pickled Ormers

| | |
|---|---|
| 12 ormers | peppercorns |
| 2 bay leaves | salt |
| 300-450ml of white vinegar | 1 teaspoon ground ginger |

Remove the ormers from their shells and scrub thoroughly under cold running water to expose the white flesh. Beat with a rolling pin on both sides. Put into a pan filled half and half with water and vinegar, and add the bay leaves, peppercorns, salt and ground ginger. Cover and bring to the boil and simmer for about 4 hours, until they are tender. Put into a bowl and leave to cool overnight, and serve them cold the following day.

Lightning Source UK Ltd.
Milton Keynes UK
UKHW041632071220
374769UK00001B/177

9 780992 711221